Exile Of Dust

Rachael S Lucas

Published by Rachael Lucas, 2023.

EXILE OF DUST

First edition. December 1, 2023.

Copyright © 2023 Rachael S Lucas.

ISBN: 979-8215300091

Written by Rachael S Lucas.

Also by Rachael S Lucas

Sarkin
Sailing For Shadow City
A Lonely Wind
The Griffin's Claw

Sci-fi and fantasy short stories
Illusions Of Steel And Sunset

Standalone
Dimensions
Exile Of Dust

Table of Contents

Chapter 1: Wizard of the Dustlands

Desert hills stretched as far as the eye could see, waves frozen in pleasing shapes of dust and sand. Nolin stood on top of the largest hill, watching a figure toil across the valley below him. His eyes lifted for a minute to view the bruised smudge rising on the horizon, before falling back down to the teenage boy in the valley. The direction that the boy was going in would eventually bring him to civilization, after more than a week of traveling. But he was already weaving from fatigue, stumbling in his steps, not paying much attention to which way his feet were taking him. And the dust storm on the horizon was going to cover that area in two hours.

Nolin adjusted the scarf around his throat so that it was not blocking his mouth and whistled, one high, sharp note. The boy looked up briefly, before breaking in to a shambling trot and heading in his direction. Nolin waited until the traveler collapsed in front of him, panting, on the side of the hill. Then he took a canteen of water from the belt which ran over his shoulder and gave it to the boy.

"Drink slowly. No one will take it from you until you are done."

Once the boy had slaked his thirst he gave the canteen back with a nod of thanks.

"What are you doing, lost in the Dustlands in front of a storm?" Nolin asked, looking down at him.

The boy scrambled to his feet. He was a tough one, with orange-yellow hair dulled by dust and an angular face, also soiled. Obviously a native by his weather-beaten, pinched skin. But not one who had traveled much alone.

"My name is Hiram," he said with a polite bob of his head, "And...I was looking for you. The wizard Nerheem."

Nolin's smile was tight. He never could get a native of the Dustlands to pronounce his last name correctly, or to call him anything but a 'wizard.' Or a Charlatan, if they did not believe in his powers.

"Why do you want me?"

"I want you to teach me your mysteries," Hiram explained, giving him a look like a hawk might use to size up a mouse. "I have traveled three days to find you and ask you to teach me."

"Brave, but stupid. I'm not looking for an apprentice." Nolin shrugged, gazing out at the approaching dust storm. Its shadow could be seen darkening the land beneath it, which was never lighter than a pale, dusty gray.

Sometimes he missed the sun and the blue sky so much that it was like a headache, ever-present and inescapable. But most of the time now, he forgot that such things had ever existed.

"I came for you to teach me. A man never knows when he will need an acolyte, because he never knows when he will go beyond," the boy remarked. He was a logical one as well.

'Go beyond' was the Dustlander's euphemism for death. Nolin's smile was still small and tight.

"That is quite true. And you will have to come with me for the next two days, until the dust storm blows over. I have found a house to shelter in, not far from here. But I can not teach anyone the mysteries of Erilaz."

Dust storms could bury a person alive, or rake them raw with blowing particles. The boy should have known better than to be traveling in the face of one.

He turned, pulling the brown scarf up over the lower half of his face again to protect it from the dust. Hiram followed him, stumbling now and then in his efforts to keep up. He could not have been more than fourteen, though he had been in the desert alone for three days according to his story.

"Why can't you? I know that you are no Charlatan, Nerheem. I have heard how you raised the Omberlings with your word and defeated King Angrist."

"Because I have promised myself that I would not," Nolin told him, leading the way down the hill of sand and dust into another valley. This one had the bed of a long-dead stream running through it, twisting away east and west. The wizard turned down it to the left, following it in the direction of the rising sun. Powdery silt puffed up at every step. The air had become still and oppressively warm, heralding the coming storm. When it hit, the wind would be like a thousand living nails trying to bite in to every object it touched.

The stream wound around the projecting arm of a low sandstone cliff, before running in to another valley. Here a worn, pale-peach adobe house stood on the bank of the lost stream, looking out on the world through windows with no glass in them. The door was made of warped, gray wood, so tortured by the elements that it screamed when Nolin opened it, dragging its feet on the ground.

"Make yourself comfortable." Nolin gestured at a wooden bunk on one side of the room, which was covered in a moth-eaten skin and a brightly-colored blanket. "I must fasten the shutters against the dust."

He went back out through the crying door, leaving Hiram in the one-room house alone. It had a rusty iron stove on one side, fitted with crooked pipes which ran up through a hole in the ceiling. Sagebrush had been piled beside it, dry and ready to burn. There was also a wooden table in the room, leaning and almost as tortured as the door. It had a few leather bags set on it and a small chest below. Other than that the only furniture in the room was the bed and a folding chair of rusted iron.

Hiram settled on the bed, running a hand idly over the woven blanket which covered it. It was of village weaving, thick, heavy and finely made. The colors were still bright even though there was wear on the blanket showing that it was not new.

The shutters slammed shut one after the other, locking the room in gray twilight. Nolin returned after a moment, carrying a tin pail of water that was only a little brown from mud.

"I am lucky to have found this house this morning," he said, setting the pail on the table. "The shutters and door will hold. The well still has a little water in it, even if the stream has gone beyond. We will shelter here just fine for the next few days."

The boy nodded. Nolin knew what he was thinking and went to open one of the leather bags on the table. Inside was a cloth parcel which he opened a little, displaying crusty, brown bread in four round loaves. Another parcel held pomegranates, while a piece of rawhide nearby contained what little was left of a butchered deer.

"As you can see, we have plenty of food to keep us as well."

"That is good." Hiram smiled, just a little shy. "I'm hungry already."

Nolin nodded, moving over to open the stove's door and throw in a handful of broken sagebrush branches. With a touch he lit a scrap of paper, which blackened and curled away from his fingers before bursting into flame. When he threw it on the brush, the fire immediately began to crackle. Cutting narrow strips from the lump of meat, Nolin strung them on a metal skewer and propped them in the grate. Soon a brown, rich smell was filling the room. While they roasted he broke chunks from the bread, giving one to the boy while keeping the other for himself.

After they had eaten and brought in a little more sagebrush the storm hit. At first it was just a light sift of sand across the roof, like rain. But it soon increased to a pelting blast of dust, accompanied by an otherworldly shrieking noise as the wind tried to claw its way in.

Dust sifted slowly in through the shutters, piling on the sill. Nolin lit a tallow candle and set it in a plate on the table, to keep the room from being entirely dark. The fire was allowed to go out, as it was not yet cold in the room.

"But why have you promised not to teach anyone?" Hiram asked as if they had been speaking on the subject only a moment ago, "I don't see why you would make such a foolish promise."

Nolin stood up from the folding chair to adjust one of the shutters a little and stayed there gazing at the dust trickling in. "I have my reasons."

With one of his fierce, hawk-like looks the boy snapped, "are they stronger reasons than my will to learn? I traveled three days to find you! My legs ached and I ran out of supplies. But still I kept searching."

"And got lost on the way," Nolin pointed out, almost laughing, before adding, "but you don't know my reasons, so you can't judge them. I will not teach you."

"Please. I will do whatever you say. I will never make you regret it. Teach me your magic, Nerheem."

Nolin glanced around at the boy once. Hiram's eyes were bright and sharp, begging for a chance to be given to him. Nolin knew that the boy had the ability and strength to learn the mysteries of Erilaz. But he also knew that he could not teach him.

"No."

Hiram's head bowed, hiding his face. It was considered weak of a Dustlander to cry, especially someone of more than five years of age. But they were still human and created with emotions that would show themselves at the worst of times. Softening a little, Nolin said gently, "we have empty days ahead of us, trapped in this house together. Perhaps if I take this time to tell you my history, you will understand my reasons for refusing you."

"Really, you will tell me all of your history?" Hiram looked up, tears instantly dashed away. Nolin was his hero. His greatest wish was to be like the legendary wizard of the Dustlands and he felt the ability inside himself. But he also knew that he needed teaching to make that ability shine.

"Everything that matters to answer your question." Nolin gave a short, dry chuckle. "We don't have time for 'everything.' But it will still be a long story, so you will have to be patient and quiet while I tell it. Then maybe you will understand and leave me without any more arguments."

"We'll see," Hiram promised, wrapping his arms around his legs and preparing for the story. Nolin came back to sit on the metal chair, pouring a little water into a clay cup to refresh himself as the story progressed. He had never told his whole history to another Dustlander. It seemed strange to be trying to make it into a story now. But it would keep the boy (both of them, actually) entertained for the next few days and perhaps convince the boy to leave him alone afterwards.

"My parents both died as slaves, working in the Neomium mines outside of a town called Ti-Gallin," Nolin began, before breaking off with a shake of his head. "Not that you know what Neomium is, or would understand where Ti-Gallin is located. Let me try again."

Chapter 2: The Story Begins

I don't come from this world. Nor am I a star from the world above, if you were going to ask that next. But we'll get to the explanation of how I came here later in my story. The world I came from has a blue sky, lit brilliantly by a great orb called the 'sun.' It rises and sets in the sky every day and night. I miss that sun and sky sometimes, but you would not understand that either.

The evening before my life changed for the first time, I was standing near the outer fence of the Neomium mine complex. Slaves were not supposed to stand there, but I was. Peering out between the woven wires of the fence I could see the city of Ti-Gallin on the horizon, a dark shape like a sleeping dragon lit by thousands of tiny lights. The golden ornaments on top of some of the buildings gleamed faintly in the fading daylight, gilding the top of the city. Ti-Gallin is much larger than any city in the Dustlands. It is bigger than the City of Markets, it is much bigger than Soleinden. Angrist's fortress could sit unnoticed in one corner of Ti-Gallin and be called a house.

As I stood looking out at it I wondered what it was like to live there as a free man. I was about fourteen years of age then and had only been in the mines for one year, but already the memory of freedom had dulled to the merest whisper in the back of my mind. I recollected, vaguely, that people were allowed to walk wherever they pleased down the streets. My parents had often taken me to a park where I had run and played, never worrying about a slave driver coming to beat me for disobedience or force me to work an extra shift. It was like a fading dream of heaven.

Then the Trackers had come in. Pieces of metal and electronics which the government fastened in people's heads to keep track of them. And my parents had both refused to wear one. They were taken away and I was put in a special orphanage to be 're-educated'.

At that time they did not put Trackers on anyone under the age of eighteen. But the next year the age limit was dropped to twelve and I was put under pressure to have one installed on me. I still refused, believing with child-like faith that what my parents had done was for the best.

So I was sent to the mine outside of town, where slaves dug up Neomium by hand and put it on trucks to send to the factories where it was used to make special commodities. Neomium is very fragile in its first state in the earth, and very corrosive to most forms of metal. It is slightly less harmful to people, at least in the first few years of contact. We used non-metal tools to find it and take it out of the ground, carrying it carefully with our bare hands.

My mother was still there, a beaten, pitiful wreck of a slave. My father had already died defending her, taking her beatings on his own back when he could and giving her a portion of his meager rations. She followed in his footsteps not long after I was brought there. It seems cruel of me, but I can hardly remember her face. Everything from before that time is just a blur in my memory.

Men, women and youngsters, all the free and rebellious thinkers in the city were made to work their lives away in the mine. Looking out of that fence at the city, I tried to tell myself that wearing a Tracker would have been worse. But I did not really believe it. Not after a year in those mines.

Hearing a sound in the compound behind me, I turned to look down at the entrance road. The part of the fence I was looking through stood on a tall embankment on the west side of the compound. The road was below me and about a hundred yards to the east. It came in through multiple baffles and gates, to prevent slaves getting out or freedom-fighters getting in.

Not that I had heard of a freedom-fighter ever trying to save us, but the government was cautious in those times.

The noise I had heard was a long, low car pulling in through the last gate, rolling slowly along the graveled road towards the main offices and barracks of the compound. It was not the armored van which brought new slaves in now and then, nor was it the commander's fancy truck. It had an old and worn look to it, though it had obviously once been an expensive vehicle.

Sometimes foreigners would come to buy slaves to work at their own Neomium mines or on their farms in other lands. With a small flicker of curiosity, I wondered if that could be what it had come for. It would not change my position much to be bought as a slave to work in a different mine, but it was every slave's last hope to be sent to work on a farm. Farm labor had jobs just as physically demanding, but the conditions were better, you did not die of the Neomium's corruption, and there was rumored to be a little more food in it.

Slipping away from the fence, I crept back down into the barracks where the slaves slept. I did not go in yet, but hid against the wall in a shadow to see who would get out of the truck. First the commander came out of the little, gray office building to look through the window and speak to the driver. Then he stepped back and the door opened to let a pair of figures out. The first was tall and dark-haired, with a ridiculously old-fashioned top hat perched on his head. He wore old-fashioned clothes, too, and a black tie. The second was a plump, bouncy man with fair hair and a purple jacket.

I could not hear what they were saying from where I stood, but it was obvious that the commander was pointing out some of the features of the place. The dull green slave's barracks, long and low. The taller, more commanding but just as bland soldier's barracks. His own office and living quarters. The mine itself, a slate-colored pit sunk into the ground with a snake of a road slithering down into it. After he had pointed out the features of our wonderful home (that's a sarcasm) the commander led the two ridiculous figures into his own quarters. That was the last I saw of them for the night.

Slipping into the window of the slave's house, I made my way to my own bunk in the dark. The barracks were not guarded heavily at night, as the slaves were too exhausted to attempt a breakout through the mine's fencing. The door was locked, but that was all. I had never heard of a slave escaping the Neomium mines alive, nor of any others getting out of the windows to look out of the fence as I did. They might have, but I did not hear of it.

After laying myself on the wooden shelf which was my bed I was instantly asleep. The next morning at roll-call the commander himself was present to read the lists. We all stood out in the courtyard between the barracks and the mine, lined up in rows on the cement. He looked us over, calling out names to which we must answer if we wanted breakfast. But this morning, the two men from the dark car were with him. I could feel them peering at us curiously, almost seeming to search through us with their eyes. Once roll-call was over the commander held us back from breakfast to explain, "these gentlemen have come to purchase a slave for their small, personal Neomium mine. One of you will be leaving with them after the hour of noon. That is all."

We were herded to the eating troughs then, before being sent down the long path into the mine to work.

It was summer then and hot. I toiled with my compatriots throughout the morning, shifting rock, dirt and the glowing yellow Neomium in strained silence. None of us wanted to be the one to go to the new mine. None of us particularly dreaded it, either. The rules were too strict and hours too tight for any real friendships to form between us, so there was nothing to be lost in the move except for the small comfort of routine.

That morning I got my right hand smashed by a falling rock. It did not break the bones, thankfully, but bruised it all over. The rest of the day until noon I fumbled and winced all through my work, biting back tears at the pain. Finally, like the light at the end of a long tunnel, the noontime came. We were not brought back to the barracks at noon, but a whistle blew and we were allowed ten minutes to get a drink of water and eat a crust of bread. They had found through trial and error that this ten minute break made the slaves last a little longer in their work, therefore paying in the long run for the work lost.

During the break the commander came down and walked among us, the two strangers trailing behind. The commander pointed out various of the slaves, extolling their strength, skill or endurance. He 'sold' us like a camel merchant trying to get rid of his worst stock. When he got to me the only thing he said was that I had not been there for as long as some, so I was not yet worn out.

"He looks like he has some skill in those hands," the tall buyer said slowly, giving me a long look from his dark eyes. I gazed back, blank and uncaring, trying to snatch a bit of rest for my bruised hand in this short break.

"Sure. Also he is young and strong." The commander whacked me on the shoulder with his cane, which he always carried despite not needing it for walking. I barely felt the light blow. I just turned my glazed eyes up at him, thinking vaguely that the white strip above one of his eyes looked funny. It was his Tracker, as he was a free man.

"Why do all of these, er, workers have white hair, commander?" The plump buyer asked in a breathy little voice, "even this boy does!"

"The contact with the Neomium bleaches it over time, of course." The commander gave them an odd look, wondering why they did not already know this, I suppose.

The tall stranger caught on to this and explained hastily, "pardon our ignorance, sir. We just bought our little mine and have not been working it for more than a month."

"Oh!" The commander laughed. "I see now. Well, they get hair like that after about half a year, I suppose. You'll soon learn. Now, did you want to see some others or have you made a selection?"

He was hoping to get rid of me, I think. I was not outright rebellious any more, as that would only get me a beating. But I had often found little things to do like sneak out to the fence, steal some of the soldier's rations or 'accidentally' break big pieces of Neomium. Always doing it in such a manner that he could not catch me, of course, though I think that he suspected. When I had first come there I had been openly troublesome all the time, but they had broken me of that. By this time, even my small pranks were starting to disappear. It was just too much effort to keep them up, too easy to become another sheep in the mass.

The two strangers consulted in low tones for a few minutes, before nodding and agreeing that they had found what they were looking for.

"This one?" The commander pointed at me. They nodded again and something shiny changed hands. One of the guards was called up to put metal cuffs on my wrists so that my arms were fixed together in front. Unceremoniously, I was marched out of the tunnel we had been working in toward the road outside. Some of the slave's eyes watched me as I left. But most of them did not even have the strength to care. Not when I was only being shipped to another mine, where I would wear out my life just as efficiently as in this one.

The two strangers came out behind me and I was put into the back seat of their car, where the tall one joined me as a guard while his companion sat in the driver's seat. They seemed to be in a hurry now, their farewells to the commander slightly strained. He was jovial, leaning on the door to chat a little before letting them go. We drove up the long, spiral ramp out of the open pit of the mine, the two strangers still acting anxious. I did not yet wonder why.

The tall one leaned forward from beside me to say quietly, "how long do you think it will be before he notices that it is only gilded lead we gave him, Lune?"

"Tallray, I don't know!" The plump one panted, gripping the steering wheel. "But don't bother me right now or I feel I shall explode."

He did not seem to enjoy driving the car. I supposed that he would have liked sitting in the back, with a slave, even less. But for the moment I was surprisingly comfortable. The seats were cushioned thickly, giving a soft, easy ride. The car drove without the rattles and bumps of the transport which we were usually crowded in to to take us to the bottom of the mine. Though my mind was still too dulled by chronic weariness to notice it much, it was the most hospitable place I had been in for over a year.

The man called Tallray sat back in his seat with a small snort, though I could tell he was still worried about being caught. It was of little importance to me, though it did seem amusing that the commander had been tricked out of his pay while getting rid of me.

I sat slumped, watching the endless gray of the mine slide past out the windows. Finally we reached ground level and drove along the road to the exit gate. Then came the checks and double-checks of the security guards to make sure that I was the only slave getting out in the car. When we had left the mine behind us a tension went out of the air and both of my new owners sighed in relief.

It's funny, but it never occurred to me during that drive to attempt an escape. Neither of the others were paying much attention to me at that point. I could have flung open the door and jumped out, or tried to throttle the driver into submission. But, really, where could I have gone with my hands locked together? If I went to Ti-Gallin for help they would have seen that I had no Tracker. If I ran away from it, I soon would have starved in the wild, if I was not simply caught again.

So I sat and listened to what went on, snatching delicious glimpses of free land and sky out of the window while knowing that a slave's lot was not to enjoy them.

"He really would not be safe at my place," Lune fussed, pulling the car back on to the road when it started to wander. "I know that was the plan, but...they'll be looking for us because of the gold."

"My friend, are you a Tracker-wearer?" Tallray, who was aptly named, stretched out a long arm towards the window and the city fading away behind us as we drove through the fields surrounding it. "Are you an inhabitant of that depressing anthill? No, so why worry? They will not think to look for him in the mountains past Sersio when he could be anywhere. We even told them that we came from the city of La'Dume, in the opposite direction."

"My name is still in the phone book of the country!" Lune snapped.

For a short space of time the man beside me did not answer. Then he murmured, "Well, he can not come with me, wanderer that I am. And he cannot be taken through a gate until the others know how we have succeeded. Besides, he does need some of your attention before he can do anything else."

"I suppose so," Lune sighed on a sour note.

From all of this I gathered that they were still worried about the trick they had played on the commander, though they had come there intending to play it. I also thought that Lune must be the one who owned the land that their Neomium mine was on, or perhaps one of a group who owned it together. Tallray, on the other hand, I put down as a speculator or stock-holder who was invested in helping him. They did not want to bring me directly to the mine until their partners had been notified, so I would be brought the Lune's private house in the meantime.

There was a few things about their words that puzzled me slightly but, as I said, I was too weary to care about anything at that point. I only hoped that staying at Lune's house would mean that I got to rest for a day or two, even if it was while locked in a cellar. Though I was already tired of listening to his whiny, breathy voice.

I must have made a movement then, because Tallray looked at me suddenly. He had a narrow mustache and thick black eyebrows which made him look like a magician under the top hat. In fact, you probably would call him a Charlatan if you caught sight of him the first time.

"Ah, all this talk of you and I almost forget that you are here," he gave me a pat on the shoulder, which surprised me so that I stared at him with wide eyes like a rabbit as he continued, "don't worry, we will get those cuffs off once we reach his place. We can't now, in case the car is overtaken or searched at the border. Awkward questions might be asked about a boy in your condition otherwise."

I just continued to stare at him, puzzled. He smiled reassuringly and leaned back against the cushions, propping his feet up on the chair before him.

"Tallray, I know he has the potential which Sultane spoke of as necessary, but I don't think he has the faintest clue as to what's going on," the driver pointed out.

The tall man jerked a little as if shocked and glanced over at me. "Egad, you're right. Worse, we still do not know his name. Do you have a name, boy, or do they just number you in that place?"

"Nolin," I told him, remembering my family title with an effort. "Nolin Nearham."

"And do you know what this is, Nolin?" He slipped his hand into a deep pocket at his hip, drawing out a piece of smooth stone. It was rectangular, about two inches wide and four long. Inset on its flawless, dark face was what looked like a triangle pointing upwards, glowing orange and yellow.

I shook my head. I suppose I could have said that it was stone, or a symbol, and been speaking the truth. But wisecracks were punishable in a slave's mouth and in my mind that's still what I was.

"This is a symbol which stands for 'fire' in a trade called Alchemy." Tallray laid the stone flat on the palm of his hand so that I could see it easily. "And this bit of rock is called a Runestone. Which obviously makes this symbol a rune, as that is what you put on Runestones."

I did not understand why he was telling this to me. Was he showing off his riches and knowledge to a slave to make himself feel more powerful? Or did this have something to do with the mining I would do for them in the future?

"Now, let me get a scrap of paper..." He dived into another pocket with his free hand, came up with a booklet, stuffed it back with a grunt and searched another pocket. This brought him three metal screws, two bits of twine and the paper he had been looking for.

"A well-stocked pocket can be the saving of a man, at times," he remarked as he sorted the paper out one-handed. To which Lune retorted, "if it doesn't drown him in old junk, first."

Tallray just smiled condescendingly and went on with what he was trying to explain to me. "Now, you can see that there is no switches or buttons on this stone, correct? So, watch."

He touched the stone gingerly to the paper. Instantly the scrap burst into flames, burning with its natural rapidity down to a stub which he smeared out on the window so that it would not burn his fingers. It left a smokey daub behind.

I frowned, looking from his hands up to his face. "It has electronics in it to do that?"

"No!" He waved it around in triumph, knocking it purposefully on the cushion, window and a gold ring he wore on one finger. It made a solid sound every time, like a pure slab of stone. I knew the sound from many days digging.

Just then our car reached the state line. A little building stood there with a raisable gate blocking the road. A man came out and glanced briefly in our car, checked the papers which Lune offered him, and then waved us on. The driver let out another sigh of relief as we left that gate behind. "So far, we are still free."

"And our new friend is just starting to learn something. The world is not so bad, Lune!"

Chapter 3: The Healer and the Alchemist

As we continued the drive, Tallray tried to explain to me that the stone was filled with a certain form of magic, which he called 'One of the greatest mysteries of Erilaz.'

I had no concept of 'magic' then. Oh, I had heard of it when I was young. Fairies used magic to make things change shape in a children's television programs (like an electronic play) or gave people gifts with it in tales. Cereal could be magically delicious. The word magic was used to describe all sorts of soft, playful things. But I had not thought that it was real or even that it could exist, which are two different things entirely. Now this strange man was trying to show me a magic stone after he had bought me to work in a Neomium mine that his friend owned, and I did not understand anything.

"Look," Tallray tapped the Runestone against his nose, "it does not burn me. It would not burn you, or Lune. See?"

He slapped it against my arm, making me jump in fear. But it just felt like a cool, smooth stone.

"But if you touch it to paper, cardboard or anything made of wood it will light that thing on fire. It is magic. It is the mystery of Erilaz. The Rune is set to the stone and imbues it with that power."

I eyed him warily. A magician might be a fearsome master. "Did you make it?"

"No, a friend did for me," Tallray sighed, "sadly, few people can make Runestones any more. Runeology is almost a lost art. My friend can do a little, small things like this, but I am only good at being an Alchemist."

Lune snorted. "Not even that. We would not have had to use gilded lead if you were any proper sort of Alchemist!"

"That is like saying that no one would die anymore if you were any proper sort of healer," Tallray shot back, sitting up straight. "A true Alchemist can only try. That is what we have done for hundreds and hundreds of years. Even such a small thing as gilding that bar of lead should be considered a great advancement. One day, with enough mercury, phosphorus and Carmot, I might be able to make a potion of youth, or the Philosopher's Stone. Until that day I can only try."

Lune just muttered to himself. I looked down at the cuffs around my wrist. The talk around me was still far above my head. So I ignored it, leaning my forehead against the chair in front of me.

Tallray noticed my slumped position. "You must be tired. You may sleep for now, if you wish."

I gave no reply except to let myself slip into a weary doze. I was still vaguely aware of the movement of the vehicle and their words for a time, through the deep haze of sleepiness.

"Do you think he will work out? It seems foolish to have gone to all this trouble instead of finding a boy in an easier position, somewhere other than Ti-Gallin."

That was Lune, fussing as usual.

"You know why we chose this area." Tallray's words had a shrug in them. "And I doubt that anyone within the city would have the potential. Besides being much harder to find and extract if they did."

"Harder!"

"To take a child away from his parent and friends, rather than buy it as a slave? Yes."

I started falling further into sleep then, the words fading away in little jerks of blank space:

"I still wish..."

"...one of the founders...Ti-Gallin."

"He has it in him, I suppose..."

My mind was swallowed by rest and I heard no more. It felt like much later when I awoke and pulled myself upright. Outside of the car windows I saw bushes, trees and steep slopes going by. We were climbing into the foothills of some low mountains and greenery was all around us. Growing things such as were never seen in either the Neomium mines nor in the Dustlands.

Bushes so thick that you could not have pushed through them, trees so tall and lush that they looked like sentries wrapped in green cloaks. I stared in silent wonder as they passed, until we crossed a bubbling stream and pulled in to a short road leading to Lune's house.

It was a solid house, build of gray stones mortared together and framed in rich old beams. It was large, too, and nicely kept, with sparkling glass windows watching over the view down into the valley. All around it was a perfectly trimmed green lawn, with flowering bushes on the upper boarder. A group of three or four pine trees grew at the upper end as well, with the clear creek running right passed them and forming the right-hand edge of the lawn. It was such a beautiful, peaceful scene that I wished with an intense fervency that I could spend the rest of my life lying on that lawn, looking at those trees and water.

"You can deal with the boy, I have to go check on Kitty," Lune said as he parked the car at the end of the drive. He jumped out, waddling away.

"Kitty is his cat." Tallray dived one of his hands into another pocket as he spoke, digging for yet another object. "That fat feline brute is wife and children to him. I don't know what he'll do when it dies."

The item he took out was a small silver key. He stuck it in the keyhole of my cuffs to release them, throwing them casually on the dash of the car. I blinked in surprise, stretching my arms to remove the cramped feeling that had grown in them from sitting so long in one position. Then he beckoned for me to follow him outside.

"That hand looks like it needs some help," he said, stopping me to grasp my wrist gently and look at the back of my crushed hand. "Wait here. I'll make sure Lune brings medicine for it."

He gestured at the ground and turned as if to stride towards the house.

"Wait," I stopped him, suddenly feeling uncertain of everything. "Why—why are you being so nice to me?"

The last words were almost plaintive, a sound which sounded pitiful in my own ears. But I could not help it. Everything around me was so nice, so clean and free. It could not be for me, I thought, it could not really be something I could have. It was all the world of someone else.

Yet, it was almost within my grasp, held out like a loaf of bread to a starving child. And the feeling that the world was changing in a way that I could not understand was a frightening one.

Tallray came back with a strange ejaculation; "Brimstone! You still don't understand, do you? But we never told you, so how should you know? You are not a slave anymore, Nolin. You are free."

"Free?" The word dazed me. "You mean I am not to work in the Neomium mines any more? But...then what do you want with me?"

He hesitated for a moment, tossing his head back and forth so that the hat almost fell off. Eventually he stated, "you will be told, when the time is right. We do want your help with something, but only if you agree. Until that time your only objective is to rest. Please, my friend, do take it easy for now."

And with that he hurried away towards the house in the footsteps of Lune. I watched him until he had disappeared around the house into its front door. Once he was gone I looked slowly around at the trees, grass and water. With a little gasp like a diver coming out of deep water, I threw myself down on that lush, green meadow. It was cool, sweet-smelling and only faintly prickly. With another little gasp I buried my face in it, inhaling the good smell of growing things. I was free. Free to smell the grass, lay in the shade, even drink the water if I wished!

With that thought I rolled over onto my back, intending to walk to the gushing stream for a taste. But laying there was too comfortable to shift myself at the moment, even for a growing thirst. Staring up at the sky, as blue as an Omberling's tapestry but with even more variety of shades, I let myself relax. I still had a hard time believing what was happening, but it had become a pleasant dream in my mind rather than an uncertain trap.

After a time Lune came back out of the house, carrying a tray of various items. He was muttering and fussing to himself all the time he walked across the lawn, and continued when he reached me.

"Tallray said that you wanted to stay out here. It really would have been easier to treat you inside. Let me see that hand. My, my, what did you do to it?"

"A stone fell and crushed it." I had sat up and held the hand out for him to inspect with the sullen compliance of a slave. The skin was various shades of blue and plum on top, seamed with the dark brown of dried blood where the skin had broken under the first strain.

He paused for a minute, staring at me and blinking as if those words took his whole mind to process.

Finally he let out a snort, "those barbarians! Or civilized tyrants, rather. My, my."

But he was a little more gentle with me after that. He probed my hand to make sure that there were no broken bones, before binding it up with herbal pastes and clean bandages. I held still, not making a sound as his pudgy fingers patted and poked the injured appendage into shape. When he was done he took a bowl from the tray and held it out to me.

"Soup. And a little bread to go with it. You are decidedly malnutritioned and it is going to be my job to get you back in shape. So eat up! There are plenty of good herbs and spices in there to make you feel better."

I did not need any encouragement to eat. It was something I felt I could have done forever without asking for reprieve. I drank the broth by tipping the bowl up, snatching bites of the soft little slice of bread in between. Soon it was all gone, so I held the bowl out to him with a hopeful grunt, "More?"

"Well." He hesitated, looking down at me with a perplexed expression on his face. Then he took the bowl, put it on the tray and hurried off towards the house with a promise to bring more soup back. Slowly, I stood up and looked down at myself. My legs were wiry from lifting and moving stones, but had little flesh on them to spare. You could run a hand up and down my ribs like a washboard. Putting my uninjured hand to my face, I found it hollow and pointed. My arms matched my legs, but were actually dirtier. The clothes provided by the commander of the mine were thin, dusty gray and only short pants and a top. At least they were not too ragged, as I had been issued a new pair only two weeks before. I guess he had reason to call me malnutritioned.

Moving over to the stream, I began to drink long, delicious mouthfuls. I had already consumed a good quart when I heard Lune's voice behind me, "oh, no! Don't drink that! It's unfiltered and might be dirty."

It tasted pure and cold to me. In fact, looking up it I could see a narrow cave and a tumble of rocks not far away which it came out of. But Lune was always worried about something being dirty, whether it was drinking-water or day-old leftovers.

"Is that more soup?" I looked up at the tray he carried, which had a bowl on it.

"Of course," he sighed, setting it down next to me on the lawn. "And a glass of orange juice, so you don't have to drink that creek water."

I accepted the food and drink eagerly, without complaint at the ban on drinking the stream. But I broke it whenever he wasn't around, too, and never suffered any harm from having done so.

Chapter 4: The Door in the Cave

On the inside Lune's house was like him; plump, comfortable and a little bit fussy. There were place mats on the table at dinner time, a doormat which must be used outside the door, doilies on the couch and all sorts of inconvenient conveniences in every room. Such as his cat's jungle and litter box in the corner of the living room. But the house was also clean, peaceful and, as I said, truly comfortable.

I spent the next week living there, being doctored into health by the peculiar little healer. Sometimes I hated him, because of his strict and unending chiding. Most the time, I was only grateful to have been given the chance to recuperate in peace. And recuperate I did, growing stronger and more awake every day. Even a boy who has been kept working in a Neomium mine eventually becomes restless with having nothing to do every day, so I soon began to explore. Tallray had left on the first day and not yet returned, so all of my expeditions were solo. It goes without saying that Lune was not the sort of person to go on an 'adventure.'

One day I was poking through the flowering bushes and climbing the pine trees in their clump. Curious to see what was beyond, I followed the stream up its bed towards the source. There was a small cliff of lava rock which had at one time crumbled in front, falling into pieces. Bits were laying all around the front of the cliff and in the stream, worn dark and smooth by the water. Taking off my shoes (for Lune had given me a whole new set of stiff but stout clothes) I waded through the cold water or jumped from one rock to the next up it. At the cliff the water ran out of a narrow crack of a cave, as I had noticed earlier. But when I came up to it, I saw that the crack widened out inside to create a cavern large enough to stand straight and move around in. I also noticed that there was a hidden path running through the rocks outside, leading from a different point along the back of the lawn and in to the cave.

"Maybe Lune has some beer stashed in this place."

I knew that the commander of the Neomium mine had kept a secret store of beer. On some nights he would gather up his favorite cronies and have a party with it, often ending in unchecked violence done to the slaves. But he had always claimed to be a teetotaler, and I knew that Lune did also. illogically, I connected the two together, believing that where one man lied another would do the same. And, as Lune was away at his work as a herbal medicine consultant, I decided to investigate this idea further.

The cave was inviting, even without the possibility of stashed alcohol. Stepping in the stream of cold water, I slipped into the narrow crack in the cliff face. It was dim inside, preventing me from seeing anything at first. Once my eyes had adjusted I saw a room about fifteen feet long and varying in width from four to six feet across. I noticed right away that something was odd about the space. Inside the crack it was not a natural cavern, as I had first thought. It was carved along the walls, roughly gouged out to make a rectangular room. The roof was arched, but the walls tapered regularly except for where a few harder rocks had been left in place, sticking out of it. Running my fingers along the wall, I could feel the dents and bumps from where tools had been used to carve it. A pick and bar had been the main tools, I thought, along with some explosive charges near the center to help clear it.

The stream flowed along a cut channel in the center of the floor, leaving a free walkway on either side. It was only a little damp, not too slippery as I made my way further towards the back. The stream appeared to originate from a fissure in the wall a few feet from the rear, where it trickled out of the rock. So far there was no beer in sight, or any other illicit drinks.

But there was a vague door-like shape at the rear of the space, which might have been an entrance to a hidden cellar. Quietly, I walked over to it, running my hand over the wall the whole time. For obvious reasons I was not afraid of being underground, but I did not want to trip in the dimness and fall into the stream.

When I reached the back I found that the lines in the wall were, indeed, a door. It was tall enough for a fully grown man to have gone through without stooping, framed in old timbers like what was used in Lune's house. The door itself was made of what felt like metal, though it was darker and smoother than any I had seen before. There was no knob or latch on it, only a pull-handle.

I hesitated for a minute, glancing back towards the crack of light at the entrance of the cave. For a minute I had the terrible feeling that someone was watching me from out there, waiting for me to go through the door so that they could shut it behind me.

"Coward," I muttered to myself, shaking the feeling off. "There's no one out there."

Though I do not mind underground places, even tight ones, it has always been one of my secret fears that I will be trapped in a small, dark place without air and suffocate there. Perhaps because I had seen workers in the mine get trapped in a collapse before, and what their faces looked like when they were finally dug out.

Bracing myself, I grasped the handle and gave it a stout pull. The door swung open quite easily, without a sound to mar the trickling quiet of the cave. Beyond it was not what I had been expecting. There were no shelves of beer, or room full of wine racks. There was not even a secret trove of gold or bones. Beyond the door was a hallway.

It was wide and tall, with a vaulted ceiling made of smooth, midnight blue stone. The walls and floor were stone as well, inky black and as fine as marble. There were lines on the floor as if it were made up of huge slabs or tiles, but the wall appeared to be all in one piece of squared rock. It was dark inside, though just slightly lighter than the cave I had been in before. I could easily see for sixty feet down the passage, but beyond that everything got dim and indistinct, as if a mystical gloom were obscuring it.

Stepping through the door, I stood in the middle of that hall. A faint humming filled the air, so soft and far away that I could only hear it by holding my breath. Other than that there was not the smallest sound to be heard. The door I had just come through was at the end of the hallway and there were others along its sides. Not at any particular place, or with even spacing between them. They were set into the wall at random intervals, never very thickly. There were five of them along the walls I could see, each made of the same material as the one I had come through. They varied in shape a little. Some were perfectly rectangular with sharp, pointed corners. Others were arched at top and had softly rounded edges at the bottom. All of them, even the first one, had a dim bar of greenish light set into the metal near the top of the door and heavy rivets around the edges.

I walked up to the nearest, on the left-hand side. Immediately I noticed something else. Under the green bar was set two smooth, red stones like counters of some sort. Looking back at the one I had come through, I saw that there was one red stone under the bar on it. My curiosity aroused, I began to walk along the hall and count stones under the glowing bars on the doors. The numbers went up to nine red stones, before being replaced with one blue one. Then there was a red and a blue counter, followed by one blue and two reds. I thought it was a sort of code, the blues standing for tens and the reds standing for ones. That way someone could know which door they were at as they walked along the featureless hall.

Suddenly I realized the dangers of what I was doing and a burst of panic hit me. What if I became lost in this place, unable to get back to the first door? What if I wandered here until I starved to death?

I jerked around back towards the entrance, intending to hurry through it into the light of the regular world. But then I stopped myself and took a deep breath of air.

"What a fool you are. You can't get lost when there is only one hall to go down," I told myself, shaking my head. Talking to myself was a habit I had acquired through so often having no one else to talk to who would have listened. When I was with others the words were only in my head, but when I was alone I spoke my thoughts aloud.

"Now, what could be behind all of these doors and why does Lune have them?"

Curiosity once again taking the place of fear, I walked over to one and put my hand to the knob. Some of the doors had pull handles, some knobs and others different sorts of latches. It seemed that whoever had built them did not buy only one sort of hardware to outfit them with.

With a twist of my hand the door came open, revealing what was beyond. To my surprise it was another cavern, this one much larger than the first and entirely different in appearance. The stone was red, a bright, hot color. The walls were formed in bubbly, wild shapes which seemed to melt one into the other. The floor was covered in dark sand.

Standing in the hall, I could not see or feel anything different about what was in that cave. But as soon as I stepped through into it a dry, stifling heat hit me, mixed with the sound of something heavy thumping in the distance. It surprised me so much that I jumped back through into the hall, where the heat and noise was instantly gone. I gazed through into that winding cave, staring at its silence. There was something odd going on in that place. Something...magic.

I tried stepping back and forth through the door a few times and found that it worked the same every time. In the hall, everything was quiet and cool. In the crimson cave there was disturbing noise and heat.

I was confused and interested at the same time. What was going on? Not only with this strange underground hallway and magical cavern, but with everything Lune and Tallray had spoken of before?

What did they want of me and how did they know of such things as magic and alchemy?

Puzzled, I slowly closed that door and began to move along the passageway again. After a time, at the seventeenth door to be exact, I came to an intersection. The hall I was in came to an end, joining into another one horizontally. This new one stretched out of sight both ways, with doors placed randomly all along it. These doors had many stones on them, handfuls of red and blue. Further along to my right, I even saw a new color of stones. Green ones, which made me wonder if they might represent hundreds.

Now my head was really spinning with the idea of all the doors in these pathways. More than a hundred in this hall, plus the almost thirty from the passage I had just left. And there might even be other hallways joining on, with hundreds of doors of their own!

I stood staring up and down, trying to think. Tallray had said something about bringing me through 'the gate' and telling 'the others' about me.

Perhaps the door I had just gone through to get here was the gate he meant. Did the others live somewhere in this warren of paths?

He had mentioned someone called 'Sultane' as well, who had seemed to be a chief among them. It was that man who had insisted the slave they bought had some sort of 'potential'. The only thing Tallray had shown me that would take any sort of magic powers to use was the Runestone, which he had hinted that few people could make.

So I came to the conclusion, standing there in the dark pathways, that I had been bought to be apprenticed to a Runestone maker and taught his trade. Which, as you will see, was not entirely untrue, though it did not hit the full scope of the mark.

As I was standing there pondering my future I heard a noise coming towards me down the hall. It was the sound of footsteps and at least one voice, echoing towards where I stood. I could not yet see who it was that was coming, but a sudden fear took hold of me that whoever it was would not be pleased to find me snooping.

I glanced around me, but there was nowhere to hide that was sure to be safe except for behind one of the doors. Deciding to take the chance, I jumped over and worked the latch of the nearest one. Just as the footsteps were getting too close for comfort the door swung open, blinding me with a bright light. Looking through the doorway, I became too stunned to make my escape. Through it was not another room or cavern. It was outside. And outside at a place which I did not recognize at all.

Chapter 5: A Friendly Elemental

A plain of knee-high, soft grass stretched before me, colored a verdant green such as I had never seen on any grass before. It was so vibrant, so lusciously alive that it took one's breath away just to look at it. The sky above was a flawless, arching lapis lazuli, reflected in the tiny bright-eyed flowers which grew among the grass. A light wind was blowing over the field and ruffling the stems. One wispy cloud moved across the sky. Other than that, it was perfectly still and empty.

Just then the voice started up again and I realized that it was singing, in a high, off-key sort of way.

"Someone told me that there's a world out there, with love in its skies and flowers..."

It broke off again, to say aloud, "now, what rhymes with 'hair' but you would find naturally on a world? Air, I guess. Song-smithing isn't always easy. Oh, hello."

The last words were directed at me. Turning slowly around I came face to face with the newcomer.

I had been afraid of some stern, wizardly personage catching me in his realm and shooting fire or lightening at me for it. But the man I saw before me was as entirely unexpected as the scene through the door had been.

For one, he was much younger than I had imagined. He had cinnamon brown hair which curled around all over the place, friendly green eyes of surprising brightness and a freckled, cheerful face which did not look to be older than in its mid-twenties. Secondly, he was not carrying a wand or Runestone to blast me with.

Instead there was a large sack slung over one shoulder, dripping with moisture and mud. Out of its top poked the tips of a few saplings, as if he had been out digging them up to move them to a new location.

When I didn't say anything he continued, "say, you must be the new boy that Tallray's been telling us about. He said that you were skinny as a starved dog. Um, no offense meant. But what are you doing wandering around here? Is Lune with you?"

I shook my head, closing the door all of the way on the bright scene beyond it before answering. "No. I—I found my way in here on my own. You know Tallray and Lune?"

"Of course. I'm a Keeper too, the newest one, besides yourself."

Seeing my puzzled expression, he let the sack slip down on the floor and stared at me in surprise. "What, don't tell me that you don't know anything about the Dark Passages yet, or the Keepers?"

I shook my head, hardening myself in case he became angry. "No. No one has told me anything about why I was purchased and freed, or what this place is. I was exploring and found it on my own."

"Well then." He looked puzzled for a few minutes, before breaking into a grin, "I guess I get to explain the Dark Passages to you. Don't know if I'm supposed to, but since you're here already it would only be more troublesome to leave you uninformed."

He picked up his sack again and continued walking down the hall, beckoning for me to follow. I fell in step beside him, looking once over my shoulder to mark the position of the hall I had originally come from, using the number of the door across from it as a landmark.

"To begin with, these passages were built a long time ago. More than a hundred years, I guess." He shrugged and gave a little laugh. "The few history books we have are pretty dull reading, but I'm made to learn them. Being the youngest and all, besides yourself. Anyway, they were built by a group of ten mysterious men, known to us as the Ten Founders, or just the Founders or the Ten for short. These fellows seem to have all been pretty powerful folks, knowing the arts of Runeology, Alchemy, Elements, Time and Space better than any of us do now. They also practiced Healing in various forms including magical and herbal, fighting skills both physical and magical, and various mental arts which I've forgotten all of the names for."

He stopped to rest the sack on the ground for a moment more, taking a breather from both walking and talking at once. I did not think to offer my assistance. Once he had caught his breath, he continued, "well, these wise old birds got together and decided to build a sort of portal system which could take people quickly between different worlds. Not just different plants, we think now, but parallel universes and things like that. So they put together these Dark Passages we're walking in."

I gave him a sharp look. "You mean these doors lead to different worlds, not just other places on my world?"

The young keeper nodded enthusiastically. "Heaps 'n heaps of worlds! You saw what was through that door, those flowers and things? Those were on a different world altogether, called Altiri. That's why they looked so...well, different than what you are probably used to on your planet."

"So, these powerful men built all of this in order to make travel between these spheres possible. But there were two problems with it, or at least we conjecture there was for them. One is that, things from the other worlds get in here sometimes and they aren't all exactly nice. You ever seen a Whistless man, or a Shadow Poker?"

I shook my head, too engrossed to interrupt him with words.

"They're things from other places." He shook his head. "Things that mean trouble if you run into one. At least one of the Founders was eventually killed by things getting in, despite all of their powers. Another problem is that the whole thing takes some maintenance. And that's where we come in. The Keepers."

We had reached the door he wanted to go through by now, so he propped the sack up against the wall and we made ourselves comfortable on the floor near it.

"You people keep the Dark Passages running and you want me to help you?" I asked, crossing my arms on my drawn-up knees. I wasn't yet sure if I liked the idea, but I certainly wanted to know more. "What do you have to do with the Founders? What happened to them?"

"Being a Keeper is pretty complicated sometimes." He shrugged, winding a finger in his curly hair. "But you'll get all of that explained to you soon enough. Now, what exactly happened to the Founders is a bit of a mystery. It seems they began to lose their members faster than they could train new ones. And it takes ten men to keep the Dark Passages going, it's absolutely necessary. So at some point they just gave it up. Locked all of the doors and left. It was not until years later that some of us, Sultane and the historian Gleeb One-step mostly, found out about it. They decided that it was a great thing, something that should be brought back up to standards and made to work again. Then came the hard part. Recruiting ten members, including me, took some doing. You have to have a...a sort of instinct for magic to become a Keeper."

I couldn't help snorting and giving a shake of my head. "I hate to say it, but I don't think Tallray and Lune knew what they were doing when they picked me up. I didn't even believe in magic until I came here."

"Well, it's not like that." The Keeper knitted his fingers together nervously, squinting his face up into wrinkles as he tried to puzzle out a way to explain what he meant. "You do have what we're looking for. I can see it in you."

"Really?" I was skeptical.

"Oh yes!" He nodded, face clearing up a little. "Everyone has a little of it, or so Sultane and Feleago say. But most people have buried it so deep, or forgotten it or something, that they lost it when they were very young. You haven't. It's just under the surface, waiting to come out. I can't explain it very well. You'll have to talk to one of the others about it."

My mouth was shut in a straight line as he said this. I felt a frown settle over my brows. Had I ever believed in magic? My life before becoming a slave was often dreamy and disconnected to me now, a bright memory hidden under pain. But I could not remember ever having thought of magic as something other than so much fairy dust in old wife's tales. There was no repressed memory of having cast spells as a toddler, no unusual happenings on a special birthday. Before becoming first a rebel and then a slave, my life had been pretty normal.

I sighed, shaking my head again. It seemed such a waste to tell the truth. They might send me back to the Neomium mines, or turn me loose to live as I could. But this young Keeper was so open and honest with me that I felt it would be a betrayal to lie to him.

"I think you've made a mistake. I don't have a mystical drop in my mind." Looking at him from the corners of my eyes, I expected to see his expression fall or become sad. But he just kept smiling as if he knew a secret that I did not.

That made me angry. "Look, how did you become a Keeper? You probably knew about all of this magic stuff from the first, didn't you?"

"Well, not all of it," he chuckled, still unruffled. "Though I have to admit, my world does know about one part of the arts of Erilaz. Most of my people understand basic Elements and are, in fact, born with clear signs of what Elements they'll be able to tap into throughout their life. I'm lucky. Most people only have one or two. I have three: Earth, Fire and Water."

"Oh?"

"See, my hair's color shows that I'll always be close to Fire." He touched his head with a rueful smile. "Which is a mixed blessing. It's the most unstable element. The curls in my hair show an affinity with water, while the color of of my eyes indicates the connection to Earth. Which is what I always feel closest to, honestly. So a few of the Keepers came to my world once it was unlocked and looked around for someone to help them in their mission. I had that mysterious extra touch of something, but I did not know it then, either. It was once I had started exploring the Dark Passages that I felt it. They saw it in me before it awoke."

By now my head was whirling with everything he had said. Elements, people and the Dark Passages themselves made a procession of images in my mind. I sat still, trying to feel somewhere in me the ability to understand those things. But I could not sense anything different about my way of thinking. As of yet, I only felt confused. A slave who had been thrust into a freeman's world and from there directly into a wizard's.

The Keeper seemed to understand my bewilderment. He stood up and slung his sack over his shoulder with the words, "you know, if we were caught here by one of the others we would get a talking-to for sitting around in the Dark Passages. Everyone says that it is too dangerous to twaddle in. This door here leads to the central meeting place of the Keepers. I'm bringing these Shevro saplings to plant there. Do you want to come and see if one of the others is there to talk to and answer your questions?"

I inched upright and shook my head. "No. I just want to think about what you have told me."

"That's what I thought." He turned and started to open the door, before pausing to say, "by the way, I never introduced myself. My given name is Corkcora, but everyone calls me Corky."

"I'm Nolin. But...Tallray probably told you that."

He nodded and winked, before disappearing through the door. It was a good thing I had memorized the number of the door across from the hall to Lune's place, as neither of us thought to have him show me the way back. The hall was not devoid of extra turnings.

In case I needed it in the future, I looked at the number of stones on the door he had just gone through. Two green, four blue and three red. Two hundred and forty-three. That was a lot of doors, but then, it was a long hallway.

Spinning about, I started to make my way back towards Lune's door. The journey seemed longer now that I was alone, without the friendly Elemental to talk to. His bright conversation had seemed to take away all of the darkness in the place, making it a world of adventure and mystery. Now, alone, it just looked like interconnected, gloomy hallways. Where was the mystery and magic he had spoken of? How could wandering these halls teach you to see magic in yourself? All I felt now was a sort of confused loneliness, and a touch of latent anger. These stupid Keepers had chosen me without asking what I wanted and now they would not listen to me when I said that there was no magic in my blood. Worse, only Corky had told me anything at all about why I had been freed. Everyone else had kept it a secret.

"Where is your magic?" I growled, looking up and down the hall as if it would appear there in human form. "Show me!"

On impulse I stepped over and jerked open a random door with the last words, hoping to see a burst of power and glory that would instantly convince or convert me. Instead I saw a windy, drizzling hillside with a stepping-stone path running along the side of it and curving out of sight.

The sky was overcast and every grass blade was tipped with droplets of water. As I stood looking out on the desolate scene a figure came into view, traveling around the path on the hill. He was tall, the tallest man I had ever seen, and he wore a straight, dove-gray robe which emphasized it. His hair was straight and gray too, falling down to his shoulders in damp hanks. But the thing which filled me with fear at the first sight of him was that he had no face. Only a blank, smooth plane of skin where his face should have been.

With an involuntary gasp of fear I slammed the door shut and scurried down the Dark Passages, not slowing until I had reached Lune's door. There I drew in a few ragged breaths of air, trying to calm my beating heart. There was no sound of pursuit behind me, no sight of a gray, faceless figure coming down the hall. He must not have seen me: I had shut the door in time.

But what had that thing been? I wondered if it was one of those things that Corky had mentioned, a Whistless man or a Shadow Poker. He certainly looked like how I had imagined a Whistless man would appear. Faceless and colorless.

Carefully, I pushed on Lune's door and stepped back out into the cave in what I still thought of as the 'real' world. It would do no good to go running and babbling to Lune, even if he had been at home. I would only have got a scolding, or worse. It seemed to me that the best plan would be to keep quiet about my trip to the Dark Passages, at least until a good opportunity came along for revealing the adventure. Corky might tell on me, of course, but somehow I did not think that he would do it in a way that would get me in trouble. If he told, it would be to someone who would at least try to treat me kindly.

Steadying myself again, I walked casually out of the cave and back to the house along the hidden path. Lune had not yet come home, but his fat, orange tabby cat was waiting inside to spike his claws into my pants and demand an early supper. As was usual, I fed him half of his meal at the moment to quiet his importuning. After that all that was left to do was wait until Lune came home.

Chapter 6: Truth

When I heard his bus pull up at the end of the road (he hated driving and had only rented the long, low car we rode in before) I sauntered out to meet him. He came panting up the drive, wobbly face tinted red with exertion and good humor.

"Were you nice to Kitty while I was gone?" He asked me first thing, trying to smile pleasantly while gasping.

"Yes. He had half his dinner for lunch, like usual," I explained, secretly turning to roll my eyes where he could not see. That cat filled altogether too much of his thoughts during the day.

"Good boy." Awkwardly, Lune pulled a chocolate bar from his pocket and held it out to me. "Generally I don't approve of sweets, but...you still need to gain a little flesh and it will help fill you out."

I took it carefully in my hands, suddenly filled with a sense of pleasant surprise. It had been more than a year since I had seen a bar of chocolate. Or any other thing that was to be eaten for mere pleasure, with no fuel and little nutrients to keep you going through the day. Struck silent, I looked from the bar up to the little, pudgy healer. So often I came close to despising him. Yet every once in a while he would do something unexpectedly kind that would nearly bring me to tears.

"No need to thank me." He fluttered a hand, obviously embarrassed. "Run along now until I can get supper on the table."

I 'ran along' to a shady place beside the house and slowly sucked that bar of chocolate away to nothing. It was much sweeter than the bars made in the Dustlands, with a milky, creamy taste that they lack. It was one of the most special treats I had ever been given.

When the candy was gone I tucked the wrapper in my pocket and stood up, coming to a decision. I would tell Lune about my expedition into the Dark Passages and trust him to treat me fairly about it. But, I thought with a tiny, mischievous smile, I would tell him in my own time and way.

Dinner was served, as usual, on the long table in his dining room. There were place mats at every seat, even though there were only two of us eating. Or three, if you count Kitty. Kitty got to eat his own meal on the table as well, though a little removed from us.

The food was not excellent, I suppose, though it was better than Neomium mine fare. Grilled pork chops, roast zucchini and a large salad on the side, with home-made croutons in it. I never really understood the croutons. There was never enough to amount to a slice of bread apiece, they were either as hard as rocks or slimy with having sat in the fridge, and they tasted like lightly sweetened hardtack.

Thankfully the rest of the salad was usually pretty good, with enough tomato slices and vinegar to overpower the croutons and beat them at their own game. I ate in silence through the pork chops and waited until Lune had just taken a large helping of salad into his mouth before remarking, "I met Corky in the Dark Passages today."

Lune chewed a few more bites with a tiny nod of his head in my direction, before realizing what I had said and choking the rest down in a rush. Still gasping from it, he said, "you met whom, where?"

"Corky, the Elemental." I looked at him over my plate of greenery. "He was carrying some sort of saplings through the Dark Passages and I met him there. He told me some interesting things. Very interesting things."

"You—you found your way into the Dark Passages?" Lune's voice was weak and disturbed. He had not seemed to notice the touch of rising anger in mine. Until my next sentence, at least.

"Why didn't you tell me about them earlier? Why hasn't Tallray returned to tell me anything? You have all been playing some sort of game with me, freeing me from the mines without a word of explanation. I am grateful, but I want to know how I am going to live from now on. If you want something from me, explain it! But don't leave me in darkness any longer."

I was a little surprised at my own outburst, honestly. A slave does not talk that way to his buyers, or his masters. You don't ask questions, you only know that the future is painful and toilsome until you die. How many times you are bought, sold, whipped and forced to eat slop until then is unknown.

It showed that I was starting to feel like a freeman.

We sat staring at each other for a long time, Lune's expression blank with wonder while mine felt both hot and desperate on my face. Finally he tidied up his plate a little, before putting a glass lid over it. Very carefully, he stood up and put a cloth over the salad bowl and my own plate of dinner. Then he beckoned to me.

"Come with me. I'll show you something. And then I'll answer your questions."

Feeling solemn, I stood up from the table and followed with the same care he had displayed. We went up the stairs to the second story, where both of our bedrooms lay. I had never been in his chamber before, as he kept it locked during the day. This did not seem odd to me, as he complained about having precious books of medical knowledge inside. He was worried that a thief would steal them if neither of us were in the house. Books on medicine could be quite expensive in that world, so it did not seem odd to me in the least.

Now he unlocked the door and led me into the room. There was the shelf of expensive doctor's books against one wall, with a glass cover over them. Near it was an elegant writing desk, with a window spilling golden evening light onto it. Unlocking the desk, he pushed open the top to take out a miniature model made of a light metal.

I came forward and gazed at it as he lay it on the top of the desk. It had pathways marked out with dark squares, with tiny walls on either side of them. Here and there along the paths was set a piece of metal painted to look like a door, though they would have been too small to see any numbers on. Instead, the numbers had been marked on the floor in front of them in Roman numerals. I, V, X and so on. It was the Dark Passages.

"I don't have a very good memory for roads, paths and things," Lune admitted with a prim flutter of his fingers. "So one of our friends made this for me. He is quite skilled with his hands, as you can see."

I reached out to touch one of the walls, which was thin and smooth under my hand. I ran a finger along it, following it until I found the door where I had stopped to talk to Corky earlier that day. Two-forty-three.

"It...it's wonderful."

And it was, in a simple way. Just a slab of wood painted dark green with the dark hallways laid out on it. I began to feel a tiny spark of enthusiasm for the subject, perhaps a little touch of the magic which Corky had spoken of.

"May I hold it?"

Lune gave it to me without a word. Cradling it carefully, I went to sit on the edge of his bed. With a finger I followed out the different paths, each one starting at door number one and running until it hit another one. But there was a problem with the three-dimensional map. Many of the paths ended at the edge of the piece of wood, with open sides to show that they should have gone on. Because of this, some of the door numbers on the main paths started at twenty, thirty or even higher figures, without the map showing the beginning. Or they trailed off into nothing, the flow of numbers cut off by the edge of the map.

"Where is the rest of it? Are there other parts of this map?" I looked up from fondling it.

Lune let out a small sigh. "There is more of it. Much more, we think. But so far that is all we have been able to unlock. The doors further on are still closed, their glowing bars dark and knobs locked. Worse, some of the paths themselves are blocked off by barricades, rubble, even ruin. That is all of the Dark Passages we have been able to get working so far."

"So far..." I repeated after him in a murmur, holding the model up to the light. It was surprisingly heavy, though the walls were thin and the metal light. The golden sun rays gleamed off of the walls, making them spark silver. I held it up for a long moment, before asking, "where are the Dark Passages, exactly?"

"Didn't you find them through the gate in my cave? What do you mean?"

"Well." I set the model on my lap. "This is here because I'm holding it here. It's resting on my lap, so it can't fall. But if the Dark Passages goes to all of those different worlds, it can't be on this planet, can it? Or is it just underground here and has portals to somewhere else?"

"Oh. No." Lune shook his head with another breathy sigh. Explaining things was hard work for him. "That is one of the greatest mysteries about the passages. The gates are in our worlds, but the Dark Passages themselves are not. If you dug down behind the portal all you would find is more stone and earth. So where are those halls? Some Keepers think that they must be on a planet that is through the doors, we just haven't found which. But most of us agree that it must be nowhere."

"Nowhere?"

"Nowhere. In a vacuum. A sort of magical black hole that exists nowhere and that nothing else exists in."

I gave a light snort, turning the map around to see it from a different angle. Something like it could not be nowhere, I thought, not really. Stone has to have a foundation to lie on.

"Why don't you just lift a tile and find out what is beneath it?"

Lune took in a gasp of air, before letting it out in a hiss. I looked up, startled, and saw his face turning red.

"That is against our laws. One day you will understand. If you join us, that is."

He turned away, folding his hands behind his back and staring out of the window, shoulders as stiff as he could manage to make them. Time passed slowly for a few minutes, until he faced around again, expression calm and face back to normal.

"Now, for your original questions. You wanted to know why I didn't tell you about the Dark Passages earlier on, I believe?" He looked at me and I nodded, so he went on, "well, it was not my secret alone to tell. You can see, looking at that map, how much of the Dark Passages we have worked to free. It has not always been easy, I'll tell you that. And we can not risk losing everything we have gained by telling anyone about them. Not yet. Perhaps not ever. If people in general knew about them, what do you think would happen?"

I tried to imagine telling anyone in Ti-Gallin about the Dark Passages. They would probably just laugh and think you were playing a game. But if they believed you, what would happen?

"They would want to use it themselves," I said hesitantly, "and maybe exploit it for tourism and transportation?"

"Exactly!" Lune waved his hands around in the air. "There would be people wandering around, getting caught by who-knows-what, trying to disassemble the doors, jumping in and out of worlds recklessly...and perhaps even some people knowingly trying to sabotage our efforts."

"So what does this have to do with telling me about it?" I ran a hand over the model in my lap. "I'm not going to tell anyone else."

Lune shook his head. "But we could not know that for sure. Take this time as a sort of, well, quarantine. Tallray was convinced that you were the right person from the moment he set eyes on you. We could both see that you had the right potential to learn the mysteries of Erilaz. But what sort of person are you, Nolin? Will you help us, keep our secrets faithfully and follow our charter? Or has your time in the mines embittered you to the world so that you will try to ruin our plans, destroy our work and take us apart from the inside out? The Keepers are still weak and fragile. We've just begun to build our world up. Are you going to help us, Nolin, or betray us?"

I bowed my head, realizing the truth of his words. They had no reason to trust me from the start. No one could be relied on without trust. I was just an experiment until I could prove otherwise.

"I mean you no harm of any sort," was my eventual reply, "like I said, I am very grateful for the opportunity you have given me to live free. But...I don't know if it is in me to be a Keeper. Everyone says that they see it there, but I don't feel it yet."

My gaze slowly lifted to his face, afraid once again of seeing anger or disappointment there. But to my surprise Lune was smiling in a way rare for him.

"You'll find it when the time is right. Don't worry, Nolin, as long as you want it, you will find it. Now! Since you know of the Dark Passages, there is no reason to delay taking you to meet the others at the meeting place. Tomorrow morning we will go there together. If Tallray is available, that is."

"Is he missing?" I asked.

Lune rolled his eyes, taking the map to put it away. "Not exactly. That soft fool is always going off on wild expeditions, to find Carmot, or dragon's blood, or some other useless, expensive ingredient for his experiments. He was supposed to have come to check on you every few days while I was at work, but he sent a message saying that he could not come. If he can't pull himself away for an official meeting, I don't know what we'll do with him!"

His tone of exasperation was reassuring to me. No one spoke of a man that way if he was likely to die. Putting my worry for Tallray aside, I began to wonder what meeting the other Keepers would be like. So far, the three that I had met were all fairly mild and kind in their own ways, even fussy, strict Lune having proven himself a sort of friend. But I had the feeling that not all of them were so easy to get along with.

Interlude 1: Dustlands

The Wizard Nolin held the clay cup in one hand, tilting it back and forth to watch the water shift. Candlelight played on it, touching the red clay with warmth. Dust continued to filter into the room, falling on sill and furniture. Looking over the top of the glass, he snatched a glance at the boy. "You must be weary by now. Shall I wait to tell the rest of my story until you have slept?"

Hiram shook his head. He was definitely stubborn. "I do not want to sleep, Nerheem. Your story has caught hold of me."

"It is...restful to have someone to tell it to," Nolin admitted, "but you may stop me if you must fall asleep. The next part is full of technical detail."

"That is what I want to hear most of all."

"So be it."

As the wind screamed and beat at the door like a furious woman, his calm voice went on.

Chapter 7: Meeting and Learning

It was difficult to sleep that night. I kept turning my conversations with the two Keepers over in my mind, trying to extract every bit of information out of them. And when I was not doing that, I was worrying about what the next day would be like. Every awakening was full of a hundred thoughts which kept sleep away.

Finally the gray light of dawn crept through my window and I levered myself out of bed. I was used to sleeping in my clothes and had not changed that habit since the Neomium mine, despite Lune's offer of pajamas. So I had nothing to do when preparing myself except for walk down the stairs and eat breakfast.

Lune was always up only a few minutes before me and had become used to my early alertness by now. He simply nodded over a newspaper as I went passed the dining table into the kitchen. It was a wonderful feeling to be able to help myself to whatever I wanted to eat. Fruit and cereal, milk and juice, anything I wanted for breakfast.

When I returned to the table with my things Lune flopped his paper down with a sniff, "terrible, terrible world! How can anyone live in it?"

"Most people can't get away," I pointed out, "Not without dying. And most people want to live."

He sniffed again, agreeing reluctantly. After watching me eat for a few minutes he put in suddenly, "you won't be staying with me tonight. Hopefully not for a week or two, if that."

He had sprung it in an attempt to get back at me by choking me in the middle of a bite, I think, but it didn't have that effect. I swallowed firmly before asking, "Why?"

"I was in communication with some of my—er, some of the Keepers, including Tallray." Lune idly began folding the newspaper up into triangles, fat fingers moving steadily across it until the whole thing was one big triangle with all the others folded into it. "We agreed that, to start your education properly, you should probably sleep at the meeting place or stay in rotation with the various members who will be teaching you their skills."

After a minute of thinking this over I decided that it would be fine by me, as long as none of the Keepers was a real tyrant. Though staying in the meeting place sounded odd to me, as I imagined it to be a sort of courthouse with hard wooden benches inside and a podium for the Keepers to speak at.

"Corky told me that there has to be ten Keepers to run the Dark Passages. Does that mean that there are nine now and I will become the tenth?"

"Oh, no." Lune looked a little uneasy, shaking his head. "There are ten of us now. You will simply be an apprentice, learning your trade until you can take your place as one of us."

I nodded, wondering privately why he looked upset. The rest of breakfast passed smoothly, after which there was a crawling, awkward time of waiting for the appointed hour of the meeting. Everyone else had to get there too and, as Lune explained, not all of the worlds were on the same time schedule as ours. For some of the Keepers it was still night time, while others had waited until almost noon to get on their way. To choreograph everything most conveniently we had to wait until near nine in the morning before leaving. It was hard for me to sit and do nothing.

Finally the hour came, Lune walked out of the house to where I was dangling my feet idly in the stream and we started along the secret path to the cavern.

It felt much less mysterious to be going into the cave towards that door with the little healer. He had a brightly colored jacket for every day of the week, today's being neon green. Beneath that he wore a gray suit of very stiff, formal clothing, presenting a picture that was not at all magical or otherworldly. But as soon as we stepped through into the Dark Passages he seemed strangely out of place. A short, dumpy figure leading the way down the gloomy, arched halls of the ancient edifice.

It almost seemed like the doors stared at us in passing, elbowing each other and whispering as soon as our backs were turned. I felt on edge, both because of the meeting ahead of us and the feeling of watching eyes all around. Last time I was here I had not experienced that feeling, but now that the passages were my future it seemed to take more note of me, and me of it.

Both of my hands were clenched tight behind my back as we went along, the smashed one having long since healed completely.

We walked down the short hall to the long one, turning to the right as I had done before. We had only gone a few steps when a sound of footsteps came up behind us and I turned to wait, heart lifting at the thought that it might be Corky. But when the newcomer came into view it was not the chattering Elemental. It was Tallray, dressed in a splendid new coat of white with gold trim and a rose in the top buttonhole.

"Aha, I find my friends on the same path as myself!" He exclaimed, as if it were a revelation. "There must be a meeting this morning."

"You know there is," Lune sighed, giving him a disapproving glance over his shoulder without pausing in his stride. I gave him a shy look, not sure how to thank him for choosing me or explain my impertinence in discovering these halls on my own.

He transferred the responsibility to say anything of the sort by catching up to me and giving me a friendly grip on the shoulder, "I am glad to see you here. We need you and, I think, you needed us."

I gave one nod in return, which finished everything that needed to be said between us.

When we reached door 243 Lune paused for a moment, hand on the latch. "Remember to behave yourself in here, Nolin. And, ahem, pay attention to your manners. And—"

"Please, open the door," Tallray interrupted him. "We do not want to be late."

Lune shot a venomous look at the Alchemist, but did as had been requested of him. Eagerly, I looked over his shoulder to see what the meeting place was like.

The first impression I got was of somewhere verdant and gray, with a sapphire sky making a small circle overhead. gradually the colors took form as a circular opening with grass and moss carpeting its floor. A cliff of stones and fern-covered earth ran all of the way around the clearing, varying in height from five feet to nearly twenty. In the tallest part of the wall there were caves, three of them. The first two were open with raw stone edges around the entrance. The last one on the right had a frame mortared into it and a door set in the frame, though the door was open at the moment to show a smooth stone wall within.

Beside the caves a few simple wood structures had been built, open shacks with benches and tools inside. Chips of wood, stone and other material littered the floors of these booths while raw samples lay in stacks outside. The last two prominent features of the cozy clearing were a pool of water near the lowest part of the cliff and a row of newly-planted saplings across from it.

Sitting just outside the central cave was a man in a wheelchair. He had no leg past either knee, just a thick, dark blanket. A cloak of violet and black patterned cloth draped across his shoulders, the hood hiding his face in shadow.

"That is Sultane," Lune hissed, leading the way towards the figure. "He likes to watch the Keepers arrive."

I could not take my eyes off of him. Despite the fact that his face was hidden, I got the distinct feeling that his eyes were locked on to mine. When we had come closer Lune addressed him with respect, "here is Nolin, Sultane. Who else has arrived so far?"

"Only Feleago and Adasian have yet to appear." Sultane's voice was surprisingly strong and vibrant, with only a touch of a crack running through it from age. Up close I could make out the face beneath the hood, old and sharp as an antique battle-ax. His silver hair was tied down one side in a braid which had nothing feminine to it, the end being tied off with a leather thong decorated in animal teeth.

Still his eyes had not left me. Feeling attracted by them, I came to stand at the side of his chair. He tilted his face up to watch me longer without saying a word. I could not speak: I was too awkward.

After a long silence he finally spoke, "the others are waiting in the cave."

Dismissed, I turned with Lune and Tallray to enter the central cavern, which was the largest. It was a shallow one but spacious inside, being almost round on its floor plan. In the very center of the circle was a rectangular table, made of solid stone rising up out of the floor. No one had ever constructed that table or moved it from its place. It had been carved directly out of the earth along with the cave.

But the thing which caught my eye first on entering the meeting cave was the assortment of characters waiting there. And it was only in the broadest sense of the word character that they could be described.

Perched indolently on the table was a man dressed in the brightest shades of orange, all of it either dyed leather or tinted metal armor. His hair was a shade of reddish gold too, sticking up in unruly spikes with a gray metal circlet around it. Beside him stood a fidgety figure with large, round glasses, the thinnest hands I had ever seen on a living being and a robe of coarse material belted on his waist. Lounging against the back of the wall was a bulky giant of a fellow with a face like a boulder set with teeth. He cracked his knuckles one by one as he waited.

Drifting about the room was a man who seemed too intent on arguing with himself to notice anything else. He had shoulder-length black hair and a quick, penetrating expression.

I was happy to spot Corky near the back wall among them, still grinning pleasantly while he rubbed one hand up and down a carved staff held in it. Leaving my escort, I made my way quickly to him before I could be introduced to everyone along the way. I felt their eyes watching me, but only with curiosity, not hostility. Ignoring them, I hurried over to the corner with Corky, who whispered as soon as I was close enough to hear, "what do you think of your first meeting?"

"Crowded. Is there only ten of you?"

"Only seven in here, right now." Corky shrugged, still caressing the staff. I noticed that it was decorated with shapes of leaves, trees, waterfalls, flames and random swirls, all carved intricately in the wood.

"Did Lune take your head off when he found out?"

"Not all in one blow," I told him, suddenly recalling what had happened after leaving Corky the day before. "But I did see something strange through another door in the passages after we were talking. I think it might have been a Whistless man or something of that sort."

"Really?" Corky's green eyes got wide. "What did it look like and where was it?"

I described the door to him and the land through it as best as I could, before going on to explain, "he was tall, the tallest person I have ever seen. He had short gray hair and a gray robe. But the strangest thing of all was that he had no face."

Strangely, Corky did not seem very worried at this announcement. Instead his face took on an expression of mirth which slowly grew with the telling. He was about to say something when I had finished, but before he could speak something behind me caught his interest. His mouth opened in a little 'o' and his eyes got even wider. Spinning around, I saw the figure I had just been describing standing there, featureless face turned towards me. I froze, hands clenching into useless fists at my side. I was too startled even to scream.

A voice came out of the figure, emanating from a point unknown rather than coming from any orifice, "I am not a Whistless man, young one, or else you would already be dead. I am Feleago."

"You're Feleago?" I could not help staring, while he continued to stand with his empty face turned towards me. He gave a small nod of his head and went on in the same sepulchral, echoing voice, "Feleago I am, descendant of Mereagi the Knower and Hallia the Wise. But I have no title as magnificent as theirs."

With this introduction he drifted away like a ghost, going to speak to the dark-haired man who still seemed to be arguing with himself as he paced the floor. I looked around at Corky, who was laughing silently into his free hand. Seeing me glance around he stopped laughing and controlled his face with an effort.

"He's the Mentalist, if you haven't guessed. Pretty spooky, huh? But that's how all of the people from his planet look, with no faces. They're called the Noomilak and supposed to be a dull, dour folk.

But somehow I doubt that they can all be gloomy. There's often a hint of amusement in Feleago's mental voice that betrays a hidden joke."

"Mental voice? You mean he put that voice into my mind, directly?"

"As far as any of us can figure."

I shook my head, already feeling like the meeting was going to be far too strange for me to understand. Deep inside, a trapped feeling was growing.

By now both Feleago and Adasian had arrived, so Sultane wheeled himself into the cave to join us. After a moment more of wandering disorder, the Keepers began to quiet and gather around the table as if on a common impulse. A solemn hush fell over the room, making me look about nervously. Everyone's face was turned towards me, eyes seeming to penetrate into my skin. I shivered a little, wishing I could hide behind Corky to avoid their gaze.

Then it struck me that this might be a sort of test, or at least an inquiry into my bravery. Not wanting to appear a coward before them, I squared my shoulders and stood straighter, giving them all back look for look. I had worked hard for my living, surviving a year that many did not. They were only my superiors in knowledge.

A small sigh passed around the table. The feeling of being examined left me, while some eyes pointed away. Tallray gestured towards me, speaking so that all could hear clearly. "This, as you know, is Nolin. He was a slave in the outskirts of Ti-Gallin, where one of the Ten Founders first came from. Because of that, and because of the potential we saw in him, we have asked him to join us as an apprentice. Is there any against this idea?"

The big man raised a hand. "How do we know that he will not betray us?"

"I already told you about that in my communication, Berune," Lune retorted impatiently, "he says he won't, he shows no aptitude for it. What more can you get out of a human or, er, any sort of person?"

"Maybe." Berune crossed his arms. "But sometimes it's the fire which shows the cracks in a stone first. I say we test him."

"That can wait," Tallray looked around at the assembly. "does anyone else have a qualm?"

The fidgety man with thin hands, whom I was soon to learn was the historian Gleeb One-step, held up one of his twig-like fingers. "Er, um, I don't want to cause any problems. And I'm sure that he would never do us any harm on purpose. But how do we even know that it's right to train an apprentice? The old books don't mention it at all. In fact, when the Ten Founders began dying is when they fell apart for lack of followers. Would it be truly traditional to keep him?"

There was a confused babble of input on this idea, which ran on until Sultane's voice broke it up.

"Quiet a moment. I think, Gleeb, that you have touched on a very important factor, in his favor. It is exactly the point that the Founders began falling apart and the Dark Passages into ruin when they lost their numbers. We are not the Ten Founders. We are the Ten Keepers. As such, it is our bounden duty to make sure that there is always someone to carry the torch and keep the passages. No matter what happens to any of us personally."

This speech was so clearly given and carefully thought out that it commanded a length of silence afterwards. A few of the members even bowed their heads as if just remembering their own mortality.

There was only one man who did not seem touched by the speech and, in fact, who had not appeared to be paying attention to anything that went on in the meeting. This was the dark-haired fellow with the sharp expression, who had spent the earlier part of the meeting sunk in monologue. Now he stood with his hands resting on the table, eyes staring at some point above our heads as if he saw a vision. Noticing him, Sultane added, "what is it that you see, Tavierfin?"

Jerked roughly out of his cogitations, the transgressor gave a small bow in the direction of the whole meeting. "Sultane, a new Rune has come to my mind. It...it's been growing all morning and now I have seen it. It is the Rune for Light!"

"Someone, give him a piece of paper," the giant Berune said dryly, "or we won't get anything else done with him during this meeting."

A piece of paper was found and passed around, with a pencil, until Tavierfin got it. He leaned over the table, scribbling feverishly.

"I think we have all overlooked one important point in this discussion," the one who had provided the paper, a man of clerical appearance, with a precise voice, spoke now, "does Nolin want to become our acolyte? It is the most critical question, as he will not get anywhere as a Keeper without the will to be one."

I had been waiting for this question to be raised, half-dreading it the while. What did I truly want? I tried to search my mind, the part of the mind they call your 'heart'. I felt in it a strong curiosity, a wish to understand the mysteries which were all around me at the moment. There was also a subtle feeling of payment due, the sensation that I should try to please these people because of their kindness to and trust in me. But as of yet, I still did not feel the full impact of the magic they had spoken of. They carried this magic with them easily, I knew that. It was a tangible thing in that room and I was outside of it.

"Well, Nolin?" Tallray urged cautiously, "what is your answer?"

I took a steadying breath, gripping the smooth stone table under my hands. "I don't feel the magic that seems necessary to be a Keeper yet. But I have been told that it will come with time. I—I don't know if you really want me. But if you do, I will be your apprentice. I will learn from all of you, anything I need to know. And...if you teach me well, I promise to be the best Keeper that the Dark Passages has yet seen."

Ah, my brave words. Such deadly, brave words, full of truths and lies like the facets of a jewel, none of which I could see yet. Don't ever promise to be the best at something. Don't let your ego carry you away, nor your trust in others. Every day will be its own guideline, no matter what you do to force it into shape in the days before.

At least I had put in the bit about 'if you teach me well.' Not that it ended up mattering, but it was a wise stipulation among foolish promises.

I had made my decision and cast my lot with the Keepers of the Dark Passages for that time. Most of them congratulated me and were cheerful about it, though Berune still insisted that I should be tested first. The rest discussed it and put it off for later, deciding that it was better to begin teaching me before giving me any sort of test.

The trapped feeling in my center fluttered and was buried for the moment.

All this time Tavierfin had been working on his Rune. He had not been ignoring the conversation entirely: he still mumbled something to me about joining them being a difficult choice and a noble one. But his mind was really more in the work before him than in what we were saying. Finally, he completed it and straightened up, showing it to us all.

"Let there be light!"

It was a simple sketch of two thick lines running vertically on the paper. The first was shaped a little like a jagged letter 'M' up on its side, while the second was more like a backwards 'Z'. Between them and on each side were hollow circles, small ones like dots. Though it was only pencil marks on paper it almost seemed to glow when I looked at it. Perhaps it was only Tavierfin's excitement and announcement influencing me, but looking at them I got the strong impression that they were light, in all of its brilliant, formless power.

"What can you do with it?" I asked, remembering how Tallray had burned the paper with his fire Rune.

"Nothing, as of yet," Tavierfin admitted, rolling the paper carefully up. "But, you see, I had not worked out the Rune for Light before. Just Fire, which is common in old scripts and traditions. Now that I have this Rune, I can attempt to place it on a stone and imbue the stone with its power, either by itself or in combination with other Runes. By itself it could, theoretically, make a stone which gave off light without any other power source. Very useful for exploring the ruined portions of the Dark Passages."

"How did you work it out, just by staring at the wall?"

"Pure inspiration," he declared, before seeing my puzzlement and adding more simply, "I'll teach you all about it soon. Runeology is one of the most important studies connected with the Dark Passages."

"Speaking of which, he should probably be shown around them and told some more about them before he learns anything else," Corky suggested, eyes suddenly sparkling with eagerness. "I could show him around, if you want. With a few other experts, of course."

"Just a minute!" Gleeb interrupted any response, jerking on a length of his white hair distractedly. "Er, um, there should be an initiation ceremony of some sort first, I think. The Ten Founders had an initiation for all of their members, administered on each other. We all followed their pattern as Keepers. Shouldn't he?"

"But he's not a Keeper yet." The man dressed in bright orange protested, followed by Berune with a grunt of disapproval.

"He's not anything yet. Not without a test! This kid can't be trusted to learn our secrets."

I soon learned that meetings could easily dissolve into mere arguments. Sometimes a meeting was as solemn, deep and philosophical as I had imagined. But most of the time it was just a collection of ten men with widely divergent characters and opinions. This was one of those times that the meeting collapsed into an argument for at least fifteen minutes solid.

I felt embarrassed, being argued over like a dinner that was not yet prepared. The trapped feeling expanded and filled my chest. I needed fresh air and space to breathe it in.

So while they were discussing how it would be best to teach me, I slipped outside. The sun was high overhead, beaming its warm light down directly into the clearing where the cave of meeting was. The grass was soft and springy under my feet, a small pleasure not to be underestimated. Crossing it, I stopped at the pool for a moment to look in. It did not have a visible source, yet was clear and mostly clean. A few strands of grass grew inside of it like seaweed, with bubbles of air caught on their sides. Some sort of underwater creature, as small as the tip of a needle, scurried in the mud on the bank.

I could have stayed there for longer and enjoyed it, but my curiosity led me passed the pond to climb the low embankment on the edge of the clearing. There was a clear path at the least steep part of it, where people and animals had gone up and down before me. The dirt showed pale and dusty there, the grass worn off from the activity. I dug the toes of my shoes in the dust and scrambled up, standing on the top of the little ridge with a hand above my eyes to block out the sunlight. On the other side it sloped down in a long, gentle hill of the same fine grass, before falling off abruptly in a sheer cliff. I drew in along breath of wonder as my gaze went out past the edge, across an abyss of broken, jagged stones to the foothills of blue mountains far away. Following them upwards, my eyes traveled high into the sky before finding their snow-covered peaks making a crooked line against the empty air.

"Beautiful, isn't it?"

With a jerk, I looked around to see Corky standing just below me, staff planted in the dusty path. I nodded, turning back to follow the path with my eyes as far as it could be seen. It wound down the hill to the very edge of the cliff, where it split into two separate paths. One followed the cliff top around the hill to my right and out of sight, while the other seemed to make a leap of faith down the vertical cliff. I could not see where that end led.

"Sorry about all of that in there." The Elemental jumped up beside me, sharing the panorama. "Sometimes our inexperience shows itself clearly. I've been a Keeper for two years and some of the others started experimenting with the Dark Passages earlier on. But we have not got all of the details worked out yet."

"Didn't the Keepers think about how they would teach me and what would be required before they purchased me and brought me here?" I asked, folding my arms on my chest.

Corky fidgeted for a moment, appearing uneasy. "Well yes, of course we did. But, er, we overlooked how we should begin the whole procedure. Don't worry, they have it figured out now."

"Do they?" I gave him a sharp look and, seeing only honesty on his freckled face, conceded, "then I should go back."

He turned with me and we jumped down the low cliff, landing with a double thump in the grass and mosses. I pulled a small clump up with me as I stood, looking at it closely. "How can this grow down in this clearing when people are always walking here? A path has been worn in this hill, but not on the floor."

"That's my doing." Corky waved his wand around proudly. "Earth is one of my Elements, remember? So I can use my connection to the land to make the grasses grow strong enough here to resist the wear of footsteps. The moss helps too, as I imported it from a place where it grows even under the trampling feet of large beasts without getting ground into dust."

"That's a good idea." I dropped the clump with a shake of my head. "I guess I shouldn't pick it, then."

"No, please don't." He gave me a wry smile, starting to lead the way back to the meeting cave. Inside, the Keepers had resumed their quiet demeanor and orderly positions around the table. Tallray was the first to speak when we came in;

"Ah, good, you did not run off. Our apologies for the delay, my young friend. These things often take time. Now, I believe we have come to a decision."

"Yes and it's historically supported, too!" Gleeb put in excitedly, before being hushed by a tap on the shoulder from Tavierfin.

Sultane took up the explanation here, "all that we require, Nolin, is that you promise to stay with us for three weeks. During that time you will obey our words and try to learn our ways. If, after that time, you still do not think that the 'magic' as you called it, is in you, or if you decide that it is not the right life for you, you may leave with no hard feelings."

"But—" Berune tried to interrupt, but he was casually slapped on the back by the slim man dressed in orange. Obviously the one in orange had more strength than was first apparent, because Berune staggered under the blow despite being the more chunkily built of the two.

This interference allowed Sultane to go on, "at that time you will be given a test, if you wish to continue your learning as a Keeper. If you pass it, which I am confident will not be too difficult if you have applied yourself, you may continue your scholarship. Otherwise you will be gently told to leave and, once again, no hard feelings will be held against you."

I had already made my decision. There was nothing to go back on or change. To his words I nodded agreement, before asking, "one question. So far as I have seen, all of you only have one specialty. I might be wrong, but it seems like it. Corky is the Elemental, Gleeb the historian, so on. Why will I be taught everything instead of just one specialty too?"

"That's a simple question to answer." The Keeper in orange grinned, his mouth making a pointy smile. "It would be better if we all could do everything. But since most of us are too old and set in our ways, we can only try to make the next generation better. That's why Corky here is still going to school on some specialties while he's a full Keeper. He's young enough to learn."

He gave the Elemental a jab with his elbow, a friendly gesture which made Corky wince. I eventually found that this bright, pointed fellow was called Firendaze and he was truly a fighter. He practiced martial arts of at least three types, all of which I had never heard of before. As well as all battle skills including proficiency with the bow, spear, firearms, brass knuckles and a strange weapon called the Staivin. I never did get to a level where I could beat him two out of three times in a fight. My swiftest movement was slow compared to his, I was not strong enough to defeat his endurance and his skill (or talent, perhaps) for always striking exactly where he wanted to with anything. Sometimes, his martial skills were almost uncanny.

Because of this it had been decided that he would act as a guard or escort while Corky, Gleeb, Tavierfin and I toured the Dark Passages. They wanted me to learn more about them and their history, including stories about the Ten Founders and the other worlds.

"Other worlds are one of my specialties too," Corky told me, twirling his staff about in excitement. "I'm on a quest, you see. The sort that can easily last a lifetime. I'm looking for the perfect world."

"Perfect for what?"

He laughed, giving me a sideways look. "Not perfect for anything in particular. Just perfect. Without flaw: full of only good."

"Which is an impossibility," Gleeb sniffed, adjusting his glasses to make them more comfortable. "Because of the statement in Genesis that—"

"Oh, it might not apply to every world." Corky shrugged him off before he could finish. "Don't be so fatalistic. Come on, Nolin. Maybe if we try a couple of new doors in the next few days you can help me find the perfect world."

I did not think then that his idea was a practical one and I still do not now. But who knows? He might still be searching for, or even have found his perfect world. One without flaw, from his own point of view.

Chapter 8: The Dark Passages in More Detail

After a few slight aspects of the tour had been decided on, we set off. The gate into the passages from the clearing was much like the gate in the cavern at Lune's house. It was made of heavy metal and riveted all around, but set into a stone lintel instead of a wooden one. We walked out of it into the Dark Passages, stepping into their gloomy lighting and distant, eerie hum.

"What makes that noise?" I asked, stopping the group with a wave of one hand.

Everyone paused for a moment and listened, before Tavierfin answered, "It's the Runestones. Or at least, that is what we believe it to be. Small ones don't make any noise that we can perceive, but larger ones do make a very tiny humming sound."

I looked around at the walls and ceiling, puzzled. "What Runestones?"

"Ah, yes." He ran a hand through his hair, making it wavy. "I forgot. You're new."

It seemed surprising that he had forgotten that already, but Tavierfin was like that. Brilliantly clever in some ways, ridiculously absentminded in others. A true genius, I suppose.

"We believe that the floor is entirely made of Runestones. Very powerful ones, of course, all with their Runes turned downwards. That would explain why the floor is jointed, instead of one piece like the walls. And it would explain the binding which holds the Dark Passages together. In fact, done by masters like the Founders, the Runestones on the floor could provide the magic necessary to make the whole place work."

He had begun walking again as he spoke, so that I had to hurry to keep up with him. All the while, I kept looking down at the giant tiles under my feet. "These are Runestones? All of them?"

"As far as we can tell. They are certainly all made of Solron, the material which tiles to put Runes on is almost always made of. Whether there are Runes on all of them or not, it is a sad thing that the Runestones were put facing downwards. Otherwise we could read the Runes and perhaps decipher them."

"Unless the legends of a Runeless Runestone are not just imaginary!" Gleeb One-step put in, "then there would be no way of telling if they were facing upright or not."

"It can't be true." Tavierfin shrugged with the prideof a practitioner. "That is like having wetless water or hot ice. It just doesn't work. It is the Runes which bind the maker's will into the stone. They must be visible, or else they would not be fastened there to keep the maker's will bound. The spirit would fly and the power be gone."

Which was poetic, but not exactly true. Is air not there to breathe because we can not see it?

By now we had walked some distance down the Dark passages further from where Lune's passage split off, the numbers on the doors climbing upwards all the while. Here and there other halls took off to the left or right, always perpendicular to our course. Some of them seemed to curve slightly or take sharp corners within my view-length, but none of them forked out of our path gently, or at anything other than a ninety-degree angle.

As we went, Gleeb began to tell me of the history of the Passages, starting with the Founders long ago. The little that was known of them before they became Founders was that they were all powerful, independent-minded and somewhat mysterious men. Some were travelers through time and space, others scholars who had poured over ancient books and writings for years. All of them had some degree of magical ability, whether Elemental, Alchemical, Mental or otherwise.

This was much like what Corky had told me before, though Gleeb gave it in more detail. He also explained to me how the Keepers thought the Founders began building the Passages one door at a time, first fitting a gate into one, central world where they had all gathered for the experiment. The books were not clear at this point, but somehow they had managed to 'lay down the tiles of the Passages on the dust of ages and build them through the realms of existence one step at a time'.

From there a door had been fitted in for each place that one of the Founders lived, nearer together or further part depending on where their homes were.

"Because the doors do give a slight indication of the proximity of the worlds beyond," Gleeb said, beginning to make my mind whirl with his large words. "Though they usually traverse more than miles of distance, the records suggest that the closer a door is to another, the nearer those two worlds are. There is even one example which we have discovered. The door into Firendaze's world (here he gave a nod to the warrior) has another next to it which leads onto the same planet, simply at a distant location. From this we surmise that the doors actually do correlate to each other in some way, suggesting the distance between not only regular planets in one universe, but that which divides parallel universes. Or non-parallel universes, for those that do not share similar traits."

I must have begun to look blank by then, because Firendaze took pity on me and broke up his flow.

"We're almost to the end of this hall. It's the longest among all of the ones we've found so far. Would you like to see what is at the end and down both branches, boy?"

He offered the distraction with a half-challenging look which instantly revived my interest in the tour. He knew how to spark competition in me.

Looking up, I could just see the end of the long hall. It stopped at a smooth, flat wall with no doors in it. Going forward alone, I found that it branched at the end in both direction. To the left, the hall did not travel far before coming to a spill of stones and gravel which entirely blocked up the passage. Before the spill there were two doors visible, but neither of them were lit up. The bar which was usually green had turned a burnt color, indicating that it was deactivated. Half buried by the rubble was another door, also lightless.

Turning to the right, I saw a path which curved slightly back on itself, so that the end was hidden from my view. Strangely, there were no doors in the walls of this hall as far as I could see. Walking down it, the end slowly came into view. On the wall in the very back I could see a door, but it was the only one.

"Now, to illustrate our theory," Gleeb One-step explained, coming up behind me with the others. "This door most likely leads to a planet very far from the rest. As you can see, no doors were ever installed in between it and the others. Either there are no worlds in between, or at least none that were of interest to the Founders."

"Has anyone gone through this door?" I asked, walking up to it. The green bar was glowing, indicating that it was unlocked.

"Oh yes," Firendaze nodded, "we've studied that one a few times because of its placing. But it is an empty world that we rarely visit it now. Why the Founders put the gate there is a mystery."

With this speech, he gestured for me to open it if I chose. It was just a simple pull handle, so I put out a hand to give it a try. It opened as easily as the other Dark Passage doors, showing a moon-like landscape on the other side. Gray stone was molded into craters, hillocks and vales, with no sign of vegetation anywhere. The sky was dark, without stars or sun. Darker than the sky of the Dustlands, though the stone seemed to be lit by a faint luminescence with no noticeable source.

Nothing moved in the scene. There was no wind blowing up puffs of dust and no grass to bend in it if there had been.

"It's like an abandoned world," I murmured, gazing out across the dead gray landscape. "Abandoned by everything, even the stars."

"Pretty empty, huh?" Corky sauntered up beside me and leaned on his staff. "As far as we know, there isn't anything alive on that world. Which is strange, as it is no colder than a normal winter's day and the air seems fine. Maybe it's just a sort of blank slate, a world that hasn't been made into anything yet."

"It feels dead to me," I told him with a shake of my head, stepping back to close the door in front of us, shutting out the scene. It seemed to me that the Founders must have built the door when there was something there worth having, perhaps a mineral or ore which they needed. But now it was gone, mined out and every trace of its existence wiped away.

"As you saw, there were no stars," Gleeb could not help inserting, "which means no nearby solar systems. None at all."

Even though I had turned away, the picture of that empty world haunted me. As we returned to the main hall I wondered if there still could be relics of an older age somewhere on that world, maybe even near enough to find. If I had a chance, I decided to return and explore it further on my own.

Still curious about where the Dark Passages themselves were located, I tapped on the walls with my knuckles at one point. The stone was too thick to make an echo or give any indication as to what the walls were built against.

"I wonder how thick this stone is?" I stopped to stomp on the floor, heels clicking on the tiles without producing any other effect.

Corky grinned, tapping his staff down on it beside me. "Thicker than we can tell from here. I don't think it would make an echo if you took a sledgehammer to it. Though it might crack, so don't try it."

"Has a Keeper ever had to replace a floor tile?" I asked.

He shook his head, brown curls bobbing.

"No. We've never seen the under side of one, remember? One or two have been faintly chipped, but never enough to impair their usability. Though there is rubble at some places, it is mysterious to us how it got there. It doesn't ever seem to have come from the walls or ceiling. It's like someone put it there on purpose. And the few places that are actually broken, like where arches are cracked off on the roof, it is not deep enough damage to pierce through the wall and show us outside."

"Sadly, we don't have the technology to completely fix those places," Tavierfin added, "only clear the rubbish and patch the ceiling up a little. If we ever came across a tile broken out of the floor, I'm afraid I would not have the mastery needed to replace it. We guess that it would make that section of the Dark Passages unusable, but we are not sure."

"What about that rubble back there?" I hooked a thumb over my shoulder to show where I meant. "Is it going to be cleared?"

Firendaze gave a sinister chuckle. "It is our next project. You'll probably be hauling stone off of it soon enough."

As we spoke we traveled back along the main hall until we had passed both door 243 and the passage where Lune's gate was. The numbers on the doors continued diminishing until we came to the fifteenth, where the tour paused for a moment.

"This door is a special one," Tavierfin explained, pulling it open. "Or at least, it is for me. This leads to the place where I mine Solron for my Runestones. The Founders cut some of their tiles from here as well, though most likely not all of it."

On the other side was a heavily-worn path of dirt leading through a short section of conifer woods towards a steep, looming hill. In the face of it I could make out the dark entrance to a mine, framed in huge timbers.

"I'll take you there sometime," he promised, before shutting the door again. We traveled on to the end of the main hall, where it ended in an archway with a circular room beyond. All four of my escorts became solemn upon reaching it, Gleeb stepping in front of the arch and turning around to announce, "this, my dear young man, is one of the most important places in all of the Dark Passages. It is one of the few rooms that is actually in the Passages, not through a door to the outside. And it is heavily guarded by Runestones with protection wards on them."

The arch was made of dark, flat tiles. The inside of it was lit up by glowing shapes and colors of every description, the tiles facing inwards towards the walkway. I stepped forward to get a closer look at them, but Firendaze put out an orange-plated arm to hold me back, "you can't enter yet."

Stubbornly, I tried to see what was inside, but a hovering darkness seemed to conceal it.

"Why not?"

"Didn't you hear our Historian? The tiles are covered in Runes of warding. They only allow Keepers to go through. Everyone else who tries is flung back by a force-field of electricity. You must be carrying the talisman of a Keeper, which is the same as that of the Founders, to go through."

I stopped struggling then to eye the Runes warily. They were like the electric fences in places around the Neomium mine. A silent guardian to keep me from going through while the more fortunate people could walk beyond freely.

"Couldn't one of you let me borrow your talisman so that I could pass through, just once?"

All four of the Keepers exchanged looks with each other, Corky smiling his 'secret' smile while he answered, "no, I'm afraid that wouldn't be possible."

I was disappointed that I could not see the room beyond, especially as they had said that it was one of the most important in the Dark Passages. But when I pressed them about why I had been brought there if I couldn't go in, Tavierfin did give a brief description of what was inside.

"It is the room where the unlocked doors are powered up so that they can be used. It is also where most of the initiation ceremony is carried out. A deeply mystical place: when you are in it you do not feel like you are part of any other world at all. There is a map of the Dark Passages there, though only the parts with unlocked doors show. There are also places for the ten Founders or Keepers to stand when powering it up. That is why it is necessary to have ten people to work it."

We moved away from the warded room then and began wandering down the other halls. The Keepers showed me how the stones on the doors could be used to count which door you were at, which I already knew but pretended not to.

Once they were done with that I asked, "if you can only power the doors up once you are a Keeper, how did you ever use the Dark Passages to find enough members to work it in the first place? That sounds like a conundrum to me."

"For that," Gleeb said impressively, "I'll have to tell you another history. This one the story of how we came together as Keepers instead of how the Founders were formed."

This sounded more interesting to me, so I paid attention and listened carefully. I can still remember the story how he told it:

"This isn't written in any history book...yet. So I'll have to tell it from my own point of view. I live on the same world as the meeting place is on, further along the path by the cliff. It's not where I came from originally: I immigrated from the nearby planet of Spindex."

"One day I was exploring and stumbled upon the meeting place. I had never noticed the dip in its cliff-faced clearing before and thought that someone might live there. But after watching it for a while, I decided that it must be abandoned. So I came down inside and looked into the three caves. None of them had doors on them at that time, but the table was still in its place. Even better, the left-hand cave held an immeasurable treasure inside. Books. Three of them being about the Founders. Others held knowledge on all of the arts of Erilaz. Which are; Herbology, Alchemy, Runeology, History, Philosophy, Elements, two types of Magic, Time, Space and Martial arts. But I did not learn all of this right away, of course. I only perused a few of the books lightly before becoming interested in what else was around the circular depression. The right-hand cave had evidently once been the home of a monk or ascetic of some sort, I thought the man who owned all of the books and perhaps had carved the table. There was also the Dark Passage gate. It looked strange there, so harshly metallic among the simple curves of cave and cliff. I tried to open it, but it would not budge. Jerking and pulling on it did no good. Eventually I gave it up."

"Upon returning to the village I live in, I asked around to see if anyone knew more about the clearing. Discreetly, of course, as I did not want a lot of tourists coming to trample around in it and ruin the old books. I had felt clearly, as soon as I stepped into the clearing, that it was a special place. Almost sacred. Honestly, I did not want to share it with anyone. And as it turned out, no one else had heard of it except for an old shepherd who thought that an evil wizard lived there and that it was a cursed location. My curiosity aroused, I returned the next day. I read the books over the course of the next week, often trying without success to open the gate, especially once I got a glimmering of what it was. Then one day I walked into the clearing to find a man in a wheelchair sitting there, three Runestones in his lap. It was Sultane."

"He had discovered a gate on his own world and, using a few fragmentary records about the Founders and Runeology, had figured out how to unlock it. You see, the doors are locked with certain patterns of Runes, mostly one or two of the four Elements. Once unlocked, they can be powered up. Usually this must be done from inside the room of Ten, the one with the wards on it. But Sultane had worked out a way to power up one door at a time using a Rune of power. He had three Runes with when we first met; Fire, Earth and the one to power doors. With them he had managed to open both his own gate and the door into my world. We put our knowledge together and explored the Dark Passages a little, teaming up to unlock all of the doors we could with just Fire and Earth. Luckily, one of the first doors we were able to open led to Tavierfin's world."

"He was already studying Runeology, an art which is almost entirely lost even now. But he did have a few old Runestones laying around, as well as having discovered how to make some types himself. A really marvelous discovery, considering how little is known now of how they were originally made and used." "So he joined us. With Air and Water we were able to unlock many other doors, though we were still having to power them up every time we wanted to go through them. The passages were much darker at that time and the ways littered with rubble. Finally we found Feleago, who had already noticed the gate on his world and was trying to discover a way of opening it. He agreed to help us right away, and with his help we recruited all the others. With his aid we were also able to get the talismans of the Founders and enter the room of Ten.

Then we truly became Keepers, promising to uphold certain laws of the Ten Founders and work only to reconstruct and keep the Dark Passages, never to harm them. That, my dear boy, is our history."

Gleeb finished speaking, one hand upheld in his favorite stance of explanation, with the pointer finger of that hand stuck upright for attention while the other hand was tucked behind his back. By now we had rambled down another long hall of the Dark Passages, to a point where more gravel and pieces of dark stone filled the walkway. The doors here were lit right up to the point where the stone intruded, indicating that they were both unlocked and powered up.

"I suppose you moved into the clearing and built the door over that one cave, to live in?" I asked the historian.

"No, Sultane moved in there, actually," Gleeb shrugged, "I still live in the village a few miles away, where they consider me a crazy hermit for spending most my time wandering the hills near the Broken Chasm and the 'cursed' clearing."

"We had better be getting back to it now," Firendaze put in abruptly, glancing around with an uneasy look. "I sense something strange moving in the passages nearby...besides, the others will be waiting for us."

The Keepers became quiet and tense. Picking up on their attitude, I fell in beside Corky and walked with him, every sense alert for something else moving around us. I could not feel it like Firendaze had claimed to, but I knew too much by now to doubt him. He must have sensed something I could not.

When we came to where the passage branched on to the main hall he gestured for us to stay back, drawing a slim jeweled dagger from a sheath at his side. Stealthily, he crept towards the intersection. When he reached it he hesitated a moment, before making a quick step into the main hall. As soon as he had moved beyond the corner of the wall there was a strange noise and something jerked out of the shadows towards him.

Corky jumped forward with his staff and I let out a small cry of warning, but Firendaze was in action before either of us. Spinning toward the shape, which appeared to be a lanky creature made of shadows, he plunged his dagger into it. The black apparition shrieked, a terrible sound, and jabbed at him with one of its long, thin fingers. The spike of a finger jittered over a piece of his armor, before sliding in between the joint at his shoulder.

Firendaze drew his dagger out dripping in darkness and stabbed at the shadow again, trying to grapple it away with his other hand at the same time.

Meanwhile Corky had darted forward to join them and now swung his staff down to crack on the thing's head. There was a strange sound like a mixture between a thump and a crackle as the wooden rod hit, sinking down into the phantom's upper part.

Tavierfin and I had also come forward, though we had no weapons and did not quite know how to come to their aid without getting in the way. Luckily the secondary thrust and the blow to the head seemed to have done the thing in. It let out a gargling cry and collapsed to the floor, where it writhed a moment like the shadows around a fire before falling still. It was shaped somewhat like a human, though much thinner and more jagged. Also, it had no face on its head and only three fingers on each hand, one of which was longer than the rest.

Before my eyes the creature faded away and dissolved into the tiles of the floor.

Chapter 9: Shadow's Touch

"What was that thing?" Stepping forward, I tried to see where the creature had gone. But there was not even a stain left on the floor from where it had disappeared.

"A Shadow Poker," Firendaze growled, wiping his blackened dagger and sheathing it with a thrust, before tearing at the plate of armor on his arm just below the shoulder.

"Did it get you?" Corky demanded, going over to help him. "Did the finger touch you?"

Firendaze had a savage look on his face. "I don't know. I felt something."

With the other Keeper's help he was able to get the metal armor off, leaving only the dyed orange leather pieces beneath. Craning to see over Corky's bent head, I saw a black mark on the leather like a burn, as if a red-hot poker had struck Firendaze's shoulder there. But the mark did not go all of the way through the leather.

"Thank goodness," Gleeb sighed, having come up from the hall to join us, "it didn't get through your armor. You know what the histories say about people who are touched by a Shadow Poker. It says that the touched spot turns black and slowly spreads until—"

"Shut up!" Firendaze waved a hand at him. "I don't need your encouragement. It still feels a little odd beneath, almost cold. Someone help me get this chest plate and arming tunic off."

Corky helped him unlace the chest plate down each side and pull it off over his head. Then the leather tunic had to be unlaced down the front and dragged off as well. Firendaze was not satisfied until they had inspected his shoulder and arm near the joint and found no dark spots on his skin.

"Heh, didn't get me." His laugh sounded more like a sigh of relief. "It couldn't get through good buffalo-bull shoulder pads. It's a good thing I wear some sort of protection, unlike other people I could mention."

He was wearing a thin silken shirt of red and white with short sleeves, under the tunic, so he rolled the sleeves back down and left his armor off to carry it under one arm as we returned to the meeting place. I felt solemn the whole way, wondering what would have happened if Firendaze had not come with us on the tour. We would probably not have known that the Shadow Poker was there and walked straight into his ambush unknowing.

At least one of us would have been touched, with no armor to protect us. And little weapons to fight him off with, either. Only Corky's carved staff, which he was now trying to rub the stains off of using a handkerchief from his pocket.

I shivered, guessing what the end of Gleeb's explanation would have been. Once you were touched the mark slowly spread until it covered all of the victim and they either died, or became a Shadow Poker themselves.

Almost as soon as we entered the clearing of the meeting place the other Keepers began to gather around us, sensing something was amiss. Soon their interest centered on Firendaze and they began asking why he was carrying his armor instead of wearing it.

"Oh, Nolin and I just decided to have a wrestling match to burn off some energy." He returned with his peculiar smile. "And, drat the luck, he beat me."

But they soon squeezed the truth out of the other Keepers who were with us, upon which Lune insisted on seeing the fighter's arm for himself. While the excitement was going on I drifted slowly to the outside of the circle, watching with an odd feeling of detachment. Most of the Keepers were friendly and had welcomed me with open hands. But I still could not quite feel like one of them. Inside, I was still alone.

It was a few minutes before I noticed that Sultane was also sitting at the outside of the group, only a pace away from me. He sat slightly hunched in his wheelchair, hood hiding his face from my view. I looked at the purple patterns on his cloak for a minute, wondering if they meant anything. He had not yet revealed his specialty, so I had no way of knowing if they were part of his trade. As if feeling my notice, he tilted his head up to meet my gaze. He met it silently until I came closer and spoke what was on my mind, "what will you be teaching me?"

His reply was unexpected, "anything you want to know."

"Anything?"

"That does not compromise the honor of any of the Keepers, yes."

I frowned, trying to read into his words. "Which means that you'll only tell me some things, not anything. You'll keep your secrets guarded jealously."

"I think you'll find that there is plenty of room for questions without them compromising our honor." Sultane folded his old hands together on his lap. "Why don't you try me?"

I glanced over my shoulder uncertainly, checking to make sure that we were not overheard. Not because we were speaking treason or any other secrets, but because I felt myself in an awkward position. Gathering my wits and courage, I looked back at him.

"What do the patterns on your cloak mean?"

A small smile cracked the hardened wedge of his face. He looked at the edge of his cloak for a minute as if remembering what it meant. "You know, there was another boy once who asked me the same thing when I offered my knowledge. No one is entirely unique."

His face became more serious as he answered my question, "I wear this cloak in memory of Merenoa, last guardian of the Tears of Shiloam. The pattern was on hers as well, though it is long since lost."

"What are the Tears of Shiloam?" I asked, taking advantage of his offer.

"Were," he corrected, "they were destroyed by the Hungry Ones, when half of Iseldome was invaded. Shiloam was a great adventurer and craftsman who discovered the secret of transdimensional thought. He built visions of what he saw into orbs of glass with changing scenes inside them. But what he saw broke his heart and he died of it, so they were called the Tears of Shiloam."

"Why did this...Merenoa protect them, if those visions killed Shiloam?"

Sultane sighed, "partially for that reason. But also because it was believed that the visions in the orbs could be images of the future, or hold powerful secrets of magic which we had not yet discovered. They were dangerous objects, but also works of beauty and power which commanded awe. Merenoa not only tried to guard them against ruin, but studied them and wrote down what she saw in case there was a secret locked in each orb that could be useful to us."

I felt that I had already asked a lot, but decided to press him on the subject just a little further. "So why do you wear that cloak in her memory?"

"Because," he said, sorrow touching his voice with its resonance, "I was her apprentice. If the Hungry Ones had not destroyed them, I would have been the next guardian of the Tears of Shiloam."

"Oh." I blinked, realizing how much of himself he had just told me. Evidently he would not conceal truths from me just to create mystery, as I had first thought.

We both looked towards the group around Firendaze then, who were all still talking over how the tour had gone and the attack of Shadow Poker at the end of it. Trying to turn my mind to more cheerful things, I asked, "why does Firendaze wear that band on his head? Is he a prince?"

"He is the king of Iseldome," Sultane stated, adding with a shrug. "Even if he usually acts like a gladiator out of the ring for a day."

I stared at Firendaze for a minute, trying to picture him as a ruler in a palace, with servants to do his bidding and officials bowing at his feet. And I could see it, if I pictured him in all of his orange armor with a scepter in his hand. But it still surprised me how varied the Keepers were in what walks of life they came from.

Meanwhile Lune had decided that Firendaze did not need to be healed in any way, though the fighter still claimed that his shoulder felt cold where the Poker had touched the armor. With a few more words to me and to each other, all of the Keepers began to break up to go home. In the meeting place it was only late afternoon, but some of them had to be going to bed, or even pretending to just get up from bed in the morning in their own world. Soon everyone had left except for Sultane, the Keeper called Adasian and I.

"Well, you had better come with me now," Adasian said, surprising me, "unless you want to find the way to Castle Georgian on your own."

"I'm going with you tonight?"

"Evidently." The Keeper had a dry, cynical voice and a face to match, with red-brown hair which looked more utilitarian than ornamental. "In fact, you'll be staying with me for a few days while I begin to teach you my specialty. Philosophy."

That was how I learned that Adasian, using his talent for philosophy, wit and rhetoric, had convinced the other Keepers that I needed to learn from him first. With no time to argue and nothing to pack, I followed him in to the Dark Passages.

Chapter 10: Adasian

The first thing I saw of Castle Georgian was a cozy turret room with tall, narrow windows overlooking a rainy moorland. There was a fireplace, bed and large chest in the room, but most of its space was taken up by an expansive writing desk and shelves of books. And scrolls. Or sheaves of loose paper tied with untidy strings. Anything that held writing or at least symbols to express an idea. Shelves lined every available space of wall which was not used for something more necessary.

We stepped into the room through a picture hung on the wall so that it could swing open like a door. In fact, it was the back of the door which led into the Dark Passages. Once we were inside Adasian swung it shut and I looked to see what the picture was of. Hung in a heavy, gilt frame was an oil painting depicting the meeting place, inside the cave with the table. I recognized it right away, though the characters shown standing around the table were entirely different than those I knew. They were all dressed in dark cloaks which concealed every feature on them except for a pair of glowing eyes. One of them was looking directly out of the image, green eyes large and round.

I noticed that his eyes seemed to be made of a different material than the rest of the picture, right before Adasian said, "it's a rather childish way to have things, but if you need to open that gate you must poke both of the green eyes at once. There's a hidden spring latch."

"Oh. Are those the Founders?" I asked, brushing my hand lightly across the canvass. It felt rougher than I expected under my fingers, the paint laid on in tiny ridges and dimples.

"Yes, a depiction of them at least, so stop stroking them like cats," Adasian snorted, "though I doubt very much that they went around dressed like that all of the time. It would be uncomfortable and they would have smothered in the heat. It is just a symbolic picture indicating their mystery and power."

"Maybe they put the cloaks on for meetings, like a uniform," I suggested, but Adasian did not reply. He was digging bread, cheese and small, purple fruits out of the chest to stack them haphazardly on a platter nearby. I started towards him, only to see for the first time that there was a lanky gray dog laying on a minuscule, ragged rug in the center of the floor. He hardly raised his head when I came to a stop right next to him, thumping his tail twice on the floor in apology for taking up the only rug space. I did not have much experience with dogs, so I did not know if he was actually lazy, or only shamming it.

"Don't mind Hunfred," Adasian told me, kicking the dog lightly in the haunches as he crossed the room to lay the platter on the desk. "He only eats people who are too stupid to stay out of the master's garden. And hardly that, either. In fact, he mostly just runs about on the moor like a lunatic or sleeps on my floor like a drunkard. Isn't that right, Hunfred?"

He threw the dog a crust of bread then, which the dog carelessly licked up and crunched on for a while before swallowing. You would expect from the Philosopher's statement that he did not have much use for his dog, but this was not the truth. As the following piece of bread revealed, Adasian was actually quite fond of the Greyhound. It was simply his manner to ridicule everybody with a sharp derision. Even beings he liked.

"Well, don't just stand there like a hat-rack," he shot at me, gesturing towards the plate. "Help me eat all of this."

I did not need a second invitation. The breakfast at Lune's house seemed like years ago and was, in fact, in another world. So I drew up a stool from beside the fire and we ate bread, cheese and a peculiar variety of extra-sweet figs until even my flourishing appetite was satisfied.

"Tomorrow you shall have milk. It's good for growing people," he decided, which pleased me well enough. For now we drank water with it, finishing the meal with a goblet each of cold mint tea.

After the meal Adasian announced that there was still daylight, so he had work to do finishing up a letter he was copying for the lord of the castle and I might do as I pleased until evening.

"You aren't the owner of this castle?" I asked, taking the plate from the desk to lick crumbs from it.

He pulled out a scroll with words written crazily all across it, as well as one which was only half-covered in a neat, curving hand. "No. I'm Sir Luthian's scribe. Now don't bother me with such foolishness any more. And stop licking that: you'll have the paint off eventually."

Used to being alone, with my head still full of the day's happenings, I was happy enough to be left to my own devices. The dog allowed me to pet him after just a cursory sniff of my fingers, so I crouched beside him for a time stroking his feathery ears and whiplash body. When the novelty of that wore off I wandered over to one of the windows, pressing my face against the glass in order to peer outside. An overcast sky ran into the distance, drizzling heavy drops across the low, soggy hills. A few bedraggled birds flew across the landscape, disappearing quickly into a copse of lonely trees. Even to me, it was a depressing scene.

I tried pulling a few different books from the shelves and reading them. It was a skill I still had from before my days as a slave, one which I had been taught and could not lose. But some of the books were written in languages I could not understand, while the others seemed lethally boring. I soon gave up on them and put them back.

The Dark Passages would have been easy to get into from Adasian's turret, but I had no wish to explore them further today, after having witnessed the attack of the Shadow Poker. There was a second door beside it, this one unconcealed and made of wooden planks painted red. But wandering around the castle would not have been a wise option for me. Even I knew that too many people would have asked awkward questions if they had seen me.

Finally I fell on the last object of interest in the room to entertain myself. The chest in the corner. It was a large, stout affair with cushions tacked to the top so that it could be sat on like a bench. Patterns of red and black depicting stags running through tangled woods lined the front of it. The hasp in the center had no lock in it, so I could easily lift it up. The lid was unexpectedly heavy, though that was no real obstacle to me.

Inside there was two compartments, separated by a thin wooden divider. On the left side was another loaf of the wheat bread and a flagon of light amber-tinted liquid which I thought must be some sort of wine. It was full and there was red wax around the stopper, so I guessed that Adasian must not drink it very often. On the right-hand side was a pile of folded clothes, the top piece being made of a shimmery silk and dyed bright blue. It did not look like the sort of thing Adasian would wear. It was far too flamboyant for my image of what his tastes would be. I lifted the piece out, unfolding it to discover that it was a sort of long, flowing cape with a high collar and bright green velvet lining the inside.

"That is something I've noticed about you all along," Adasian remarked without turning from his work, "you have no manners. You don't say 'please' or 'thank you' or ask permission before you do anything."

I froze, my face slowly feeling warm and uncomfortable all over. A flash of memory showed me my mother scolding me for spilling a glass of milk all over the table when I was very young, then holding up her finger and prompting, "now what do you say when you make a mistake of that sort?"

Blinking back into the present, I mumbled, "I'm sorry."

Hastily, I tucked the cloak back into the chest, slamming the lid down on top of it.

"That's better. We'll work on your manners this evening, along with teaching you what Philosophy means. Manners are not a strong point of my own, I must admit, but they are useful when dealing with fine-grained folk," Adasian remarked, making a flourish with his pen as if to punctuate his words. "Now, there are two puzzles in this drawer beside me if you are bored and don't want to go outside. They've occupied me on many rainy nights when there was nothing else to do."

After staring out of the window until my face had cooled a little, I took his offer and stepped over beside him to open the drawer he had indicated.

Inside there was a small box with a smooth, patterned lid in two different shades of wood. Beside it sat a pyramid of wood, made up of petite, carved blocks. As they were the only two things in the drawer, I guessed that they must be the puzzles. Lifting them out, I carried them over to set on the floor next to Hunfred, where I collapsed beside them.

There followed a pleasant time of twisting, pulling and jiggling as I tried to figure out how the pyramid came apart and how the loose pieces of wood that were in the box could be put together. I worked on them alternately, so that the pyramid was a third deconstructed and a cube of the other parts equally built when Adasian interrupted me to announce that his letter was done being written and he must deliver it now.

"But I'll be back in only a few minutes, when we may start our lessons," he told me, making me look up to see that the clouds had parted a little and the sun was beginning to set in an aura of red-gold outside the windows. The time had gone rapidly, I had been so concentrated on finishing the pair of puzzles.

They had challenged my mind in a way which was both unusual to me and pleasant, after more than a year of brute force labor. Little did I know then how often my mind would be challenged in that way over the course of the next weeks, until running, playing and fighting were pleasures for their use of my pent-up energy.

Adasian was only gone for a short time, as he had promised. When he returned it was with a basket, which smelled temptingly of roast meat. But it was set aside on the desk to be saved for dinner, while the scribe made himself comfortable on top of the chest and gestured for me to sit on the floor before him. Moving into position, I folded my legs and rested my elbows on them.

"First, for your lesson in manners," my initial teacher announced, making me turn a little red again and feel childish as he continued, "let us say one man says to another: 'Give me that book. You do not read it, so I will'. How can you rephrase that to sound more polite?"

"Can I please read that book," I muttered, looking down at the floor between my legs. This was going to be an arduous session, I could tell.

Adasain was silent a moment, before speaking crisply, "Along with Philosophy it is my idea to teach you Rhetoric. Do you know what that is?"

"Something to do with conversations, or arguments," I returned, unclear on the subject and grasping at straws.

"It is the art of speaking so as to convey an idea to the best advantage. Not just a way to converse, but a style of speaking, so as to make a deeper impression on your listeners." The scribe nodded, trying to encourage me. At the time, I thought this sounded like a pointless subject to learn and one that could be of no advantage to a Keeper. On the contrary, it has often come to be of use in my life and, in fact, I could not be telling this story to you now in a clear, concise way without Adasian's lessons. It is due to him that you are getting a story at all, instead of just a rambling tale of hazy adventures.

Soon I was given another sentence to convert, then made to do various tasks around the room which forced me to ask him questions or ask for permission first. I was thoroughly wearied of the subject once we finally stopped.

"You are making some progress," Adasian sniffed hypocritically, "though I think that you'll always be a very direct person when it comes to speech."

After that we were allowed to have dinner and he pointed out a few books that I might want to read in the future, to help 'direct my course in the field of Rhetoric.' Once dinner was over he asked me to bring in a few armfuls of wood from a stack that was just outside the turret in a shed on the ground. No one was around, so I went out of his door into a hall of the castle, down a spiral set of steps and out a door into the wet, graying evening. The smell of the damp moors struck me first, wild and almost wistful. I paused to draw in a deep breath, enjoying the fresh air after the frustration of lessons on manners in the cramped, warm turret.

A few trips up and down the stairs later I was glad for the rest when Adasian said that it was enough wood, though this signaled the next set of lessons to begin.

Chapter 11: Philosophies

"**P**hilosophy," the scribe explained, settling himself once again on the padded bench, "is the way in which an individual looks at the world. It can encompass his moral code, his sense of honor and his ideals on such subjects as death, love, revenge and forgiveness. Or any other part of life, for that matter. Philosophies can be shared with others, or even taught as a code of their own. Many are connected to religions, though that is not necessary for a philosophy to exist. for the use of this course, we will try to disconnect Philosophy from religion as much as possible, though a person's convictions can not help swaying their ideals. For instance, what do you think of death?"

"Death?" I stared at him. Sadly, I had seen death before, many times. It came when exhaustion felled a slave to the ground, or made him stop working long enough that the guards beat him unmercifully. It came when he began to cough and choke because of the poisoning of the Neomium working in him. Though we had possessed little to cling to, no slave wanted to die. We all had regarded the dead with some superstition, speaking their names as little as possible in the hopes that it would forestall our own fate in following them. But I knew nothing of it in a philosophical sense.

"Well...it's not something anybody wants to happen to them," I said, frowning as I tried to work out anything more erudite to say on the subject.

"Then how to you explain suicide?" He asked, folding his hands on his lap and watching me with interest.

I couldn't think of an answer. Not a good one, at least. I mumbled something about some people being in such bad places that they wanted it, I supposed, and left it for him to explain. Instead, he introduced another question for me to answer, on another basic fact of life. The conversation wound on through different subjects from there, not so much as a lesson in what I should think, as an attempt to make me think about what went on around me in a deep and purposeful manner.

When the time to go to bed finally came I was ready for it. My head was so packed full of new thoughts, images and ideas from the day that it made me almost feel dizzy. Adasian took some blankets from under his bed and threw them on the bench for me, apologizing for the narrowness of it as a sleeping place. After Lune's spare room it was a little cramped, but compared to my old cot in the mines it was the height of comfort. I lay for a few minutes, trying to think about all of the opportunities that were opening up in front of me. But I could not keep awake to think them through as much as I would have liked to. Philosophies and Rhetoric still swimming through my mind like wordy fishes, I fell into a deep sleep.

THE NEXT DAY ADASIAN had to attend a gathering in the castle for the first part of the morning. A round, yellow sun had taken the place of clouds in the sky, so Hunfred and I were sent out to amuse ourselves on the moors until lunch time. Adasian led us down the stairs and put us out of the door with a reminder to stay out of sight of people as much as possible. The ground was still wet, the grass soaking our legs at every step. For a little while we shivered as we walked. But when the sun came up over the distant hills enough to light the land it became comfortably warm. Then we ran and romped and played, that whip-lash greyhound and me, searching out gopher's holes and bird's nests in the grass or playing hide and seek in the scattered copses.

When I began to feel hungry again and the sun was far up in the sky we wandered back towards the castle. It was not a very practical fortress, being more of a lord's manor than a stronghold. A square base with battlements on the walkways supported three square towers, two smaller ones in the back and one fat, short one in the middle. Turrets and gables protruded from it all around, with narrow glass windows peering out of them at every angle. Banners flew from the peaks, purple and blue in the light wind. The stones were an old, mossy gray stained with rain having run off of the tinted roofing slates through the years.

I was not worried about anyone on the wall tops seeing us. We were at such a distance that I could have been any farmer's boy and his dog out in the fields. But once we got closer in we went more cautiously. Hunfred seemed to understand my anxiety to remain unseen and followed my example of caution.

We made it up into Adasian's turret without being caught to find that he had just returned from the gathering a few minutes before. He appeared pleased to see us, though he hid it under a chiding manner, "all wet and dirty, both of you. Well, Hunfred will soon dry and clean himself, but I have no extra clothes that would fit the boy. Stand by the fire, Nolin, and I will give you your lunch there."

Though I was not cold I obeyed him, standing by the smoldering coals of the hearth to dry off. He gave me lunch, too, which I was eager to have. When it was gone he said that it was time for another lesson.

"Today we will hold a debate," He decided, moving to pull a pair of slim volumes from a shelf full of them. "You will uphold one set of Philosophies while I shall assault it from the vantage point of another set. You will have to study a little first, of course, to understand what you are arguing for. Would you like to be a Stoic, or an Epicurean?"

I took both of the books he proffered, seeing those names on their titles. "What are they? Stoics and Epicureans?"

"Ancient schools of thought. They were rivals in their time and, I suppose, still are wherever they are taught." Adasian went around me to settle himself at his desk. "Pick one and study it, then I'll take the opposite school to uphold and we will debate Philosophy. It is a good exercise in logic as well as the other two forms of thought I am trying to teach you."

Well, I did not know then what Epicurean meant, in either sense of the word. But I had heard the word 'stoic' applied to someone who did not show pain or fear. That appealed to me, so I chose the book on Stoicism and lay the other aside on the mantle. Making myself comfortable on the bench, I opened the cracking pages.

After I had read most of the book (skipping places where the words were just too complicated for me) I set it aside. I did not feel much more prepared for the debate than I had before, so I said nothing while I tried to process all of the ideas I had just taken in. But Adasian was waiting for me. As soon as the book was closed he declared, "well, now we shall begin. You may have the opening statement."

How do you start a debate on a dead subject? I tried to play my part, with the feeling that nothing which was said really mattered.

"Um...I think that virtue is the goal of all actions."

Adasian snorted dryly, "wait a moment. 'Um, er, ah' are not good ways to begin a statement, no matter what Gleeb One-step seems to think. Also, you should not affix the 'I think' to the front of your argument. In a debate, we are supposed to be convincing each other that what we are saying is the truth. A valid statement. The Only Philosophy, not a philosophy."

"But how can I argue for that? I don't really think that it is the truth, so it would be a lie," I protested.

"Now we are getting into the principals of logic," Adasian commented, "and the difference between sound logic and valid logic. You see, any tenet which makes sense is called 'valid' logic. That is, it makes sense within itself even if it is not the truth how we use that word. For instance, I could say that, every day we do lessons we have soup. Today we are doing lessons. So today we must be having soup."

He gestured at a pot hanging by the fire as he spoke, illustrating the statement. "Which would be a valid argument, even though it is not the truth. Sound logic is an argument which has a basis for every tenet it makes, so is in that sense true. A sound statement would be like this; every day Adasian teaches Nolin. Today is a day. So therefore Adasian is teaching Nolin."

I nodded slowly, beginning to understand what he was getting at. "So you want me to play this debate using valid logic, but not sound logic?"

"Exactly. Convince me that Stoicism is right because it is a valid argument, not because you believe it is true yourself."

"It still sounds like lying to me," I sighed, "but I'll see what I can do."

We began again, this time with Adasian making the first statement to show me how it was done. He won the debate, of course, almost actually convincing me along the way that Epicureans had the best Philosophy of life. But when I thought it over at a later time I realized that I did not believe either of those philosophies entirely. They both had problems, as far as I could see.

Later on that evening we had to play another debate, this time with me acting the Epicurean and Adasian being a Stoic. He beat me again, though I had remembered many of his arguments and tried to employ them against him. His quick wit, exact choice of words and large knowledge of the human mind always left me fumbling.

I give this as an example of the thinking skills that man taught me. I still don't think that I could beat him in a debate, but over time he showed me how to think about the worlds and their inhabitants analytically, reasoning out both their motives and my own in connection with them. He also taught me how to express those ideas, both vividly and tacitly, if I chose.

It is hard to decide, in the end, just how much impact his teaching has had on my life. Would I still be where I am today without them? Perhaps, but I tend to think that I would be moldering in a dungeon or bleaching my bones in the sand if he had never taught me his invisible skills, which a man can never lose.

Interlude 2: The Constraints of Time

The candle was starting to gutter. His bone-white hair catching the flicker of shadows from it, Nolin turned and looked at the flame. It went out, a thin line of smoke rising from the charred wick. He brought out a second candle and touched it with the tip of his finger, making it ignite. Hiram watched solemnly.

Caught in the weave of his own narrative, the wizard stood and paced around the room once. He was remembering the hard shell he had held around himself at first, still afraid that the world would shift back to the horrors of the mine. He felt again how it had slowly fallen away, opening up into a bright new world.

Eventually, Nolin settled back in the creaking chair to explain, "I do not have the time to tell stories about all of my lessons, even those brief ones I learned in the first three weeks before the test. All of my teachers made an effort in one way or another, but some teachings simply are not important enough to go into detail about."

"I wish to hear everything that you will tell, Nerheem. Do not shorten your story on my account. I have the patience of a Sandthistle."

"No man has that kind of patience." One eyebrow quirked on the wizard's face. "And we do not have that kind of time. There are many small adventures I must leave out of my story, or else we would be here for uncounted days sharing it. The constraints of time dictate that I end when the storm is over."

Chapter 12: Elements

I have already given an example of how Gleeb taught history. All of his lessons were that way, long and full of complicated context. I learned a lot more about the Founders and how the Dark Passages were ran at first, but none of it particularly useful to this narrative. The only thing of great interest I learned was how Gleeb had earned his last name, One-step. It seems that he had been working on a Spindec dictionary for the last few decades and every time he was asked how he could take on such a complex project by himself, he would answer, "oh, I just take it one step at a time..."

He had a few other writing projects of this sort as well, but they got much less attention than the dictionary. His answer to questions about them were always the same, so the name stuck and he kept it proudly.

Lune also tried to teach me during a few days of those first weeks. He showed me how to make salves and tinctures, how to bandage a wound or make an herbal tea. Unfortunately, not much of his teaching ever stuck with me. I can still remember some of the herbs and processes, but not enough to save anyone's life if they needed something beyond basic first aid. It wasn't a specialty that I was interested in.

Feleago's teaching did not benefit me much at that time either, nor Berune's.

Berune, I found, was an expert in certain magical skills used for attack and defense. He called it, 'Powerpointing' and showed me that he could destroy a stack of bricks or light a fire using it. But he did not like me and I still had not found my connection to magic. So though he told me to concentrate, explained how to focus my energy and gave an example by shooting bolts of weak lightning at me until I collapsed half-conscious to the ground, I still could not master Powerpointing.

On the other hand, I enjoyed the teachings of Tallray and Corky like a special treat. They are more important to my story, so I will explain them in a little more detail.

After Adasian and Gleeb had been in control of me for about four or five days altogether, it was Corky's turn. We were both excited when the council decided that I should go to stay with him next and learn about Elements.

"You'll like it on my world," Corky promised, "my people always try to settle where all four Elements are present nearby. There's a forest, lake and mountains all within walking distance of my home. You'll see."

I had not yet had time to explore the Dark Passages more on my own, so I kept my eyes open as we traveled down them. My senses were also alert for any sign of Shadow Pokers, lurking around corners or hiding in the gloom.

"Corky, why is there that dark mist down all of the passages? I could understand if it were regularly dark in here, even with the green bars, but the shadows here always seem thick in odd places," I pointed out, waving a hand toward the darkness both ahead of and behind us.

"That is a mystery we have not solved yet," the Elemental explained, turning down a hall to our right. "And may not ever solve, either. Some of the Keepers think that it is only like that because we have not powered up all of the doors. But, like you said, there is not really enough light made by those neon beams to illuminate the passages. So in some ways the fact that there is light to see by in here is more mysterious than the darkness. I think that the entire atmosphere might be created by the Runestones of the floor themselves."

As we stopped in front of his door, which was number ten on that particular hall, I asked, "are light and dark considered Elements, as well as the other four you've told me of?"

Corky paused with his hand on the knob, letting out a light chuckle. "That was a fierce debate on my world for many years. We came to the conclusion that since none of use were ever born with only the light or dark Element, they must not be Elements at all. For instance, my sister is only an Air Elemental. That is the only connection she was born with the signs of or can tap in to. But there has never been a record of someone being born with none of the four great Elements, in which case they might have been pure Light or Dark. So my people decided that all four great Elements have both light and dark in them, Water both refracting and reflecting light, Earth supporting both plants which need light and stones which are often in the dark, and so on."

"I see. But—" I began, still curious about the subject.

Before I could go on further Corky stopped me with a wave of his hand and another laugh. "Wait. We'll discuss Elements in detail later on and I'll teach you whatever you want to know. But for now...I want you to enjoy seeing my world."

With his last words he swung the door open, sweeping a hand towards it in a grand gesture for me to proceed. I stepped through directly into the dappled sunshine and gentle rustlings of a forest. A mixture of grand, spreading old oaks and slim, young trees with a white bark grew all around me, only a narrow pathway running between them where I stood. Looking back, I saw that the gate we had stepped out of was set in the face of a mossy boulder, with ferns and grasses growing thickly around it so that it would have been hidden except for Corky's irregular use of it. Tilting my head back, I could see small gaps of sky between the green leaves of the trees, which were spaced far enough apart that it was not actually dark beneath them.

"This is the forest, of course," the young Keeper remarked, "our village is a short walk this way. Come on."

He began to lead me along the path, which wound naturally through the tree trunks and around more mossy rocks of varying proportions. I could see by Corky's step that he loved it here, in these woods. He had said that Earth was his favorite Element and it showed in his manner while he was this close to it. His hands caressed the rocks we passed close beside, while his green eyes sparkled up at the branches and leaves whenever they were not watching the path before him.

After perhaps half a mile of traversing the woods we began to come upon signs of civilization. Trees had been cut down here and there, their stumps growing more colonies of the thick moss or holding acorns for the hardworking squirrels. A fresher stump gleamed golden in a beam of light, sawdust sprinkled brightly around it. The path joined in to a wider one, which began to run beside a wide stream. It gurgled so noisily over the rocks that we had to speak in loud tones to be heard.

"The village is just ahead!" Corky pointed out a gap in the trees ahead, where sunlight was gleaming off of slate roofs.

"I see it."

The stream curved away from the path a little, but still ran on towards the sunlight ahead. Soon we were coming out into the edge of the forest, where the trees were even sparser and the path widened out into a large area of hard-beaten dirt. Arranged somewhat erratically in the clearing was a group of houses, half in the forest and half in the plains beyond. They were built of wooden planks fastened in overlapping layers down the side, with thin stone slates shingling the roofs. Some had boxes of flowers growing at the windows, or large raised beds growing garden produce behind them.

Altogether there were about twenty houses, not including the larger buildings which were obviously a bakery, sawmill and smithy. None of them displayed technology as advanced as I was used to. Like Adasian's castle turret, everything seemed to be caught in a time-period before the advent of combustion engines, electricity or perhaps even steam power. It made me wonder how the shock of traveling between worlds had first struck the Keepers.

"See the Earthwind mountains and Undina lake?" Corky spread his hand out and I followed the pointing fingers across the plains. Against the skyline a range of low, jagged mountains rose, gray rock and green forests rising in majestic cliffs directly from the plains below. A large cone-shaped mountain on one side puffed smoke slowly into the air. In the near distance a silver-blue lake rippled gently in the wind, a structure of pure white set so near the shore on one side that I wondered how it avoided becoming flooded in the wet season.

"There are extensive mine systems below the mountains, where iron and coal are mined almost every day," Corky explained proudly, "while a type of large, silver fish called Slivfin are brought from the lake. Water, Earth, Air, and Fire in the live volcano are all amply represented here."

"Aren't you worried about the volcano burying the valley in ash and lava?" I asked, gazing at the burning mountain.

"No. Those strongest in the Fire Element keep an eye on it and make sure that it does not erupt. Come see my house." Corky started into the village with an eager step. Following him, I noticed the people for the first time. They had been there all along, of course, but my attention had been drawn to the scenery too strongly to pay them any mind at first. Now I saw the inhabitants of the village moving between buildings about their chores, working in the fields beyond or, if they were children, playing in the streets. They were all dressed simply, but to me it seemed like there was an extra vibrancy to the colors of their hair and eyes so that, even from a distance, they seemed brighter and more defined than any people I had seen before.

We had not gone far into the settlement when a girl came running towards us, shouting, "Corky!"

Skidding to a stop before us, she waved a little banner of bright red which she was carrying in one hand. Her hair was a pale, wild blonde and her eyes the color of the edge of the sky. I guessed that she was only a few years younger than me.

Corky laughed and patted her on the head. "Hello! I've come back, you see, and brought my friend Nolin with me. I told you about him. Nolin, this is my sister Airlee."

She made a face at the introduction. "And it's a stupid name, too. I wish my name could be Sylvia or Rowena. It's silly to name people something just because it's their Element."

"It's a tradition in our land," Corky explained to me, "especially when someone is strong in only a single Element. My father's name is Ember because of that."

"Does Corkcora mean anything?"

"Hah. No, I have too many Elements to be called any one thing. Rocky-Flame-Cascade would be too much of a mouthful."

Airlee was jumping around by now, fluttering her banner and waving it near our heads. I was not quite sure how to react, or if I should do anything at all. It had been so long since I had played with any other youngsters that I did not feel like I was one. Neither did I feel fully adult. I was caught somewhere in between.

"Are we just going to stand here talking, or can we take him home now?" The girl asked her brother breathlessly, stopping beside him. "He's staying here to learn about Elements, right? Because this secret club of yours off in the woods wants him to learn about Elements?"

"Yes. Run ahead and tell our folks we're coming," Corky told her, giving her a friendly shove in the right direction. Once she had scampered off he told me in a lower tone, "I had to tell them something about you, as you were coming to stay with us. I have already told them that there is a secret club of inventors and adventurers that I joined, who have meetings off in the woods. It explains my disappearances. So I said that you were one of them who was interested in studying all of the Elements."

"Alright. Sounds good to me," I agreed. It was not far from the truth and I realized that we could not reveal the Dark Passages, even to Corky's own family. Word might spread around then, people start to search for the gate in the woods. And it was not so well hidden as to stay unseen if someone was looking for it.

By now we had reached the house where Corky's family lived. It was built just like the others, but with a piece of stone laying outside carved roughly into the shape of a mermaid holding up a flower.

"My mother is Earth and Water," he stated with a wave of his hand at it. "She does rock carvings as a hobby and that is her favorite one, so she keeps it. Most are smaller figurines and are sold to the traveling merchants whenever they come by."

The door burst open at that moment and Airlee came dashing out, followed by a boy with curly brown hair and eyes as green as Corky's. They both came up and danced around us, before grabbing both my hands and dragging me towards the door. With a sudden feeling of panic, I glanced over my shoulder at my friend in hope of rescue.

Corky just smiled gently. "Don't worry, they're not cannibals! And I'm coming too."

He began to follow after us, making me feel less afraid of being hauled off by his younger siblings. It sounds silly to be afraid of friendly children, but the unknown of meeting a family for the first time since my freedom made me both shy and confused.

I was pulled up in to the house, where it immediately opened into the main room. Shelves held a few stone figurines, plants in pots and dinnerware painted in delicate patterns of flame. A table spanned the center of the room, set with simpler plates and utensils as if for the mid-day meal. Corky's parents stood nearby, waiting to greet us. His father was thin and agile in appearance, with fierce red hair and angular features slightly marred by the fact that he wore glasses. The woman next to him was stouter and rounder, with twinkling blue eyes and a merry smile.

"Mother, father, this is Nolin," Corky introduced us, rescuing me from his brother and sister with a wave of his hand. "Nolin, Ember my father and Ada my mother."

They greeted me kindly and invited me to join them for lunch. Still feeling awkward, I thanked them and agreed. The meal was simple and good, though I felt as stiff as if I was at a grand banquet. It was not the fault of Corky's folk: they were just as kind and unaffected as if I were a neighbor. But as I said, I still did not know what to do with myself among a friend's family.

The part I enjoyed the most began after lunch. Then Corky took me to his own room, where there was a small brick hearth on one side.

"This is the first lesson in Elements, as it's traditionally taught." He went over to stir up the coals so that they glowed brightly red. "Watch."

Reaching over, he picked up a less seasoned billet of wood from the stack nearby and threw it on the coals. Blowing on it, he made flames begin to lick up around its edges. Smoke curled upwards, out of the chimney and sap hissed out of its cut end into the coals.

"See. Wood comes from the Earth. Fire burns. Smoke moved upwards as Air. A little Water bubbles out. And it slowly collapses into charcoal, which becomes Earth again. All four Elements are present, in motion."

"I see." crouching beside him, I watched the four Elements mingling. After a moment I looked up and asked, "what about things like metal, wood and lightning? Aren't they Elements in a sense?"

"No. Even the electricity that people on worlds like yours use would probably not be considered its own Element here. Metal comes from the earth, wood from the trees, lightning from a mixture of air and water."

Corky sat back on the floor, propping his head on a hand. "Elements are the basic building blocks of the world. Everything around us has a combination of Elements in it. Sometimes they are complicated combinations, even so complicated that we can't figure out exactly how they are mixed or what Elements are in them. My people have learned how to control many of these parts of the world, allowing us to manipulate them beyond what other people might expect or think possible. But we do not consider it magic to do these things, because we can't use an Element to do anything beyond its natural potential. A strong Fire Elemental can direct the course of a fire as it burns, know when it is present nearby without seeing it or hold flames in his hand without being burnt. But he could not use Fire to do anything that it does not naturally do, like make a cool drink in an empty cup."

He paused, giving me an anxious look. "I'm not boring you, am I?"

I shook my head, still watching the green log smolder away into coals on his hearth. "No. But...you said that the Keepers saw magic potential in you before you knew it was there. How can that be, if you don't believe that working with Elements is magic?"

Corky was silent for a minute before answering, "I said that my people do not believe it is magic. And, how they use it, it is not part of the arts of Erilaz at all. Because they can not do anything with the Elements that their Element does not naturally want to do. They feel connected to them, study and understand them beyond what most worlds think possible. But most of my people see using it in a 'magical' way as silly superstition, just myths from the legends of long ago. Like most peoples of the many worlds, they have buried the spark of Erilaz deep under the practicalities of life. They could not do anything like this..."

He held up his right hand slowly and made an orb of fire appear there, floating in the air above his fingers. I watched with widened eyes and a sense of awe as he held up the other hand and made an orb of water appear above it, floating just as the fire was. They swirled and flickered just as water and fire should, but neither spilled over the bounds of their orbs or dripped on the floor. Corky's face showed deep concentration as he brought the orbs together before him, clashing them into each other so that the fire hissed and the water steamed. They bubbled and fizzed together until, in just a moment, there was nothing of either orb left. Corky gave me a crooked smile, "this is my favorite."

Reaching out a hand, he touched a cooled bit of charcoal which had rolled from the fire. Slowly, it disintegrated into a pile of dust. From the pile of dust a little sprout began to grow, then sprang upwards into a fuzzy, green stem rich with life. A moment later a yellow flower budded and burst open at its top.

Corky gave a little sigh and sat back, grinning. "It takes energy and concentration, but not even Berune can grow a flower from a lump of charcoal."

I reached out hesitantly to touch the petals, half expecting them to crumble away under my touch. When they did not I picked up the whole plant, turning it to look at all of the thin, hair-like roots which had spread out from the lump of dust searching for sustenance. Already the flower was beginning to droop without Corky's energy to keep it alive.

"How did you grow a flower with no seed to start it from?" I held the plant up, looking from it to Corky's head as if to figure out how that object had come from an idea in one man's mind.

"I've memorized the pattern of that sort of flower. They are common around here and easy to study. With it in my mind, I drew on the Earth element to form it from the little energy in that lump of charcoal, taking whatever else it needed from me."

"If only—" I set down the plant with a little sigh. "I could understand this spark of Erilaz that you Keepers are always speaking of. You have said before that it is in me, but I only felt the tiniest stirring of it once, when Lune showed me his map of the Dark Passages."

"You'll find it when the time is right," Corky told me comfortingly, "in fact, maybe if you knew what your Elements are, it would help. Let's see, your hair is white, but that is only because of the Neomium, isn't it?"

"Yes," I replied mechanically, my thoughts still far away, before realizing what he was insinuating. "But does everyone have Elements in them? I thought only your people were born that way."

Corky had to admit, "well, I'm not really sure. It's a pet theory of mine that other people must have Elements, even if they aren't obvious. But some people are so difficult to connect to any combination of Elements that I'm never sure. Firendaze, now, is easy to see as having a Fire Element. And Tavierfin's would be Earth and Water, I think. But most of the others I haven't been able to figure out. Sultane is always a riddle, Lune is too fussy to see what he is actually made of, and so on. Anyway, what color was your hair before?"

"Er...some shade of light brown, I think." It had never concerned me enough to remember it clearly. I had been a fairly plain child before being taken to the Neomium mines. Afterwards, I was more remarkable for an oddly skinny, angular, bleached look than anything else.

"And it is straight, not curled. Then, your eyes are a gray-blue like Airlee's." Corky said, inspecting my features closely. "Hmm. It seems like you would be an Air Elemental. Maybe Air and Earth, in different proportions. Do you feel drawn to any particular Element over the others?"

I thought of how it had felt to lay on Lune's green lawn for the first time, considered how good his stream had tasted, remembered watching the sky at Adasian's world with the good feeling of the wind against my face and pictured the flames around the log which Corky had thrown into the hearth just a moment ago. With a shake of my head, I replied, "no. But maybe you are right. I do enjoy being outside, in the fresh air, a lot."

"Well, we'll try a test which is sometimes used to determine what Elements a child has if the signs aren't as clear as usual." Corky got up and began collecting assorted items from around his room, then left for a moment and came back with a few more. In front of me he lined up a little platter of garden soil, a small bowl of water, a candle and an empty glass. With a flick of his fingers he lit the candle, before telling me to close my eyes tightly and not peek.

I heard him shifting things around, before he told me to find the Earth Element without opening my eyes, by sticking out a hand to touch it. I did, and surprised myself by touching the soil in the first try. Next he told me to find the water, the flame and the empty glass. Each time I was able to do it, though the first try for Water I missed all of the containers and hit the floor.

"This is peculiar," Corky said, a frown in his voice, "you're not looking, are you?"

I shook my head, keeping my eyes shut.

He had me try to find them again, rearranging the containers between each try. I missed the containers altogether a few times, though mostly I hit just the item I was searching for. It was beginning to make me feel strange and shivery, because I did not know how I was doing it. There was no careful time to consider: each time I stuck out my hand I did it at random, not thinking about the consequences. It was such a strange sensation to hit the right Element every time that I began to wish that I would not. It was those times that I hit the floor the most.

"You can open your eyes now," Corky said in a puzzled tone, "this isn't working. I thought you said that you did not feel any spark of magic in you?"

"I don't." Opening my eyes, I sat staring down at my muddy, scorched fingers. "Is it possible for a person to have all four Elements at once?"

The Keeper twiddled his thumbs, chewed on his lower lip and fiddled uncomfortably with the containers of natural material.

Finally he said, "in the old legends there are hints of characters who do. But as there has not been a person born within recorded times who has possessed all of them, it is considered impossible. The wisest of my people say that no person can have everything; we all get our own portion out of the universe, no more. The legendary characters who wield all four Elements are thought to be just myths. So either you are a myth, or the spark of magic in you was working to find the Elements without you actually feeling it."

We stared at each other solemnly over the top of the containers for some time. Eventually Corky broke into a grin. "But you don't look like a myth to me, so it must be that you have a very strong potential, even though you can't tap into it yet. Besides, I don't know if the Element test works on people who are not from my world. We'll forget the whole thing and go on with your education."

I still wished that I knew what Elements were mine, if any, but I agreed with him that it was better to go on with the lesson. Corky put away the little containers and candle, before fetching paper and pencil to draw diagrams with. With them he illustrated the connections between the four Elements, how they worked with and against each other and the four traits (heat, cold, dampness and dry) which could be rearranged to describe their properties.

After some book-work of this sort, he took me outside and we went to the lake. On its shores he lit fires and put them out with waves of water, bored holes in the earth to find water, made grass grow in the sand and did other experiments to teach me about the Elements which he could control. He could not do anything with Air, as it was not among his own connections, but he told me things about it which he had heard from others.

Corky tried to teach me to feel the Elements and use them as he did, but that was one of the things I could not do. All the information he gave me my mind absorbed greedily, but I could not find the spark of Erilaz. He told me not to worry about it, assuring me again that time would give me the key to my powers.

After our lessons, I looked across the waves of the pretty lake and saw the structure of white marble still standing there. It had docks running into the water in front of it, and stairs going down into the lake. The front of it was open, with pillars supporting the roof in orderly lines.

"What is that building for, Corky?"

"Oh, that." The Elemental turned a cold shoulder towards it. "That is part of a foolish idea which some of my people have. You see, traditionally we regard the Elements as part of ourselves, links we have been given to the world and may use, somewhat like special tools. But some people have decided that the Elements are actually gods, each one controlled by its own divine power. So this temple was built on the edge of the lake to Undina, the supposed goddess of Water."

Turning to point at the mountains, he added. "There is a temple to Slyph of the Air up there, on that crag. You can just see the white dot of it. In the cone of the volcano there is a temple to the Salamanders, joint ruling spirits of Fire. In the woods to the north there is a temple made of dark stones and vines to the gnome king, deity of Earth. They are all foolish cults, with 'mysterious' occult rites and punishments for those of their members who do not attend the right meetings. They even claim to be able to shift, add or remove Elements for a person, so that they can worship at any temple they wish. But that is all foolishness too. No one can change the Elements we were born with, even if they change the outward signs of a person in an attempt to do so."

After that we returned to his house for the night, where his family entertained me with kind simplicity.

The next day Corky taught me more about Elements, leading me on walks through the woods and to different places along the stream. There was a waterfall where many people who were both Air and Water oriented came to meditate, and a smooth rock in the center of the stream where Earth and Water people did the same. Corky showed me the secrets of tiny plant life, explaining how some plants worked together to grow bigger, where as others fought bitterly over patches of ground or sunlight.

The young Keeper tried to show me how to absorb the knowledge of an Elements structure so that I could recreate it with my own energy, as he had done with the flower and the orbs. Needless to say, it was beyond me, as it was still too close to magic for me to grasp.

Chapter 13: Lines of Power

Eventually I was sent to learn from Tavierfin in his booth at the meeting place.

"I suppose we aren't going to your world to study?" I asked him the first day, surprised when we did not enter the Dark Passages.

"Not unless you can hold your breath for days at a time," he replied absently, starting to take angular, sharp tools from a drawer under the bench in the shack. When I did not reply, he remembered. "Oh, yes. You don't know what my world is like. Well, it's mostly underwater; the gate is on a small island among some old ruins made of Solron, the stone of Runes. My house is at the bottom of the sea near the city of Chexselz, where I work as a decorative stone mason. All of my people live under the water. We do not need as much air as you humans do."

I stared at him, searching for any sign of gills or scales. But he appeared perfectly normal with his dark, shoulder-length hair and fine, pale face.

"Oh, I don't wear my legs underwater," he added, catching my look, "it's much easier to swim with fins on that end. You know, like mermaids are always pictured with. But not quite as sparkly or mystical looking. They're very comfortable, under water. That's what my name comes from; Xavizzirzine translates to 'strong fin' in my tongue. But that was far too difficult for our friends to call me, so Sultane suggested that I be called Tavierfin on land, an easier to pronounce version. It is strange that you land dwellers cannot say things like Fiziquizix'a'jaxiziq with any accuracy."

I couldn't help laughing at that. It sounded like he was just making up a word by sticking the most difficult letters together in random order. He gave me a hurt look and explained that it meant 'stone pillar' in his language.

"But how do you put the fins on or take the legs off?" I asked, hoping to avoid being made to learn any of his crazy words.

In answer he pulled up a thin chain which was around his throat, displaying a small Runestone suspended on the end of it, which had been hidden under his shirt. It had a complicated embroidery of Runes across it, more than I have ever seen on that size of Runestone before.

"This grants me human-style legs as long as I wear it," Tavierfin held it out carefully on the palm of his hand. "It is the first Runestone I ever found, hidden in the ruins on the shore. Which was very useful, as crawling around in the sand on your flukes is a dry, slow business, you know. Or you don't know, I suppose."

I shook my head, which he took as a signal to drop the subject of living underwater and get down to the business at hand. Runestones.

I LEARNED THAT THERE was actually a variety of materials which could be used to create Runestones. Tavierfin showed me samples he had found of Runes carved on quartz, obsidian and even a fine-grained river rock of dull gray. But none of them, he said, were as powerful as those made on Solron.

Pure Solron is a black, dense stone with no other shades of color in it. It is found on different worlds but usually only in comparatively small veins that are pure enough to use for high-quality Runestones. According to Tavierfin, it 'carves like butter' when using the right tools. When he demonstrated it looked to me more like it chipped away in small, jagged shards, but I learned later what he meant. Compared to the other usable types of rock, it rarely cracks or chips beyond where the mason wishes it to.

But geology and stone types is only a small part of the knowledge it takes to make Runestones. Once the slab is cut out, the runes must be carved.. And this is the part which takes it from being a practical skill to a powerful art. First of all, the mason must know the right Runes to carve. If one knows a master, as I did, he can show you the Runes he knows and tell you their meanings. Or someone can look at already carved Runestones and try to guess what their meaning is based upon the use which has been made of them.

But just cutting the lines into the stone is not enough. It is the concentration of willpower into the Runes and the graceful flow of making them which gives them their potency. Few people can make even a simple Runestone because of the immense amount of concentration and connection with the material which is required. Tavierfin could make a handful of simpler ones which were functional, such as the fire lighter which he had given Tallray or the Lightrune which he made and gave to me on that first day of teaching.

It was fascinating to watch as he carefully squared up a small slab that could easily rest in the palm of my hand. Then he lay it in a frame made of wood which had knobs at the corners to adjust it until it held the black Solron securely. Once it was in place Tavierfin picked up a little chisel from beside him in one hand and a light mallet in the other. He had already warned me to be quiet so that he could concentrate while he began to carve the Rune.

I stood in silence as he stared at the shining tip of the tool for minutes on end, apparently lost in a world of imaginings. I was just beginning to wonder if I should remind him of his task, when he began to move again. The chisel tip came slowly down and touched the stone, scratching across it a hair-thin line as he moved the chisel in a careful pattern. It was the light symbols, such as he had drawn in the cave during my first meeting.

Once it had been marked out he began to work it in. With careful taps and a concentration so steadfast that I could feel it in the air around him, he gouged out perfect little troughs where all of the lines were. Then he used other tools to smooth them, finishing off with a piece of sandpaper so that there were no bumps or jags in the pattern.

"This is the most important part," he whispered to me, eyes full of something I could not yet see. With precision he lay the tools aside and began to run the tip of his finger down the lines of the symbols. For a moment, I wondered what was supposed to be happening. With a start, I saw it. Behind his finger a line of brilliant yellow was left behind, filling the troughs with a smooth radiance. It was like the stone was growing back again, or a ghost of the stone was appearing in glowing lines.

I breathed as quietly as possible, afraid to disturb him even a bit. Slowly he drew the lines across the face of the slab, until all of the lines were filled in. He paused then, for a moment at the end, before drawing his hand away with a small gasp. As soon as his finger was no longer touching the stone, it began to glow. The whole slab lit up with a soft, bright white light which threw an aura of brilliance around it. Just as suddenly it went dark, leaving only the Rune sparkling on its face.

"Now," Tavierfin said in a practical voice, all of the concentration and power going out of the air around him. "If I linked everything correctly, the slab should light up whenever it is being held in someone's hand. Take it out of the frame and try it."

Feeling strange with excitement and wonder, I undid the tightened bolts and picked the slab out. As soon as it was held in my hand it lit up, glowing brightly as it had before. If I set it on the counter or put it in my pocket, it went out again. But every time it came in contact with my skin, it lit up.

"It's wonderful," I said, holding it up to light the shady corners of the simple wooden workshop.

Tavierfin smiled appreciatively. "It is. And now it's yours."

I tried to thank him and promise to keep it safe, but he waved my words away.

"I'm glad you're pleased. It is a real pleasure when a Runestone works out right. Especially a new type like that, which I have never made before. It's a thrill like no other to put your mind at the tips of your fingers and create something powerful with it."

He showed me the tools which he had used and taught me both their names and uses. I had to hold them, not just any way but exactly how he wanted me to. Then he made me sketch on pieces of river rock with them, making meaningless patterns at first, and then making symbols which he taught me.

Tavierfin knew many more symbols than he had ever been able to use in making Runestones. He said that some he understood the meaning of but had never been able to put onto stone with enough power to make them activate.

He went on to explain that there were three basic types of Runestones which he knew of.

Active Runestones, which were always using whatever had been written on them, such as the ones which the Dark Passages were made of.

Sleeping Runestones, which had an Element or other power bound to them but did not actively use it, such as the Runestones they used to unlock doors in the Dark Passages.

And Trigger Runestones like my Lightrune, which would only activate when the right stimulus was applied.

"The one I wear around my neck is a Trigger Rune also, with an input much like the Lightrune," Tavierfin pulled it out for me to see again. "It only works when it is touching a living being. That's why I have to be so careful to keep it on the palm of my hand, or else I would instantly have fins again and probably fall all over the floor trying to get my balance back. But it is, of course, much more complicated than the Lightrune, which only has one symbol on it. This has so many and so fine that it is difficult to make out where one begins and the other ends. I've never been able to read all of them."

"I suppose that Tallray's Runestone is also a Trigger Rune?" I suggested, carefully slipping mine into a pocket, where it would not glow.

"Actually, it's a form of Active Rune. It burns anything made of wood that is touching it, all of the time. It's simply that wood products are not touching it all of the time, so it can't use its power." Tavierfin pulled open a drawer and rummaged around in it, speaking as he searched, "Trigger Runes are excellent at making traps, of course, or wards to keep people out of places. Sleeping Runes are keys or used in conjunction with other Runes to create special effects. Active Runes can be used for a myriad of ways, including making hovering walkways, giving their wielders extra powers or even cooking meals. It all depends on the imagination and mental powers of the Runestone creator."

Finally he pulled out a handmade scroll with jagged, sloppy handwriting across it, interspersed with diagrams of Runes. Tavierfin told me to study it that evening, before stating that we were going to work in the Solron mine for the rest of that afternoon.

I was not, as you might think, afraid of going to work in a regular mine. I knew that it was a simple tunnel in the mountain with stone in it, without guards, fences or slave-masters. He was not taking me there to labor until I dropped. So I went with him willingly, looking forward to doing something more active than we had been.

When we reached the mines he showed me the veins of Solron and how they ran sideways away from where the main tunnels had been carved. They had to be followed carefully, the stone dug up so that it would not shatter or be cracked. This was a job that I understood and was practiced at, though it had been with a different material before. Tavierfin gave me a pick and we began to work together, chiseling out a section of the black rock which had already been brought to the surface. It did not take long before Tavierfin commented that I was better at the mining than he was. "I'll have to ask for your help more often."

"Not too often," I returned, setting aside the pick to grab up a shovel which lay nearby, before remembering to add, "please."

When evening came on we returned to the meeting place, where it had been arranged that I would stay with Sultane, as Tavierfin could not take me home with him.

Sultane's house was behind the wooden door set in the cave. Unlike the bare, cold cave that Feleago lived in, it had been made as cozy and comfortable as possible. There was a wooden table to eat off of, sleeping benches covered in thick furs set into opposite walls and a wood stove set up in the back with its chimney pipe running out of a hole in the roof. The walls were whitewashed, except for where a picture had been painted on one. In shades of brown, tan and dusty red, deer had been painted, leaping and browsing through a forest of fall colors. They were not three-dimensional or excellently drawn, nor were the trees realistic looking. The image was made to give the impression of deer in the forest and tell the story of their being there, not represent it in a photographic fashion.

I sat and talked to Sultane that evening before going to bed. He wanted to know how my training was going, not only in the sense of how much progress I was making, but how I was enjoying it as well. I told him about my lessons, displaying the Lightrune Tavierfin had made and elaborating on the adventures I had gone on with Corky. But I tried not to tell him how much about the disappointment some of my other lessons had been.

"Don't worry," He intuited when I had finished, "you will find your way, Nolin. You did not tell me about what Berune taught you, or how. But you do not have to, nor any other lessons you want to keep silent on. Just remember, the rougher a path is the more sure you will be on your feet once it is over."

That night I slept soundly, feeling safer in Sultane's cavern than in any other house I had been in before. Not that I slept poorly as a rule, being generally too tired out by the days to afford anything else, but that cave felt deeply secure.

In the morning Tavierfin came back to teach me more about Runes and Runestones in his little workshop. I had studied his scroll a little the night before, though not perhaps as much as I should have, and found that it was a record of all the Runes Tavierfin knew at the time. The next morning he had me practice sketching different ones of them, memorizing what the shapes and figures meant. In the evening he had to leave again to meet someone in his underwater city of Chexselz on business, so our lessons came to an end. But Tavierfin promised that he would continue to teach me more once I had passed the test.

It was not yet time for the evening meal. Everything was quiet in the clearing. Finally, there was some time to explore on my own.

Chapter 14: Shadows

My idea was that I could either explore the world I was on, or enter the Dark Passages. The memory of the Shadow Poker had faded by now, but my curiosity about the empty, moon-scape planet at the end of the main hall had not.

Sultane was reading in his cave, so I did not bother him with questions. I left the clearing of the meeting place quietly and entered the Dark Passages. The trip down the main hall seemed longer than it had been before, dark tiles and doors stretching out infinitely before and behind me. Dim neon bars of green slid slowly by, accompanied by their pebble numbers; two hundred and seventy, two-seventy-one, two-seventy-two...

Finally I reached the end of the hall. On my left was the heap of rubble and deactivated doors, while on my right the last path curved away into darkness. I stopped for a moment at the intersection, glancing over my shoulder with a sudden, eerie feeling that I was being followed. But no one was there, no one I could see through the hanging mist of darkness. And if I could not see anyone, that meant no one should be able to see me.

Turning down the hall, I hurried up to the only door on it. Its single red stone seemed lonely, staring out at the world with no companions in sight. Reaching out, I pulled open the door and, before my nerve could fail me, stepped through it.

The first thing which hit me was the cold. Corky had said that it was no colder than a normal winter day. But it was no warmer, either, and I was still dressed for springtime. With a half-repressed shiver I reached into my pocket to pull out the Lightrune. Not because it was dark there. The ground seemed to glow with its own white illumination which left everything in clear, though flat, detail. But the sky was dark above me, such a heavy, black darkness that I felt a light would be comforting to carry.

With it glowing brightly in one hand, I pulled the door shut behind me. On this side it was set into a low cliff of the hard white material which coated the whole world as far as the eye could see. Still mentally fighting off the cold, I surveyed the scene. As I had noted before, there were craters, hills and valleys of pale, whitish-gray, all flowing endlessly towards the horizon. No stars interrupted the sky and nothing grew to break up the monotony of the land. It was barren.

Taking a few steps away from the door, I felt the stone grit under my shoes, though it was quite solid to the touch. There was a faint, sandy powder over the top of the stone, like dust blown onto a clean surface by the wind. But there was no wind, not even the faintest breeze.

I moved forwards into the silence, the only thing alive or active in the entire scene. In front of the gate the land sloped down in a gentle dip, where what looked like an empty stream bed no wider than my hand twisted across the valley floor. Its walls were smooth, lined in tiny, soft ridges as if the water had been eating into the sides and then dried abruptly in its path. Past it the land rolled into a low ridge, with craters on top of it. There was nothing in them, no bubbling acid or pooling steam. They would have made good places to store dried beans or eat a large amount of cereal from, if they had been somewhere else.

The cold was slowly making me feel numb, so I hurried down the next slope of the ridge in hopes of warming myself with the motion. Here there was a wide plain interrupted with miniature hillocks and larger craters, the biggest being wider around than I was tall. I ran up and down the hills for a few minutes, until I did not feel so chilled. Then my curiosity led me to peer in more of the craters, always looking for something interesting that could have been left behind by the Founders. Most of them were just as empty as the rest of the breathless, silent world. But the last one I peered into contained something out of the ordinary. A pool of darkness sat in the bottom of the crater, filling it like a blackened sea. I stared at it for a moment, before reaching out a hand tentatively towards the shadows. Just before my fingers came in contact with the pool it began to swirl and bubble, as if coming to a boil.

A shape began to materialize in the basin, unfolding towards my hand. With a little cry I drew back, just in time to avoid the blackness grasping me. Something angular and jagged drew itself up in the stone bowl, towering over the rim. An angular head tilted up on top of it, without eyes or mouth to be seen in the shadows. A long, inky finger reached towards me on a hand with only three fingers. It was a Shadow Poker.

I stumbled away backwards, too afraid to turn my eyes away from it. I had no weapon with me, nothing to fight it off. There was not even loose stones on the ground to throw. In one stride the creature stepped out of the crater, coming towards me with lithe, swift movements. It was larger than the one which had attacked Firendaze, with a touching finger twelve inches in length. I watched it for one more moment, backing away, before I broke and ran. Up the ridge, down the other side into the valley and up to the cliff where the door stood. Gasping with mixed fear and exertion, I stopped at the door to look back. The shadow stood on the near slope of the ridge, a black shape outlined against the pale stone and dark sky. It seemed to be watching me, but it made no other move to follow.

I stared at it for a long moment, almost fascinated by the closeness of something so terrible. As I watched two more Shadow Pokers came up over the ridge to stand beside it. Both of them were smaller, but just as dark and frightening in appearance as the first.

With a jerk, I pulled open the door and dashed through. It was not until I was in the Dark Passages that I realized how cold I had become from standing still in the empty world. My fingers felt icy and stiff, while my nose tingled from the warmth in the passage and almost made me sneeze. Cramming my hands under my arms to warm them, I found that they were shaking with fear.

One touch was all it would have taken. If the Shadow poker had awoken in his stony nest or if I had moved my hand away just a little slower, he would have got me. Then I would have been marked like the leather on Firendaze's shoulder, and it would not have stopped there. It would have spread all over me...

With a shiver that was not just from cold, I began to hurry towards the main hall of the Dark Passages. Someone should be told about what was behind that door, what lurked in the craters of the otherwise empty world. Sultane would know what to do if I told him. Though the Keepers had no elected leader, his experience and wisdom gave his words an extra weight among us all.

When I reached door 243, I did not stop or slow before opening it. The sight of the three Shadow Pokers had stirred me strangely, so that I felt as if a dark magic had touched me to the core. I was worried that they might be hunting me now, still following through the passages. I needed to warn the Keepers in case the Pokers found a way to the meeting place behind me.

Dashing through the door, I stumbled in surprise when I found that the clearing was dark. Night had fallen while I was away, filling the sky with stars in the blackness. A stream of yellow light spilled over the grass of the clearing just ahead, picking out each blade sharply. A dark shape hunched in the doorway, bright light behind it making it appear solid black. Sultane was waiting for me.

My steps slowed with hesitation as I approached him. Would he be angry that I had left without permission? Adasian's words came back to me, pointing out my rudeness and disobedience.

"You've come." Sultane's voice held no anger, only a calm acceptance of my arrival. "And you are breathing hard. Is there someone in pursuit?"

"I don't know. Maybe. There were three Shadow Pokers. I'm not sure if they followed." My words came out in a hectic rush as I stopped and looked over my shoulder, still expecting to see the dark shapes moving after me.

"Three Shadow Pokers in the Dark Passages? Were you touched?"

"No. In the empty world." I steadied myself with a breath, collapsing onto the ground beside him. With his calm questions the whole story came out, until he knew all that had happened.

After a pause he spoke again, "some people would scold you for having gone to the empty planet and awoken the Shadow Pokers. You should have told me that you were leaving, in case you were missed. But I do not want to hold you in or take your freedom away. You have just as much right as any of us to decide where your footsteps lead you. And the discovery of so many Shadow Pokers might be a good thing hidden inside a bad."

"How?"

Sultane sat in silence as if he had not heard, before giving himself a little shake and answering, "how, you ask? Because, we have never before found where the Shadow pokers come from. We've only seen them in the Dark Passages. It has been speculated that they are formed there from evil magic lingering in the air. But your new discovery may prove that this is not true."

"You mean...I might have found their homeland?"

"Yes, perhaps." Sultane was nodding slowly to himself. "We will have to discuss it with our friends. Tavierfin is still busy in his city and cannot get away, so we can't hold a meeting tonight. But I have called Firendaze to come take you to his world. You will be safer there than here, if the Shadow Pokers have tried to follow you.

Besides, it has been proven that you need to learn martial skills and carry a weapon. If you are to be exploring other worlds through the Passages, you will need to be able to defend yourself. Firendaze's lesson can come next."

"What about you?" I looked up at him where he sat in his wheelchair, illuminated in the light from the room. "What if they come and find you here alone?"

"I will keep the door locked for tonight. And it is more important that you are safe. You have a long life before you." Sultane turned his chair and began to wheel it into the room. "I doubt they will come this far anyway. And I am not helpless, you know."

He looked back at me, a twinkle in his fierce old eyes. "stop lying in the doorway and come eat."

I ate the dinner he had prepared, then sat back on the second bed to wait for Firendaze. The day catching up to me, I leaned back against the wall, eyes almost closing as sleep began to stalk my mind. I had blinked once, almost losing contact with the world, and in that time Firendaze appeared.

He looked like a king from a fairy-tale, striding suddenly into the door. The light from the lanterns played over his armor, glinting off of the circlet in his shining hair. He gave me a grin, then turned to Sultane with a stiffly respectful bow. "I've come to take the baggage."

"Take him, then, and be careful with him." Sultane turned to me. "I will see you tomorrow, Nolin, at the meeting."

"'Til next shift." Yawning, I stood up and followed Firendaze out of the door. I still felt dazed with sleep, as shown by my giving the typical slave's farewell without thinking about it.

Firendaze did not comment, keeping silence until we reached his exit. Then he warned me that it would be dark on the other side at first, but that I was not to use my Lightrune despite that. Warning given, he pulled open the door and led the way through.

It was dim on the other side, not the dark of a starless night but the pitch black of a room with no windows. A dusty, musty smell filled the air, not what I would have expected from a palace. Firendaze stepped away from me and there was a clicking, clunking noise, followed by a thin beam of light entering the space which we occupied.

It illuminated a pile of old cloth in one shadowy corner and outlined Firendaze at the top of a wooden staircase.

"Good. The servants didn't forget to light the lamps while I wasn't around to tell them to," the warrior snickered, pushing back the sliding door which covered the stairs so that the illumination became brighter. I followed him out of the small cellar-like space we had been in, into a tall, spacious hall. The walls were lined in what I took, rightly, to be gas lamps, while the windows were covered in heavy draperies of green and gold. Arches and pillars of orange stone upheld a vaulted ceiling high above, making our every step echo majestically. The sliding trap which Firendaze had pushed aside was concealed by a throne, plated in gold and ornamented with a pair of bluish diamonds. Knobs of a gray metal also decorated the back of it, gleaming dully in the lamp light.

"Welcome to my throne room." Firendaze waved an arm casually around. "It's not as big as the main hall, or dining room, but it is nice to receive a few hundred foolish ambassadors in. Make 'em line up in this place without their guards and they start losing a bit of their pride."

I was impressed, but so sleepy that my awe was dulled by the wish for a bed. Thankfully the king seemed to understand my wish, leading me over to a set of stairs in the rear of the room after he had slid the throne back into place.

"It would be dreadful if the servants found out about the gate to the Passages. Then they could hunt me up whenever I disappeared. And they would probably wander around cleaning and lighting them, if they thought it was a subterranean part of my palace."

He stopped talking as we passed through a door and into a long hall, where halberdiers stood on each side and at both ends, holding their tall weapons upright. I hesitated, afraid of what discovery might mean, but Firendaze simply nodded in return to their salutes and continued down the hall. The guards did not pay any attention to me, coming behind him. At the end of the hall was a regal door inscribed with a gray crown, which was surrounded by pictures of animals which I did not recognize.

"That's my room, if you hadn't guessed." The warrior king pointed it out, steering me towards a door about three down from it. "And the next one belongs to my chief military man, while the second from it holds Lady Valenzeel. An, ahem, 'friend of the king's' by official order. So you'll have to take this one."

He pushed me into a sumptuous room which was lit only by the reflected light from a lamp in the hall, and the last glow of a red sunset coming through a large window. The suite of chambers was so ornate, complicated and full of conveniences that I hardly knew what to do once Firendaze had slammed the door behind me. But, luckily, I recognized a large, fluffy piece of furniture as a bed and was soon out of my confusion upon it.

Chapter 15: Iseldome

I awoke gazing up at a shimmery peach-colored canopy which topped the bed and was decorated with golden embroidery stars. Turning my head, I saw a room littered with graceful wooden furniture, thick rugs and precious nick-knacks in every shape conceivable. All four walls had yellow suns painted on them, with red glass ornaments hanging in their centers. The window was framed by thick, green drapes of a fancy fabric for which I did not have a name.

Altogether, it was the richest room I had ever been in. It was so fancy that it was frightening. In fact, I have not since seen a place more magnificent than the king's palace in Iseldome.

It was early morning now, the light coming through the window a predawn gray. After being awake for only a few moments I heard a tapping at the door. Thinking that it would be Firendaze, I jumped up and hurried over to open it. My face must have shown shock when I saw a neatly-uniformed maid standing outside, a silver tray balanced in her hands.

"Your breakfast, sir," she said, giving a polite half-curtsy. It must have taken some effort for her not to laugh. Though perhaps Firendaze's whims had trained it into her.

"Thank you," I stammered after a minute of blank staring, taking the tray from her hands. Breakfast delivered to my room, on a silver tray! Breakfast under a domed lid, with delicate aromas trickling up from the edges like the ghost of feasting past. I had never before been given such deference, though the maid seemed to take it as routine.

She gave a slight nod and added with practiced ease, "his majesty wishes me to inform you that he will be busy in the throne room for the next half-hour. After that he will be disposed to see you. Until that time you may wander the palace as much as you like, but in thirty minutes you are to join him in the throne room. Also..." A flicker of expression finally touched her face, a small giggle escaping the corners of her lips. "He also says to avoid his stupid officials if you can, sir. But his words were a lot stronger than that."

After that she gave another quick curtsy and hurried away. I closed the door softly, carrying my tray over to a desk near the window. I think it was a writing desk, not one meant for eating at, but to me it was simply as a horizontal surface on which to set my breakfast. Taking off the cover, I found white, spongy bread spread with thick preserves, thin strips of grilled meat much like bacon and a miniature omelet filled with mushrooms and cheese. The cutlery was just as fancy as the rest of the trappings surrounding me.

After breakfast I decided to stay in my chambers until Firendaze was done with his business. Though he had given me permission to wander around his palace, I did not feel like trying to find my way around it while avoiding his 'stupid' officials.

I had no way of knowing where they would be lurking, or what passages would take me into their grasp. It was better to explore the rooms I had been given, instead.

The room I had slept in was not the only apartment in the suite. I passed through an open doorway into a room with a large hearth place, thickly cushioned couches to lounge on and bizarre old paintings hanging on the wall. It was not a large space, but just as well furnished as the last. Through a door on one side was the bathroom, with porcelain tub and washstand. There was no water piped to them, so I supposed that one was to request it brought up every time one wanted a bath.

On the other side of the bedroom was a small space which I took to be a 'dressing room' as there was a long mirror on the wall and a huge wardrobe across from it. The wardrobe was empty, so I did not stay in there long.

There was no obvious way to tell time in the rooms except for by the lighting outside the window. I was not sure if it had been half of an hour since breakfast when I set out for the throne room. The sun was just starting to crest a distant ridge outside, throwing golden beams across the roofs of many buildings which stood between the palace and the highland. Golden, domed or pale peach, they all reflected the light. I did not know exactly when the sun rose or set on this world, but my inner sense of time said that it was time to go.

Out in the hall, I had to brave the guard's stares alone. But if Firendaze wanted me to meet him in the throne room, I reasoned he must have made provision for it with his soldiers.

As you can see, Adasian's first bit of training had already given me a more objective turn of mind. Enough, at least, to force myself to walk under the fixed stares of the guards without flinching. At the far end of the hall one of the soldiers gave me a salute, to which I returned a surprised nod. They were paying more attention than I had first imagined.

At the end of the hall there were two doors with staircases behind them, leading in different directions. Going by memory from the night before, I took the one that was straight ahead. The steps were carpeted, muffling my footsteps so that I was moving silently. Half way down I heard the sound of voices in the throne room below. Creeping softly to the doorway, I peered into the large hall. The curtains had been pulled aside from the windows, letting in streams of natural light. The lamps were all put out, their glass covers shining in the sun.

From where I stood all I could see of Firendaze was a part of the back of his head over the throne, with the red-gold hair sticking up in every direction and the gray band of his circlet just visible.

By the upper part of his head alone I could tell that he was sitting very straight and erect in his chair, looking directly in front of him. Beyond the throne was a group of men of all sizes and shapes, dressed in uniforms of pale orange and cream. They were just taking their leave of the king, bowing and exchanging courtesies before backing out of a door on the side of the hall. As soon as they were all out of the way Firendaze called over his shoulder, "you can come in now, Nolin. My officials are out of the way."

I trotted around the throne to the front, where he jumped off to meet me. "That meeting lasted a little longer than I expected. The rebellious Cheri bands along the edge of the Cherial desert are starting to become restless again. Commander Grelious is worried that they might unify to create an insurrection...but perhaps you don't care about all that."

I shook my head, "I don't know about that sort of thing. Shouldn't we be going to the meeting?"

"Well, not everyone will be there yet, with the differences in time. But I suppose we can leave now. Let me tell Nana that I'll be out."

"Nana?"

"My old nurse." Firendaze smiled a little sheepishly. "She took care of me most of the time when I was young, as my parents were busy with affairs of state. When the queen passed on, Nana took care of me even more until I was old enough to be sent to the barracks for my education. I always tell her when I'm going out so that if the palace starts to explode with worry over me she can deal with it. A wonderful woman for dealing with explosions of emotion. She needed to be that way when I was young."

He strode away up the stairs, leaving me to wait for him below. It was only a few minutes before he returned, shaking his head. "She never asks questions. It's extraordinary."

Together, we shoved the throne back on its hidden rails and descended into the cellar below. I could see, with the brighter light coming in, that the gate looked much like the others that went into the dark passages but set into the wall of the cellar. After giving me a moment to look around the room, Firendaze used a handle on the bottom of the throne platform to slide it back in to place, sinking the space into darkness.

Chapter 16: King's Weapons

The journey to the meeting place was routine. When we reached it the sun was just starting to shine down into the clearing, making long, morning shadows from the plantation of Shivro saplings. Some of the Keepers had already arrived, standing outside of the meeting room, talking in hushed voices. Others came soon after.

The meeting was a brief one, as far as meetings with the Keepers went. Some of them wished to punish me for having strayed into the Passages alone, but Sultane explained to them how the information I had found could be useful to them, even praising me for my bravery as if he had been there to see it. Which he had not, and would probably not mention it if he had.

Eventually it wound down to the decision that they would have to lock that door so that nothing could come out of it. Also, everyone was warned to be alert in case a Shadow poker had already infiltrated the Dark passages. The idea of the empty world being a spawning point for the creatures was discussed, but no solid agreement reached on the subject. Immediately after the meeting, we left to complete the work on the door.

The Keepers sealed the exit by putting a steel bar across it. That way it could be unlatched and opened from our side if we wanted to go through, but any more Shadow Pokers would be held out. Firendaze wanted to go hunting them across the moon-like world, but the other Keepers held him back for fear that he would get overwhelmed far from the gate and be touched. They also reminded him that he was supposed to be teaching me today.

"Oh, yes," he said with a touch of bad humor, "that's right. Come along, Nolin, so that we can beat the lubricant out of each other on my world instead of looking for Shadow Pokers on this one."

Which did not sound very promising to me. But I was supposed to be learning from him, so I followed behind as he led the way towards his door. It felt like a bit of a let-down to be going back to normal training after the excitement of the morning. I think now that a tiny touch of the spark or Erilaz had been arouse in me at that point, though not enough to be obvious to either me or the Keepers. Facing the Shadow Pokers and exploring the passages alone had made me feel a faint draw towards magic, a yearning for things just beyond my reach in the normal world. And that is always how the spark of Erilaz is found.

As we walked, my mind went back to the door we had just sealed and I thought that it was funny that the hall leading to it did almost nothing now.

Firendaze was the only one who wanted to go through the door and his impulse was really only a whim to satisfy his enjoyment of combat. So there was a length of Dark Passage with nothing in it, no other doors or splits leading in any direction. Just the Rune tiles of the floor and the carved rock all around. It was thinking about the emptiness of that hall which led to the actions which would change my life for a second time.

Firendaze took me into his palace, still fuming to himself at not being allowed out to hunt monsters on the empty world.

We scrambled out into the throne room, where he pushed the chair back into place before declaring abruptly, "well, you should have a weapon to carry with you if I'm going to go through all of the trouble to teach you fighting skills. Besides, there might be more Shadow Pokers left in the Dark Passages or some other form of dangerous creep. You need to be able to defend yourself."

Giving me no time to reply, he strode out of the throne room through one of the many doors along the side. Following him, I found myself in a long, narrow hall with doors on each side and one at the far end. We traversed it to enter this door, which had a sword and bow painted on it.

It was not locked, though the door was built stoutly and had a keyhole so that it could be. Once inside I stopped in wonder to gaze around me. The room was large, about fifty feet across and perfectly round with a domed ceiling. At the apex was a circular plate of glass to let in sunlight. The walls were almost entirely covered in different sorts of weapons and armor, hanging on hooks or resting on stands. There were the classic swords, bows and spears, with shields, chest plates and helms to match them. Near these hung war hammers, crossbows, maces and flails. I saw pole arms with long hafts, clubs with short handles and weapons I did not even know the names of. All of them were made of a variety of materials, some highly ornamented while others were plainly utilitarian. The different forms of armor were also in great variety, some so outlandish that I wondered what sort of person would use them in a battle.

Firendaze went to the center of the room, spreading his arms out wide, "my personal collection. It's a hobby of mine. You may choose anything that is hanging on the walls as your own."

I gaped at him, then around the walls at the hoard of weapons displayed there. What young man would not be delighted and overwhelmed by the offer to have any weapon he chose from a huge assembly?

"Anything?"

"That is on the walls." Firendaze pointed to a large, red chest which sat against one wall. "But not the weapons in there. They are the inherited weapons of the Kings of Iseldome."

"Can I see them?" The promise of seeing an ancient king's armament was an even greater attraction.

The warrior gave a thin smile and moved over to unlock the chest with a key that was in the lock. He obviously trusted his servants not to steal or play with his collection. I was not sure if this was because they loved him as their king, or feared him for his quick temper and fighting skills.

"This is called the Hand of Kings," he explained, drawing the first weapon out. It was a gold-plated staff almost as long as he was tall, topped in a gray metal ball with spikes set in one half of it. The staff was stylized to look like a golden hand gripping the ball and holding it in place, almost as if it were about to throw it.

"An unwieldy weapon, but powerful for breaking through armor or knocking armored men off of horses."

He let me hold it for a moment, the butt end steadied on the floor. It was heavy, even for me, and the thin gold plating made it slippery. But I would not have wanted to be the person struck by that studded ball. It could have torn a man's head off in a single blow.

As I inspected it he pulled out another item. "This is Invincible, sword of the kings."

We swapped so that I could look at it. The blade was shorter than I had expected and broad, angling to a heavy, sharp point at the tip. A thrusting blade, built to withstand any parrying blow. The metal it was made of was the same solid, dark gray as Firendaze's circlet. I had never heard of a metal that color before, so I fingered it curiously.

Seeing my interest, the king paused to tell me, "Rellite. It is a durable, rare and hard to work metal that does not break easily. Because of its rareness it is only allowed to be used by the rulers of Iseldome. That is why our crown and throne are decorated with it, as a sign of our rulership. Luckily, it is not a heavy metal, or else it would bite into my head all of the time."

The sword was lighter than I had expected it to be. Handing it back, I was given the last tool from the chest. A crossbow, fitted with trigger and other hardware made of Rellite, though the crosspiece was of another metal. The stock was carved of dark wood, inlaid with silver, and the grip was wrapped in soft black leather to pad the wielder's fingers.

"Pierce, our long-range weapon." Firendaze showed me the bolts which went with it, a dozen of them in a leather pouch with their razor-sharp heads. "It was made before the advent of firearms. But sometimes I think it is even better than them, for its silence when shot and sheer power."

He waved a hand in the direction of a selection of black-powder rifles and pistols hanging on the wall. They had as much variety of make as the rest of the weapons, each one unique in some way. Many had silver or Rellite inlays, some even depicting Iseldome's crown.

Firendaze put all of the weapons of the kings away again, standing back in the center of the room. "Now, make your selection."

I walked slowly around the domed room, inspecting all of the weapons in it. There were long ones and short ones, heavy weapons and light ones. Some were long-range. Others were for hand-to-hand combat. A few seemed to be only for ornamental purposes, though the numbers of these was very small.

Finally, I came to a decision, "I can't pick a weapon without knowing how they are used. I don't have any experience with weapons. Maybe after we've trained for a while I'll have a better idea of what I want."

A smile lit up Firendaze's face, bright and fierce. It made me wonder if sending me to choose a weapon had been his idea of a test. "A wise thought. I'll let you return later on in your training to pick one. But for now...every person needs a knife."

He moved over to pick a blade off of the wall and fit it to a sheath. I took the weapon and drew it out again to admire.

The grip was made of a smooth, dark wood with bright copper rivets to hold it in place. The blade itself was stout and long, sharpened on one side, angling to a narrow point. A faint film was on the metal when I touched it; oil, rubbed on to preserve it from rusting.

"This looks like a good knife," I said, though I really had no experience with blades of any sort. Even knives to eat with had been scarce and flimsy in my past.

Firendaze nodded once. "It will do. Now, on to the training grounds."

He led the way out of the weaponry room, through the throne room to another passage. This one took us to the main hall, a huge cavern of shining windows and chandeliers. The guards here gave us salutes as we passed, to which the king always replied with a nod. The trip to the armory had improved his mood greatly, so that once we stepped outside he began talking cheerfully to me.

"Don't worry about any of my guards stopping you or asking questions during your stay. I've made it quite clear that you are to be given the run of the palace, as long as you don't cause mischief."

"Do they know why I'm here?" I asked, wondering what Firendaze had told them I was.

"Nearly. I told them that you were a prince from a nearby kingdom called Krackin, which has fallen into ruin from the attacks of the Hungry Ones. They know that you are here to learn fighting techniques from me, they just think that it will be Krackin you are returning to afterwards, not the Dark Passages."

I stopped, looking at him in surprise. "You told them I was a prince?"

Firendaze chuckled. "Just a very minor sort, as you come from Krackin. But they would not have given you any respect or thought it mete to let you stay in a room near mine, otherwise."

"I don't see how they can believe it." I looked down at the plain, stout clothes which Lune had given me, now beginning to get worn and dirtied from use.

"Oh, they'll believe anything I tell them to," the king said confidently, leading me around the outside edge of the palace.

It sat in a wide green lawn of trimmed grass, with gravel paths running through it in all directions. Around the lawn was a twelve foot wall of pale colored stone, built to allow guards to walk along the top of it. Hedges and ornamental trees grew in luxuriant clusters here and there, carefully groomed by the gardeners, which could be seen going about their business nearby. Looking up at the palace itself, I saw for the first time what it looked like on the outside.

The walls were painted a pale salmon pink, accented by stripes of a darker orange that were supporting ribs on the outside. Though it was hard to tell from this close, the structure seemed to be hexagonal in shape, with a domed roof over it all. There were a few turrets and low towers attached to it, for mostly decorative purposes. On each side of the palace wide wings stuck out, one of them containing the throne room and its connected rooms while the other, Firendaze explained, held the kitchens for the whole place. Our bedrooms were in the main building, along with the dining hall, library, war room and hundreds of other chambers too numerous to count.

Around behind the throne room's wing there was a cluster of courtyards, each separated from the other by a low wall or hedge. One of these, right up against the palace, Firendaze had confiscated to be his private training grounds. Others were tennis courts, swimming pools, croquet grounds or herb gardens, all for the amusement and enjoyment of the people who lived at the palace.

The training ground was a little larger than most of the courtyards, with a thick, even turf only a little worn down in the center. Stuffed dummies stood at one end, while round targets with red rings were set up on the other. In between, on the palace wall, hung an assortment of wooden weapons, plain steel ones and simple bows with their arrows on a rack beside them. Nothing as beautiful or well-crafted as the ones in the armory, just tools for practice.

"We'll start with sticks and rocks, the basic weapons from which all others stem," Firendaze announced, taking a pair of stout, knotty rods from where they leaned against the wall. "Sticks first. Or 'staves' if you want to be technical about it."

Turning without warning, he tossed one towards me. My reactions were barely quick enough to catch it before it fell, though the top end still banged painfully on my forehead.

"Reflexes," the warrior remarked off-hand, "are a fighter's best asset. When they're quick ones, that is."

Rubbing the bruised spot, I moved further into the courtyard. I still had the feeling that this lesson was going to be a difficult one, despite Firendaze's improvement in mood. And I was not mistaken.

To be fair, Firendaze took off all of his armor and left it piled by the wall. In just his thin shirt and leggings he was more open to any attack, I thought. But without further instruction, the king gripped his staff in both hands and charged at me.

I held the stick up, somehow expecting to easily hit him on the head with it as soon as he got in range. But he did not wait for me to make the blow. As soon as he was close enough he jabbed me in the stomach with the tip of his stick so hard that I doubled up. At the same time he flicked my weapon out of my hands with an easy movement. It pattered to the ground nearby while he laughed and I coughed.

"Don't wait for the enemy to hand you their head on a tray. Fight them off!"

Then began a series of staff duels which always ended in me getting whacked on the arm, jabbed in the chest or smacked on a thigh. I was strong and had the endurance to take a beating, but after getting trounced for an hour by a man who almost seemed to glow with agile fighting energy, I was starting to get frustrated. Not to mention hot and bruised all over.

This time Firendaze charged at me and leaped high into the air a few feet away from me in a move that both of us knew was more frightening than useful. Tired of being played with, I drew back my hand and threw my stick at him with all of my strength.

It twirled through the air, meeting him as he landed. Somehow, his vaunted reflexes did not save him this time and the stick bypassed his blocking swing, bouncing off of his face. A feeling or horror took me as it slammed point-forwards into his cheek. My only thought was not one of triumph, but 'everyone's going to kill me now!'

Firendaze was taken aback for a moment, coming to a halt as the stick bounced away onto the grass. Blankly, he raised one hand to touch the bleeding mark which was starting to swell up on the side of his face. Blinking, he turned away to stare over the hedge wall at the sky.

After a moment in which I felt frozen cold and rooted to the spot, he turned back to me.

"It seems it's time to start practicing long-range skills now."

Finally his face broke into a wide grin. "That was using your mind for once! Not what I expected at all."

"You're alright?" I actually wanted to know if he was mad, but that seemed like a suicidal question.

He just chuckled. "If I'm injured with this one little bump, you must be a permanent cripple."

Looking down at all of the bruises on my arms, I had to admit that he was right. I was hot, hungry and aching by then, ready to quit for the day. But we had to go on to long-range practice, because Firendaze would allow no complaints. As he had promised, the practice was with the simplest of projectiles, rocks. We picked them up around the edges of the yard. With rocks in hand, we lined up near the side with the round targets. Facing the dummies, Firendaze demonstrated how to throw a stone effectively, with a whip and a snap of his arm so that the missile bounced off of the stuffed mannequin's head and left a dent there.

For another forty minutes he showed me how to throw rocks the right way, until my arm was tired of the whiplash movement.

Finally, he declared that practice time was over for the day, "it was a short session today, but we were busy all morning. Now, what do you say to going into town for a meal?"

Food of any description was just what I wanted.

We washed in a fountain in one of the nearby courtyards and left the palace grounds on foot. The palace was on top of a low hill, so that the town lay spread out below us just outside of the gates. Most of the buildings were painted the same creamy color as the palace, often accented with blues or brown.

There were many with domed roofs, which I learned helped keep them cool inside, for just on the other side of the far ridge was a desert. Not the fearsome Cherial desert, full of rebellious tribesmen and vast wastelands much like the Dustlands. It was the smaller, gentler Dusna desert, containing many famous palm-tree oasis and spectacularly colored rock formations.

Some of the buildings in the city did not have domed roofs, instead being topped by flat, walled spaces where children played games, women wove or spun yarn and men perched to talk business. These were covered in colorful rugs, giving the town a holiday feel.

It was not, of course, as large as Ti-Gallin. But Iseldome, the capitol of the kingdom of Iseldome, was still vast enough to confuse me once we were down in it.

Crooked streets ran off in all directions, the main street was full of busy traffic and old-fashioned automobiles ran honking through the crowds now and then, almost seeming to stir them up on purpose.

"Do you have a car?" I asked Firendaze, surprised to see that innovation in the streets. So many of the Keepers came from low technology planets that I had come to take it for granted.

"Oh yes." he nodded, strolling along one side of the road with all of the passerby's attentions following him. "But I never get to drive it. Just the chauffeur does, with me stuck in the back. So I prefer to walk."

"The people seem to like you walking, too," I commented. Many were following us, calling greetings to their king or throwing him flowers. He nodded easily to them all, throwing small coins to the children who ran behind us screaming his name. If the servants of the castle feared and revered their fiery king, the people of his city obviously loved him with a childish glee.

A camel driver pulled his ugly beasts up in front of us, forcing them aside with prods of his elbow. "Ay, Sheba, Granite. Back. Can't you see that your rightful ruler comes this way?"

He swept off his hat and bowed to Firendaze, who absently patted one of the animal's slimy noses in passing. The driver looked as pleased as if he had dropped a sack of gold coins at their feet.

"This is where Sultane comes from originally, isn't it?" I asked, remembering the explanation of his cloak.

A dark expression crossed my companion's face, but he nodded, waving a hand towards the distant ridge. "Oh, yes. That is the ruined tower of Merenoa up there. Do you know how Sultane got his name?"

I shook my head, scrambling around a pair of fighting dogs to catch up with him. "No, how?"

The king's face still wore a strangely stormy appearance as he replied, "before he abdicated to become Merenoa's apprentice, he was one of my predecessors. One of the few kings of Iseldome to have ever gained the favor and faith of the desert tribes without a bloody war. Because of that, the title of 'Sultan of the Cherial' was added to his name. But the tribesmen themselves, when they came with presents and gold, could not pronounce that word correctly. It is one of our titles, not theirs. They called him 'Sultane' and the old king was so pleased at their efforts that he insisted everyone call him by that name. It stuck. A bit of childishness, if you ask me."

"Then what is his real name?"

By now we had reached the sprawling, cool restaurant which Firendaze had in mind. I barely heard his reply as he turned in the door. He muttered it in such a tone that I did not dare ask for a repeat. It sounded like; "Hizendar."

This story eventually changed how I viewed Sultane from then on, but at the moment I did not give another thought to it. As soon as we entered the restaurant we were surrounded by waitresses, escorted by the owner to a balcony overlooking the city and fed a huge, resplendent meal.

Chapter 17: Alchemy is Energy

After the first taste of Firendaze's training regime I was handed over to Tallray to learn Alchemy. But before beginning, we stopped off at Sultane's cave, where Tallray had a small packet to give to the old Keeper.

Sultane asked me how my training had gone and listened intently as I described it. When I told him, half-ashamed, how I had hit Firendaze with the stick he shook his head. " Be careful not to follow his impulsive ways too closely, Nolin. If you must fight, always do it with a cool head. His impulsiveness has led him to regret his actions deeply, before now, and I would not have you experience the same thing."

"Yes sir." I bowed my head, impressed by his somberness.

"Now that you have talked fighting enough, we must be starting for one of my workplaces," Tallray told me, pulling a fob watch from his pocket to look at the time it displayed. Which was not, of course, the same time as it was in the meeting place.

"Aren't we going to be working out of your shop here?" I pointed out at one of the wooden shacks, which was outfitted with a bench and equipment to be a small Alchemy lab.

"No, no!" Tallray tucked the watch away with an impatient gesture. "Though I do not have a home anywhere, I do have a few larger work places scattered in the worlds. In one of them I left a potion brewing this morning and I must check on it now. So come along!"

With a nod to Sultane, I followed after him. His long legs took him quickly into the Dark Passages and through them, so that I had to trot to keep up. As we wound our way to the correct door, he explained, "this is the planet I was born on. Like many worlds, it is simply called Terra Firma. Dirt, Soil, Engrast and Earth are all variations of that same name. My workshop is in a friend's house, in the attic. So I try not to make too much noise with all of my experiments..."

"How did the Keepers first find you?"

"The gate is in my workshop. I had tried to unlock it many times before, but could never succeed. One day Tavierfin and Sultane just came through it, saw the spark in me and sold me on the idea of world-travel right then and there. You would not believe how prosaic my world is, Nolin. There are no dragons left to get blood from, no Carmot to be found and very few people who believe in any magic except for the evil, half-witted sorts."

At that moment we stepped through the door, into his attic workshop. A mixed smell of burnt feathers and boiling salt hit my nose like a blow. It was dim inside, as the single window was covered in a light curtain. But when Tallray had shifted it aside, pale gray beams of light stole in and I could see what was around me.

The boards of the attic floor were old and warped, worn to a brown sheen by the tread of boots. The walls were also worn, showing chinks of plaster like white mold.

But all across one side of the room was a long work bench, strewn with fascinating, gleaming equipment. There was glassware of every sort, arranged in racks of retorts, lines of bottles and a giant, curling distiller which fed from a huge tank into a tiny bowl. At one point the bench was broken by an open space where a cauldron sat on a wood stove, steaming under a heavy lid and letting out the pungent smell which had hit me at first.

Yanking out his watch again, Tallray hurried towards the cauldron, muttering, "almost a minute late! I hope it has not gone too far..."

He burnt his fingers grabbing at the lid, before remembering the heavy, leather glove which lay nearby. Picking it up, he used it as a pot holder to pull the top off. Immediately swirls of yellowish vapor curled upwards, making him cough and squint as he peered into the pot. "Just in time, I hope. Nolin, help me get this off of here onto the floor! Quick, quick now."

Snatching up another glove, I slipped it on before grasping one side of the pot. Leaning my head as far away from the noxious fumes as possible, I lifted one side while he pulled on the other. Together we set it on the hearth stones, where the steam began to dissipate. Eventually we could see down into the bottom of the cauldron, where it was covered in a mass which looked like a mixture between burnt dog hair and vegetable stew.

"Excellent, perfectly dry. Now all we have to do is find the center and retrieve the seed." Tallray took up the fire poker and began shoving it into the mass, which cracked and pulled reluctantly apart wherever he prodded it. After it had been broken up, he took a pair of tongs and fished something out of the mass. Moving over to a sink, he began to rinse it off. Soon an oval-shaped object about as big as a plum was revealed, smooth and bright green.

"What sort of seed is it?" I asked, piqued by the mysterious energy of everything in the room.

"It isn't a seed at all, in reality." Tallray shook the object off and laid it gently on a towel to dry. "I simply call it that to symbolize its use. You see, this is part of my recipe for alkahest. The nucleus of the recipe, the seed which is the beginning to the end. Mixed with certain sulfurs and acids, this is what makes the alkahest."

As he spoke he laid one hand proudly on the object, tucking the other into the front of his coat.

I nodded slowly. "Ah...what is alkahest?"

"That," Tallray said with a flourish, "will be our first lesson today."

While the 'seed' dried, he took me over to a rack of test tubes, each with a different colored liquid inside of it. One of them had a little yellowish, putrid looking liquid in it, and this one he held up proudly, "this here is alkahest. It is one of the great works of alchemy to discover an alkahest and not all are as good as this one."

He went on to explain that alkahest is the theory of a liquid that can dissolve any material into its pure elements, without either ruining them or using itself up. Many people had tried before to make alkahest, with varying results. Some would dissolve almost anything, but would contaminate the subject in the process. Others only dissolved one or two items easily. But he had discovered, through dint of much effort, an alkahest that really worked. It dissolved almost anything (which I found is not exactly anything. Some things, like glass, it still did not work on) and always separated itself from the dissolved material in the end, so that it could be easily drained away and reused.

All of the tubes nearby contained different materials which had been dissolved in this manner. There was gold and iron, wood and bone, as well as many different types of vegetable matter and animal parts.

"Do you use all of these things?" I asked, picking up a tube which was supposed to contain the alkahest separated eyeballs of three geckos. It looked like three different shades of yellow liquid, sitting in layers one atop the other.

"Of course." Tallray went to get a book down from a shelf, returning to open it out beside me. It was a hand-written one, all of the pages being stained and much-used. The words were arranged like recipes, with a list followed by solid paragraphs. I bent closer to read one of these recipes, but found that I could not understand the writing. It was a strange sort of language, all of the letters looking like fishhooks or eye-bolts jumbled together with little, round dots mixed in.

"This is my book of personal recipes and ideas." Tallray ran a finger down one list, which had other strange symbols marked beside each ingredient. "See here, one drop of juice from a gecko's eye."

"Is this the writing of Terra Firma? I can't read it," I pointed out.

"Ah, how silly of me." The Alchemist slapped a palm to his forehead. "No, we use the same Latin alphabet as you do, in Terra Firma. This is written in my private code, which I developed just for my experiments. It's something done by most Alchemists so that no one can steal their secrets by looking at their journals. I will have to teach it to you as we go along."

"Don't Alchemists also draw stars on the floor to summon spirits or something?" I asked, remembering vague rumors of that practice.

Tallray drew in a quick, shocked breath at my words, making me look up in surprise. When he spoke it was firmly, "yes, my friend, some do. But those are only the evil Alchemists, the ones who have gone wrong in the head or heart somewhere. All of this—" he swept his hand around to show his work space full of gear, "is only for scientific and magical experiments. I never dabble in the spiritual with them. You see, the problem with calling on spirits is that the only ones who would obey such quibbling magic as chalk lines on the floor are evil spirits. And all evil spirits wish to do people harm, either directly or through manipulating them to do wrong in their world. Not only that, but all evil spirits are stronger than a person once he invites them into his world and himself. So yes, there are some Alchemists that dabble in necromancy. But I never do."

He spoke in such a tone of firm, quiet gravity that his words instantly marked themselves on my mind. I did not ask him again about the darker, necromantic side of Alchemy and he taught me never to go searching for that side of Erilaz myself.

We did not stay in that mood of solemnity for long, though. Soon he was showing me how he crushed the 'seed' of his alkahest and mixed it with the acids needed to make the concoction whole. His teaching was always easy and carefree, a stream of friendly chatter flowing with it.

Tallray was not merely an Alchemist because he thought he could get rich or obtain living immortality with it. He could not have been anything but an Alchemist no matter what station in life he was born in to. It was his passion to mix odd potions and messes together to see what they would become in the end. And a little bit of his enthusiasm rubbed off on me during his lessons.

Soon I was mixing, liquefying and distilling strange liquids of every type at his orders. We also measured salts, weighted metal bars and discussed the properties of mercury, poisonous and otherwise.

Tallray's teaching was much more informal than any of the other Keeper's. While we worked on a dozen projects, some just started and others part of the way through their cycle, he explained to me that the Magnum Opus, or 'great work' of most Alchemists, was trying to create an object called the Philosopher's Stone. This powerful stone could be used to transmute base metals such as lead into precious ones, especially gold. Also, small flakes could be taken off of the Philosopher's Stone and used to make the Elixir of Youth, which was known by about twenty other names by as many different Alchemists. This elixir was supposed to be able to heal any illnesses or wounds, along with granting the one who drank it living immortality and perpetual youth.

There was also a theory that the Philosopher's Stone could be used to see into or even travel to different worlds, something which made it of interest to the Keepers as a whole. Gleeb could not find any mention of a stone like that in the Founder's books, but some of the Keepers still believed that the Ten must have had one.

"How else could they have known where to put all of the doors in the Dark Passages?" Tallray argued, "they would have had to build it from the inside out before being able to travel to different universes, I would imagine. So how did they know where to place the doors in order to reach the correct planets? My theory is that they had a Philosopher's Stone and used it as a sort of sight, like on the top of a rifle, to 'aim' the doors at the right places."

"But if that were true, wouldn't they have been able to make the Elixir of Youth?" My hands were busy mixing a bowl of various salts at the time, so my words were slower than usual as I concentrated, "and if they had the Elixir, they could have cured people who were Shadow Poker touched, right?"

"Unless." Tallray held up his hand with a flourish. "They did not know how to apply it correctly to heal the black mark. Just drinking it might not cure anything."

"Maybe..." That theory did not sound right to me. "But then, wouldn't there still be some of the Founders left alive? I mean, wouldn't they have all drank the Elixir of Youth, so that some could still be alive?"

The Alchemist stopped what he was doing, which was measuring out various acids into a separate bowl, and gave me a mysterious look, "ah, my friend, that is just what we do not know. Are there still some of the first Ten Founders left alive? For the books do not say that they all died. Only that they abandoned the Dark Passages when some of their members had been killed. So, for all we know there are still some of the Founders out there wandering the worlds. We might meet one of them any day."

I stopped mixing to stare at him, caught up in the fantasy he drew of being able to meet one of the men who had built the Dark Passages, and being able to ask him all of the questions we did not know the answers to.

How were the Passages built, what prompted them to choose the locations for the doors that they did and why was there rubble filling some of the passages that had been abandoned?

I did not know it then, but only one of these questions would be answered in my time as a Keeper. Most of them are probably unknown quantities yet.

Tallray told me that there was a few other, smaller, works that Alchemists are always striving for. One of them is alkahest, which Tallray himself had almost perfected already. Another is called panacea and is a healing medicine which, like the Elixir of Youth, is supposed to be able to cure any illness or wound when ingested.

But it does not grant long life, so it is not considered to be part of the Magnum Opus. There is also the making of a Homunculus, which is considered part of an Alchemist's final goal. When we were done mixing potions to set boiling, Tallray took me to show me the Homunculus he had been working on.

"I have made it's body and finished it, physically," he explained, moving across the room to the bookshelf, which also held a few small chests and bottles. "But I have not yet found a way to give it an Animus. Not without using those evil methods we spoke of earlier. But I believe there must be a way, a good way, so I keep working in hopes of finding it."

Opening one of the chests with a little, golden key, he took out a narrow wooden box with a glass cover. It was padded inside with cotton, which had a tiny figure laying at full length upon it. It was like a miniature human, only eight inches high but almost perfectly formed. He had hands with four fingers and a thumb each, feet with the correct amount of toes and a head of dark, smooth hair. His face was a little bit blurred, it seemed to me, with a very vague expression on it and something missing in it's composition. But otherwise, the little being looked like Tallray. It even had a tiny top hat, though it was only dressed in what appeared to be a short, white toga.

"This is my Homunculus," Tallray said proudly, holding the box with great care. "A tiny copy of myself, a human just waiting to come alive. But without Animus, a mind and spirit, how will he ever awake?"

Feeling the Lightrune in my pocket, I asked, "I wonder if there are any Runes that could make him come alive? A 'Life' Rune maybe...or something like that."

A twinkle came into Tallray's eyes which meant that he was pleased, "that is very clever of you, Nolin. But, sadly, I have thought of it before and discussed it with Tavierfin. We both agree that, if there was such a thing as a Life Rune, it would be practically the same thing as the Philosopher's Stone. And what other Rune Stones would be sufficient to bring something alive?"

I pondered the question carefully, but did not have enough experience to come up with an answer. Could an expert make an Animus Rune, or was it a word only used in Alchemy? What was the limit to Runes for a theoretical 'all-powerful' Runeologist?

If Tavierfin had a charm which could make his natural fins turn into legs, it seemed there was not a limit to what could be done. It was just knowledge that was needed.

"Anything can be done, with enough knowledge," I murmured dreamily, caught up in a vision of the power that the Founders must have wielded before their fall. I realized that it was partially the fact that all of the Keepers knowledge was divided between them rather than cohesive which led to inefficiencies in rebuilding the Dark Passages.

Overhearing my muttered words, Tallray added, "do not forget energy, my friend. Knowledge and energy together are needed for all projects. That is what Alchemy is about, shifting the energy of one item, or a group of them, so that they become something else altogether. At its core, Alchemy is energy."

As if to prove his point, a slowly-heating bottle of experimental fluid exploded at that moment, splattering glass shards and gunk across the room. It made me jump, and Tallray dashed to turn off the alcohol burner it had been sitting on.

The next fifteen minutes were spent in cleaning up the mess, another thing which I found was integral to Alchemy.

As we were finishing there came a knock on the trap door which led to the rest of the house. Tallray started, before a small smile flitted across his face. "Nolin, open the trap door, please."

I hurried over to the cumbrous trap door, which was barred on the inside to prevent unwanted visitors. Pulling aside the bar, I grasped the iron ring on top and hauled the door open. It was lighter than I expected and fairly easy to open. Flopping it all of the way over onto the floor, I looked to see who had knocked.

A woman stood smiling on the steps below, a tray held in her hands, "Hello. I heard you two working up here and thought you might like some dinner."

Tongue-tied, I stepped back into the room and let her come up. Tallray came to meet her with a smile, taking the tray from her hands to lay it on one of the nearby counters.

"Thank you, my dear. We were just about to starve up here in our slavery over Alchemical concoctions."

"You would have been down soon to raid the pantry, if I had not come up," the woman returned, before glancing over at me curiously, "so this is your new apprentice?"

As Tallray agreed and began telling her about all the things we had been doing that morning, I continued to watch the newcomer curiously. She was tall for a woman, coming to Tallray's shoulders, and had an abundance of rich red hair partially done up on her head. The rest flowed behind in a narrow stream which reached her waist. Her dress was full-skirted and had a high, stiff collar which looked very uncomfortable to me, especially as it had two large, gold buttons on it. The dress was made of a stiff, white material edged in soft blue at the hems, giving it a seafaring appearance.

Her hands were slim and nervous, wrapping themselves in the skirt of her dress while she talked to Tallray. I wondered at first if she was hiding something, or afraid of the Alchemist, but soon put those ideas aside. She spoke so quickly and honestly about any subject he introduced that she could not be afraid. Her hands were simply fidgety.

Once she was gone Tallray and I began to eat what she had brought us. There were triangular sandwiches on soft bread, filled with ham and cheese, as well as fried chicken, deviled eggs, carrots in a cheese dip and lemonade to drink with it all. A real summer picnic-style lunch, though when I looked out of the attic window I saw gray skies hanging over a cobbled street, with grim, muddy buildings on the other side.

"Tallray," I asked when we were almost through with our meal. "None of the Keepers are married, are they?"

The Alchemist jumped, looking faintly guilty. "Eh, no. In fact, the Founders had a law against getting involved too closely with any person from any single world. We've somewhat, ah, unofficially kept up with that rule. Why do you ask?"

"I was just curious...none of the Founders were women either, were they?"

Tallray shook his head. "No, no my friend. Founders and Keepers alike, we've always tried to devote ourselves to keeping the Dark Passages going and the arts of Erilaz alive. The Ten Founders were all men and thought that there was sure to be unpleasant entanglements if that ever changed. Why do you ask such odd questions all of a sudden?"

He did not really look at me when he asked this. I did not want to offend him by suggesting that it was his red-headed friend who had prompted me to ask, so I sidestepped the question. "Corky still stays with his family. I guess that isn't against the rules?"

"As long as he knows that this is his job and life now, it will not distract him." Tallray bounced up, hastily putting all of the bones from the chicken back onto the tray. "Come now, let me show you where you shall be sleeping tonight. It is small, yes, but not unpleasant."

The place he showed me was a closet to one side of the attic, which had in it a cot, a lantern on a hook and a short, empty shelf. It was a little cramped for size, but it was better than some places I had slept before. Tallray said that he had his own little room just below the attic, which was almost as cramped for bed-space as mine.

"But as my legs are a little longer, I do need more space than an apprentice takes up," he chuckled, closing the door of the closet again, "now, let us go back to our experiments for a short time before we stop for the night. I will show you the steps I have taken to make the Philosopher's Stone and why I think they have not worked..."

I went back to work with him gladly, enjoying the thinking challenges and puzzles that Alchemy threw our way.

Chapter 12: The Test

One more day of learning Alchemy was all I got, before my pre-test instructions were completed with Sultane. Every one of the Keepers had spent a few days teaching me something, except for Sultane. I spent the last couple days of the allotted three weeks with him, living in his cave at the meeting place. My respect for him had grown since I learned that he had once been king of Iseldome and sultan of the Cherial desert, as well as the apprentice of Merenoa and a wise Keeper. But when I tried to tell him this he only shook his head at me gently.

"Nolin, do not base your evaluation of a man on the titles he has held in life. Some of the worst scoundrels known to man have been given the title 'king' or another word for ruler. I am honored to gain your respect, but only if it is because you know me and know that I am worthy of it."

Like many of the things Sultane told me, this made me think more carefully about the values I placed on things and how I viewed the world. Though he did not teach me any special skills, he let me rest and helped my mind expand so that it could be large enough to meet the test.

I was worried about one thing. I had not yet found the root of magic. It worried me, as I did not know what the test was going to involve. It seemed to me that my teachings over the last three weeks had fully tested my loyalty, which was what Berune had been worried about. Other than that, I had only gained a foothold in a few skills and some confidence in my companions, nothing more mystic.

The morning of the test a full meeting was called, with all of the Keepers present. I wore a new embroidered coat with the sleeves rolled back so that they would not cover my hands. It was a gift from Tallray on the last day of his teaching and was splendid, but a little too large for me. I fingered the brass buttons and maroon cloth when I put it on, thinking that it was the most fancy piece of clothing I had ever worn.

At first I was not allowed to enter the cave of meeting, or even come near it. The Keepers told me to stay in the library, where the thick stone muffled their voices so that I could not hear what was being discussed.

I guessed that they were talking over my performance in the last weeks, trying to decide if it was worth continuing my training. Frustrated that I could not hear their conversation about me first-hand, I stalked back and forth in the library like a kenneled dog. I considered sneaking around the wall to get a better vantage point, but I knew that Firendaze's sharp senses would find me quickly, even if none of the others noticed me first. They might even have had a sentinel posted to watch for me at the entrance.

Stopping at the back of the room, I pounded a fist against the wall. What were they saying? A hundred little things I had done wrong or spoken too hastily came back to me, laughing and pointing fingers at my discomfort. Perhaps they would be offended at my questions, or angry at my slowness to find the spark of Erilaz. They might even decide that I was no good as an apprentice altogether! What would I do if they threw me out?

I tried to imagine going back to my own world and living a regular, singular-world life. With no arts of Erilaz to learn, no friends or family to look after me or be glad to see me, I would feel sunk. I realized for the first time how much learning the ways of the Keepers meant to me and how much I had come to rely on the ability to shift through worlds. If it was taken away my life would feel empty.

Finally, when I was feeling both hot with excitement and cold with depression at once, Corky came to get me. There was a smile on his face as he came in and said, "come on over, Nolin. The first part of the test has to begin."

I knew that Corky would not be happy to see me kicked out, no matter what the others thought. Taking heart, I followed after him.

In the other room the other Keepers were waiting, excitement and curiosity plain on their faces. It hit me when I saw them that they wanted me to succeed at least as much as I wanted to myself. Of course, they had brought me there to train as their apprentice, but I had not been sure any more that they were satisfied with their choice. Seeing their expressions, I knew that only Berune among them had any hope at all that I would fail the tests. And even he only half-hoped it out of sheer spite.

Sultane beckoned me up to the table, where the Keepers moved away to gather at the far end, facing me. I stood before them with my hands resting lightly on the old, solid stone, trying to steady myself with it.

"First, we will each ask you a question that you must answer to the best of your ability," Sultane explained, "After that, a few of your skills will be tested directly. But the most important part of the test will begin afterwards. Then you must stay a vigil in the Dark Passages."

Before I had time to do more than nod my head once, Adasian shot off the first question, "what are you doing here?"

It was such a sharp, unexpected interrogation that I was at first thrown off-balance. For a minute, I thought he meant it as a true challenge.

But I realized after a moment that he was just testing my Rhetoric skills in his old way. After a moment of thought, I replied, "learning to keep the Dark Passages and the ways of the Founders."

He nodded, gesturing for someone else to speak. Gleeb asked me a historical question next, which I answered only half-correctly. For a minute I was afraid that I had failed, getting half of it wrong, but I soon learned that there was no failing this test. It was to see how far I had progressed and feel out my loyalties, not decide if I was knowledgeable enough to stay. One by one they all asked me a question, some about the skills they had taught me and others on more general subjects. Firendaze appeared bored of the whole thing and asked, "what is the name of the kingdom I rule?"

"Iseldome."

"Very good," he yawned, muttering aside to Adasian a moment later, "I already struck his metal the other day. This is a pompous charade."

"Only to some of us, leg-lopper." The scribe returned, which made the warrior's face turn such a dark shade of red that I thought he was going to explode outwards like a volcano, or punch Adasian's head in.

Luckily, Sultane was asking the last question at that moment and it was one which drew everyone's attention back to the test. "Do you desire to continue training to be a Keeper, Nolin?"

Every eye became focused on me in a moment. Except for Tavierfin's two, that is. They were fastened speculatively on the wall off to one side of my head.

"Yes." I bowed my head in acquiescence. "I do."

Sultane looked around at the others, who gave their nods of approval.

"Then your vigil in the Dark Passages will begin."

I hardly knew what a vigil was, or how I would perform it, but I waited patiently, knowing that they would give me more of an explanation before sending me off.

Gleeb pulled a scroll of cracked paper from a pocket in his robe, unrolling it to read.

"In those times the first of the Ten went alone into the Dark Passages and stayed in their halls for three days without seeing anyone. He only brought one jar of water with him and fasted all that time. When he returned his companions marked a difference in his attitude and asked what it meant. In reply he said, 'I have seen wonders. I have been tested and returned whole. The Dark Passages spoke to me. If they had not, I could not continue to be among our companionship.' After that time all of the Ten Founders of the Dark Passages went into them alone for three days, one by one, and all returned having passed the test."

The Historian stopped there, rolling up the scroll with a snap and looking around smugly. "I told you that the idea of a test for the Keepers was historically grounded! In fact, we really all should have done it by now."

"I have," Sultane told him, "or else I would not wish Nolin to try it, for fear that it would demand too much of someone without enough experience."

All of the other Keepers looked at him in surprise, except for Tavierfin, who agreed "actually, I have too, in a sense. Not because I read the ancient script and thought that it was a good idea. I just got lost in speculating on the Runestones of the floor one day and stayed for some time. Though perhaps not three whole days."

"Did you see what I saw?" Sultane met his gaze solemnly.

The Runeologist's dark eyes held a spark of wondering mystery for a moment. "Yes."

By now I was shaken by both anxiety and wonder, as you may imagine. I could not guess what they would have found in the Dark Passages that would affect them so strongly, other than perhaps something of the Shadow Poker sort. Waiting to be told what to do in order to prepare myself became a more difficult task than it had been at first.

"Do I have to bring only one jar of water? And how will I know when the three days are up?"

Sultane turned to me with a small smile on his fierce old face. "You will have the strength for it, do not fear. As for the water…it will be a large jar and you will be given a small amount of bread to go with it. I do not think that it will harm the test at all. Someone will be sent to find you when the three days are up. Until then you must speak to no one that you recognize and you may not go through any gate in the Passages. In fact, as our Passages are a little more cramped than the Founder's were, you must stay on the higher-number side of this meeting room door. On our part, we will try to avoid going that way unless it is necessary. That way you will be alone."

That last word sent a shiver through me, but it was not only of fear. It was the first awakening of a nameless feeling which swirled together anticipation, mystery and a sense of the unknown.

After it I was outfitted with a half-gallon jar of water, a single loaf of bread and a warning to speak no more words to the Keepers until I was sent for. Then, with no more ceremony, I was set loose in the Dark Passages.

Unsure of myself and what I was doing, I wandered slowly down the dark hall towards the far end. Part of the way down, my eyes fell on the glass jar and lump of food in my hands. Bread and water. Prison fare, or the meals of a slave. Suddenly, I was not afraid of going without anything else for three days. I had eaten little more while doing hard work and survived. Sitting around in the Dark Passages should be easy enough. Especially as Sultane had said nothing against either sleeping or running about if I felt like it.

What I did not know then was that three days is a long, long time to wait through with nothing to do. At first I set the bread and water next to the wall and ran up and down the Passages, just to burn off some extra energy from the excitement of the meeting. After becoming tired of that, I picked up my supplies and wandered slowly down to the very end of the long hall. There I picked through some of the rubble which had fallen into the tunnel on the left-hand side, hoping to find some sort of ancient relic or even just a lost button. But there was nothing except for the dark stone, broken off in jagged, hard lumps. It looked just like the material which made up the walls and roof, as if the ceiling there had collapsed into the path to block it off. Though the Keepers had told me that they had cleared spaces like this when originally opening up the Passages, they yet not found any sign of breaks in the hall walls.

"Maybe someone put it here on purpose to close the Dark Passages off," I said to myself, in a sudden stroke of brilliance, "it might have even been the Founders when they left. By hand it would take a long time to cart all this in. But with magic it would be easy."

Tossing one more lump idly into the pile I had been building, I sat on the edge of it lost in thought. What seemed like a long time later I stood up slowly to stretch my arms above my head, "it's only late morning now. I'd better wait before eating or drinking anything."

Getting a drink of water was appealing, but not because I was thirsty yet. It was simply that it would have been something different to do. Trying to forget the idea, I rambled up and down the main hall of the Passages again, carefully inspecting every nook and cranny of its design. For a while I sat and stared at the misty darkness in front of me, then lay on my back and stared at the ceiling.

A sensation of impatience crept down my back, into my feet. Jumping up, I ran quickly back to the place where I had left my supplies. The sound of my footsteps echoing behind me was eerie, almost as if I were being followed. Stopping suddenly, I looked over my shoulder. But there was nothing there and only the faint, breath-like humming of the Dark Passages themselves filled the air. I went on more slowly, huddling down beside my jar and loaf with the feeling that eyes were watching from the empty walls. Boredom held sway with Uncertainty, the king and knave of the ceremony.

It would be tiresome to go into the details of the first two days. Or I should say, the first two spans of time. I slept twice, heavily, in that time so I guessed that the second time I awoke was at the beginning of the third day. Though I did take short naps in between, time had slowed to a whisper by now so that it was hard to tell how much had passed at all.

Through the first two stretches of time I ate and drank sparingly of the provisions, but still they went down at an alarming rate. At the beginning of the third period I only had a quarter-inch of water left in the jar and a tiny crumb of crust left to consume. Worse than that, I was beginning to see and hear things which other people would have said were not there.

I had taken up permanent quarters in the branch of the passages which had the door to the empty world at the end of it. It felt safer there when I slept, because nothing could come at me from any way but one. Or that's what I thought when I had settled down for the first sleep.

When I awoke on the third bit of time it was with a start. My mouth was dry with thirst. Something was looking down at me from the vaulted ceiling: I was sure of it. Straining against the never-changing gloom of the Dark Passages, I searched for the eyes which must be watching. But there was nothing there, nothing to see.

The feeling still persisted. Drawing myself up against the right-hand wall, I crouched with my hands on my knees, face tilted upwards.

Nothing.

Then, a sound off to my right, in the direction of the barred door. I could not quite see it from where I sat because of the curve of the path and the mist, but it sounded exactly as if someone had unbarred the door and opened it. Which would be impossible, without having first stepped over me...unless they could open it from the other side.

My hand slid to the hilt of the knife at my side. My eyes strained for any sign of movement down the hall. And all the time I was dreadfully thirsty, without daring to move far enough to reach the jar of water set upright on the floor not far away. Every nerve strained to see what was to come after the noise. But for a long time, there was nothing.

Eyes falling to the water again, I slowly began to stretch a hand towards it. Inch by inch, those pale fingers of mine glided towards the glass jar.

Before they reached the jar, though, I remembered that those were my very last drops of water. If I drank it all now, there would be nothing for the rest of the day. Nothing to wash down the bread when I ate it. My hand was stilled, but I continued to watch the jar with a heightened interest.

Water...it was so beautiful. Silvery clear, vaguely reflecting the darkness around it. Drinking it would have been better than being given a handful of diamonds. It would taste like diamonds, I thought confusedly, clear and sparkling, cold. Ah, the trickling coldness of water!

But I mustn't drink it yet. Sitting back, I let my eyes droop to half-shut. Perhaps I would just sleep a little longer to let the time pass...but then there was a sound again. It jerked me awake, hand reaching for the dagger and gaze searching the darkness. I knew that I was not asleep.

Something stirred down the hall towards the door, flickering black in the darkness. Small shapes like rats or mice scurried by, half-seen as shadows against the opposite wall. I let out an inadvertent gasp and scrunched up against my side of the hall, trying to keep away from them.

Once they had gone passed there was a deep, awful silence. It seemed that even the humming of the Runes had been stilled for the moment. A larger shape loomed out of the mist, a figure made of shadows. Sure that it was a Poker, I drew my knife and waited in fear of it seeing me.

The shape had seemed huge at first, bigger than the largest man. But as it drew closer it dwindled down to regular human size. After a second I realized that it was shaped like a man as well, not jagged and flat like a Shadow Poker. I still did not know how it would have come through the door, or why it was coming so slowly and silently towards me.

Finally the form was just a few steps in front of me and it looked up with eyes which glowed in flickering rainbow colors. It seemed to be a man dressed in a shadowy cloak, like the portraits of the Founders which hung on Adasian's wall. But this one was even darker and more ethereal, with eyes which never stayed the same color for more than a heartbeat.

Strangely, I was not afraid any more. My hand relaxed on the knife. I was only curious about who he was and what he was doing there. I leaned forwards to speak my questions, but my mouth was so dry I could not form any words. Like a wraith, he crouched before me, holding up one shady hand to command silence.

Using a finger, he began to draw lines on the floor. Where he drew, beams of fire lay like coils of burning string. He made Runes on the tile of the floor which he crouched on, tracing them out all across it. When he stopped, they faded away. The figure looked up at me, meeting my gaze as if to show me something.

I could not talk, but I tried to look my questions at him. What did he want me to know?

Again he drew the Runes, this time in brilliant green like leaves with the sun through them. Then again in liquid blue. Finally he drew them without a mark, invisible on the smooth black of the tile. As soon as he had finished it he looked up once more with his iridescent gaze, then was gone.

I blinked, pulling myself to my feet. No one was anywhere in the hall as far as I could see. The sound of the Runes humming was still going somewhere in the background.

Fire, Earth, Water and Air. He had drawn the Elements on the stone in Runes.

"I must be going crazy," I muttered thickly, settling back onto the ground and sheathing my knife. There could not have been any shadows like mice, or like a man with glowing eyes. I had been seeing things. But was that what I had come here for?

I dozed again, before awakening thirstier than ever. But I was also just as determined not to drink the little water I had, not yet. I gazed at the crystalline jar, tapped it with the toe of one shoe to make the water slosh inside. It looked so good that I had to close my eyes again to avoid snatching it up and gulping it down. With them closed, I began to hear voices talking somewhere far away, apparently in the wall behind me. At first, I could not make out anything of what they were saying. Slowly the sounds became clearer and more understandable, until three words fell on my ears with perfect clarity, "don't perfect weakness."

After that the conversation fell to a distant muttering once again. My eyes jerked open and I sat up straighter. Don't perfect weakness. The water shimmered in its jar. I would not drink it. My determination became an obstinacy.

Standing up, I paced back and forth down the little side-hall, avoiding the provisions on the floor. The air seemed to get thicker and more oppressive as I walked, until I felt smothered by darkness all around me. Light, just to have a little light!

Remembering my Lightrune, I jerked it from my pocket and set it on the floor, crouching over it like a cold man by a camp fire. One hand had to hold it, of course, or else it would have gone out, but I let the back of that hand rest on the ground limply. White brilliance pooled up and around me, reflecting on my face and picking out a strand of hair which had fallen in front of my eyes. White hair, white light. They both gleamed with a living comfort...then it went out.

Though I was still touching it, the Lightrune stopped glowing. The darkness pressed in even tighter than before.

I must have really gone a little crazy at that point. I can only vaguely remember shaking the Runestone, throwing it on the ground and jumping up to run away. I ran wildly, hunting for a way out of shadows and darkness. Suddenly door number 243 jumped into my vision, my hand on the doorknob. I almost went in, out of the Passages into sunlight and fresh air. But the words echoed in my head again. "Don't perfect weakness."

With a gasp, I flung myself around and ran back in the other direction...

The next thing I knew I was laying face-down on the tile which the shadowy man had written on. Lines of fire were trickling and pooling over the floor like spilled water. I tried to touch one and it jumped away from my finger, skittering into a new course. Sitting up, I watched the fire outline the tile in glowing orange, and then flicker out in an instant. Leaning over and looking at the joint between that tile and the next one, I inspected it with insane care. It was a fine joint, but with my eyes close to the ground I could see a narrow line of gray mortar holding the tiles together. One tiny flake of it had cracked loose, so I peeled it away with a fingernail. What was beyond the tile, below it? Was it nothingness more empty than outer space, or another world which no one had seen before?

I tried to find other chipped flakes to pull away, but the rest of the mortar was smooth and unbroken. I realized with dawning eagerness that this passage was a hidden one, which no one could see from the main hall and none of the Keepers would be likely to traverse anytime soon. I could get tools sometime, maybe break the rest of the mortar away and lift the Runestone, just a little, to see what was beyond it. They would not like it, but they would never have to know.

After this series of thoughts the pressing darkness came back even worse, filled with voices just outside the range of my hearing. I jumped to my feet, deciding to find out who was talking and where, even if it meant going to the ends of every world in the Dark Passages to get the answer.

At the moment of my decision the voices all fell away and a bright light, white like my Lightrune, filled one end of the hall. It shone on me so brightly that I had to blink rapidly to adjust my eyes to it. Shimmering waves of cream and gold vibrated through it, accompanied by a far-away noise like music. It was just in front of me, with the darkness still behind. I moved towards it, trying to reach the center of the light. It seemed to retreat away, fading as I drew closer until I felt a solid surface beneath my hands and knew that it was the door at the end of the hall. The golden pleasure was going. A longing filled me like no other I had ever felt before.

"No, please, come back..." I wanted the light. I needed it's power in me more than I had felt the urge to own anything else in the worlds, even freedom. It was still fading as I pressed a hand against the wall towards it and tried, with all of my will, to take the light into me.

Something broke in my center and filled with light, before it all faded away like a dream upon awakening. Though I'm ashamed to say it, I leaned against the door and sobbed openly with discovery and loss until the Keepers found me.

Three had come to tell me that the days of the test were over. Berune, Gleeb One-step and Firendaze, the warrior carrying my jar of water with an odd expression on his face.

They stopped abruptly, seeing me crying there like a brokenhearted maiden. Gleeb was the first to speak, "are...you alright Nolin?"

Berune cut him off with a snort of derision before I could answer. "Look at that crybaby! He thought he saw something that scared him and so he weeps. Or maybe he didn't pass the test by finding his spar—"

He never finished the sentence. I spun around, filled with sudden anger at his constant antagonizing. Without thinking, one of my hands whipped up in a furious gesture at him and I poured all of my frustration at him in a beam of solid energy. Like a whiplash, yellow light swung from my hand and swept him off of his feet against the wall. He struck with a solid thump, before falling to the ground limply as I released him.

I had not meant to use Powerpointing against him so viciously, or any magic at all for that matter. My anger had simply gotten the best of me. Once he fell to the ground I stood staring at him with just as much surprise as the other two Keepers were regarding me with.

Slowly, Berune jacked himself up on one arm, then on to his feet. He ran a hand dazedly through his hair, standing it all up on end. He looked over at me and said, "that was more like it!"

Tension went out of the air in a gasp.

"I—I didn't mean to—" I tried to explain, looking down at my hands in wonder.

"I know," he laughed mirthlessly, "you've got some power now, kid. But you've also got a temper to match, and that could be dangerous. Next time you might kill somebody if you don't stop to think."

But his words held less venom than formerly, so I did not take offense. Wiping a sleeve across my face to dry it, I turned to look at Gleeb and Firendaze. "Did I pass the test?"

"Oh, eh," the Historian sputtered for a moment, "of course!"

Firendaze just held up the jar and looked at me through it. "You didn't even drink all of your water! What was it like, the test, I mean?"

I shook my head slowly, still feeling out of touch with the world. It had been insane, I had been insane. But I had found the spark of Erilaz and I would have had it no other way.

Interlude 3: Memories

"I suppose you could say that my training truly began after the test. Everything else had been an experiment up until then, to see if I would make it. Now I was the Keepers' apprentice. And I had magic to aid me." Nolin's eyes gleamed in the dim light as he relived that time. His coarsely spun, tan clothes and scarf were lined with dust, just like those of anyone who lived in this world. His colorless hair, too, was speckled by it. But the expression on his narrow, bony face hinted at things which most Dustlanders never thought about or knew.

He was remembering the long weeks and even months of training with one Keeper or another. How Firendaze had made him and Corky fight in practice duels, until Nolin had once angered Corky and seen the Fire Element light up his whole face. The times learning how to sense a person's intentions, staying in the bare, cold cave which Feleago lived in. All of the days experimenting with Tallray and Tavierfin, or arguing history with Adasian and Gleeb. Lune's failure to teach him anything but the most basic of first aid skills.

Everything that the Keepers had told him, all the adventures he had been on. The worlds he had helped to uncover and explore. Just in the few short years of his apprenticeship.

Hiram made a small noise of impatience. Nolin's gaze focused on him. Sitting up straighter, the wizard apologized for halting the thread of his narrative.

Abashed at being apologized to by his hero, Hiram bowed his head. "Think all that you wish, Nerheem. It is not my place to interrupt you. An apprentice must be obedient."

There was a slight tightening around Nolin's mouth as he shook his head. "You are not my apprentice...besides, I was not a perfect student by anyone's standards."

"You weren't?"

Nolin sighed, "of course not. In fact, I turned out to be the worst sort of follower. A traitor. But that will be soon to come. When we left off I was still just learning to become a Keeper. We acquired the secret of how the Dark Passages had become filled with rubble. An ancient book uncovered in it told that the Founders had put it there magically, just before they left, to prevent things like Shadow Pokers from drifting between worlds."

"And I learned a lot about each Keeper's secrets, on the side. Berune's indebtedness, Adasian's hidden, insane brother, the imminent war between Iseldome and the tribes of the Cherial desert... But none of those are the worst mystery I learned. The one that was hardest for me to take was when I discovered the secret that all of the Keepers knew, the secret of why I had been needed so urgently as their apprentice."

Chapter 18: Sultane

I learned the truth on a cool fall evening when Lune had come to visit Sultane at the meeting place. It was one of the times I had been given a few days off from formal studies to rest and learn from the wise old Keeper and, like usual, I was enjoying it. After the Healer had sat talking about nothing interesting for a few minutes, a peculiar look passed between him and Sultane.

Then the eldest Keeper looked to me and said, "Nolin, would you go fetch some of the firewood I had you stack outside of the meeting place yesterday? It will be cold tonight and we will need it."

I knew right away that they were getting rid of me to say something secret. But it was true that we needed more wood before nightfall, so I nodded silently and got up to leave. Just outside the door I stopped, closing it gently before pressing my ear against the crack to listen to what was said.

Sultane was usually entirely open and free-spoken with me, so I had always returned the same to him. But if he was going to play the childish trick of sending me out of the room on an errand in order to speak privately, I thought that I could pull the equally childish trick of eavesdropping on him.

The door, though, was too thick for me to hear anything through very well. All I could pick up was a few intermittent words.

"—lately?"

"Worse..."

"—double dose—"

"Hah...no need—"

Frustrated, I reached over and slowly pulled the door open, working the latch so carefully that it made no sound. I opened it no more than a crack, so that the saffron light of the fire inside pooled out into the fall twilight around me. Putting an eye to the widened crack, I could both see and hear what was going on inside. Lune was leaning over to give something to Sultane. I caught a glimpse of it as it changed hands: it was a small, tinted bottle such as doctor's pills were kept in.

Instantly, I remembered once before when I had seen Lune giving Sultane a bottle stealthily. Also the many times when Lune had come to call on the old Keeper and left something, a small package or bundle, behind for him. I had never seen what was in the packages and had usually been too busy to pay much mind to it. I had thought that it was merely old friends exchanging little gifts. Now a shaft of fear pierced me straight through from the top to the bottom. Did Sultane's wounds from losing his legs simply bother him, or was he falling ill?

Lune was straightening up now, so I shut the door and hurried off for the wood. When I returned with it, he was coming out of the door. It shut behind him with a fussy clicking sound. I dropped the wood in front of the house and stopped the Healer before he could get to the Dark Passage gate.

"Lune, what are those bottles and things you are always giving Sultane?"

The Healer stopped, turning to look at me in the bluish twilight, "well, you've noticed them, have you?"

He was blustering, so I just nodded and looked at him steadily. I had grown in the two years since coming to learn from the Keepers and was a little taller than the Healer by now.

Lune let out a sigh, turning to look longingly at the gate before focusing his attention on me again, "the others did not want you to know, but I see no reason to hide the truth if you are going to ask questions. Those 'bottles and things' are medicine, of course. I am a Healer. Sultane never quite recovered from the poison of his wounds, so I have been doing all I can to stave it off. But I'm afraid there is little I can do any more. The poison is terminal."

"You mean—" I clutched at his sleeve so he could not move away, "—Sultane is, dying?"

Lune nodded once, "why do you think that we needed to train an acolyte to be the next Keeper so suddenly? The time he has left will be just enough for you to learn everything."

"There must always be ten," I whispered hoarsely, more to myself than to Lune. It was an expression that had reinforced all through my training.

The Healer nodded slowly while the truth sank into my mind.

Sultane was dying.

My being brought in to replace him when the time came.

The Dark Passages without Sultane...being a Keeper without his advice to call upon.

I suppose that I had always known that one of the Keepers must die before I could become one myself. But life had stretched on before me with no sign of changes ahead. I had felt that I would always be in training, just waiting until the far-off day when I would somehow painlessly become a Keeper.

A shaft of brighter light shone on both the Healer and I. Spinning around, we saw Sultane sitting in his wheelchair in the open door, dark against the light.

"I never told you the story of how I lost walking to gain wheels, did I Nolin?" He asked, voice as low and vibrant as ever, "come inside again, both of you. I feel the urge to talk tonight."

As if drawn by a string we followed him back into the cave, firewood forgotten just outside. Sultane rolled himself over beside his bed where, with a small feat of dexterity and strength, he used his arms alone to lift himself into it. Lune and I settled nearby in a pair of chairs, mine pulled up right next to the old Keeper's bed. He touched my hand once, with the tip of his finger, a gesture as intimate as a pat but less soft.

When he began, it was with an explanation first, "I never told you this before, not because I am ashamed, but because it might hurt your opinion of one of our friends. I hope now that it does not, as you seem to have become fast friends with him as well as Corky, you all three being energetic young men. It is Firendaze I speak of."

He paused for a moment while I nodded slowly, tensing against what I was about to hear.

"You know that when Firendaze was younger I was the ruler of Iseldome. There were many things I had to attend to and many people who wanted my attention. Even so, I took notice of his fighting abilities and courage, which he showed on the practice field or in the few skirmishes along our border that he was allowed to join. Without immodesty, I can say that I was a great fighter in my own time. I began to invite him to join me in practice, or fight against me in informal duels. It was only for our own amusement and to keep up our practice, you understand."

"But in those days Firendaze had a hot, wild temper which he had not learned how to control. The smallest things could make him angry to the point of reckless acts, or depressed into a sullen gloom. He has learned how to restrain himself now, else I never would have invited him to take the throne when I abdicated."

Sultane fingered the animal teeth tied to the end of his braid for a moment, putting together his next words carefully, "It was mostly one of our play duels which taught him the need for restraint, a hard lesson. But I blame myself equally with him. Firendaze had become excellent at any form of fighting by that time. Though I was older than him by many years, we would often come together like a pair of young stags, struggling and striving for supremacy. One day he brought an old sword with him to the playing field. It was a strange sword from a time of darkness in our land, the blade imbued with an exotic poison and sharper than most blades can be."

"I teased him at first for carrying that sword, calling him taunting names. It was known to have been last wielded by a weak coward, so it had a bad history. I reminded him of this and asked him if he was that coward's heir. Firendaze did not seem too angry at first, just laughing with that bitten-off, sharp laugh of his. He said 'are you afraid to face this sword in play? I thought you were too swift to be touched by any blade.' Foolishly, I retorted that I was not afraid of any sword he could wield. I suppose I did not really think, then, that he would touch me with such a weapon. I had an idea that he would pull the blow if I was not swift enough to avoid it.. Besides, my ego was pricked and I still imagined that I could beat him in a duel any day..."

Sultane coughed, shaking his head and wagging a finger at me, "remember never to be so stupid as I was and you will spare yourself much, young one. We fought for half an hour, getting more tired and angry as time when on. Finally I managed to give him a heavy blow to the side of the head with the flat of the blunted sword I carried. He stumbled to the ground, stunned, and I'm afraid that I laughed at him. 'Finished!' I told him grimly, bending forward in a mock gesture of stabbing him through the heart. It was at that moment his temper, always fragile, snapped. He scrambled to his knees shouting, 'I'm not finished yet, you old fool!' and swung the poisoned sword at my legs with all of his might while he yelled it. It is kindest to think that he forgot the danger of that particular blade, or that he had lost his mind altogether in that moment of stress. Which is quite likely, with how I had stirred him up."

"The blade took off one leg below the knee and bit part way through the other. The court physicians amputated both in hopes of stopping the poison, but it did not work. Merenoa had some knowledge of healing and was called to help me, but all that she could do is slow the poison's work. Lune only has the power to do the same. It is not because they are poor healers. They are, or were, the best. The poison is unstoppable."

By the end of the story I was looking away, throat aching with unspent emotion, "that is terrible. I—I'm sorry."

"Nolin, every road must end sometime," Sultane's voice forced me to look back and meet his gaze, "and the end of every road is the beginning of another. It may not be an easy, paved road. It may be only a path through the thorns. But no road leads nowhere. I forgave Firendaze long ago. It took some time for him to forgive himself, too. Both of us have learned to live with life as it is. Who knows, without having lost my ability to walk I might never have become Merenoa's apprentice. And I might never have gone looking for the Dark Passages. I would not ask for my legs back and a few extra years of my life if I had to give up those things to get them."

Lune was fussily rearranging some things on the table, using the act to disguise the fact that he was wiping at his eyes with the other hand. Eventually he rose and blustered, "well, hum, I must be getting back to my home. Kitty will be missing me. I'm sorry, Nolin, that we had to tell you the truth so suddenly."

With a mumbled word of thanks to Sultane, I followed the Healer outside, "how long has he got?"

"To live? Whew," Lune blew out his chubby cheeks and sucked them in again uncertainly, "two more years, at the outside. I think. I'm really not sure, having never seen the poison on the blade or anything like it. But he is a fighter still, in spirit, and will not go quickly. I'm sorry, Nolin."

His repeated words had little effect on me. My mind was sunk in numbness since learning the truth. It seemed cruel, somehow, to keep training to be a Keeper now, knowing that I was only waiting for him to die. And yet, I knew that he had sent Lune and Tallray to find an apprentice to take his place when he went. My thoughts were so mixed and depressed that I could not go back into the cave right away. I went for a long walk on the edge of the jagged cliff nearby, watching the stars and moon turn in the night sky.

Chapter 19: Becoming a Keeper

I could not give up easily on the idea that there still might be a cure for Sultane using all of our arts and skills. But when I put the idea forward to the others they held that they had already researched cures and tried everything they could. The only hope we had of saving Sultane was if Tallray could invent the Elixir of Youth or a Panacea to heal all ills before too much time passed.

This put an edge of urgency to my learning with that had never been there before. Instead of having fun experimenting with anything that came along, I devoted myself seriously to aiding Tallray in creating his Magnum Opus. A Philosopher's stone was needed to make the Elixir of Youth. I tried hard to discover how one could be made.

I borrowed old books on medicine from Lune, had long talks with Tavierfin on possible Runes of Life or Healing and questioned Gleeb on any texts having to do with the Founders' studies in Alchemy.

All this time I did not forget the vision I had seen of the rainbow-eyed Founder pointing out the one tile on the floor of the Dark Passages, or how it had been outlined in fire. Sultane was the only one I had told the full story of my test and he thought that the vision had been a sign that I would one day become an expert in Runeology, being able to use all four Elements to aid me in their creation.

But I had other ideas.

When I had time away from my studies and endeavors with the Keepers, I would often go to look at that tile and investigate how it was mortared into the floor. You may think that it would be impossible to find that one tile again in the middle of the hall, with nothing special to mark it out. But I always found it by instinct and then by looking very closely to find the missing chip in the mortar.

I found that the mortar lines were exposed on two sides, where the tile jointed to the other stones in the floor, but the short ends were slightly covered by the bottom of the wall. If I wished to raise it or cut it out, I would have to remove a thin strip above it in order to reach the mortar there. Also, I did not know if there was anything below the tile to catch it if it fell once released. If there was a universe of nothingness outside of the Dark Passages, the tile could fall forever and be lost once dropped.

To prevent it from falling away, I would have to chip a few holes in the mortar along both sides, figure out how thick the tile was, insert hooks underneath it and fasten them to a board laid across the other nearby tiles to support it. Either that, or I would have to find a way of using magic to levitate the tile before chipping it loose.

It was such a large undertaking that, though I thought about it often, I did not yet begin work on the project. I knew that when the project of lifting it was started, I would have to complete it quickly and have a way to put the tile back into place afterwards. For the Keepers would not be happy to find I had been desecrating (in their eyes) the Dark Passages. But what they did not know could not hurt them or, more importantly, me. So the project would have to be a swiftly executed one.

Even chipping up the mortar was going to be a difficult undertaking. I tried to pry up bits with the tip of my knife as an experiment, but it was far too hard for me to crack. Even gouging at it with all of my strength, I was in danger of breaking the knife before the mortar would split. Stronger tools were needed, ones more fit for the job at hand. Which was another problem that made me set my ideas aside until a later time.

As time went on I grew in more ways than one, as everyone does. Not only did the coat that once was too large for me start dragging at the cuffs and showing too much waist for comfort, but my responsibilities and ability to handle them also grew apace.

I found myself often called on by the Keepers for ideas, aid in using magic or even, to my great surprise, advice.

My reputation as a person with the ability to solve problems grew among the Keepers, young as I was, helped by the fact that I practiced all of the arts of Erilaz at once instead of having a single specialty. At any one skill there was a Keeper who could best me, but my having been taught all of the types to some extent made my skills more versatile. I could Powerpoint with Elements, use Alchemy to help in Rune making or know a person's outermost thoughts with the art Feleago had taught me before attacking them with physical skills.

It was a little less than two years after I had learned the truth about Sultane, almost four years since I started training to be a Keeper, when the summons came. I had been looking at the tile in the Dark Passages again, considering ways to use Air and Powerpointing to make it levitate.

Arising to head back towards the meeting place, I was startled to hear footsteps coming down the branch in my direction.

What would I tell one of the Keepers if they found me here and asked questions? Telling them my ideas would get me a lecture, if not worse, and most likely prompt them to forbid my experimentation with it. Going out into the empty world would have been almost as dangerous in their eyes, though less evil, perhaps. And it was the only other reason I would have been in that hall. I was just deciding that my best excuse was that I liked to come back to the place I had experienced my test, when Feleago came into view. He was walking slower than usual, with his shoulders hunched forward as if against a rain. Instantly, I knew that something must be wrong.

Hurrying to meet him, I asked, "what is it? Are you looking for me?"

"Yes, Nolin," Feleago lay a hand on my arm as he spoke, a rare gesture for him. It made his mental words jump into clearer focus in my mind, as if they were being written there with electricity, "it's Sultane. He's going."

I don't remember running through the Dark Passages, but I must have. For I reached the meeting place long before Feleago and was out of breath when I got there. Sultane had seemed a little more tired and worn that morning, but not enough to worry me. If I had known he was so much worse, I would not have gone exploring in the passages or stopped to look at the tile. It is a possibility that he had hidden his weakness purposely for that reason.

All of the other Keepers were already there, summoned by telepathy no matter the time of day that it was in their world. I got there just in time for Sultane to give me his last words, "remember, no road ever truly ends."

Then he died like a warrior, silent and calm. There was a stunned silence among the Keepers for a long time, while I put a hand over my face and bowed my head in sorrow. We had not found the Philosopher's Stone in time. Sultane was beyond healing.

He had been a great friend to me, a teacher and wiseman equaled by no other. I would not say that he was like a father to me, because he never expected me to obey him like a father or follow his guidance as strictly. But my natural respect for him had prompted me to give him my trust whether he expected it or not.

My eyes were dry, the sorrow too swift for physical reactions to follow. But when I looked up I was surprised to see tears running down Firendaze's face. All of the other Keepers had fallen back near the cavern door and were talking in low voices. Thinking that the warrior blamed himself for the old Keeper's death and his tears were in shame, I came over to say quietly, "he forgave you long ago. He said...he would have rather had it this way than any other."

"I know," The warrior made no attempt to dash the moisture away, though his voice was still steady, "but he was my father."

I was taken aback by this statement, though I should not have been. It made sense that Firendaze would inherit the kingdom from his parents, as that was common practice among royalty. And I knew that Sultane was the king before him. But I had assumed that Sultane had no children and that the crown had passed to Firendaze out of preference rather than bloodline.

Now I understood the bitterness in the warrior's voice whenever he spoke of Sultane, who was once King Hizendaze. Because of the stubbornness and hot temper they shared, Sultane had been cursed to die. I could not imagine being Firendaze at that moment.

Moving away from him, I joined the group of Keepers at the door, "where did he wish to be buried? Or did he?"

"That is what we were just discussing," Adasian sighed, "there is a small but knotty problem with the answer. You see, the people of Iseldome do not know where their former king is, but they think he is still alive somewhere in Iseldome. If they knew he was dead, they would want to give him an Iseldomic funeral, which includes a huge, fancy pyre with lots of gifts and a ceremonial cremation. But the Founders had their own place for laying their dead, catacombs in the Dark Passages, and that is where we think Sultane would have preferred to be put. Unfortunately no one thought to ask him before he passed away!"

Though the scribe glared around at the others and spoke sharply, I could see that he was just as distressed as all of us by Sultane's death.

"He'll lay in the catacombs," Firendaze spoke firmly, moving to join us.

His answer seemed to surprise the other Keepers, but the tears were gone from his face and his eyes sparkled with their normal fiery energy as he added, "Sultane gave up his place as a king when he became Merenoa's apprentice. Just as he gave up his place in Iseldome when he moved here. The Dark Passages were his discovery and passion more than they are for any of us. He will stay in them, as the First Keeper."

The words of the king of Iseldome and the son of the dead man were accepted as law. When I asked, I found that I could not come with them to the catacombs for the funeral. To reach the catacombs you had to pass through the warded archway which only Keepers or Founders could pass. The circular room had a trap door leading down from it, into a sort of basement below the Dark Passages. That was where the Catacombs of the Founders were. It had many niches which were not yet filled.

"They must have expected to have more members later on, or ones following them, but never did," Corky told me in a hushed voice, "it's a spooky place and the tombs of the few Founders who were laid there only have bleached bones left on them now."

So I stayed behind while they left, sitting in the cavern which had been Sultane's while they carried him gently away. His wheelchair still sat behind, open and empty as if waiting for him to return. The bed that had been his was rumpled, but I straightened the covers back out. He always liked his cave to be neat and tidy, though not uncomfortably. Just enough so that it did not look unkempt. He would have liked the gesture.

After that I just sat at the table, staring at the picture of deer in the forest which was painted on the wall. He had made it himself, I knew now, to recall a scene of hunting in his youth. What it lacked in art it made up in spirit.

My mind was blank and tense as I waited for the others to return. Three things kept playing over in it like an echo which would not stop; 'Sultane is dead, they are putting him in the catacombs and now I have to become a Keeper'. But though the words played there, they meant little to my conscious mind.

When the remaining Keepers returned they were pale and solemn. Even Tavierfin was paying his full attention to the matter at hand. They came into the cavern and stood in front of me in a half-circle, which only Tallray broke by coming forward and bending down to meet my eyes.

"Nolin, there are only nine Keepers now," he spoke carefully and quietly, penetrating the emptiness in my mind to focus my attention, "will you fill the gap?"

I sat up straighter, realizing that the time had come for me to do what I had been bought from the slave mines, housed, fed and taught to do. For a crystal-clear moment I felt my childhood slipping away. It might not have been much of a life while I was a slave, but it was all I knew of being a boy. Now I would have to take my place as a man with a position to fill. Just as Sultane had told me, no road truly ends, though it might keep going in a new direction.

"Yes." I stood up, looking around at my companions with a mixture of nervousness and determination. "I am ready to become a Keeper."

Gleeb clapped his hands together at my words, knotting them into a tight ball with excitement, "then we will have to follow the prescribed ceremony of induction! First the talisman, then the oath—"

"One step at a time, One-step," Tavierfin reminded him, cutting off his flow. I had heard small bits about the ceremony in my time as an apprentice, but not enough to give me an idea of the whole thing.

It seemed to be a closely guarded secret. But I knew that most of it took place in the warded room, so I would have to be given a Keepers talisman before entering.

"Am I to be given Sultane's talisman now?"

Feleago shook his head and beckoned to me, "the Keeper's talisman cannot be shared. A new one must be made every time, because it is not a physical object. It is imprinted on your mind."

"You must be really sure you want to be a Keeper," Tallray told me, seeming as nervous as if he was becoming the new Keeper himself, "Brimstone! After this there is no going back."

"I'm sure."

Too much had happened for me to feel surprised at the nature of the Keepers talisman, though I was slightly uneasy about having anything 'imprinted' on my mind from an outside source. I trusted Feleago, but my thoughts had always been my own.

"Come. Kneel here." Feleago gestured at the floor. A little self-conscious in front of everyone, I dropped to my knees in front of him. The stone floor was hard and cold, but familiar. I had knelt on it a few times before to scrub it for Sultane, a task that had become almost impossible for a man in a wheelchair. I had felt it under my feet when I got out of bed in the morning, when I had been staying with the old Keeper. Or before getting into bed at night.

The Mentalist opened his hand and lay his palm gently against my forehead, speaking words through it that were only for me, "may your time as a Keeper be long and fruitful. Beware the seeds of unhappiness."

I don't know if those last words were usually part of the ceremony. Were all Keepers given a warning?

Before I could respond to the invocation, a beam of light seemed to travel from his hand into my head. Like a Rune being carved on Solron, I felt it touch my mind and draw lines there. My eyes closed, I could see the lines, glowing in a strange symbol that must be a Rune, though it is not one that I had ever learned the meaning of. The symbol glowed white-yellow, warm and full of energy. It was made of the same material as the light I had seen during my test, which had originally given me the spark of Erilaz.

Feleago's hand was gone before I knew it. Opening my eyes slowly, I found Corky there now, pulling me to my feet, "I'm so glad you've joined us."

His face was bright with well-wishing. I couldn't help smiling back, though I still remembered that the only reason I was there was Sultane had gone.

The talisman gave me a feeling of being connected to all of the Keepers which I had never experienced before. I knew, just by looking at them, that they carried the talisman as well. I could not see it glowing in their heads. But it felt like I could. And I knew that the Rune-symbol was in me as well, glowing on my forehead for them to feel though they could not see it.

"Come, we must finish the ceremony before celebrating," Firendaze reminded us, striding back out of the cave towards the gate of the Dark Passages. I followed after him, dazed by the light I carried. Everything looked different now, the walls holding hues of blackness I had never seen before. The others came behind in a file.

Chapter 20: Room of Power

It only took a moment to reach the room with the warded door. My guide passed through it quickly, disappearing into the room beyond. Though it was an open doorway, I could not make out much of what was inside. It was round and dome-shaped, but other than that the whole place was shrouded in shadows impenetrable from outside. Steeling myself to feel a blast of energy holding me back, I walked towards the door. The Runes glowed brightly as I passed beneath them, set in darkness like colored stars. But no ward stopped me.

Inside, the room seemed to open out like a flower in bloom, the dark mist clearing away before my eyes. There were ten rings etched on the floor, arranged in a circular pattern around the center. Each one was filled with a complicated swirl of Runes, marked in five different colors. In the wall behind the circles there was a big, flat stone sunk part of the way in, rectangular in shape and stark raven. Traced on it were lines of pale ash-gray, outlining the paths of the Dark Passages to make a map of all the halls with activated doorways. The doors were indicated on the stone with yellow dots which glowed like miniature lights.

On one side of the map was a red stone the size of my fist, sunk half-way into the wall and polished to a smooth sheen. I was led to this by the Keepers, who then pointed out that there were words written on the wall above it in gold.

"These are the laws that the Founders lay down and we follow," Gleeb explained, "there are ten of them, just like the original Commandments, matching the number of Founders or Keepers there must be at any time. There are other traditions we follow, of course, but these are the laws we must swear to uphold."

I read down the list quickly, seeing my future printed in gold:

'I; Thou shalt keep all of these rules honorably.

II; The Dark Passages can be added to, but no doors may be taken wholly away.

III; The ten men who make our members must be as one in these matters.

IV; No member of this ten may be placed above the other in rank or worth. Whether he be king or beggar, healer or murderer, he may not rule the others.

V; The Spark of Erilaz must be bright in every member. If one loses it, he must leave our company.

VI; The Dark Passages shall not be disassembled, mutilated or destroyed in any manner. Graffiti on the walls is forbidden.

VII; The Dark Passages must be kept in good repair, so as never to cause harm to pedestrians.

VIII; A member of the Ten shall not have anything to do with marriage, romantic love, women, ect.

IX; No member shall destroy the life of another member unless his own is threatened and there is no alternative.

X; Any crimes committed by the Ten are only punishable among the Ten by exile from the Dark Passages and our company, or death. Any crime not worthy of these punishments shall be forgiven among us.'

These rules did not seem harsh to me. I felt a slight twinge of guilt when reading numbers six and seven, but I told myself that I was not really planning to harm the Dark Passages in any way. Only investigate what was beyond them, then seal up the hole before it could cause trouble. The Founders must have seen what was beyond when building them and probably took out stones now and then for repairs, or at least planned to. So I believed that it was not really wrong to promise to uphold these rules while planning to lift one of the floor tiles afterwards.

And if a few of the Keepers (such as Tallray and Firendaze) were edging along towards breaking the eighth rule, I would not be one to tell on them or hold it against them.

I could not help feeling a touch of amusement when I read the extra injunction against graffiti on the walls. It made me wonder if one of the Founders had ever been caught writing on them and that rule had been added to stop him.

As for killing or banishing any of my fellows for any reason, the thought was abhorrent to me. Even Berune I would not want to destroy or make give up his place as a Keeper.

"You must lay your hand on the red stone and swear an oath to keep all of these laws." Gleeb added, "it's traditional."

"Is the stone magic?" I asked uneasily, hesitating.

Berune let out a grunt, "no. If it took magic to make a Keeper uphold the laws, there would be little point in having him. Your conscience should be enough. This is just tradition and a way to make stupid initiates remember the laws better."

As I had said, there was no love lost between us. But his rough dismissal was oddly comforting to me, as it entirely removed the fear of a powerful magic binding my mind to its will no matter the circumstances.

Calmly, I lay a hand on the red stone and promised to keep and uphold all of the laws written above.

"Now initiate, you must walk the Runes," Tavierfin told me with an intense look in his sharp, dark eyes.

With one hand he waved around at all of the circular Runes on the floor, while the other hand beckoned me towards them. He escorted me over to the nearest one, which was a brown Rune furthest from the entrance door.

"Stand on this one. Face the wall on the right side (as compared to the door) and close your eyes so that you cannot see."

With my eyes closed the sounds in the room intensified. The Keepers' breathing, the sounds of their clothes rustling and my own heartbeats seeming to echo all around me. I heard Tavierfin's voice close to my shoulder, "do not open your eyes until all the rings of power have been walked. Start moving, using the feel of the power of the Runes to guide you."

At first I felt lost when he moved away. I was sure that I would not be able to find the Runes, so that the Keepers would laugh at me.

But once I had forced myself to relax and feel what was around me, I knew that finding the rings would not be hard to do. Though I did not know what they accomplished, the rings of power were strong enough that they impressed themselves on my mind while my eyes were closed. It was like rays of warmth coming up from the floor, or beams of sunshine. When I left the first one the floor in between felt empty and cold, while I could sense the location of the ring ahead. Stepping on to it filled me with warmth in a powerful surge.

The next space in between the rings seemed even colder, more empty than before. It was a relief to get onto the Rune and experience its power. I could feel the different colors as well, brown, green, yellow, blue and gray as I walked on to them.

It was like different flavors of energy, each bright and tangy. But the floor in between became more frigid the further I went, so that it took a real effort to leave the rings by the time I was half way around.

The crossing to the seventh ring left me shivering, dreading the steps ahead. None of the Keepers spoke a word, though I could feel them hoping for me to go on.

Taking a deep breath and holding it, I stepped into the floor between. Waves of cold air wafted up my legs, sending frozen rays to hold me back. Every pace was a fight against the iciness which had to be tactically won with my will. The eighth ring felt like a warm fire on a winter night by the time I came to it. There was just two more crossings left.

I don't know how I made the last one. It was so cold it burned and so empty I thought that I had fallen into a world of dark nothingness.

I almost opened my eyes at one point, just gave up and told the Keepers to make it stop. But some hidden willpower in my core asserted itself and forced me to make the next strides to safety. Perhaps it was only pride, as I felt elated as soon as I reached the ring which was both beginning and end.

"You may open your eyes now." Tavierfin's voice told me. My eyelids sprang open and I looked around the room, feeling surprised to see the Keepers so near to what had felt like a frozen void. But when I walked tentatively back over the space, there was no change in temperature. It was simply the floor of the Room of Power.

"Cold, wasn't it?" Corky smiled with surprising grimness in memory, "if there was such a thing as an Ice Elemental, I would have become one walking the Runes."

"I hardly felt it, enjoying the power of the Runestones in between so much," Tavierfin admitted, locking his hands together in front of him. All of the other Keepers also began to reminisce about their time walking the Runes, until I asked them, "what do I have to do next?"

"Do?" Gleeb blinked at me, "why, nothing. You are a Keeper now. Talisman, oath and walking the Runes is all it takes."

"A Keeper." I said the words quietly, without any inflection. Somehow I had expected more of a ceremony than this, something like a grand finale.

A moment later it struck me in full force what I was, at the same time as Firendaze stepped forwards and snatched me by both shoulders, giving me a hard shake which made my teeth rattle together. I was almost as tall as him now, but he was still far stronger and faster than me, so that I could not break away.

"You're a Keeper!" He exclaimed, giving me an extra shake before letting me go with a flashing smile, "so stop looking so glum. Gleeb, you forgot one thing to finish the ceremony off!"

"Oh, er, I did?" The Historian looked puzzled.

"Yes, the use of the Runestones, all of us together."

"But that's not part of the traditional ceremony..."

"Then it should be!" Firendaze turned back to look at me, "you see, we must each be standing on one of the rings of power to make any of the unlocked doors in the Dark Passages power up. They show as blue dots on the map when unlocked and unpowered, but yellow when ready to use. On the circles, we're all linked together through the Talismans. We must each will the energy to flow into the door for it to do so. It is a very important part of being a Keeper and one that you should know. Don't you agree?"

His last words were directed at the other Keepers. Corky nodded, grinning, while Tallray also gave his assent. The others looked more or less willing, with Berune giving a snort and a shake of his head. But after a moment they all agreed to show me the linking of the Runes, though we had no doors unlocked which actually needed powering up.

I think Firendaze had suggested the experience as a way to get Sultane's death off of both of our minds. Though he was just as energetic and steady as ever, there was something in his manner which showed me that he had not yet been able to forget the cause of the old Keeper's passing. He was too quick to look for diversion, too cheerful for the circumstances.

To power up the doors, we each stood on one Runestone ring in the circle, facing inwards. Each Keeper had his own circle which he always stood on: mine was the brown ring I had started walking on, furthest from the entrance. When we stood on them, they glowed even brighter, almost hiding the Keepers in a haze of light. I saw the brown light come up around me, felt its power reflecting off of my bare arms and face.

A feeling of other presences filled my mind. Realizing that it was the Keepers, I did not fight it. With a feeling akin to jumping off of a cliff and finding that I could fly, I let my mind pool with theirs. Our power came together into one force, the Runes glowed so brightly I could see nothing but light within me and without. For a brief moment I was not myself at all, I was not one person called Nolin Nearham. I was the Keepers and we were all one. The Dark Passages scrolled out beneath our eyes, doors glowing with pinpoints of light. Halls, passages, all laid out like a map before us.

The image held for just a split second, then shivered and faded away.

I blinked and gasped to find myself standing on the ring of power, which had gone back to its usual faint glow. The other Keepers were also coming to themselves, shaking their heads or blinking while they stepped off of the Runes.

"That was...exquisite."

I joined them in the center of the ring.

Tallray smiled, "that, my friend, is being a Keeper in the truest form of the word."

We were all tired and filled with a dazzling mixture of sorrow and joy. Soon we left the room of power and split up to go to our own places. I went back to the house that had been Sultane's and fell onto my bed, not even having a moment to realize how dragging my tiredness was before I was asleep.

Chapter 21: Power and Exile

Many of my studies continued with the other Keepers, though some paths I followed alone. Sultane's house had become mine naturally, with no questions asked and no real thought given to it on my part. I slept there, worked odd jobs in the nearby village to earn my bread and prepared it in the cave when I earned it. There, I studied the books in the library until I knew them all from front to back. I practiced Elemental magic in the clearing outside, helping Corky keep the grass green and Shivro trees growing for their shade and beauty. Or building bonfires out of thin air, raining water on them with a wave of my hand and making the water dance in the sky with gusts of air.

I became so powerful in Powerpointing that Berune could teach me nothing more. In a duel between us, I used my inner energy to fray his attempts away into nothing and knock him from his feet at a distance. He avoided me from then on, except for in meetings, because I could beat him at his own game.

Firendaze had already taught me to shoot the crossbow he had given me both accurately and swiftly. He could throw a gold coin into the air and I would knock it out of the sky with a bolt, or strike down a pigeon on the wing when we went hunting together in the Dusna desert. I was a little less proficient. But not far behind.

In hand-to-hand fighting he had begun to teach me the fierce, difficult martial arts of Iseldome. With it, a person did not need a weapon to be deadly. Their hands and feet became striking forces faster and more dangerous than an untrained person's dagger. Firendaze could turn handsprings across the training grounds quicker than a steady walk, hit a two-inch-thick board so that it broke in half and knock a strong man down with a single blow. In the year which I spent as a Keeper I did not become that lethal, but I could still hold my own in a fight against most brawlers.

The warrior's sense for danger was harder to acquire, and seemed to me to be in the realm of Feleago's training. But he said that any person with a touch of intelligence and intuition could learn to sense things amiss near them. It only took concentration.

Alchemy I excelled at in partnership with Tallray, learning the secrets of metals and chemicals so that they became as simple to use as flour and sugar were to a baker. All of the arts of Erilaz I excelled at except for the skills of the Mentalist and Healing. Even Runeology, which I never became a master at, I know better than most people who try. As I had promised when I started learning, I became the best Keeper in every way possible. My combination of skills became powerful and with it grew my pride.

I'm afraid that I often avoided learning more from Feleago. He was the only Keeper who seemed to guess what I was up to in the Passages.

Now that I had the freedom to chose my own studies and duties as a Keeper, I spent as much time as could be safely spared working on the tile in the blocked branch of the Dark Passages. And I was afraid that Feleago's mental powers had picked up a little of my guilty intentions on the day of my ceremony. But he did not say anything or interfere.

It would have been too difficult to suspend an object the size and weight of the floor tile in the air with magic, for as long as I wanted to work on it. So I built a sort of crane, with metal hooks to go under the stone and a wooden frame to hold it up on the tiles to each side as I worked. With the arts of Erilaz I was able to discover how thick the tile was, using a mixture of Powerpointing, Mental arts and Elemental magic.

But I still did not know how to break the mortar easily, nor replace it once I was done. I tried 'borrowing' a few of Tavierfin's chisels from his shack in the meeting place and using them, but they only chipped it slowly. His cutting tools from the mines worked better, especially on the walls above the floor, but they were still to slow for my liking.

By now it had become my consuming passion to find out what was beyond the Dark Passages. When I was not helping the other Keepers clear rubble, unlock doors and power them up, I was researching Solron, mortar and the building of the Dark Passages by the Founders.

Soon my friends noticed that I was distracted and often absent on mysterious missions. Once Tallray almost caught me at my work when he was passing by and I had to make the excuse that I had been studying the walls of the Dark Passages in an attempt to find out how they had been constructed. Which was not far from the truth, even if it was not nearly the whole of it.

Another time Corky remarked during a meeting that I was getting to be as absent-minded as Tavierfin and insisted that I explore a few new worlds with him to 'lighten me up'.

I went on the expedition, but mostly daydreamed about what was beyond the Dark Passages the whole time.

I was obsessed and I knew it.

But it did not seem to be a harmful obsession to me. I thought that it would all end once I had seen what was beyond the Dark Passages and put the tile back into place. Then I could go back to a normal, quiet life among the Keepers and they would never know what I had seen.

It did not work out that way. My pride and power took me too far. Near the end of the year of my Keepership we found another apprentice. This time, no one was immediately dying, but Gleeb and Feleago were not young any longer. And there was always a danger of attacks by strange beings in the Passages. Everyone knew that it was better to teach an apprentice before someone died and left an irreplaceable gap in our numbers. As it turned out, someone took their leave without dying.

As I had been chosen from Ti-Gallin because one of the Founders had lived there, the new apprentice was brought from the world of AlterTerra for the same reason. Adasian and Gleeb went to fetch him, as they could both speak a smattering of the language and they taught him our common tongue when he was brought. He picked it up quickly, as well as the habit, irritating to me, of calling everyone 'sir'.

I think Adasian taught him that trick.

I had promised myself that I would be a good friend to the new boy. I thought we would have things in common, being the first two apprentices of the Keepers. My plan was to help him learn from the others, teach him things only I knew about being an apprentice and give him warm support. But life never worked out like that between us.

Bensi was a small, slightly plump boy with a pointy nose that he was always sticking into everyone's business. He had been an orphan too, but had never really known his parents and was brought up in a rich, kindly orphanage all of his life. His manners were fine, his curiosity unmatched and the spark of Erilaz in him bright. Bensi did not find it the first day, but it was only two days later that he discovered his magic.

Most of the other Keepers seemed to think that his ways were winning and his interest in everything 'cute'. Sadly, I only thought that he was a bit of a wimp and could not help feeling a little jealous that my position has been usurped. Which made it no better for either of us when he stumbled right into my project.

By that time I had discovered a way to cut the stone of the Dark Passages and the mortar between the tiles quickly. Using one of Tavierfin's Solron chisels and a mixture of Runeology and Powerpointing, I could make the tip sharp enough to cut the materials as if they had been wood. Slicing off sections of the wall was risky and troublesome, but it was the only way to get the tile up without breaking it. Cutting the tile would not have been a good idea, as it was a Runestone and I could not have repaired it once destroyed. I thought that the wall could be patched up with the same mortar as the tile would be replaced with, so that it would not cause long-term harm to cut it away.

With my new cutting methods and the crane I had built to lift the tile, work progressed swiftly. I chipped both long sides of the mortar up so that the tile was free, slipped the long, thin hooks underneath to hold it up. Once everything was ready, I used a winch to raise the tile about two feet above the others. The timbers on each side of the gap creaked as they took the weight. A groan seemed to echo down the Dark Passages from it.

Excitement pulsing through me so that my hands trembled with it, I locked the winch and fell to my knees. My finger tips gripped the stone beneath me, feeling its cold, hard edge. For the first time in more than a hundred years, someone in the Dark Passages looked outside.

At first all I could see was darkness and a spot of light. As my eyes adjusted a wholly new scene came into focus. I was looking down from the top of a cavern roof, which was made up of the tiles of the Dark Passages. The walls and floor were made of a coarse, tan sandstone, worn by a rain which had not fallen on them for many years and covered in a fine layer of dust. A dim, grayish light streamed into the cavern through a tunnel, which held its course away from me in the same direction as the Dark Passages. It was a wide, tall tunnel carved naturally by forces which had then been blocked out by the Passages being built on top of it. Long ago, it had been a canyon rather than a tunnel, open to the air. I could not see what was at the end of the tunnel, but I thought that light must mean an open sky. And an open sky meant a whole new world.

I almost hugged myself in the triumph of discovery. There was not nothingness outside of the Dark Passages, nor open space (which would have pulled me out and killed me, most likely, yet I had taken no precautions for it.) There was not even a blank area of solid rock. The tile the Founder had showed me in my vision had led right into a tunnel and to whatever world lay beyond.

Just as I was trying to decide if I should fetch a rope to climb down and see what was beyond the tunnel entrance, I heard a small noise behind me. With a stab of fear, I turned my head to see what was there. Bensi was standing behind me.

His eyes were wide open above the pointy nose, his mouth hanging slightly agape. I've never seen anyone stare with the mixture of horror and fascination with which he gazed at my contraption or the project it suspended. Slowly, his gaze fell to my face. Without a word, he turned suddenly and began to run the other way.

"Bensi!"

Jumping up in anger, I drew on the power in my center. I knew that he was running off to tattle on me, like a stuck-up schoolboy. In that moment I wanted to stop him more than I had ever wanted anything else, except perhaps to see what was beyond the Passages.

In that moment, I was on the edge of smashing him against the wall or burning him to a cinder with my power. But just before I released it, better sense prevailed. Instead of hurting him I only made a curling tendril of energy whip out and wrap around the boy's legs, tripping him. He fell heavily to the floor, breath knocked out in a grunt. In a few strides I was beside him and he rolled up onto one shoulder to look at me. Fear was in his eyes.

The fear made me even more angry, because he thought that I was going to hurt him badly and I almost had.

Bending down, I gripped his arm and held him in place, "Bensi, where are you going?"

"I—" He gulped, before whispering hoarsely, "I had come to get you, sir...I was going back to the one who sent me."

There was no noise this time, but I sensed that someone else was watching. Looking up, I saw Corky standing just a few paces away. His staff was in his hand, end set solidly against the ground. His eyes were hard and hot like I had only seen them a few times before, while sparring with him. But now they were fiercer.

"Let him up."

"Corky—"

"Let him up. Now."

I let the boy go, straightening up as he scrambled to his feet and ran to stand just a little behind Corky, as if the Keeper needed to protect him. Helplessness swept over me in a sickening wave. The Elemental's gaze moved over to the lifted tile behind us.

"What are you doing, Nolin?"

Like always, I could not betray him by lying to him, no matter the consequences. I looked from the lifted Runestone and removed slices of Dark Passage wall back to him.

"Finding out what is beyond the Dark Passages."

He stared at me for a moment, before spinning on his heels and beginning to stride away, Bensi's hand in his free one. He spoke only one word over his shoulder, "come."

"But Corky...there's a whole world out there! If only you could see—"

"Come on."

He did not let me get any further. I had never seen him so mad, nor had he ever treated me in that way before. My mind, so clear with elation a few minutes before, was now fuzzy with bewilderment and dread.

As I have said, Keepers could speak to each other telepathically, mostly in a limited manner. It was not like holding a conversation with someone you were standing near. Instead it was more like talking on a telephone: you had to think things slowly and distinctly for the other person to pick the, up, before they could send something back. Corky must have sent short, angry messages, garbled with emotion, to the other Keepers, asking them to meet us at the normal place. When we arrived, Tallray and Feleago were already there. Others began arriving soon after. All of them had confused and anxious expressions rather than the hard distrust I had been expecting.

"Corky, Nolin, Bensi, are you all unharmed?" Tallray came forward to look at us, apparently imagining that we had been attacked by some dangerous being in the passages.

"No one ended up getting hurt," Corky told him, inferring that it had been a near miss. "But Nolin has a lot of explaining to do. And I don't think any of it will help."

Firendaze came in the door behind us then, snorting, "what, did he kill someone in the passages?"

"Worse." The Elemental would not even look at me now, "he's destroyed a part of the Dark Passages, attacked our acolyte and betrayed everything it means to be a Keeper!"

"I have not!" I shouted back, tired of being the helpless target of his wrath, "all I did was raise one little tile! And Bensi tripped."

"You tripped me with magic," the boy sniffled, "and you were going to hurt me so that I would not tell them what I saw."

"I was not!"

"Please my friends, please be calm," Tallray waved his hands at all of us with a sorrowful expression, "there is no need to shout. Wait until everyone is here. Then we will have it all explained in a rational manner."

My hands were knotted into fists at my side. I had not done as much wrong as Corky was accusing me of. I felt betrayed that someone I had thought was my friend would lie about me. But when he turned towards the table to sit at it I saw the tears in his eyes.

He believed everything he had said and hated me for turning against the Keepers' laws, but no more than he hated himself at the moment for being the one who had discovered it.

It was not long before everyone was assembled in the room. The Elemental's message had evidently been worded so that everyone thought that a disaster had struck. I supposed that it was less than that, though only time would tell.

"Now Corkcora," Tallray used his full name in a formal manner, "please tell us what you saw that is making you so upset."

"I sent Bensi to get Nolin because I wanted to take them both exploring a world through the doors more fully. Then I remembered that I had not told Bensi where to meet me, so I went off to find him." Corky explained in a strained voice, before going on to describe the scene as he had seen it when he came upon us, "Nolin had knocked Bensi to the floor and was bending over him with a threatening expression. Beyond them pieces of the wall had been cut out and thrown aside in pieces, while there was a big gap in the floor from one of the large Runestones being taken out. Chips of mortar and gray dust lay all around. You can see it for yourselves: just go down the side-hall with the blocked door at the end. It's all the truth."

The other Keepers were all solemn now. I felt their eyes pierce me, already convinced of my guilt.

Fury bubbling inside me at the idea of their narrow-minded, prejudiced thoughts I only said, "I was not going to hurt the boy. I just did not want him to cause something like this."

I waved a hand around at the meeting, "a big upset over nothing. The damage I have done can easily be repaired. Nothing terrible has happened."

Tallray spoke to me with surprising gentleness, though it did not soothe me, "please do not be sullen, my friend. Just tell us everything you have done, in your own way."

His words were meant to calm me, but they did not. Instead, they made my feelings snap, "I am not sullen, I feel betrayed! The only wrong I have done is to look beyond the petty rules you have imposed upon yourselves. I've discovered what none of you dared know, though the Founders before knew of it and did not look upon it as a desecration. If you want to condemn me, do so! But give me no charades of kindness and understanding until then."

Tallray looked hurt, falling back a few steps away from the table. Many of the others looked shocked as well, though Adasian was simply watching me with professional interest and Feleago could not show an expression on his face. When he spoke, the words echoed around to all of us, quiet and calm, "Nolin, we do not want to condemn you. Nor is our sympathy a charade. But you have stepped beyond the bounds of our laws. We are called Keepers, not Breakers, for a reason. Tell us why you have done so and you might win our understanding so that you will not see it as a farce."

I sighed, trying to pull my frayed beliefs together. It all seemed so empty now, so inexplicable. But I still did not think I had been wrong. And in the back of my mind, the obsession to find out what was through the mysterious tunnel grew.

In clipped, spare sentences I told them about collecting the tools and knowledge to break through the floor of the Dark Passages. I explained that my thirst to know the truth drove me on, nothing more heinous.

I did not reveal the vision I had seen of the lines of fire picking out that one tile, or of the rainbow-eyed Founder who had written on it. When the story had been told in brief, I added, "it was my plan to seal it back up when I was done, so that no one would know of it and be hurt by the knowledge. But now that you know, I don't see why we can't leave it open for a time, to study what is beyond. Think of the opportunities! We might even find more clues to show how the Passages were built."

The Keepers looked at each other uneasily. Bensi had been forgotten in a corner and was watching with his eyes even wider than before, if that were possible.

"He—he seems to be obsessed." Gleeb suggested hesitantly, pointing a crinkled finger at me from inside the wide sleeve of his robe, almost as if to hide it. And with that, the debate began.

I'll spare you the details.

As I said before, the Keepers really were just ten men of very different backgrounds and temperaments, even if magic held us together on some subjects. The conversation went up and down, around and around. I refused to say much, even in my own defense. I thought that condemnation was already sealed in their minds, so any extra words would only tell against me. A few of them, I knew, were more sympathetic with me.

Gleeb thought that perhaps I had simply gone mad and was out of my mind. Tallray wanted to pardon me because I was, according to him, 'young, inexperienced and full of investigative vigor'.

But with my silence and the hole in the Dark Passage floor weighing against me, most of the Keepers found me guilty of treason. Full of wrath and conflicting emotions, I almost welcomed the verdict.

"You have broken three of the rules you swore to uphold," Feleago pronounced, "number six, The Dark Passages shall not be disassembled, mutilated or destroyed in any manner. Number seven, The Dark Passages must be kept in good repair, so as never to cause harm to pedestrians. And number one, thou shalt uphold all of these rules faithfully."

And with this, even my supporters were silent. Soon they left me under the watchful eyes of Corky and Firendaze while the rest went to see the tile I had lifted and the hole that was made. They came back even graver and less inclined to feel sympathy for me.

"Why did you have to do it, Nolin?" Corky whispered in my ear, "we could have had so much more fun together..."

"And found the perfect world? Where no one in condemned for following their dreams?" I retorted viciously. He retired with a hurt look to stand against the wall. Meanwhile Firendaze just shook his head and muttered, "fool!"

I knew what he was thinking. But I was the best Keeper yet, altogether, and it was silly for them to punish me for a harmless experiment.

"Rule ten says that there are only two punishments allowed for a Keeper who breaks the rules." Gleeb reminded everyone. "Exile...and death. Either that, or the Keeper must be exonerated of his crimes. The laws also state that all of the Keepers must act as one man on any problems concerning the Dark Passages. I think that we should cast an anonymous vote, aiming for unanimity."

Meaning that they had to decide whether I should live or die, stay or be cast away. I waited in stony silence as they decided that the best way to cast a vote was with symbols on slips of paper. An X was for death, E was for exile and A was for forgiveness. They were letters easily told apart and not easy to confuse, so the voting would be incorruptible.

The votes were put in a box and then counted by the Keepers, each one spoken aloud so that I could hear it. Every one was for exile.

I can't tell you how I felt at that moment, or what I thought. Everything started to feel numb and pass in a blur for me. The sentence of exile was officially pronounced on me, the name of Keeper struck from my titles. Then, while I could think of nothing of any use, Feleago removed he talisman from my mind. His touch was cold and distant. For a moment, when I felt the glow leaving me, I almost drew on my central power and blasted him for it. I felt the energy in me swell with anger and pain, wanting to pour it all into him as a punishment for taking part of my mind away.

Just in time I held myself in check. It would have been a step too far to hurt any of these people who had raised me from the living tomb of the Neomium mines and given me a life. It was their mistake to send me away, I told myself, they were the ones losing me in the long run.

Then the numbness came back and I did not really hear or see anything until I was told, "you are an exile, never to walk the Dark Passages again. You may pick any planet to stay on, but you must stay at least a mile away in radius from any known gate. If you are found closer, or trying to enter the Passages, the Keeper's duty will be to give a stern warning to leave. If you do not obey, your life will be in your own hands. You are forbidden to enter the Room of Power before you leave, so your talisman has been taken away to prevent it. You are forbidden to enter this sacred meeting place again."

I looked up, mouth feeling dry and lips stuck together at first, "May I choose any world to live on?"

"Yes, Nolin." Tallray answered with a look still touched by sympathy.

"Then I choose the world beyond the lifted tile. The world that the Dark Passages are built on!"

There was a small space of silence before Adasian replied, "then you shall be conducted there and set at your liberty. You may bring anything which belongs to you, that can be carried."

Still in a daze, I walked to Sultane's cave with the Keepers trailing after me. I heard Lune and Berune murmuring together and even managed to hear what they were saying. But as soon as I understood it, I stopped listening. They only claimed that they had never expected me to do much good as a Keeper.

Inside the cave, I gathered a few items which I thought would be useful to me, no matter what world I came out in. My crossbow and quiver of bolts were slung over one shoulder, then a worn backpack I had once found discarded in the nearby village was hung next to them. In it was put a loaf of bread that had been bought from the baker recently and a piece of dried meat.

I also stashed a bottle of Tallray's alkahest there, not because I had any reason to, but because my mind was on autopilot at the time. With my knife at my belt and the clothes I stood up in, the only other thing I brought was a tiny model of the Dark Passages. Because of my fascination with Lune's model, Tavierfin had once made me one as well. It was a miniature, small enough to rest on my hand comfortably, with the walls being less than an inch high.

With these things packed, the Keepers escorted me to the spot where I had raised the tile. Coming to a stop in front of it, I looked up and down the hall at the place where I had passed my test and worked so many hours on the project before me. It was a familiar space now, the particular curve of the walls and number of tiles imprinted on my mind.

I would never see it again. It, or my home in the cave, or my original city of Ti-Gallin. None of those places would hear the echo of my footsteps in the future. All because of that obsession.

I looked down at the gap which had been opened below the tile. Whatever my future was, it began through that slot in the stone. My life was changing for the second time.

The Keepers used the crane to lift the tile higher, then dangled a rope down into the hole. Firandaze and Berune held on to the end of it, while I was expected to climb down to the bottom.

"Are you sure about this?" Corky did not look at me as he spoke, "there are a lot of more certain worlds out there, even if none are perfect."

I said nothing, but went over to the edge of the hole and sat with my legs dangling out of the Passages. Gripping the rope, I wrapped myself around it and slid my way into a new world.

The dust on the floor puffed up around me as I landed, swirling tarnished brown around my head. I gave one jerk to let them know that I was at the bottom, then stepped back. The rope was pulled up and the tile lowered back into place, though the crane still had to hold it until it could be mortared. I was sealed off.

The cavern did not become much darker than it had been before, as the passages above contained little light to shed. The light was coming from somewhere at the end of the tunnel.

I followed it quickly, a sudden fear striking me that there would be nothing but a dead-end there. It was something I had not thought of before. If it did come to an end I would be trapped. The tiles of the Dark Passages were too thick for the Keepers to hear me through, even if they would have listened. I could have stood shouting beneath that loosened tile until my voice gave out and nothing would have changed.

But there was the light ahead. A gray, lifeless light unlike anything the sun shed. Pace lengthening, I strode down the tunnel until I came to its end. The Dark Passages still stretched above, reaching across a gray sky like an inverted pathway. Branches, curves and straight halls were all outlined in solid black against the light gray. Beneath it lay a vast, rolling landscape of dust. Hills shaped by the wind, cliffs worn bare by the same force. Plantless, sunless and all but empty, the Dustlands were before me for the first time. This was the land on which the Dark Passages had been built. And in it, I was an exile.

Interlude 4: In the Storm.

"So is that why you won't teach an apprentice?" Hiram turned his sharp eyes on the wizard who had once been a Keeper, "because you failed as one and were found out by one?"

Nolin sat on the creaking chair, hands folded and stuck between his knees. His eyes did not meet Hiram's, watching instead the flow of dust trickling in the narrow cracks of the shutters over the window. It had built up by now to cover the sill in a thick layer and cascade down onto the floor in a brown stream.

"That is one of the reasons, I suppose. Or the seeds of the reason. But you will have to listen to the other part of the story to understand it all. Being exiled to the Dustlands was not the end for me. No, there is more to come."

When he finished speaking, Nolin lit two more candles to replace the one which had just gone out. The dust storm blocked out all light that would have been sifting in the little house, if it had been daytime. But as it was night in the Dustlands, a night with stars but no moon for those who did not have a storm on top of them, it would have been dark anyway.

"Will you tell me more, Nerheem?"

"If you are not yet too tired."

"I will listen. Sleep is far from me still."

Nolin twiddled his fingers together and sighed, "and from me. As it almost always is now...but enough of that. The Dustlands. You know them, though I did not when I first came here. So I will tell about it as I perceived it then, even if you already know what I was just learning."

Hiram nodded in acceptance. That was how stories were often told in his land. With explanations and descriptions so that the listener could see everything clearly in his head.

"Telling you about my younger days has brought them back to me sharply," Nolin admitted, "sometimes I even forgot that I was telling them rather than reliving them. So forgive me if I spoke too long, or of things strange to you. But now begins the part of the story you may have heard tales of. Because my later adventures are told in this land, even if in highly embellished forms."

"But you did defeat Angrist and raise the—" Hiram began to protest, only to be cut off by the storyteller.

"Of course. Just not always the way they tell it. As you know by now, I'm not actually a wizard," Nolin shrugged, "only one who practices the arts of Erilaz. Now, when I first came out of the cave all I could do was look about me in wonder..."

Chapter 22: Exile of the Dustlands

I was on a rise overlooking dunes of dust rolling far off into the north. Round boulders and flats of sandstone pocked the sharp slope below me. Behind me, a line of jagged cliffs ran to my left as far as eyes could see. To my right, they petered out in tall, inaccessible spires of sandstone. The tunnel I had come from looked like a simple crack from where I stood, like many which ran into the rock all up and down the cliffs. But it was deeper and more shadowy, with the Dark Passages sitting on top of it.

The Passages looked like a giant, black creature stretching onto the horizon. From where I stood they seemed to angle upwards so that they were high in the air above the dunes, like a part of the sky. Like a strip of storm clouds which did not blow in the wind.

Looking at them, I realized that something was odd about the tiles which made up their floor. There was no symbols on them, no glowing lines of Runeology. Were they Runes at all? Tavierfin had seemed sure of it and there were solid records of the Ten Founders using Runes to build the passages.

I stared at the tiles with my mouth closed in a straight, hard line. The Keepers were not right about everything.

These must be the legendary Runestones which had no visible Runes upon them. There was actually such a thing, right below the Keepers' noses the whole time. But they could not know of them without being brave enough to see the underside of the Dark Passages.

The discovery seemed to clear my head of all the uncertainty which had filled it before. I looked about me with fresh eyes, taking in the gray sky and seemingly endless wastes. Was there anything alive here, or had the Founders built their invention on a dead world so that it would not be disturbed?

A flash of movement caught my eyes and I turned to see a speckled yellow lizard dart into a crack under a rock nearby. As small as it was, the creature almost made me jump in surprise. I moved forward to peer in at it with a feeling close to kinship. There was living things here, if a lizard could survive. He would need insects to eat, and the bugs would have to have some sort of food to live off of as well. Plants with flowers, most likely. And even if the food-chain was that short, bugs eating flowers, feeding lizards, which then fertilized the plants, it was life. And where there was life of some sort I was sure that I could survive. Most importantly, there must be water where a plant could survive, even if it was simply seasonal rains.

Heartened, I stood up again and began to make my way down the steep slope, almost sliding from boulder to boulder because of the steepness of the hill. On the way, I passed a group of dead plant stalks, dried and sere with rattling seedpods on top. They were only about a foot tall and growing in a crack of the rock, but they too fulfilled me with a hope of life.

By the time I reached the bottom of the hill I was already covered in dust and coughing it out. This land was not going to be easy to travel in.

Looking around, I found myself in a sort of wide draw with a gentle slope of dirt leading up to the top of the next ridge. I crossed the draw and climbed the first dune, before slipping down it into another shallow depression and scaling the next. Stopping at the top of this hill, I looked back behind me. The cliffs loomed there, dull tan against the somber sky. Ahead, more dunes seemed to roll on endlessly.

Toiling on, I spent hours crossing hills of dust and climbing through bone-dry ditches at their bases. At one place, I found a little flat of dried grasses growing in clay soil. They were tiny, stubbly things with grain heads like feathers, all a light yellow in color. But I sat in them and pictured myself in a field of green as I ate a little dried meat and bread.

I had not thought to pack any water, which was beginning to be a serious issue. No Dustlander would go far from his home without bringing water. But I did not know much about traveling in deserts then, despite having been in a few with Corky before. But then we had only stayed an hour or two and had returned easily to our homes afterwards. Homes where water ran in wide streams or sat in still pools, with greenery all around them.

Fighting down my thirst as I swallowed dry crumbs of bread, I stood up and went on. Hill after mound of dry dirt passed under me as my thirst slowly intensified. With no sun, I could not tell the time of day accurately. But at some point I looked up and saw that the gray sky was darkening. As I watched, it turned an inky black as light faded from the land. The dust hills turned from brown to shades of darkest midnight blue. Then I saw the stars.

There is nothing like them in the worlds I had been in before. In those worlds, the stars fade in slowly and glow like little pinpricks of silver in the sky. They are just far-away suns or planets, reflecting light back to your eyes.

These stars were larger, brighter and came sweeping in from the east in a moving tide. Like a web of diamonds in a sunrise they were drawn across the blackness, moving in a stately spill from one horizon to the other. Except for where the Dark Passages blocked them out, the whole sky was thick with the brilliant stars. And unlike any other world I had been on, I could see these stars moving. Not quickly, it takes hours for one on the horizon to cross the sky, but enough so that if you stopped to tie your shoes, then looked at them again they would have shifted.

Filled with their beauty, I forgot all about the lack of water. Laying back on the top of a dust dune, I watched them moving. Patterns I had never seen before flowed before my eyes, glowing white against silky onyx. Just before I fell asleep, the thought crossed my mind that these stars must be much closer to the world than any I had seen before.

In the morning my thirst had intensified. Opening my eyes to the pale, gray sky of the Dustland's dawn, I felt like I had been swallowing the dust I slept on all night. Stiff and cold, I stood up as slowly as an old man. Desert hills spread on all sides, seemingly endless. Where should I go now?

Water, I needed water before anything else. But where to find it in this wasteland?

"It can't be endless," I muttered thickly to myself, "somewhere there has to be a green land, or at least an oasis. All I have to do is find it."

But of course, the wasteland can stretch for miles in all directions before it reaches another type of terrain. Hundreds of miles, even. I could not travel that far without something to drink.

Picking a direction at random, I stumbled off, sucking on a bit of dried meat to sustain me. I was too dry to eat any bread or really chew the meat. My feet sunk into the dunes at every step, dust sloshing up into my shoes. There was no sun to beat down upon me, but the air did become fairly warm with the blank, directionless warmth of this land. It made the sweat stand out on my forehead, losing more precious liquid by the moment.

I tried to Summon Water with my Elemental skills, but both the land and I were too arid. I should have tried earlier on, when I was less parched, but now it was too hard to bring any water to the surface.

By the time nearly two hours had passed, I was walking in a feverish haze. I could not have chosen a cardinal direction if I tried. Where the stars had risen must be the east, while where they set would be the west. Making the Dark Passages run north-south, a fairly simple marker. But I was too sunk in apathy to look up at them.

It must have been at least four hours since dawn when I stumbled against a hard, smooth object at the bottom of a small valley of dust. Blinking grit out of my eyes, I saw that it was a little structure made of polished sandstone. Stone bricks had been laid into a circle and fitted together so that it was jointless on the outside. On top of them was a lid made of cement, fashioned into a thin disk with a piece of metal bar set into it as a handle. The whole thing was about waist-high to me and at least eight feet around. Imprinted into the top of the cement lid was a strange symbol, like a bird's claw holding a squiggly line.

Curious, I climbed up onto the sandstone rim and gripped the curved bit of metal in my hands. It was rusty and sharp-edged, biting into my palms. But in the back of my head something was telling me that salvation was under that lid. Pulling with all of my remaining strength, I lifted the lid a little on one side and slid it backwards off of the ring of stone. It grated horribly as it went, leaving tracks of cement powder across the rim. But as soon as it was out of the way a cool, moist breeze rose up from below. Looking down, I saw a deep hole in the center of the ring filled with darkness. In the shadows, something glittered with an oily sheen.

With a sob of hope I snatched up a pebble from the ground and dropped it into the hole. It fell about ten feet, before hitting something with a loud plop. The sound made me feel even drier than before.

There was no rope or bucket in sight: I would have to improvise. Hastily, I tore off my belt and shirt, tying them together into a rough rope. Then I emptied my backpack out onto the ground, careless of where the items fell. It was made of a water resistant cloth, tightly woven and slick. With it fastened to the end of my shirt, I climbed back up onto the rim of the well. Leaning down as far as I could reach, I dangled the pack towards the water. I was in such a state that my mind might have snapped entirely if it did not reach.

But it did, the cloth draping down into the water and slowly filling with it.

I don't think a dipper has ever been drawn up from a well so quickly as that one was. Much of the water still leaked out through the backpack's seams, trickling with maddening sounds into the well below. But some was left, enough to dump into my mouth heedless of dust and debris, gurgling down my throat in wonderful waves of moisture.

I sucked every drop from the cloth, then dipped it in for another round. This one was even better than the first, so I went for a third, then a forth. I had just drunk the fifth backpack of water when a strange sound struck my ears. Far over the dunes, but approaching rapidly, there was a rumbling, clattering sound. It was muted as it rolled down into a draw, then gained in intensity as it climbed the next rise. Not knowing what it could be in this strange land, I hastily dropped to the ground and stuffed everything back into my soggy backpack.

Chapter 23: King's Men

As the sound approached, I could make out the tortured roar of a small engine, mixed with the clanging of metal against metal and the screech of poor brakes. A shape crested the nearest ridge, sliding down over the near side with even more screeching noises. As it came nearer I found, to my amazement, that it was a sort of vehicle. It looked like someone had taken an old, rusty car and cut off any top or roof it might have had. Then they had welded on beams and bars in the back to hold an assortment of rags, bags and buckets which all clattered together with a deafening sound.

Shouts and rough laughter came from the vehicle, announcing the first people I had seen in that world. Five or six men, all as dirty as the tires on the car and dressed in sparse clothes of leather and fur, were riding in the crazy contraption. Most of them were perched up by the bars, or sitting precariously on the edge of the wall. I could hardly make out the driver from a distance, but he seemed to be wearing an ugly creature's head as a hat, with the rest of it's fur flapping behind him.

There was no way to tell if they would be friendly or not. Quickly, I pulled my crossbow down and cranked a bolt into place. Looking up again, I saw that they had spotted me. Their laughter had gone quiet and only their shouting remained. Over the top of the car sounds, I could make out what they were saying.

"He's been foolin' with the well!"

"That's the King's well."

"Get him!"

Obviously, they were not friendly. The car's engine growled louder as they bumped over shallow dunes towards me, snatching up weapons from the floor of the vehicle. These ranged from what looked like black-powder rifles with feathers tied to their stock, to spears decorated in rodent's skulls. So far, they were just waving these weapons menacingly and calling threats of what they would do when they caught me. I only had a few seconds to decide what to do about it, before they would either catch up to me or opened fire.

In one smooth motion I shouldered the crossbow and shot the readied bolt. A crossbow is powerful and accurate, but slow to reload. I only had one chance to make the shot right. The bolt whipped off of the stock with a swish! and flew straighter than an arrow could have. In a split second, it had plunged into the front-right tire of the oncoming vehicle.

As swiftly as it was moving, and being poorly balanced from the start, the driver had no chance to correct his rig. It slewed to the side, bounced once on a small rock and stuck in a mound of dust. There was a shout of wrath from the vehicle's owners and a long cry for revenge went up.

Without looking back I turned and began to run. Past the open well, across the little valley, I was almost to the top of the hill when I heard thumping feet coming behind me. A rifle shot cracked in the air and something hit in the ground nearby with a dirty poof.

Turning, I saw one man reloading his gun at the base of the hill while another took aim and a third was more than half-way up it behind me. He had a weapon like a sickle on the end of a pole, decorated in long stripes of bright red paint. Far too bright to be blood, but it was suggestive. There was no opportunity to get another bolt into place before I was taken down. Now was the time for some magic.

I felt the core in my center burning bright with energy, strong from the fear and excitement of a fight. Snatching a great fistful of it, I threw out my hand in a sharp gesture towards the man climbing just below. An invisible flow of energy whipped out and slapped into him, sending him flying off his feet and tumbling down the hill with a scream. Others had started to climb after him, and now darted out of the way as he came scything past. I wouldn't be surprised if he had some more red streaks to ornament his weapon by the time he reached the bottom.

Immediately after knocking him down, the sound of a second rifle shot blasted through the quiet air of the Dustlands. Drawing more energy, I spread it out into a wall of air in front of me. Invisible, it would be impenetrable to most substances.

Something splatted with a thudding sound just a half-inch in front of my upraised palm. I felt the core in my center go dim from the amount of energy it took to block the shot. A flattened piece of lead fell softly to the ground at my feet. It was time to be leaving, before more could be fired and wear me out. I turned and ran again, over the crest of the hill.

Between keeping a hold of the swinging backpack, banging crossbow and trying to get away from my pursuers as fast as possible, I suppose I did not look where I was going. I crossed the hill out of sight of the rag-tag gang before they could take another shot at me, but stumbled over a head sized stone on the other side. Some people may feel inclined to laugh at that, a wizard holding off bullets with a wave of his hand just to trip over a regular stone a moment later. But, unhappily, that sort of thing happens in all worlds quite often.

Before I could stop myself I pitched head forward down the hill, which ended up being more of a cliff than a slope. Banging off sandstone ledges, slithering in the dust, I tried to claw a hold and stop my decent. My hands were only scraped on the rough rock, fingernails almost pulled out by the force of the fall. And I lost the grip on my backpack, so that it went clattering down wildly beside me.

At the bottom of the cliff was a crack in the ground, a miniature canyon eight feet wide and more than ten feet deep. I bumped off one more ledge and fell down into it, mouth clamped shut on a frightened cry.

Hitting the bottom must have stunned me for a time. I don't remember anything but blurry images of stone until I found myself wiping droplets of blood off of my scraped hands onto my shirt, while laying flat in the dust at the bottom of the crack. My head felt beaten and bruised, my joints like someone had been bending them the wrong way and my hands as if they had been put in a sandblaster. I lay still, trying to get my breath back and wondering if there was any exit from the hole I had fallen into.

Dust trickled down onto me in the darkness.

Voices echoed from above, "He's gone!"

"Must have fallen down there."

"Well, if he did he's dead. No one could come off of that hill and survive. Even if they did, they would break a limb and not be able to climb out."

"Hah! Fool saved us the work of killing him. Still, too bad about the water he must'a drank."

"What the king don't know won't 'urt him..."

Their voices faded away. The gang had decided that I was dead, or at least far along the road to the reaper's doorstep. Once they had gone I sat up with a low groan. Perhaps they were right: I did not feel like moving more than a few inches from my resting place. And one ankle was beginning to throb above all of the other pains.

With a burst of fear, I wondered if it had been broken by the fall. Reaching down, I poked and prodded at the bones until I felt fairly sure that they were all in place. Then I turned the foot from one side to the other until I was satisfied that it still worked properly. I must have simply caught it and twisted it during the fall. As long as no bones were broken, my prospects were not quite so frightening to me. I had been beaten and bruised in underground places before, yet survived. The thing to do was find a way out as soon as possible.

Standing up, I gingerly put weight on the sprained joint. It protested so that I had to lean against the stony wall nearby, taking part of the weight on my hand. Above me, the stone went up in ragged walls towards the edge of overhanging dirt which indicated ground-level. There was small bumps and cracks in it here, but none I could really get a grip on. The opposite wall was the same or a little worse, as it leaned over towards me at a slant.

Behind me, the walls became narrower and drew together until the canyon petered out in a smooth slot reaching towards the surface. I thought that this was where water must flow down it and cascade in a waterfall to the bottom of the gorge during the wet season. If there was such a thing as a wet season: I did not know. The stones did indicate that water fell in large amounts from time to time, but not how often.

In the other direction the gorge ran on much the same as far as I could see, sloping slightly downhill the while. There was no sign of a better place to scale the walls, but it was the only option available to me. I would have to forge ahead.

Not far off my backpack lay on the ground, contents once again scattered. I picked up the dusty food and brushed it off before putting it back in. The alkahest was miraculously unbroken, but my little model of the Dark Passages had become sadly chipped and cracked. I stuffed it into the pack as well, keeping it through habit more than for any use it would have had for me. My crossbow and bolts had also made it down, though two quarrels were missing and one cracked, other than the one I had lost in the gang's car tire.

My gear retrieved, I began to limp down the narrow crack, leaning on the wall now and then to take the stress off of my sprained ankle. The ground sloped gently downwards, both on the floor of the canyon and, apparently, above. The floor of the canyon was mostly smooth, except for at places where rocks had broken off of the wall and fallen into little heaps on the floor. None of these were high enough to help me escape, only enough to make my progress more irksome.

The walls were always too high and often angled inwards, so that the gray light of the sky was only a narrow slot above me. At places, the overhangs even fused together so that the light was blocked off entirely, forcing me to navigate through the dark to the other end of the tunnels. Luckily, I still had my Lightrune, so if the going got too dim I could hold it in one hand to brighten the way.

The crack went on for what felt like miles before it closed off again abruplty into nothing. The walls just came together in a sharp angle before me, with a shallow depression of sand at their feet. The walls here were even higher than before, being about fifteen feet above my head.

I stopped, frustrated, to pound a fist against the stones. I had been hoping to find a way out without relying on the arts of Erilaz. I was tired and injured, so it would be hard to concentrate on any power strong enough to get me out right away. Levitation and shifting the Earth took more energy than most other works, as they had to directly defy gravity. As it was, it would drain me too much to use those powers to get out of the trap I had worked myself into. I would reach the top, but if any hostile beings were about they would be able to catch me easily.

Besides the fact that I had, admittedly, grown soft in my life as a Keeper and did not feel like traveling on any further after my fight and fall.

Slumping down on the floor by the wall, I leaned my back against it. In my pack the bread and meat had become dusty and damp from the sack having been used as a dipper and then spilled down the cliff. I still ate what I could, crunching through the grit or spitting it out when it became too hard to bite. As I ate, I thought about the gang of men who had chased me in the old car. Water must be very precious in this dusty land, I decided, as they had evidently been angry at me for taking even a small amount of their supply. Or their king's, as the truth might be. They had shouted something about it being the king's well. But did their king have lands, cities and villages in his realm, or was he a nomadic warlord who only kept a vague territory under his sway? Either one could be true. If the men in the car had been a sample of his people, he must be a savage king indeed.

Once there was nowhere else to go with my cogitations, I told myself that I would awake at the beginning of evening when less bandits might be about, before falling asleep on the hard ground.

I dreamed of the Founder who had showed me the tile with lines of Fire, Earth, Air and Water. Even in my dreams I wondered if he had purposely betrayed me by showing me a tile I could lift, or if he had only been trying to explain that the Runestones had no Runes on either side. Was I the only one to blame for my predicament, or had he made me want to come here? Perhaps he had only been a figment of my hidden desires, awoken in a time of stress.

When I awoke the sky had turned dark, though the stars were not yet far enough over head for me to see them from inside the crack. I felt stiff, but also rested. Standing up, my cuts and scrapes protested all over. I stretched my arms above my head, yawned and slung my gear back over my shoulders. With a glance up at the wall, I tried to decide what the best course of action would be.

It was higher here than where I had first fallen in, but I did not want to hike back along it just to find a lower spot. Here, I could either make a channel through the stone to walk up like a ramp, or lift myself with the Air Element up to the surface. The second sounded like the easier of the two, though I had only experimented with self-levitation a little in the past. It was a dangerous art, because if you lost concentration for even a moment, you could fall back down to the earth at the speed of normal gravity.

Closing my eyes, I felt the currant of Air around me. It is the breath of most living worlds, not simply oxygen mixed with other gases but the flow and movement of currants which bring rain, fan flames and cool the worlds. Air is in people as well, in every breath they take. It is also one of my personally bonded Elements.

Reaching out my hands, I felt the air brushing through my fingers. Bending it to my will, I forced it to form a solid slab of pressure below me, pushing upwards. Slowly, precariously, I lifted up. Wind ruffled my hair, making it tickle my face. Opening my eyes, I saw the gray outline of the cliff roll past, until the top of it was within an arm's length. Then it was at eye level, so that I could just see out over the dunes of dust beyond. Just a moment more and I was tumbling over the edge into the dirt.

"Now that is the way to get out of places like that," I muttered, standing back up to brush the dust from my face. Out on the horizon a long, low cloud seemed to be resting, blocking off the first of the stars. Naively, I thought that it meant rain was on the way and felt pleased about it.

In front of me the plains went on in smaller, more compact dunes, while behind, on the other side of the crack and to the north of it, ran a low line of jagged rock cliffs, an extension of the ones I had fallen off of. As I was looking about a noise came to my attention, a quiet, steady noise approaching from the south. At first I thought that it might be the gang returning with their car, but after a pause I reconsidered. The car made a lot more noise than what I was hearing. This was just a low, continuous creaking sound mixed with a light tinkling.

Still, there was no way for me to know what sounds meant trouble in this world. As far as I could tell, any person I met would be hostile towards me.

Taking advantage of the darkness, I crouched down to see what would appear. Meanwhile, a new bolt was stealthily loaded onto the crossbow.

A shape appeared over one of the nearer dunes, or rather a group of them traveling together. They were outlined against the sky clearly for me to see. There was what appeared to be a cart, pulled by a creature akin to a donkey or mule. The wagon was what was making the creaking and tinkling noises, and now I could hear the dull footfalls of the beast as well. Beside the creature walked a figure which seemed, oddly, to glow with a faint luminescence as it came nearer. Though it was in the shape of a man, it could be seen as a faint pale blur against the hills even while the other two shapes were hidden by shadows. This man seemed to be trying to hurry towards the low cliffs, though the beast simply plodded along heedlessly.

The caravan had come abreast of me, about ten yards off, when the man stopped suddenly and looked over towards me.

"I can see you, you know, so there is no good in hiding. And if you are not every sort of stupid in the Dustlands, you'll want to take shelter."

I straightened, offended at his insinuations, "I'm not hiding, just watching. And what would I want to shelter from?"

Stopping his cart and beast altogether, the strange man approached me. As he got closer I saw that his hair was a pale, shimmering blue and his skin so pale that it looked silver in the darkness. In fact, he seemed to gleam with a silvery light all over, as if he had a Lightrune hidden under his clothes. The people I had seen earlier did not have this appearance, so I gathered that he was of a different race. Either that, or the all inhabitants here shimmered at night like some sort of phosphorescence.

He was looking at me as if I was just as strange. Stopping a pace away, he regarded me in the gloom for a long moment. Then he said, "you're not from here, are you?"

I shook my head, "No, I—I come from up there."

With one hand I gestured at the black streak across the sky, while still keeping the crossbow safely held in the other.

"The Dark Passages."

The stranger continued to eye me, before glancing at the storm that was building on the horizon. It had expanded now to blot out most of the eastern sky, blocking all but the first star from being seen.

"We have to hurry to shelter now. That is not water you see in the sky: it is dust. You have a lot to learn if you are to survive this land. I know. It is not my native environment either. I am Eoan of the stars."

"The stars?"

"No time to talk now. If you want to live, hurry!" Eoan turned and darted back to his beast, which he gave a slap on the rump and ordered, "up now, Snufflar! Hup, girl, hup."

I fell in behind the cart as it rattled past the end of the canyon, headed for the low cliffs. In the dark, all I could make out in the wagon was clusters of bumpy items, some stacked in large wash pans, others hung on hooks around the edge of the cart or simply rolling on the straw-sprinkled floor. They clinked together like glass and thin metal, making a racket as Eoan had his creature break into a trot. We hurried up to the edge of the cliffs, where a wide crack ran into them like a canyon. Eoan slowed his beast and led it into the slot, which the wagon barely fit into.

After traveling down it about a hundred feet he called back, "this is far enough for Snufflar. She's used to the Dustlands. Let me cover my wares, then we will continue into a cave. Out here we would smother."

He came back to unroll a large square of canvass, which I helped him tie down all around the cart so that it covered the box snugly. By now a fierce wind had started to blow, whistling down the canyon and fighting us as we secured the thick cloth. When it was done Eoan took me by the arm and led me to a hole bored back into the wall of the crack. It was about four feet high and the same size in width with a sandy, soft floor. If I had been claustrophobic in the least, I would have been afraid to crawl in.

As it was, I went without hesitation when Eoan pointed the way. It opened up inside to a rough grotto, which I could feel but not see because of how dark it had become. There was little, shelf-like protrusions on the walls, a few stalactites connecting the floor to the roof and an open place to sit. Eoan came in behind me as I fished the Lightrune from my pocket. Instantly the stony room was lit by white brilliance, showing the brown rock in all of its convolutions.

Eoan settled across from me and we listened as the dust storm came on. Inside the cave, very little debris or wind could find us. But I heard the savagery of it outside and shivered. If I had been left out there on my own...

It would have killed me.

# Chapter 24: Eoan of the Stars

A few minutes after the commencement of the dust storm, my companion looked over at me thoughtfully. His face was pale, without line or scar, eyes a glistening, icy blue. He looked like someone who had been frozen in the ice for too long, or kept in a cave until he learned to glow in order to see his way. I had the feeling that he thought I was almost as odd. His next statement proved it.

"So, you come from the Dark Passages. A descendant of the builders?"

"No. I was...helping take care of them. But I was not born there. My home world is through one of its doors. But you know of the Dark Passages and the Founders?"

Eoan smiled thinly, "I saw them built when I was still on my father's ship. We all watched as the builders constructed the stones across the sky, fitted the doors and roofed it in. I have wondered, since, if they still lived there or had turned to dust like other humans."

"You saw the Passages built?" I leaned towards him, astonished, "but that was over a hundred years ago!"

"Those of the stars do not go beyond as quickly as humans." Eoan shrugged, "Many Stardwellers live for a thousand years before their ship is sent flaming across the sky in farewell. But that is in the pure atmosphere of the darkling sky. Here, I may only last another century before my light goes out. If violence does not smother it first."

An image of the bright, near lights of the night sky flashed into my mind. They were not only closer than the stars of my home world: they were inhabited. But what ships was he speaking of, and how did they live on them in the sky?

"What are the stars? Planets you live on and fly between?"

The Stardweller shook his head, staring off into visions of the past, "they are the ships themselves. Shining, silver ships with sails of purest white and rigging that glows like the coals of a fire. In the formations passed down for ages we sail across the sky, only altering the fleet when a man reaches his eightieth year and can be given a ship of his own, or when a fellow dies and must be sent beyond in a ship that flames and streaks across the sky in farewell."

"Shooting stars." I realized with a gasp.

"So some of the Dustlanders call them. But they don't shoot too anywhere, they simply burn away with the captain who has lost his light. My ship was burnt as well, though I was not on it. They only did it as a sign that I could never come back. I watched from the ground and knew that I was condemned to wander the dust until I became one with it, like any of the Dustlanders below."

I nodded slowly, took off my pack and dug the model of the Dark Passages out from it.

Laying it on the floor between us, I said, "this is what I know of the passages. It's not all of it, not by many halls, from what I have seen out here. I helped clear much of it, opening passages that had been filled with rubble for years. But because I became too curious about what lay outside, the other Keepers made me leave. You are an exile as well?"

Eoan picked up the model to look at the tiny walls and smooth tiles, before setting it back down between us. He glanced towards the dark entrance of the tunnel, then back at me, "yes. I'll tell you why, if you will explain to me more of the reason for your own exile. It will pass the time during this storm."

So, just as now, we told stories in the dark of a dust storm to pass the time. In compact form, I explained how I had become a Keeper and been trained by them, before being discarded because of my wish to know what was outside. Then Eoan told me his story;

"In the beginning, the Stardwellers were all captains of their own ships. Men, with no wives or children among them. They sailed the skies alone, or threw rope bridges over to nearby ships while they were sailing and had parties together. But still, something seemed to be missing. One night a great, white ship was moving over the Dustlands and its captain was watching what went on beneath him. It is a little-known fact that the Stardwellers can see and even hear what goes on down on the land as if they were there themselves. But only what is happening directly below them and only if they take the time to look."

"Well, this captain saw two girls of the Dust camping outside, watching the stars. Whispering and giggling, they pointed out the great white ship and a smaller, reddish one nearby, 'If you will marry the white star, I will take the red one, sister.'"

"Hearing this, the captain of the great white star threw his bridge across to the nearby red one and told its captain what he had heard. They tied together their spare rigging and made a knotted rope to drop all the way down onto the Dustlands below. As the ropes end trailed along, they climbed down and found the girls asleep. Awaking them, the captains promised them a long life among the stars if they would come to be their wives. And so the first women came to the stars."

"Their children were of the stars, brilliant and long-living. But there has always been few children among the Stardwellers and little of them are female. So we still descend to the Dustlands and take women of the Dust up with us, from time to time, to live in the stars.

"One day I and a few of my friends who had just been given our own ships made a rope and dropped down in the night to find wives to bring back with us. There was a beautiful girl of one village which one of my companions wished to take with him even though she did not want to come. She pleaded that she was already promised and asked him to leave her. He would have carried her off by force, but

I stood between them. And when the captain tried to force his way passed me I hit him between the eyes with a fist. He fell down and hit his head on a sharp stone, which made his light go out."

"No Stardweller destroys another without great reason, or stops him from making a choice among the Dustlanders. My companions saw what happened and ran from me, back to the rope we had thrown to the ground. They climbed up and drew it up behind them while I stood, bewildered at what I had done. The next night I saw my blue-white ship streak across the sky as if I had gone beyond. It was a signal that I had been exiled to live and die in the dust."

"I burned my dead companion's body to keep him from turning to dust, though I knew that I had done the right thing in stopping him, even if I had made his light go out without meaning to."

"The girl thanked me and her father promised me any reward I wished when he heard of it. I asked for a skin of water and provisions to last me three days, then moved on."

Eoan finished his story with head bowed, hands clenched together on top of his up-drawn knees. I was struck by the similarity between our stories. Though his had been, perhaps, a less selfish reason for exile, we had both done something we felt was right but was beyond the regulations set by our peers. This had led to our being cast aside as worthless, the way back to our worlds shut behind us.

I remarked as much to the Stardweller, who nodded slowly in agreement.

"This Dustlands is a harsh place, perfect for exiles. You must learn a lot yet, to survive. I had to learn it painfully, alone. But I can tell you some things to make it easier for you, tomorrow. Now it is time to rest."

The dust storm beat down on the thick stone outside, whistling through the canyon where the beast and cart stood. By late morning it had blown itself out, leaving behind it drifts of the land's material. The canvass over the cart was heavy with it, like an extra blanket of shifting particles. The beast was sifted over with it but did not seem to care. She had a long, drooping nose with a soft, hairy end which well earned her name. Her eyes were sleepy-lidded and had long, heavy lashes like a vain maiden's. But these were to keep the dust out, not improve her decidedly ugly appearance.

Eoan gave his beast a friendly slap on the back, before going to roll the laden cover off of his cart. I helped him, unfastening it and pulling it off before shaking out the dust and packing the tarp back in the cart. The wheels were buried six inches deep in the soft particles, so that it took a bit of a heave and jerk to get it loose. All of the objects in the back clinked together as we got it going.

I could see now that they were a mixture of tinware, pottery and glass bottles, the more delicate of which were packed in straw or colorful folded blankets. These were his stock-in-trade, as he intimated as we got the cart ready. He traveled from town to town buying tinware from the places that made it, bringing it to famous potters or glaziers and trading for their goods, as well as a little extra coin. He also carried a private collection of fancy bottles with him. This was only about six items altogether, each one he had found separately, lost out on the dunes, and kept for their unique shape or style.

"They must have come from somewhere," Eoan commented, fondling one carefully before putting it back in a padded case with the others, "but nothing like them is made in any town I have been to. I have never heard of a great kingdom spanning all of the Dustlands, but even the Stardwellers do not remember everything. Perhaps, long ago, this land was greener and there was a kingdom great enough to produce vessels like this."

Once he was done repacking his stock, we trudged out of the canyon with the Snufflebeast between us. As we turned to travel beside the cliffs towards the north, I asked, "is this land ruled by a king now?"

"Nominally," Eoan looked over his shoulder as if to make sure that no one was near enough to hear us. In this part of the wasteland, it seemed like a superfluous action, "Angrist is more of a bandit lord and a tyrant than the people's king, though he puts on a great show of ruling fairly when he thinks it will impress anyone. His soldiers are mostly mercenaries and thieves, mixed with a fair sprinkling of deserted caravan guards, or bored ones. He pays them a little better than what they could make otherwise and gives them a safe position in society to occupy, as well as a home in his castle, Hahstgart. In return, they pillage where he wishes and kill whomever he wants dead."

"I think I ran into some of them the other day," I muttered grimly, remembering the topless vehicle full of savage men.

Eoan gave me a sharp look, "then you should be careful in the future to never meet them again. Stay away from Soleinden, the capital city, and Hahstgart. If you have got on the bad side of Angrist already, things will go poorly for you if you go near them. On the other hand, some of the braver villagers or nomads might help you secretly when they know of it. Most won't guess it unless you tell them, so just stay away from the capital, the soldiers and any other brigands of the desert."

"There is probably no easy way to distinguish between them, is there?"

My words were immediately met by a shake of his head. We walked in silence for a few more minutes before Eoan went on, "not until they are trying to slit your throat or take your goods. But that is the one good thing Angrist has done as a ruler. There are less other bandits now, as they are too much competition for him. Unless they are paying him tribute from their levies, of course. But that is enough on that subject; you understand that danger well enough. Now I must tell you a little more about how to survive."

He detailed ways to find the nomad's hidden wells, how to tell when a dust storm was coming and a few important landmarks to keep an eye out for. He also imparted a little wisdom about how to speak to friendly tribesmen or villagers, as well as creatures to be avoided in the dunes.

"If you are stung by an Anrow scorpion, get help as soon as possible. A medicine man or woman can sometimes cure the sting, if it is brought to them in time. Furstal snakes also have a deadly bite which must be treated quickly. Diamond spiders, rare and as big as your outspread hand, there is no way to cure the bite of. The dust will always reclaim you. Just as it will at the bite of a Scurry."

"And what do all these things look like?" I asked, shivering internally at the thought of what I might have been sharing the ground with at night without knowing it.

"Anrows are smaller than the Red scorpions and have long, whip-like stingers. They are a dusty yellow in color. Furstal snakes are not the only poisonous species, but they are the only type with black and yellow bands between head and body. The Gripsnake which looks much like them otherwise is harmless to people, though it strangles small animals to death with its coils before eating them. As their name suggests, Diamond spiders are shiny purple with either a white or pale blue diamond on their back. They are the biggest type of Dustland spider and are, as I said, rarely seen. Most people kill them on sight."

He also told me a little about what fruits could be eaten and which could not, though I had not yet seen anywhere that fruits of either sort could grow. When we got to the end of the cliffs he turned towards the east around their nose.

"Now we must part ways, I'm afraid. I would invite you to come with me so that I could teach you more, but I am going where you must not come. To Soleinden. But first, take these."

He gave me a skin of water and a few small loaves of bread from under the bench in the front of the wagon. Then he pointed me in the opposite direction, where he said a village lay after two good days of travel.

"Thanking you for everything you have done in this short amount of time would be difficult," I looked down at the provisions he had given me, remembering that first day when Adasian had tried to teach me manners. Meeting his gaze again, I added, "let's just leave it at that I owe you a return in the future."

"That," Eoan told me over his shoulder as he began to walk away, "is a powerful token, in the Dustlands."

I looked up at the Dark Passages in the sky, using them as a marker to set my direction. Then I started walking. As I went, a little of the food and water was consumed before being crammed into my backpack.

All that day I trudged across the low dunes, turning over in my mind the things Eoan had told me. When it became dark the stars sailed across the sky in their ordered formations, flaming silver. It was difficult to picture them as inhabited sailing ships, despite how close they were. But I believed everything Eoan had told me, laying for a long time watching while imagining things that could be happening aboard them. I wondered if they ever broke formation or fought with each other, or if there were pirates who sailed the stars as they sailed seas on some worlds.

The next morning I walked on, crossing a low canyon on a natural arched bridge of stone. Passed it more jagged rocks stood up, not in any particular formation but in random spires. Then on into another sweep of open dunes to camp in before I reached the village.

Chapter 25: A Magician's Life

It was built on the banks of a yellow, sluggish stream, with hardly anything growing naturally along its banks except for hard, rattling reeds of jointed brown. But it was water, a fact the nearby people appreciated fully. They had planted crops on a mudflat not far off and watered it with many hand-dug irrigation ditches no more than a six inches wide. The crops looked poor, but they were something growing and mostly green. It was a sight to rest sore eyes upon.

As I approached the village, men working in the fields stopped what they were doing and drifted towards me, fingering their tools warily. They were dressed in ragged clothes of homespun cotton and they looked as worn and toughened as old leather. One of them, a man wearing swathes of white which left only his eyes free, had not been working in the fields. He had been standing on the top of one of the small, flat-roofed adobe houses, keeping a watch. He was the first to approach me, carrying an old rifle rather than a farming tool.

Remembering what Eoan had told me, I held both hands up palm-out to show that they were empty. The man in white stopped three paces in front of me, while the farmers made a half-circle just behind him.

"You are alone." It was a statement that the man in white made, his piercing blue eyes sweeping the landscape behind me, "what do you want here?"

"May your water always flow. I am Nolin Nearham. I come only looking for shelter and a place to ply my trade."

"Nerheem." I thought that he had misheard me, but did not interrupt to correct him. "I am Coloth the Hunter, guardian of this village. What trade do you practice?"

Eoan had not advised me on any trade to profess, since I had not told him much of what the Keepers had taught me. Being a healer would have been the most useful, since everyone needs one at some point and they are usually considered innocent. But I had not learned enough of that skill to lay it down as my highest card. Instead, I gambled on rousing his curiosity.

"If you give me food and shelter I can make your crops grow better. They look a little poor, for having plenty of water."

The men bristled at the slur given to their hard work, so I added, "Despite obviously having the best of care given to them. Some years are more difficult than others and normal means can do nothings."

"We do not accept Charlatans here." Coloth warned, "if you try to trick us that you are using magic on our field, we will throw you out."

He said the word charlatan as if it was a name, a type of people who had tried to play tricks on these villagers before. But I could use the Elements to give a boost to the plants, as well as knowing of a mixture of bone meal and ashes that Tallray had invented to make some of his Alchemical herbs grow better. As long as the villagers did not see my movements as being an empty show of magic, I was safe.

"I'm not going to trick you," I explained, sweeping my gaze over them all to show that I meant the words for every one of them, "I know a mixture of minerals to fertilize them, if you will let me collect the materials. And I can make them grow better by touching them."

"That sounds like a Charlatan's work." Coloth shook his head, as if dismissing me. Wishing to have a night with a cooked meal, somewhere other than the dirt to sleep on and a few people to talk to, I offered, "I will show you before you give me anything. Let me prove that I can make the crops grow. If I am lying, you will see it and can still throw me out with nothing lost."

All of the men hesitated. Finally one of the farmers spoke, "let him try. You can watch him, Coloth, so that he makes no mischief."

Another joined him with the words, "yes, he does not look like a Charlatan. They wear fancy clothes and big boots."

Though one of the villagers did turn away as if in disgust and would not look at me at all.

Under the supervision of the village guardian, an official that Eoan had warned me most habitations in the Dustlands kept, I was marched into the little group of buildings. There the work-worn women glanced curiously at me, while the almost clotheless children stared openly or ran away to hide. The guardian allowed me to collect a basket full of cold ashes and a handful of cracked bones from the village women, the latter which I crushed using Powerpointing until they were as fine as the ashes. This made the men begin to watch with interest, though still not with complete trust.

When the mixture was ready, the guardian took me out onto the field. Then I saw that many of the plants were not only yellowish and poorly: most had been bent or partially crushed by the weight of the dust from the storm. The only reason they were not buried entirely was that the villagers had seen it coming and used every spare blanket, sheet and strip of canvass to cover the fields with before it hit. Even then, about two acres of the grain had been buried in dust, so that it did not even appear to be part of the field any more.

First, I spread the ash mixture across the ground around the plants, letting it sift slowly through my fingers. This took some time, in which many of the farmers became bored and went back about their chores or into the village. But it was earning my keep, at least partially, so I did not care. And it gave me a chance to get a feel for the land, how the plants grew and what their needs were.

When the mixture was all spread I stopped in the center of the field. With my eyes closed, I felt the currant of life around me, flowing and growing. Roots sunk silently down into the ground, moving nutrients up into the stalks of the greenery. Sun rays were lacking, but the ambient light was enough to make these plants grow. They were adapted to it.

Letting the feelers of my mind go out all through the field, I could sense how they struggled to grow back after having been crushed. All of the sprouts wanted to become large and make seeds for the next generation to grow from. It was their imperious command and goal in life.

Feeding them images of rich, lush greenery, I began to bend them to my will. It was easier than bending the Air, as what I wanted was the same as what the plants naturally strove for. Giving them a trickle of my own energy, pouring the light from the spark of Erilaz on them, I made them grow. You could hear it, a soft, crinkling sound as the stalks straightened and reached upwards. Grains, fruits and vegetables, all strange to me a moment before and intimately linked in that moment, became richer in their growth.

There was an assortment of exclamations behind me, followed by a faint clicking sound. I opened my eyes on the waving, bright green field and turned to see Coloth with his rifle shouldered, pointing at me.

"Come here." He commanded, not shifting his aim. I stepped carefully around the crops until the gun was almost touching my chest.

"You are not a Charlatan," the guardian's voice was low and steady, "you are a Wizard."

I looked down at the barrel of his weapon, "are wizards shot in this village?"

There was a short silence, in which I heard both our breathing and the sound of the soft wind through the newly raised crops. Slowly, he moved his rifle aside and pointed it down at the ground, "not without reason."

Raising a hand to show once again that it was empty of weapons, or even a magical glow, I told him, "I mean no harm to you or your people. I am only a hungry stranger, passing through. If I can give you a little help in return for shelter and food, everyone will be the better for it."

Coloth held my gaze steadily for a moment, before turning to look at the other men standing near. One by one, they gave nods of assent.

"Very well, Wizard Nerheem. You may stay the night. And thank you for saving our crops."

Led to the village, I was explained to everyone within hearing and paraded through it to a comfortable adobe house at the far end. This was where Coloth's family lived and where I was given a bowl of a delicious stew, which seemed to be made of some sort of grain like barley, boiled and mixed in a thick gravy including chunks of meat. Though there was no sun, it was not cold in the Dustlands at that time of year. But it had been many meals since I had eaten something cooked and warm. I did not even mind the bits of bone or cartilage which was sometimes mixed in with the meat. I just threw it to the huge tame canine which lay by the door (it was a Gorewolf, but I did not know it then) and kept eating.

That evening I had the children bring me bits of smooth stone and carved Light Runes on them with the tip of my knife before giving them back. They made a poor Lightrune, being the wrong type of stone and carved with the wrong tool. But they still glimmered a little, making a faint halo around the young one's hands as they ran about admiring them. This was enough to delight them, as well as their parents.

A strategic move, as well as a pleasant way to spend the evening. When it came time to sleep, I was given a pile of colorful blankets on an adobe shelf built into the wall. No more or less than anyone else in the house received, including the wolf.

In the morning I moved on, given a pack full of basic supplies by the villagers, who had come to look at me with a shy respect instead of their normal wary caution of strangers.

Leaving their village, I crossed the stream and wandered out into the dunes, never stopping at one place for long. Days and nights passed as the full realization of my exile sunk in.

I had no home, no friends by me and no real goal in life except for to see the next gray dawn. I wandered in places with giant arches and boulders of sandstone, where the ground was swept almost bare and hard by the wind. I walked in a dried marsh where the ground was desiccated peat moss as fine and crisp as frost on the window and the trees were white-hulled skeletons with little branches left on their trunks. It had once been green, but the water did not flow there any more.

Lessons were still learned every day about surviving in the Dustlands. I barely escaped with my life when I learned that a nomad's smile is not always friendly, or that Gorewolfs will hunt a man at night even when he is healthy and has not troubled them.

I found that hot herb tea by a camp fire made of snufflebeast droppings is one of the best treats to look forward to in life and that poetry sung to the stars alone is never given the cold shoulder it might receive among men.

I might have lived alone and half-mad for much more of my life if I had not accidentally wandered near the capital city of Soleinden.

I did not know I was getting close to it until I crested a hill and a sense of great turmoil hit me like a bad stench. Below me a road, pounded into the dust until it was a pair of hard ruts, wound in from between hills to my left. It ran down a low slope into a great valley, which had a muddy, low river flowing through it from east to west. Along the banks of this river, overshadowing it on either side, was the city itself. Adobe and sandstone structures built in the classic Dustlander fashion of boxy walls and flat roofs, but on a larger scale than I had seen before, stood in rows. Some were tinted dusky purple, faded orange or pale rose. Arched windows looked out of the upper stories, with colorful cloth overhangs on the lower stories and roofs to sit under. It almost reminded me of Firendaze's capital, except for that it was much smaller and there were no domed buildings.

Raising my eyes, I saw the castle on the far side of the little city. It had square walls made of great sandstone blocks, topped with battlements and triangular watchtowers all around. Inside was a tall building of pale adobe and sandstone, carved with a pair of fantastic griffin-like creatures acting as pillars to hold up the roof.

Other than this one ornament, the castle was plain and militaristic in appearance. It may have been the palace of the acting ruler, but it was more of a fortress than a place of riches and frippery. As if drawing away from such low scum as dwelt in the town, it was built at a distance of about two miles from the buildings. Around it was a wide, slightly sloping space of empty dust.

The feeling of unrest was coming from the town itself rather than the fortress. I did not have Feleago's disciplined mind powers or Firendaze's accurate instincts to tell me exactly where it was coming from, but I knew that the turmoil was in the buildings somewhere. I knew that it must be something big to have caught my attention at all.

The sound of a wagon rumbling over the road out of town made me become fully alert. Laying flat on the crest of the hill, I watched as it came nearer, to a sharp little dune which lay on the opposite side of the road not far from where I lay. The wagon was pulled by what looked like a pair of shaggy snufflebeasts, both a nondescript grayish color. The figure on it was also a smeared color much like the dust, so that it was difficult to make him out against the terrain. But by watching closely I saw that he had jumped off of the cart and was taking things from the back of it.

Sticks of what appeared to be wood, which he brought to the top of the hill and began to lay out as if for building something. The sense of unease hung over him as well, like a dark cloud.

He brought out tools from his wagon and began to beat hurriedly on the pieces of wood. Under his hands, they took shape into what looked like a large picture frame, set up on legs so that it could support itself.

Wood was rare in most of the Dustlands, as it is now, so I did not think that he was simply building himself a shelter to camp at for the night. Neither did it look like he was framing a house, since it stood on angled legs. Besides, there was still the feeling of dark energy which hung over him and meant trouble.

From the wagon he pulled a few short coils of rope, which he dumped unceremoniously at the foot of the frame. Then he turned to watch the city with what was, I fancied at a distance, anxiety and repressed excitement. Following his lead, I also watched the city once again.

The sense of turmoil bubbled up and came boiling over the edge of the town. It poured out along the road in the form of a throng of people. Leading them was the car I had been chased by before, with a repaired front wheel, to go by how it was driving. Beside it was also a large pickup truck, just as beaten and misused as the car was.

This truck had spikes on its wheels, sticking out like scythes, and a large, barred bumper with rusty spikes on it. Painted on the sides was a ghoulish, twisted woman, reclining with an eagle perched on her arm. The eagle had a snake grasped in one claw, painted in a shade of slime green. In the back of this vehicle a handful of men stood, wearing metal helmets which gleamed dully under the gray sky. Every one of them was armed to the teeth.

Behind the two vehicles, the people tromped in a solid stream except for where there was one large opening in their center. This was taken up with another wagon pulled by a pair of camels, a creature which dwells in this world as well as others. In the middle of the wagon a figure stood, guarded by two more men with helmets. As it drew closer I saw that he was holding his hands together in front as if bound and that his head was bowed sadly. By then, I could see him a little more clearly and noticed something odd about his appearance. He glimmered silver-blue all over, like a distant star. It was Eoan.

Chapter 26: A Wizard's Rescue

I drew in a hissing breath of air and lay even flatter on the hilltop. The bound figure in the wagon was Eoan.

He was obviously being taken to the hilltop for some sort of gruesome punishment or execution. I could see no other reason for the wooden frame, ropes and excited crowd of people all coming together with him captured in their midst. The car must mean that the execution was sanctioned or even instigated by Angrist, as those were his bandits in it.

It was a bad place for me to be, because it would be easy for the soldiers to add one more victim to their list for the day. The question was, what was I going to do about it?

The safest plan would be to crawl back over the crest of the hill and make tracks for another part of the territory. It might even be what Eoan would have advised me to do, if he were with me instead of down in the valley. But he wasn't and I would not leave for the very reason that he would have told me to run. Because I already owed him a favor and could not let him die without repaying it.

Pressed into the dust so that it almost stuck to my lips, I tried to think of what to do. Rescue Eoan, of course, but that was not an easy proposition. I had a crossbow with three bolts (all the others had been broken or lost by then) a knife at my side and the spark of Erilaz in my chest. How could I use those to save the Stardweller from a few hundred angry people and at least a dozen of Angrist's vengeful men?

I needed a plan of action, one that could be thought up and began in less than ten minutes.

While I was thinking, the deadly parade moved up to the low hill and spread out around it on almost every side. There was a slight gap on the side facing me, as it was the direction away from town, but other than that the dune was surrounded. The vehicles had parked nearest it, the truck disgorging its load of helmeted men onto the ground. From the cab a pair of men got out, one dressed in a black uniform with a floppy hat pulled down over his face, while the other was wearing bright red robes. Both startlingly vibrant colors for the Dustlands.

They climbed to the top of the hill, which the frame-builder had discreetly melted away from at some point in the past. Eoan was brought up to them and the soldiers began to tie him into the frame, spread-eagle so that he could not move hand or foot. He must have been thinking then that his light was very close to going out. Perhaps he even believed the sooner it did, the better.

The man in black moved back down the hill a little ways, while the one in red began to speak. I could not hear his words from that distance, but I could make out that he was speaking loudly for the benefit of everyone below. I guessed that it was the denouncement.

It was time for me to do something.

I had acquired, by then, a tan-brown cape of coarse material which blended nicely into the dirt. Using it as camouflage, I worked my way stealthily down the hill to the bottom, where I crawled into a low ditch beside the road. From there I could just make out what the man in red was saying. He had a pompous, round voice like an actor from a play, the one who pretends to be the reluctant father of the hero's sweetheart.

"—So you see that our great ruler, Angrist of the Dust, finds this man guilty of the charge. As a lesson to you this man will be put to death today, by the Death of the Iron Whip. Let all take heed and never do ought against our gracious king! May his rule be triumphant!"

The man in black was returning, followed by a thickset beast of a fellow wearing nothing but boots, a loincloth and a suit of heavy muscles. In his hand he carried what looked like a three-pronged whip, which glinted with a metallic sheen.

Now it was really time for me to do something, but I did not yet know what to do. The executioner was approaching the wooden frame on top of the hill, twirling the whip lazily at the end of his arm.

Looking up towards the scene, I saw three black shapes circling in the sky above the crowd. Avisha, a crow-like scavenger which lives near most villages and is as big as a large eagle. They had come for the feast when the executioner was done, but they gave me an idea.

Focusing on their life forms, I tried hard to summon all that Feleago and Corky had taught me. They were of the Earth and Air, Elements I understood, and they had clever minds somewhat like a man's. I did not have much skill in mental magics, but using my link to their Elements I was able to touch their minds for a moment. In that second of time I impressed it on them that the executioner was a walking lump of meat, just waiting to be devoured.

With screams of avian hunger the large birds dropped from the sky. The executioner had placed himself in front of the frame and was drawing back his arm for a blow, but now he paused to look up in surprise. The three black birds hit him with all of their weight, moving at speeds that would terrify a human in the air. He went down with a growl of mixed anger and pain, flailing out at them with his spring-steel coiled whip. There was a small murmur in the crowd and a few of the soldiers rushed forward, trying to come to their compatriot's aid. Just as they reached him I did a cruel thing, to the birds. I used the Elements to light them on fire. And the executioner as well.

The screams from the wiggling mass became terrified, the crowd let out a concerted gasp. I surged up out of the ditch and ran bent almost double, straight up the hill in the gap between edges of the crowd. As I went I pulled all of my power into a great pool of energy in me, holding it penned up like a dam about to burst.

Just as I reached to top of the hill people began to take note of me and the soldier's attention was diverted away from their flaming companion and the tearing, burning birds.

"Hey, what do you think you—!"

Before they could get any further I released the energy in a sweeping tide, pushing down from the top of the hill in a cone of power which struck everything in its path, but left the very peak where the frame was untouched. The soldiers were knocked over and rolled on the ground as if hit by a colossal wind. The Avisha were blown smoldering into the air and the crowd below was pushed flat on their backs in a struggling, heaving pile. I staggered, slumping against the wooden frame beside Eoan's bound figure. His head had whipped up as he whispered incredulously, "Nerheem!"

So much energy had left me at once that I felt the spark in my center dwindle and almost go out. The world blurred before my eyes for a moment, before I forced it back into focus. It was no time to lay about. There was work which had to be done.

Pulling my knife from its sheath, I slashed through one narrow rope, then sliced off the other across. Half-freed, Eoan began to work at the knots on his other side. I passed him the knife with the words, "cut free and run. I'll keep these folk busy before following."

He hacked furiously away at the ropes while I straightened to look about me. The crowd was still fighting itself madly, but the soldiers were gathering themselves again and the man in red was standing just a pace away from me, staring with big, fishy eyes. Galvanized by my glance, he jumped forward and grasped me by one sleeve, "I have him! I have the—!"

Without pausing to think, I slammed my other fist into his flabby throat as hard as I could. It bruised my knuckles so that my hand went numb, but the orator fell down as if electrocuted.

"Grab him! Cut him down! The prisoner is escaping!" All of the solders shouted at once, charging at me.

'Calm is the ability to think in any situation and react accordingly' I heard Adasian's dry, cynical voice repeat in my head, from some long-ago lesson. Pulling up the Elements once again, I summoned Fire all around me. Shaping and forming it, mixing it with Air in subtle shapes, I created the image of a towering, fiery being in the air around me. A cloak of pulsing red, mask of burning orange and eyes of hottest white loomed up above the soldiers so that I was hidden in it. Voice cracking with concentration, I shouted above their cries, "Do not anger Salamon, lord of the Fire!"

While they fell back in fear, I stumbled out from inside the image of fire, hair singed by its heat. The wooden frame had lit as well, though Eoan was nowhere to be seen. Half-blinded by my own workings of energy, I tumbled down the hill and fell into the ditch at the bottom. There I lay, trying to get up, as the image of Fire faded away in he sky above.

I could not move, my powers were so spent and mind addled. Even the thought of the soldiers finding me could not make me move. But after a long moment I felt hands grasp my arm and help me up, pulling me out of the ditch on the far side. Blinking, I saw that it was Eoan again.

In that crazy moment we grinned at each other like naughty children, before half-stumbling away behind the dunes.

I did not really recover my senses until I found that we were somewhere in a maze of sandstone pillars, sheltering behind a wide one with a dent in one side like a shallow cave. I was sitting with my back against the stone, head cradled in my hands. Beside me, Eoan knelt looking anxiously into my face, "are you awake now, Nerheem?"

"It's Nearham." I muttered thickly, "Nolin Nearham. Keeper of the Dark Passages."

Then I realized what I was saying and shook my head, straightening, saying inexorably, "not any more. Exile of the Dust. I'm fine: you're the one who was going to be executed. Were we followed?"

He sat back on his heels and shook his head, "not that I know of. Hopefully a wind comes up and wipes out our tracks. I have never seen anything like that before, Nerheem. Not even among the stars."

I noticed for the first time that his face was bruised, turning a purplish color around the cheekbones and dark around the eyes. It looked strange on a man glimmering silver. He was speaking of my feats of Erilaz and I knew it.

"The Founders could have done better," I told him, "they knew the secrets of Time and Space, which have been forgotten by now so that the Keepers could not teach them to me. You saw the Founders build the Passages. It must have been greater than what I just did."

"I suppose so. They did use the powers of nature like you," Eoan looked thoughtful, then shivered, "though when it saves you from the Whip of Iron, all feats are the best you've ever seen."

"What were they punishing you for? Did you save another maiden?"

"Hah. No," Eoan gave a crooked smile, "It was just my temper which got me in trouble this time. I did not tell you last time, but I was on my way to Soleinden with a special commission from the king."

"Angrist? You were working for Angrist?"

"Only to bring him a specific type of glassware he asked for. Omberling black vases and pitchers. Two of each. They are rare and beautiful works, though somewhat depressing in style, if you ask me."

"So he asked you if you had them and that is how you got in trouble?" I still wanted to hear the full story.

Eoan shook his head again, "no. He had me bring the glassware to him in his castle, where we dickered over it. The price he offered was far too low, but I gave in eventually, knowing how he treats those that get in his way. The next day he had me brought back to his palace and began claiming that I had demanded too much for the glassware the day before. He wanted a refund: the glassware wasn't as good a quality as he wanted."

"It was in perfect shape and I knew it, so we argued for a time. Then he demanded to see my whole stock of wares, glass, tin and pottery. Before I could start to bring it in he sent his men out to get it themselves. They brought in everything, even my personal collection. I stood watching uneasily, sensing impending trouble. The king had them bring him different pieces, turning them over and setting them aside. He looked through most of my wares before telling them to bring up the case with my special bottles in it. I tried to intervene, but he silenced me with a look."

Eoan paused for a moment in telling the story, eyes bright with anger, "Angrist took my bottles from the case and looked at them all. Then he picked up my favorite one, the golden-clear one with flakes of sparkling metal suspended in the glass, and held it carelessly in one hand."

'This is far better than the Omberling trash you brought me,' He said lazily, 'but still...it is no good.'

"With a swift move, he smashed it on the arm of his chair. It shattered into a hundred fragments, beautiful glass laying broken on the floor around him. He laughed and added, 'don't you agree?'"

"I couldn't stand it any more. Instead of answering, I slapped him across the face. Hard. His guards took me a moment later and were not gentle with me. He was furious, accusing me of 'attacking' him and attempting to 'murder' him. All of the guards were sworn in as witnesses to this attempt at 'regicide'. The news was spread abroad in the town, which went wild with a mixture of fear, amazement and hate. For me and the king, both. Not long after that I was brought to where you found me..."

"I see now," Leaning my head back against the rough stone wall, I closed my eyes and saw the whole scene played out in my imagination. The king's baiting, the Stardweller's anger and the people's mixed reaction, "I would have slapped him too. In fact, I would have fried him with Powerpointing if he had done that to me. Then someone could have complained of assassination, but not him. I don't blame you in the least."

With a small snort, Eoan said, "I should have held my temper, still. Then I might have left with what remained of my stock and been allowed to leave unharmed. As it was, I almost died a terrible death. But you saved me with your strange mysteries. Thank you."

"I owed it to you." I gave him a quick look, reminding him that I would not be there at all if it was not for his warning about the dust storm, "But I am tired. As long as they are not on our heels, I'm going to sleep."

And with a former slave's carelessness of place or time, I did.

They did not catch up to us at all, because a wind rose in the night, fierce and full of dust, to cover our tracks. In the morning we shared what food I had and traveled on together.

Though we did not reference it aloud, we both knew that we were a team now. Instead of going our separate ways, we found villages where both of our skills could be used and stayed in them the same amount of time before moving on together. Eoan began trading for a small stock of glassware right away, though he could only transport a few pieces at a time without a wagon to carry them in. He made a pack out of a blanket and stashed them in there, carefully using bits of old leather to keep them from rattling together.

We never went in to larger villages, or any near the capital. Angrist would be looking for a wizard and a Stardweller, especially traveling together. Most of the people disliked the king's rule and would not have informed him of our whereabouts, but there was too great a chance of running into soldiers or spies in the few larger towns spread throughout the Dustlands.

In this way we made a living, not a bad one under the circumstances. Things did not always go right, of course. We would argue over the silliest things when both of our tempers flared, like who was to collect fire material for the night or if we should assume false names when going into a specific village.

Often these arguments would end in one or the other of us going off in a sulk to sit on a dune and look the other way until his temper had cooled. Eventually we would fall sullenly back together in camp and the next day the incident would be forgotten.

One time, this sulking out of camp led to a nice little discovery which ended the argument quickly. I had been the one to stomp out of camp and sit on the far side of a dune staring at the sky turning from ash to ink, this time. As I sat muttering to myself about stubborn star-men and how much better it would be to travel south in the morning instead of east, I dug my fingers angrily into the dust. At first I paid no attention to what they were doing, but when I felt something smooth and hard under my fingers it made me pause in my personal rant. Brushing the gouged dirt aside further, I saw a curved piece of dark glass buried in the dune. Interest caught, I began to dig it up. Soon it became evident that it was not just a loose piece of broken glass: it was a whole bottle.

"Eoan!"

"Shut up!"

"There's something here you need to see, Eoan."

"If it's just more navigational blathering—"

"No, really, there is something here you'll want to see!"

I had been scraping around the buried shape all the time and could now make out that it was a tall, slim-necked bottle with the form of a cluster of grapes protruding on one side. It was of a very dark glass" it looked black but I could not be sure. By then Eoan had reached me, a scowl on his face and mouth working in suppressed words of anger. But as soon as he saw what I was excavating his face cleared like the sky after a dust storm.

Falling on his knees across from me, he began to scrape around it as well. Together we carefully unearthed the bottle and emptied the sand out of it so that we could see what color it was. Eoan held it up for the light to go through, making the sides a gloomy, smoky color that I could not quite name. It was somewhere between black, purple and brown, with hints of dusty gray. Caught in the dark glass were tiny flakes of silver. They sparkled like stars in the night sky.

Now a smile was on Eoan's face such as was rarely seen there.

"It's a good piece," he said with a professional tone in his voice, "very nice indeed. See how fine the grape cluster is? And the flakes of silver are all evenly distributed. How did you find it?"

"I just dug my fingers into the dust and it was there," I shrugged, "it's like the others from your personal collection, isn't it?"

"In quality, yes. Though I've never found a bottle of exactly this color before. It is more lucid than the Omberling black. Someone many years ago knew some secrets about glazing that we have forgotten by now..."

"If you saw the building of the Dark Passages more than a hundred years ago," I said, deep in thought, "and the bottles were made sometime before then, it could easily be two hundred years old."

Eoan shook his head and wiped a finger delicately over the rim of the bottle, "more than that. My father did not know of a great civilization here that could have made these, though he had been a captain of his own ship for four centuries before my light was lit in the stars."

"So at least six hundred years of laying buried in the dust...I wonder what that ancient civilization was like?" I pictured great, glistening domes of gold, with spires of purest white between them. Rivers of clear water spanned with beautiful stone bridges, contented farmers crossing them with wagons piled high.

"It was wide-spread, whatever it was like," Eoan stood up, carrying the glass container carefully in both of his hands, "and must have ended in violence the likes of which we have never seen, there is so little trace of it left. Either that or they were all wandering nomads of cloth tents and great skill. Even then, what has become of their tools? Did they all return to dust so quickly?"

I followed after him, still trying to picture the scenes of long ago. In that time, there would not have been the Dark Passages stretching across the sky. It would have been an unbroken expanse of gray during the daytime, spangled black at night.

"Eoan, what makes the sky light?"

He stopped in his quick stride, turning to look at me blankly. So I hastened to explain, "in most of the worlds I have been on, the brightness was made by what we called a 'sun'. It's a big light, a little like a candle's flame, which moves across the sky during the daytime (orbital mechanics are too complicated to explain, either in conversation to a Stardweller or in this story). But I don't see any source of light here. It's just gray."

"Ah, I see what you mean," The Stardweller nodded, sitting down beside our smoldering camp fire to tuck the bottle carefully in his bundle. Once it was secured to his liking, he tilted his face back to stare up at the sky as he explained, "the people of the stars can only sail so high before the air gets too thin for our ships to rest on. Just beyond where we can sail the Great Mist covers the world. It is like a roof, but it goes around everything. It is a pale, billowing mist like a thick cloud, laying in a solid blanket. The ships with the tallest masts have sometimes come so close that their tops brushed the Great Mist, where moisture gathered on the rigging and spars. The captains of these ships always say that they hear strange voices in the mist, or distant singing."

"So that is what we see during the day? The Great Mist?"

"Yes. But no one here knows what makes the light beyond it in the daytime. Because of this, some of my people say that on the other side of the mist is heaven. That this is its reflected light we see."

I pondered this for a moment, but thought that it was more likely that there is a sun on the other side. I still do not know the answer to this, though if I ever gain access to one of the star-ships through the ropes that get let down on some nights, I might find a way to discover the truth.

After a minute I asked him, "what about the other side of the world, Eoan? The stars have to go all of the way around it. Do the Dustlands cover everything?"

"The other side of the world is dark all of the time," Eoan moved his gaze back down from the endless field of gray above us, "as far as I have seen, this side is all waste. There might be something else far to the north or south: I do not know. Most people in the Dustlands do not go beyond the edge of the darkness on the other side of the world. They believe that it is where condemned spirits are forced to dwell in bonds for eternity."

With this he got up and left to find more fuel for the fire, inadvertently stopping me from asking my third question: how the Dark Passages had been built across the sky.

But that night we were attacked by Gorewolves and had a fierce fight of it, so that those questions were put aside for a time. I was bit on the side by one of the large, shaggy canines, forcing us to stop in the next village to have it seen to. Luckily it had not got a deep grip before Eoan struck it away with a stone, so nothing vital was pierced. But it did make a nasty wound on my side, forcing me to stay in bed for many days afterwards.

Once I was well again we went on, wandering through the wastelands making our living on cookingware trades, Runeology, Elements and Alchemy. I even taught Eoan a little of Elemental magic, though he seemed to possess some Element that I could not fathom. Air was in him strongly, but there was something else that I believe had to do with the stars. It was like a fifth Element not seen on earthly planes. He never learned to use any Element with the ease that I did, but he took a childish joy from making little whirlwinds go across the dust or sparkling lights appear in the air around us at night.

In return, he taught me a lot about the Dustlands themselves and eased my sense of exile with his company. I had a friend then, someone to live for besides myself. And with that, I became almost content in my surroundings.

Chapter 27: The Midnight Maw and the Omberlings.

One day in the 'wet season' of the Dustlands many months after I had been exiled, Eoan and I were traveling through a long, narrow valley with sandstone cliffs rising sheer on either side. As you know, the wet season simply implies that it is colder most of the time and that a few bursts of rain will fall on random places in the Dustlands, from time to time. When Eoan had mentioned it before I had hoped for a long space of rain and moisture, after which there would be a bright spring of desert greenery. And I learned later that grass or flowers did often sprout after the rains coming, in the places that the moisture fell. But for the most part, life just went on with heavier clothes all around to hold out the creeping chill.

The valley we traveled was set, here and there, with pillars of a whitish, smooth stone unlike any I had seen yet. Eoan had been this way once before and discovered something that he wanted to show me, though he was stubbornly close-mouthed about what it was when I tried to press him. In the morning we had been on our way west, passing by the opening of the canyon, a narrow, jagged crack in the rocks which looked like it did not lead anywhere good. He had seen it and insisted that he show me a 'surprise' down it, though he made it sound as if it would be just around the corner inside. Instead we had been walking all morning and into the afternoon, the cliffs drawing back and hidden valley widening around us all the time.

"Does anyone live here?" I asked innocently, wondering if it could be a special village that he wanted to show me.

He just turned his gleaming face towards me and grinned without speaking a word. With Eoan, there was no way to tell if that was an admission of the truth or a mocking laugh at a pitiful attempt. I fell quiet for a few hundred yards, before probing gently, "you know, our water bottles are getting low. Do you think there is water ahead?"

"There is a nomad's well near the entrance to this valley," Eoan returned easily, "we'll refill when we go back out."

So it was not a lake, waterfall or river that he was going to show me. I frowned to myself, trying to think of a way to ask him more questions about where we were headed without seeming like I was doing it. He shot me a look that was openly mocking now, with the words, "we're almost there. Look up ahead."

Glancing up, I saw that the walls of the cliff suddenly came together in front of us, terminating in a jagged heap of rock that reached into the sky. At the foot of the cliffs was a wide, black hole leading straight down into the ground. Jags of white stone stood around it like sharp teeth aimed at the sky.

"The Midnight Maw, I call it," Eoan told me with some satisfaction, "I don't know what could have made it and have never met anyone else who knows that it is here."

Hurrying forwards, I bent down to look over the edge of the hole. It was at least forty feet in diameter, drilled roughly into the earth like a gopher's tunnel. It was almost vertical, with little angle to it. For the first twenty feet I could see the dirt it was burrowed into along the walls, bronze and crumbly, but then everything disappeared into the shadows.

Eoan came up beside me, careful not to step too close to the edge. I was just on the brink but felt little fear, even while grains of dust were trickling away passed my feet into the hole. Curiosity overwhelmed any fear I might have felt.

"But what made this hole, and why? It doesn't look like either a water sink hole or a volcanic tunnel."

Eoan did not have the answers for my questions and, though we talked about it for a long time, we did not come to any solid conclusions. All it did was make me want to find a way to descend into it and see what was at the bottom. But as this was impossible without ropes, climbing gear and other supplies, I had to give the idea up.

About a week later we ran into another odd phenomena of the Dustlands. This one more people know of, but we did not seek out on purpose.

As it signals the beginning of the end of my story, I will describe it in more detail. But I warn you that parts of it will not be easy to tell. I may not find the words to tell it as easily as I have the other parts of my tale.

We had swung around in our long wanderings to end up, inadvertently, only perhaps fifteen miles from Angrist's capital city of Soleinden. Eoan did not recognize the country we were traversing until we came upon a large village hidden in the folds of the dunes. Or at least, it looked like a village at first sight. But there was no water or wells in view, no crops or animals to support a family on and no sight of people moving among the small, brown adobe buildings. The only thing which moved in the whole village were a few Avisha hopping unafraid on the roofs.

Upon catching up to me at the top of the dune, Eoan stopped abruptly to stare down at the village, which seemed abandoned. He looked at it under lowering brows for a moment before pronouncing quietly, "I know this place."

I looked quickly from him to the buildings below. The only thing I could see which looked different from any other ghost town we had seen before was the pillar standing in the center of the place. It was taller than the houses, set with a long, rusted spike of metal on top. The bricks it was built of were a dark, almost-black color that gleamed with purple glints in the gray light.

"What is it?" I asked, not seeing anything to occasion the expression on his face.

"The last city of the Omberlings," he said solemnly, "few dare walk those streets. I have a few times in search of Omberling black glassware. But it is...eerie. I do not care to go into it very often."

I felt a chill move across my shoulders, as if a wind had just blown up from the dark side of the world. One of the Avisha cawed roughly, before flying away in a flash of black.

"I did not think that the Omberlings were alive any more. Everyone speaks of them as if they are a lost race."

"They are, but it's not because they died out. Not exactly." Eoan waved a hand at the dust-covered buildings below, where gloomy windows stared, "as you can see, none of them are walking the streets. And it is not a large town, either. But it holds all the Omberlings who were alive here when the plague called Jer-duv fell upon them. To escape the death which was felling hundreds of their fellows in other cities, they put themselves into vaults below the houses, to hibernate in a magical sleep until someone who can cure them arrives. Then they have promised to rise and follow that person, no matter his commands."

I gazed down at the village in wonder. "Truly?"

Eoan just nodded once in reply.

"Then why hasn't anyone came to cure them? I'm sure someone like Angrist would love a band of followers who would do everything he says."

"Jer-duv has no cure," the Stardweller shook his head sadly, "it always kills. Many Dustlanders of every sort died of that sickness. It was eighty years ago, yet still old men and women mourn the ones who were lost in that time. The Omberlings were especially susceptible to it. Most of their towns were burnt and destroyed to be rid of the last traces of Jer-duv."

"Do you think that the sickness is still active in there? I mean, would we catch it if we looked around in this town a little bit?"

"I never have caught it,' Eoan gave me an annoyed look, "but we don't need to go down there. Let's continue on. But not towards the south: Soleinden is only about fifteen miles in that direction. Let us leave this area before some of Angrist's followers find us."

"It won't take long to look around down there," I shrugged, making sure that there was no sign of movement on the horizon, "you can stay here and wait. I'm going in."

"Very well," Eoan still frowned, but made no effort to stop me, "if you see any black glassware in good shape, please bring it back with you. Though I don't think that you will want to be in there for long."

I shrugged again, before loading my crossbow, dropping off my pack beside him and descending into the valley. The dust slipped under my feet as I made my way down the slope, making trickles run before me towards the village. Half way down I stopped and looked back, to see Eoan standing with his arms crossed watching me. He expected me to stop any moment and return, afraid of the silence below.

I looked back at the village, setting my gaze on the pillar in the center. I was not going to be afraid and turn back. He could wait there all he pleased: I was going to explore the city at my own pace.

It seemed like a long time before I reached the first houses, though it must have only been a few minutes. They were smaller than normal homes, little adobe houses with square sides and empty, arched windows. The only thing which set them apart, on closer inspection, from many Dustlander houses I had seen before was that the doors had a strip of black-dyed clay all of the way around them and strange, twisted markings in the same color above that. I thought that the symbols must have been like a street address, because every one was different from the next.

Making my way through the buildings towards the center, a deep quiet settled around me, broken only by noises that accentuated the silence. The rustle of wind through dead weeds in a dooryard, the distant scream of the departing Avisha.

The windows seemed to be hiding invisible people that watched me as I passed, their eyes boring into me whenever I looked away. No one was there, but it felt like it. Finally I reached the pillar in the middle of the town. It was set in the center of a courtyard tiled in smooth, plain slabs of sandstone, with flat pieces of grim stone bordering it. Looking at it closer, the pillar appeared darker than it had from a distance, the purple glimmers almost lost except for around the edges. It was built in three layers, the first being a short, thick block of solid stone, carved straight at the edges so that it was a perfect cube. On top of this was a longer section made up of large bricks of the same material, stacked six wide and about eight feet tall. On top of this was the last layer of stone, the same bricks stacked three wide and many more feet tall. The rusty metal rod stuck straight up into the air above the stone. It looked like some sort of arcane antenna.

Circling it, I found that the stone base was not the same on every edge. The far side had an indent on it, slightly angled as if something was supposed to rest there. It was only a few inches deep and about six inches square, with words carved into the bottom.

Running my finger in the troughs, I read the words, "The White Stone here."

After reading it I gave a little start. The White Stone is another name for a Philosopher's Stone, an Alchemical goal which I was not even sure any more could really exist. For a moment I thought that the words meant that the White Stone was already there, hidden in or under the pillar. But after a minute of thought I realized that it was a sign telling whoever read it to put the stone there, if they had it.

"It must be the trigger to awake the Omberlings," I murmured to myself, "which makes sense. It is the best thing to cure a cureless disease."

Just then something moved on the edge of my vision, making me flinch and turn towards it. A shape darted into one of the buildings, running low and fast. For a moment I began to whip the crossbow up to my shoulder, surprised.

But then I had to give a faint chuckle at myself. It had only been a wild Dustfox, those small animals which live in sandstone burrows and hunt for lizards in the dunes. Harmless to people and rather pretty in a ragged, rakish way. It was probably living in the abandoned house, making a burrow out of the preformed shelter.

My attention diverted from the pillar, I decided to explore some of the houses myself. There was little hope of finding glassware or anything else of great interest outside, where any traveler would go. Choosing the building opposite the one the fox had run in to, I walked cautiously up to the door. Just outside I stopped and put a hand to the black strip of clay, trying to sense any sort of trap or magic that could have been woven into it. But I did not sense anything out of the ordinary, and Eoan probably would have warned me if the buildings were rigged.

With one hand on the hilt of my knife and the other holding the crossbow, I went through the open doorway. The first thing I noticed was that a lot of dust had blown inside. It covered everything in a thick layer. Floor, furniture and hangings.

The house was fairly normal inside for a Dustlander's dwelling, with a worn wooden table, shelves built into the walls for sleeping and an open-hearth fireplace constructed into one wall. The only thing which was strikingly different was the wall hangings. Many

Dustlander houses have cloths hanging on the wall to brighten the room and give more insulation to it. But they are colorful, cheerful pieces of cloth with simple designs. These were of solid cobalt cloth, finer and smoother than most Dustlander weaving. Depicted on them in silver or purple was animals, weapons or even people.

There was one on every wall, or two where they would fit. Moving over to look at one closer, I saw that it had a picture of a woman woven into it. Her face was made of a shadowy purple, her hair a long silver stream. She wore a robe of slightly lighter purple shades, while her dark hands held strange weapons or tools that I did not understand.

"Is this what the Omberlings actually look like?" I muttered, feeling the silky fabric of the hanging. If so, they were more than a different tribe of Dustlanders. They were an entirely separate race.

But there was no glassware or other loose items in the house, so I left it to look in another. This one must have belonged to a rich Omberling, for it had two rooms rather than one and the walls were covered in the hangings, some of which had golden threads woven into the edges. I was surprised that nobody had taken them away by now, though perhaps nobody else had come this far into the city through fear of what might lie here. Taking a larger, gold-woven hanging from the wall, I rolled it up and tucked it under one arm. It might sell for a good price in a village that had money to spare.

Going into the next room, which had evidently been used for sleeping and storage, I also found a shelf which had two pieces of plain pottery and an Omberling black vase set on it. Careful not to drop it or handle it roughly, I pulled the vase off of the shelf. It was not large, probably holding only a quart of liquid, but it was finely shaped. The bottom had a wide, round base to sit on, then narrowed almost immediately to be only as big around as my thumb. From there it went up in a graceful, flower-like shape with veins worked into the outside. Knowing that Eoan would like to have it, I wrapped it carefully in the hanging before tucking them both back under my arm.

On the way out of the room, I stumbled over something on the floor. Luckily I was able to recover without falling and breaking the vase, afraid as I was that my friend would have been very displeased with me. Turning back, I looked to see what it was I had tripped over.

Buried in the dust, with just its top sticking out, was a metal handle. I brushed the dust away around it, slowly revealing a removable tile with the handle on top. It swung up easily, set on hinges hidden in the floor. Below the trap was a ladder leading downwards into what looked like a cellar.

But Eoan had said that the Omberlings laid themselves to rest in some sort of vaults below the buildings, so I guessed right away that it led to one of them. The question was, could I go down into it safely?

The plague might still be lingering around the vaults. Or there could be phantoms haunting the places...or, more realistically, a magical ward set upon them.

A dark sort of silence did seem to creep up from below, so eerie that it made me feel cold. A shiver ran down the outside of my arms. On the other hand, unknown places always call to me strongly, no matter what might warn me against them. Summoning my courage up, I dropped through the gloomy hole to climb down the rungs of the ladder. A cold, damp air seemed to press against me. Stepping to the hard surface of the floor below, I drew the Lightrune from my pocket. Its bright, white light flooded the small space, outlining everything in sharp detail. The vault was lined in solid black stones, much like the floor of the Dark Passages. In fact, upon closer inspection I was sure that they were Solron, perhaps even large

Runestones, either turned so that the Runes faced away or made mysteriously without them like the Passage's tiles. But the floor of the vault was simply hard-packed clay, like that of the buildings above.

The only things in it were a hanging on the wall and a set of bed-like shelves let into the walls. Each of these held a reclining form, laid out flat and peaceful in the manner of corpses. Between them and the vault was a single sheet of thick glass, sealing them into their deep sleep.

Walking up to one of the three beds in this vault, I held out the Lightrune to get a clear look at the person within. Thin, gauzy black clothes tending towards a robe or gown sheathed it from shoulders to thighs, while its ankles and feet were bare. Unlike I had feared, its skin was not a deep purplish color. Instead it was a shade of slate gray, almost as if it was a dead body.

I could not see it's chest moving in breath, nor any other sign of life. I thought that perhaps the spell they had put themselves under to sleep had failed and that they had died in their beds years ago. But it was difficult to tell if the Omberling was sleeping or dead, because its face was covered in a wrapping of filmy black veils. I could not even see what color of hair it had, nor tell under all of its wrappings whether it was a man or woman. Looking in the other two beds, I saw that they all looked almost the same, except for slight natural variations in size or shape.

"Are you Omberlings still alive?" I whispered under my breath, almost jumping at the sound of my voice echoing around the chamber. Feeling spooked, I climbed swiftly back out of the place. Dead or alive, the Omberlings were a wraith-like scene in their black shrouds, laid behind glass.

As soon as I had climbed out of the vault and shut the door behind me, I heard a sound like a voice calling from outside. At first I stopped still, staring with wide eyes towards the doorway. Was it a specter, or an Omberling raised from their living tombs?

But then the call was repeated, louder.

"Nerheem!"

Chapter 28: My Last Friend

I recognized the voice as that of Eoan. It sounded like he was in trouble. Fear of more earthly things, like Angrist's soldiers, came back to me and I dashed out of the door into the central plaza of the city. Once again I heard Eoan's cry for help, spurring me on to dash out of the village towards where it came from. My crossbow, still loaded, swung from one hand and bumped against my legs as I ran, telling me that it was ready to be used.

When I came out of the town at the base of the dune, I did not see Eoan where he had been standing when I left him. But I guessed that he would have moved down into one of the shallow valleys between hills, to avoid being seen by others. Swiftly, but still with a touch of caution to my quick steps, I made my way to the top of the dune. The third cry for help had not been followed by another, but now I heard a muffled growling and thumping noise from a gully off to my right to guide me. Sweeping my gaze that way, I saw vague shapes moving down in it, dark gray and Stardweller pale.

"Gorewolves," I gasped, turning to dash in that direction. But that is not what it was.

When I got closer I saw a dozen or so small creatures, about the size of a fox but built more like rodents, attacking Eoan. He did not usually carry any weapon besides a rather blunt boot-knife, which he used more for cutting up his meals than fighting wild animals. When it came to wolves, stone or brands of fire was his usual choice of defense, but he had not started the evening fire yet. Because of this the rodents had all but swamped the Stardweller, pulling him to the ground as he struggled and struck out at him.

With a cry of frustration I threw my crossbow aside, because shooting it would have been just as likely to hit my friend as the wild creatures. Fire too, might have burnt Eoan just as well as the giant rats. Drawing my own long, sharp knife I slashed at the brutes, or kicked them away with the toe of my boot. But they only squeaked and turned on me, or continued with their attack on their first victim. Large, luminous eyes burning like coals, long teeth stained a putrid green, about half of the maddened beasts started trying to attack me. Kicking them away crazily before they could sink their fangs into me, I began to pull together the power in my center. Though there was no time for calm concentration, I had learned to use Powerpointing in difficult situations by now.

Using the energy like a feather duster, I raised my hand and swept it sideways through the air. Below it the rodents were knocked tumbling off of Eoan and wiped across the dust into a heap to the side. The ones in front of me were swept aside as well, scraped up and shot over onto the heap. They were heavy for their size, thickly built with weighty haunches and long, skinny fingers on their front feet. I felt the toll of energy it took from me to move them, but did not stop to count it. Jumping forwards toward the heap, I Linked my mind to the Elemental Fire and summoned it onto them. My fear for Eoan and anger at their attack was so strong that the flames did not appear gently. They made a streak in the sky and struck the creatures like a lightening bolt, burning all of the giant rodents until they stopped moving and the Fire went out. Behind it was left a pile of scorched fur and glistening fangs, connected raggedly with blackened bones.

With a stagger, I turned to drop to the ground beside the fallen Stardweller.

"Eoan?"

He sat up slowly with a groan, fingers covering his face. The backs of his hands were pierced with purple tooth marks and scratches, while thin, bluish blood ran down his arm from a deeper bite.

Afraid that they might have hurt his eyes, I reached out to pull his hands away from his face. His eyes were both closed and looked unhurt except for light scratches near them, but there was more scrapes and teeth marks on his face.

"Eoan, what were those things?" I gasped, astounded at the ferocity that would drive a rodent to knock a man down and tear at him in that manner.

"Scurries," he said hoarsely, jerking his hands away to cover his face again, "always hungry. Forgot to tell you much about them...water. I need water, Nerheem."

Too tired from running and fighting to stand up, I crawled over to grab the water skin and take it back to him. I thought that he wanted a drink, but he began pouring it out in his hands to splash it over his face. Seeing what he wanted, I took the bottle back and poured it into his cupped hands for him. The bites were a nasty, dark purple color on his glimmering skin, and with the condition of the Scurries teeth I began to worry that they might get infected despite his cleaning.

"We should find a village and have someone look at those," I told him, knowing that many villages had an herb woman or wiseman that could heal wounds, "let me help you wash the ones on your face, then we will go."

To my consternation, he just pulled away from me and covered his face again, rocking back and forth as he moaned, "not enough time. Not enough time!"

"What's wrong with you?" made rough by alarm, I jerked a hand forward and grasped his wrists tightly, dragging them from his eyes, "what is it, Eoan? Look at me!"

His eyes opened, silver orbs of fear. They looked at me wildly for a moment before seeming to focus. Gradually the pupils narrowed. He let out a shaken sigh and the fear was replaced with a defeated calm.

"The dust will claim me now, Nerheem. The bite of even one scurry can be deadly, if not treated by special herbs by one who knows. So many...they are poison, Nerheem, because of the fungus that Scurries breed and consume in their underground burrows."

His hand stretched out, shaking just a little, to point out the small tunnels dug into the bank of the gully, "I did not notice them when I stopped here. Now the dust will claim me for sure..."

"No." the word was soft and harsh as a fall of cold snow. Standing up, I tried to force the Stardweller to his feet.

"We will find a village with a healer to cure you. You can't just give up and die because some rodents bit you!"

He stayed on the ground, pulling his hands away from mine again. Bowing his head into them, he would not look at me any more, "do not make it harder, Nerheem. There is no village close enough to save me. I saw a man die of Scurry bites once. The beginning will overtake me soon. My ship has already been burnt, now is the end."

For the second time in my free life I was overcome by helplessness. I paced back and forth, stomping as I tried to think, "what about Soleinden?"

"You know that it would be worse than poison for us to go there, even if it were close enough. A Stardweller and a white-haired wizard are hard to disguise, if we tried. Still, it is too far."

I threw my mind back to Lune's teaching, wishing, not for the first or last time, that I had paid more attention to him when I had the chance. What would he do for a venomous bite? For he would say that it was not poison unless you ingested it, while an injected bite or sting was venom. He had spoken of herbs for snakebite, but their names all escaped me, besides the fact that they probably did not grow in the Dustlands. He had also showed me how to put a tourniquet on the bitten limb and use a sharp knife to drain some of the venom away.

I threw a quick glance at Eoan. You can not put a tourniquet on someone who has been struck on the face. It would have to go on their throat, which would destroy them much quicker than the poison. And Eoan had already washed the wounds on his face in an attempt to get rid of the venom. All I could do was hope to lessen the amount of evil absorbed through the bites on his hands.

He patiently let me wash them in more water, trying to squeeze the venom out of the cuts. But even the deeper one on his arm had stopped bleeding by now, they were so narrow.

All he said to me was, "even a wizard cannot stop someone's light from going out when it is time."

I remembered Sultane and ground my teeth together. All the arts of Erilaz that I knew could not help him. If only I had possessed the Philosopher's Stone then! I would still have a faithful friend at my side, an ally in every extremity. But once again I had chosen to follow my inquisitive mind, search for knowledge beyond the normal, rather than listen to given council and stay with my companions. The Omberling's city had drawn me away to explore its mysteries while my friend unwittingly stepped into a trap alone.

Bitterly I rued that decision and hated myself for it as the day turned into darkness and that terrible night drew on.

I will not describe it in detail. Every moment was a year of the grimmest battle as the venom flowed through Eoan and destroyed him before my eyes. But as the stars covered the sky and he lay weakly with his head pillowed on my lap, he spoke of things which you must know for this story to be concluded.

First it began with wandering stories of his time as a captain of a star ship. Interspersed with Stardwellers slang which he never used otherwise, he described every rope and bit of rigging on his ship, telling me the shape of the hull in detail as if he saw it before his eyes at the moment. Eventually his stories went back in time, slowly, until he was remembering his childhood. He said a little about his parents, whom he had greatly admired even while rebelling against them in many aspects of daily life. His father had taught him to navigate the sky, so that when he was given his own ship one day it would fly perfectly in formation with the others as it should. His mother had told him legends of both the Dustland and the stars, as she had once dwelt long ago in the dunes below, before being raised to the sky by his father.

Then there had been the day when his parents called him to the railing of the ship to see something strange that was being built beneath them, in the air just above the Dust.

I gave a small start at Eoan's next words, though I soon calmed myself so as not to disturb him.

"The Dark Passages, Nerheem! That is what was being built beneath us. The dark figures that you call the Founders were putting it together across the Dustlander's sky, blocking a strip of gray from them and brown from us."

Eoan explained how he had leaned over to watch them with a Stardweller's long sight, saw how they used magical powers to lift huge slabs of stone up into the air to form a roofless bridge, first writing inscriptions on the stones with tools that left no mark, in colors of Fire, Air, Earth and Water.

"Then they sealed them one to the other with those same powers of nature that you use, Nerheem, all four to seal each stone. It was done so carefully, with each strand of power interlacing with the next across the tiles. I could see it all, like the finest lace wrapped around every stone! You must have broke that when you made the tile fall, my friend..."

He trailed off for a long time, before continuing to tell how the Founders had raised walls of stone, carved with the powers of their minds, around the bridge tiles until the Stardwellers had sailed passed and could see no more. The next night Eoan had looked again, but the dark figures were already far across the sky, building under other gleaming ships.

"From one side of the lit world to the other, with many branches, it runs. But does it go into the dark?"

This idea seemed to frighten Eoan, who grabbed my hand suddenly and begged for me not to let him fall into the dark side of the world. With tears in my eyes I promised that he would go beyond the mists into the light, where his ship was already waiting for him.

Near the last, darkest part of the night it all came to an end. When I was sure that he was gone, beyond all shaking and pleading, I stood up stiffly and wiped the tears from my eyes, "but the Dust shall not take him! He will have a pyre to send his light beyond the Great Mists."

Until almost dawn I dragged tables and chairs from the Omberling's houses below, smashing them with rocks, Powerpointing or my hands alone until I had a great heap on top of the dune overlooking the hibernating city. Then I laid a blanket on the top slab, making it as straight and comfortable as possible. Eoan's light had truly left him, so that he no longer glimmered in the night and felt cold to the touch.

As soon as he was set on the blanket I stepped back and made a light and warmth around him that I will never forget. Fire scorched from me until I was empty and the pile of old, dry wood burned like a monster unleashed.

As it burned to coals and there was nothing but ashes and a fled spirit left of my friend, exhaustion overcame me. Dizzy, I slumped to the ground nearby and fell into an unconsciousness more close to a dead faint than sleep.

Blackness was all that I saw until sometime in the late morning, when my instincts forced me awake at a light sound.

I reached for my crossbow, but it had been left in the gully along with the supplies. My eyes were sticky and gritted as they blinked open, trying to find the source of the noise. It came again, a faint shifting of dust and ragged breathing. Looking towards the fire, I saw a woman crouched beside it. Her face was dirty and streaked, her clothes ragged and torn. There was more fear in her eyes as she turned from warming her hands at the dying coals than I felt in all of my mind.

Chapter 29: A Bargain

"Who are you?" I asked in a hoarse, dead voice.

I did not really care for the answer, I simply felt that we should do more than stare at each other forever.

The woman gazed at me without answering. I had the faint feeling that I should know her face and that she was trying to recall my own. Most Dustlanders do not have red hair, but hers was a bright red, clipped short and spiky around her head. Though she looked worn by recent sorrows, she was not old. Only middle-aged, perhaps on the younger side of the slate.

In better circumstances she was what would have been called beautiful, though at the time she was too tousled and I too weary for me to see it. But I could not remember her, so after a short effort I discarded the idea to ask roughly, "what do you want?"

"I—just..." she gestured at the fire, obviously unable to say more. Her voice sounded dry, so I bent to drag up a water skin from nearby and toss it to her.

"Oh, thank you. I hope you don't mind—" Another gesture at the coals. She looked at the water like a hungry man gazing at a feast.

"It is my best friend's fire," I told her with a grim smile, "it is not for me to say if you can warm yourself at it or not."

At that she looked around wildly, until I added, "I burnt him to ashes on it last night. After he went beyond."

"Oh!" She snatched up the skin and took a long drink, before saying in a softer tone, "I am sorry. This is a cruel land. As to your question...I am Swiftwing."

The name was pronounced as if I should know it and, perhaps, condemn her for it. Instead I grunted and crossed my arms on my knees, leaning my chin on them to stare at the red coals.

Swiftwing looked over her shoulder once, towards the south, before settling at a little distance from the coals in front of me. She had been panting when I first awoke, but now her breathing was steadier.

"You don't, ah, do you come from Soleinden or near the king's castle?"

"No." I looked at her once, then away.

"I'm sorry," she repeated, bowing her head, "I hate to intrude on your grief. What is your name?"

"Nerheem," I said without thinking, before giving myself a shake and correcting the statement, "Nolin Nearham."

A light seemed to come on in her eyes and she asked, "the wizard I have heard tell of, who makes crops grow and water fall from empty skies?"

"Perhaps," wary now, I eyed her more closely. She could be someone from the capital city, or even one of Angrist's informers sent out to find me. The light of the pyre must have been visible for many miles in the dark.

Noticing my distrust, she shook her head quickly, "I mean you no harm, Nolin. Please...do not look at me that way. I would never betray you to the king if that is what you are thinking. In fact, I need your help if you will give it to me."

Her hands had clenched together anxiously, turning white at the knuckles. They were slim hands, but capable. As we spoke they often fidgeted, clasping and unclasping or twisting into the fabric of her clothes.

"Tell me what you want." I said, giving no inflection or kindliness to the words to encourage her.

Swiftwing heard the inelegance of them, but did not comment or let it affect her. She just nodded slowly before explaining, "I have heard that you are not friends with Angrist, or else I might not trust you with this story—"

"Trust can be dangerous," I interrupted, to which she only shot me a quick look, before going on.

"My husband and I were...traveling through the Dustlands on a quest when we ran afoul of Angrist's men by drinking at one of their wells. We were attacked by them and my husband told me to run, turning to fight them in order to give me time to escape."

Her face contracted with the memory, eyes filling with unshed tears, "I ran, but not for long. Turning back, I followed the soldiers secretly. They took my husband to their castle, where I could not follow any further. I would have bribed my way in, but I have no money. So I, well, stayed stealthily in the town trying to find out what had happened to him."

"Brave of you."

"I had to know. Anyway, I learned that he was being held in the castle's dungeons until the king could decide what to do with him. But, unfortunately, I was discovered by soldiers soon afterwards and had to flee again. Do not worry: I was not followed out of the town. But I resolved to find help in order to rescue my husband as soon as possible. Will you help me?"

My feelings were too drained to be diplomatic or empathetic, "what would be in it for me?"

An expression crossed her face at those words, one which I could not read though it contained measures of hope and despair equally.

"I already told you that I have no money," Swiftwing said carefully, "and you can see that I have nothing else of value with me. Even water and warmth I must borrow or beg. But my husband does have a powerful Runestone with him. He would give it to you if you set him free, I'm sure."

That stirred my interest, beginning to pull me out of the apathy I had been sunk grimly in before, "a Runestone? What sort of Runestone?"

Swiftwing shook her head, "a very powerful one. He keeps it concealed in his coat and does not tell even me its meaning. But he said that it was the most powerful Runestone ever made, being more than just Runes on a stone, whatever that means. Once, he said that it would cure any ill known to man. I don't know what he meant, but if it is that powerful it must be valuable. A wizard...might wish to possess something that potent."

Moving closer to her, I picked up a partially burnt splinter from the pyre. Passing it over, I made the demand, "show me what the Runes on it looked like, as close as you can remember. Please?"

I recalled myself enough to add the polite word and correct tone at the end. Taking the twig between her fingers as if used to sketching, she shut her eyes for a moment in concentration.

Upon opening them, she began to draw in the dust, "I've only seen it once or twice, briefly, so these may not be accurate. They glowed a yellow-gold color, almost like sunlight near the end of the day. The stone itself was white, very pure and smooth."

"White," I breathed, leaning over to study the Runes she was making in the dirt. Solron was not white, not naturally. And quartz was supposed to be an inferior stone to make Runes on. But she had said that this powerful stone was supposed to be able to cure any ill known to man, according to her husband. Could it actually be the Philosopher's Stone? Or even a strong panacea?

Either way, it was something I could not pass up lightly. My deepest frustration was that it would come just one day too late if I were to rescue this Runestone carrier now. But for future use it would be invaluable.

If I was to rescue this man, I would have to go into the very castle of Angrist, King of the Dust, who already had a few grudges against me before I tried freeing one of his prisoners. I would have to wear a disguise. And find an excuse to enter the castle and move about it freely...

Standing up, I looked down at the red-haired woman, "I'll free your husband. But do I have your assurance that he will give the stone to me if I do?"

Swiftwing hesitated just a moment, before nodding, "I can't promise what he'll say, of course. But I think that he would be happy to give it to you in return for his freedom. How will you rescue him without danger to yourself?"

"There is always danger," I pulled off my cape and began slicing it in half lengthwise with my knife, "But I will make it as little as possible by a disguise."

"What will you pretend to be, to get into the castle?"

I gave her another grim smile, "what better to pretend to be, than what everyone already thinks you are?"

Leaving the strips of thick, brown fabric on the ground, I turned to go down the hill to where Eoan had brought our camp gear the day before. His pack of bottles, my backpack and the bundle of Omberling treasure I had dropped during the fight were all laying in the bottom of the gulch. There was also a few extra water skins, the crossbow and Eoan's fire starting tools. I began to gather everything up, hanging it from my shoulders or sticking it under my arms. Swiftwing had followed me hesitantly, and now took some of the bundles from me to help carry them back to the top of the hill beside the burnt-out pyre.

Once everything was laid out, I opened Eoan's pack and took the strange black bottle with the silver flakes from it. Leaning over the hot coals of the pyre regardless of the heat, I stuck it deep down into them. It belonged to the Stardweller and no one else should have it. I put it where the heat would melt it beyond use, so that it would not be picked up later.

Then I carefully unrolled the Omberling hanging with the vase inside. To my surprise the glass was unbroken, even the narrow stem still firmly attached. Setting it aside, I picked up the hanging to look it over. Swiftwing gave a soft gasp as it glimmered in the light and I saw her fingers itching to touch the gold-laced fabric.

"It would make a fine wizard's cloak, wouldn't it?" I said, holding it out so that she could feel it. The nervous fingers ran over the edge of it carefully as she nodded without a word.

The hanging was wide enough to cover my shoulders, falling to the backs of my knees behind. Using a bit of string, I tied it in place. The cloth was silky smooth against my back, seeming colder than it should have been. Picking up the pieces of brown fabric from the old cloak, I wrapped them carefully around my head until hair and face were mostly hidden.

Only my eyes and nose would be clearly visible which, hopefully, would not be recognizable enough to give me away. Nomads often wore such a headdress to keep out the dust, though it was usually made of a finer material. A wild wizard would not seem too strange for wearing it, or too suspicious. And my other clothes were much like those of any Dustlander by now. As a last measure I tucked the alkahest into one pocket, while carrying the Omberling vase in my hands.

"Will you stay here and keep the rest of these things until I return?" I asked, gesturing around at our packs and camp gear, "it may take a few days, but there should be food to last you in my pack."

Swiftwing nodded, standing up to offer me her hand, "please, be careful. I'll be fine here, just bring me my husband as soon as you can."

I shook the proffered hand briefly, feeling awkward while doing it. Then I looked once more at the heap of glowing coals and ashes on top of the hill, thinking a silent farewell to my lost friend. I knew that, if he could see me now, he would be pleased that I was not spending my days in moping or weeping, instead setting off on a new journey.

As I turned to go, Swiftwing added, "oh, yes. You'll know my husband because he is tall, with dark hair and a mustache. Also, his coat has gold buttons."

I gestured understanding, moving on my way. Down the hill towards the south, over many dunes towards the valley where Soleinden and Hahstgart castle lay.

Chapter 30: Into the Castle

Near noon I reached the low cliffs which bordered the valley on the northern side, giving a clear view of the castle and city. Laying in a pile of small boulders on top of the cliff, I watched for any sign of unrest below. A vehicle was moving down the road from the castle towards the town, but not hurriedly. Dust spurted lazily from under its tires, drifting up in the warm noon air. I could not make out the shapes which would be bustling about their business in the town, or the ones which must be standing on the wall tops of the castle. They were there, undoubtedly, but there was not the sense of evil foreboding hanging over the valley that there had been last time I was near it.

"Now for the plunge," I muttered under my breath, prying myself off of the stones. From there I my way around the edges of the cliff into the dunes. The castle was set at a distance from the town, so it did not take me long to reach it from the cliffs. Before I had time to procrastinate any longer, I was knocking on the spike-studded, wooden gates. The arch which held the frame was fancifully domed, with one single, large blue stone set at its peak.

A man wearing a helmet and a shirt of scale armor leaned over the wall top above, "what do you want, desert scum?"

Making my voice rougher and deeper, I called back, "I would not speak of someone who brings a gift to your master that way. Especially one versed in deep mysteries."

At that moment another shape appeared beside the first on the walls, this one with a red cloak thrown energetically over one shoulder. They spoke for a moment, before the one with the red cloak called down, "what name do you go by, and what gift do you bring?"

"They call me Amulet, of the Omberlings," I swirled my own cape of re-purposed hanging behind me, "and I bring a vase of that kind to your king. I have heard of his fame even in my sequestered vaults and wish to see him in person."

This statement made them have an even longer, deeper discussion before the first man told me, "we are opening the gates. But if you try anything tricky, we won't hesitate to gut ya' so be on your best behavior!"

I allowed a small smile to creep up under the cloth covering my face as I replied, "my best and my worst are never far different."

In a few moments I heard gears being worked inside, along with the creaking of ropes. The gates swung open inwards, allowing me to enter. The arch was thick, displaying the stoutness of the walls, while the road was paved in pale sandstone tiles the size of a comfortable bed. Just inside the main courtyard, a group of rag-tag soldiers waited to escort me. The courtyard was wide and about fifty paces across to the steps leading up into the castle. I could make out the strange carvings of griffin-like creatures on the walls more clearly now, as well as noticing for the first time a garage, stables and barracks to the sides of the courtyard. In the open door of the garage I could see the roofless car which had once chased me for having stolen water, as well as two of its drivers lounging nearby.

Not letting my eyes rest on anything for long, as if it did not interest me in the least, I walked between the wary guards up to the door of the castle. The door was opened by a sort of page or door boy who was waiting outside of it, dressed in a gaudy uniform of sand-cat skins and gold medallions. Beyond it was a series of shorts passages, leading to a heavy door plated in iron. As I stepped inside, images from Eoan's story of capture began to flicker through my head. It was with an effort that I pushed them aside.

At the far end of a long hall, tiled in colorful stones, sat a hard, square sandstone throne. Near it were a pair of potted plants with feathery, drooping limbs, a show of wealth in this land. Behind the throne stood a young woman with despair planted on her face, waving a silken fan over the head of the man occupying the seat of power.

This, I knew, must be Angrist. He was just a little over average height, with powerful shoulders and a heavy, red face. But there was nothing lax or stupid about him. His chin was firm, nose sharp and eyes twinkling brightly. The hair which hung down the back of his head was a plain brown, ornamented with two amber beads near the temples on one side. His clothes were good and there was a golden buckle on the belt which crossed his chest at an angle, but other than that he wore no decorations to show his rank.

Followed by the soldiers, I came and knelt before him. For just a minute I saw an image of Eoan slapping him across the face and could have laughed bitterly, but the moment passed as quickly as it had come. This was serious business.

"My servants say that you are a wizard," Angrist spoke in a rumbling, confident voice, not without arrogance, "how are we to believe this claim?"

"I could easily prove it to you," tilting my head up to look at him, I added, "but first, I bring you a present from the sleeping place of the Omberlings."

With these words I held out the vase of black glass, letting the light of nearby torches play over its silky sides.

With a gesture, the king had one of his soldiers bring it to him. He turned it around slowly, before nodding once and waving a servant to take it away, "it will join my collection. Few venture into the city of the Omberlings, once known as Ombreel, to bring such things out. But you claim to live there. Very interesting."

Still disguising my voice, I returned easily, "the places few dare tread are the ones I cherish. The spirits that few dare face are my chosen companions. It is only word of your bright fame which drew me from those vaults to see the man which had won it."

Angrist seemed pleased at my silvered words, though he only drew his hand in a caress over the arm of the throne to show it. When he spoke again it was with an edge of cunning, "so, perhaps you have heard word of another of your cloth, even in Ombreel. A young man, with white hair, who is a wizard. He disrupted some of my plans with his magic a time ago, then disappeared into the desert. Have you heard of him?"

His gaze was sharp on me.

I bowed my head slightly, before raising my eyes to his again, "I have heard of him. In fact, I have heard that he died, bitten by Scurries beyond saving. But that is only a caravan's rumor, no more."

"I see," Angrist grunted, "show me some of your magic, wizard, so that I may be entertained."

Guessing what he was watching for, I did not use Fire or Powerpointing in my display. Instead I summoned orbs of Water and had them dance above my hands, before dropping them with light splashes into the feathery plants. Then I made one of his soldiers levitate using Air, much to the soldier's discomfiture, before setting him safely on the ground again. My last feat was to make my knife levitate through the air along with a group of Water orbs and slice through them repeatedly, flashing around as if possessed. In the end, it zipped back to my hand, while the water flew towards the roof and disappeared.

"Pretty." Angrist observed, "though hardly practical. Even some Charlatans have done near as much, claiming that they were wizards."

"That was just a small sample of what I can do. Though to a man who lives alone in the Dustlands, being able to summon Water is not impractical." I told him calmly, "is there anything in particular you wish to see?"

The king's eyes narrowed, "yes, in fact, there is. I wish to see your face clearly. Remove that headdress so I may see what Amulet of the Omberlings is really made of."

This was a problem which I had foreseen, but had still been anxious about. The king would not be diverted by white lies and simple tales, of that I was sure. His persistence in baiting Eoan had shown that clearly. He needed to be shown what he thought was the truth, in order to believe the fantasy I was creating.

"King, I have sworn to never show my face to any man. My life in the Omberling city has imprinted marks on it so deep that I wish none to see it." I said, forestalling his comment by a raised hand, "but to you, I will give what none other would recieve. I only ask that you let your servants go and tell your guards to stand in the outer chamber. Unless you are afraid of being alone with me?"

The last was said with no antagonism, but still the king turned a little more crimson in the face over it, "I do not fear any man, wizard or otherwise, when he is alone."

With a wave of his hand, he sent the soldiers away. The girl also departed, clearly relieved to be on her way. As soon as they were gone I began slowly unwinding the brown cloth from my face, at the same time weaving strands of Elements and Powerpointing around it. Earth made my hair dark like mud, even to the eyebrows, while I used Air and power mixed to distort my features into deep lines and a flattened chin. Water gave a wet gleam to my eyes. It was uncomfortable to hold, but I could not risk being recognized at this point in time.

Angrist looked at me closely, before grunting, "I can see why you hide your features. I've never seen such a strange face in all the Dustlands. Though it seems to me that it is only vanity that makes you wear those wrappings and no kindness to others."

Letting out an internal sigh of relief, I put the headdress gradually back in place while releasing the magic, "every man has his little bit of pride, your majesty. I'm sure even you feel it."

"Now you mock me," but the king did not seem displeased, only thoughtful, "I wish that I could get my hands on that Wizard Nerheem. He killed my chief steward and orator, you know, as well as injuring the executioner. I will have to send out spies to see if he still lives, or if your rumors are true."

He seemed to be lost in thought for a time, while I stayed kneeling on the hard floor before him. I knew that his cruel whims could make me dance for the smallest of infractions.

Eventually his gaze came back to me.

"You are a strange one, Amulet of the Omberlings. Most flee from me if they can, or only bend their backs because I force them. Unless they have something to gain. What do you want in return for your gift?"

"Gifts do not need repayment," I said slowly, but the king gave me an impatient tilt of his head, so I went on, "but if you will grant me a boon, I will ask one thing."

"Yes?"

"Allow me to stay in your castle for a day or two. It has been long since I saw human faces or spoke to anything but the half-dead."

"I can do better than that," Angrist jumped up from his throne to stride down to me, "I can offer you a place as one of my servants. I have never had a wizard working for me before: it might be useful. Especially if I need to send you to hunt down that other magician in the future. What do you say?"

His tone did not make it much of a choice. Luckily, it was a better favor than I had hoped for.

But I pretended to hesitate, "exalted king, I would like nothing more to serve you, because your path is one to greatness and power. But I have lived alone for many years, as I said. Though I may seek to speak to some of your followers at times, I would not like to be bothered by them when I wish to be alone."

"They won't bother you," Angrist waved his hand lightly in the air, before clapping both of them together, "I'll tell them not to. But you will come at my call and respond to me whenever I wish, won't you?"

"Your conversation will never seem low or tedious to me," I agreed, rising as he gestured for me to get to my feet.

"Good. I would hate to have to have such a powerful wizard gutted and hung on my door as a warning to others of his creed."

His soldiers came back with a tramping of feet and he gave them instructions to find me a room in the palace, as well as to let me roam where I wished without being heckled.

He did pull the chief of the soldiers aside and give him some extra commands, watching me out of the corners of their eyes. I stood quietly, apparently watching everything without seeking to spy on anyone. After a moment the officer came to lead me to a small cell built into one wall of the inner keep, only one hall away from where Angrist himself took his repose. It was bare except for a bed, but after so long spent living on the dunes it seemed like a luxury to have a cushion, blankets and a roof over my head.

The day was still not spent. Except for a small canteen of water, I had no goods to unpack in the room. Taking Angrist at his word that I may roam the castle freely, I left the little chamber to explore.

While I searched, I made sure to speak to servants and soldiers now and then, with the sort of light, earnest gossip that a man long unconnected from civilization might enjoy. I found the kitchens and borrowed a bottle of wine, brought it out to share with men lounging in the courtyard and even spoke to the scruffy bandits who drove the ragged car. The man with the Sand cat skin over his head was wary of me at first, but the wine soon warmed him. He talked about the long patrols he had to lead to protect the far-flung holdings of the king, and of the rough 'jokes' they played on the farmers along the way. He even mentioned the time he had chased me and the search that had ensued.

"Heck, I thought that wizard must 'ave died, falling down that crack," he grunted, "If I had known how much trouble he was going to cause, I would have sent a man down there to finish him off. But I suppose wizards can heal themselves with their voodoo, huh?"

"Some can," I shrugged, "healing has never been my type of magic."

"It wouldn't be," the driver slapped me on the shoulder with a rough chuckle shared by some nearby companions of his.

All that day, I noticed the officer Angrist had spoken to earlier, trailing me. He did it stealthily, at a distance, but still I noticed that, where ever I went, he was sure to follow. So when I found the passageway leading down to the dungeons, I asked the guard curiously where it went, but did not follow it when he told me.

I just shook my head and muttered, "stupid prisoners" before wandering off. That night I resisted the impulse to go searching there immediately. Instead, I made myself as comfortable as possible on the bed and slept lightly, senses alert for anyone slipping into the room. But no one came.

Chapter 31: The Prisoner

The next day Angrist called me up to entertain a group of rich merchants who were visiting him. They sat in a dining room in a separate hall, with another sandstone chair at its head for the king. The merchants were richly clothed in the simple Dustlander way, with layers of white and red fabrics as fine as a lady's handkerchief. I felt the king's eyes still on me, so I did not play with Fire at first. Instead I jumped up on the table and skipped lightly between the plates, making tiny flowers grow in cups of water or moss sprout across the edges of plates. It was Firendaze's training which kept me from spilling anything as I whirled across the well-laid board, before springing off the end with a cartwheel. The guests laughed, while Angrist clapped his hands, but still with a cautious eye upon me.

"These pretty games, you learned them in the city of the Omberlings?" the king asked, picking up a petite pink flower and shaking all the petals idly off of it, "I've never even seen flowers of this type before."

I bowed to him respectfully, "the city of the Omberlings brings strange dreams, your majesty. I've seen places in my mind, while meditating there, that are stranger than a Charlatan's claims of divine descent. Fields of green brighter than jade, skies of lapis blue."

He just grunted with a small touch of surprise in his face, so I added, "but perhaps this play is too minor for a great king like you. Allowed me to send for some items from the kitchen and I will make something a little more impressive to entertain important folks."

Angrist gave his sanction, so I gestured to one of his servants and whispered in his ear, "Bring me strong spirits from the kitchen and alum from whoever dyes the cloth in this castle."

He nodded once, with a frightened look at being sent on a mission for a wizard, and went running off. While he was gone I cleared a place in the center of a table, before calling up another servant that was waiting nearby, this one a young woman.

"Sit up here, girl. Prettily now, I'm not going to turn you into a spider or anything." She reluctantly arranged herself on the table, while the merchants laughed and nudged each other to see what I was going to do next. I took empty goblets and a golden plate from the table, making the girl hold a goblet in each hand and balance the plate upon her head. It sat there glittering on her smooth, dark hair, like some sort of ridiculous bonnet.

At that moment the manservant returned with my requested materials, one of each type which I promptly poured into the goblets.

"These are favorite drinks of the spirits of the dead," I announced, speaking in the rough, dark tone I had adopted for Amulet, "now, will someone give me a fowl's bone for the spirit's platter? Thank you."

I took the bone that a merchant proffered, laying it carefully on the plate on the girl's head.

Then I turned to the manservant abruptly. "You, get up on the table behind her. Take this torch from the wall and hold it in both of your hands. Steadily now, I won't have the picture ruined."

Now it was time to play with Fire, but carefully, so that Angrist would not suspect me of being the same person as Nolin Nearham. Stalking slowly back and forth in front of the servants, I began to mutter incantations and mystical words. They were humbug, but I knew how to make them sound impressive. When I was ready, I spun about and flung open my hands, pointing at the goblets, "come to me spirit of Malkin, ghost of Til and phantom of Shadus-Corom. Eat with us today, drink with us in your fiery forms!"

Blue flames sprang up in one goblet, narrow and graceful, jumping into the air in thin tendrils. Green ones in the same form arose from the other goblet, making the girl gasp and tremble. On her head the plate erupted in a pillar of plain orange flames, sizzling eerily while consuming the fowl's bone. The servants were both frozen in fear, watching the flames from the corners of their eyes. Colored light played across the two faces.

As the fires burned I made them dance, swirling about and catching at the flames in the torch that the manservant held. Sometimes they seemed to dance with each other, supple forms moving to unheard music. Other times they bent low and trembling as is weary.

Then, slowly, they died down, bowing once to the audience before disappearing. Once they were gone I gave a small sigh of weariness as I released the concentration and energy needed to uphold the flames. Controlling them had taken all of my mental powers.

I was just about to relax and let the servants down when the catastrophe hit. A small ember jumped off of the torch, burning into the manservant's arm. Strung up as he was at the idea of participating in summoning spirits, he startled and dropped the torch. It fell onto the girl's head, knocking the plate off before rolling back onto the man's feet. He jumped around wildly to put it out, while the girl screamed and leaped off of the table, dropping goblets and spilling unused alcohol behind her.

In a moment, Angrist was on his feet glaring at the manservant, who crouched pitifully to the floor with fear stamped on his face.

"How dare you interrupt the wizard's show, dog?" He shouted at the servant, making him shake all the more, "he told you to stand steadily and you did not! Now you will pay the price!"

I raised a hand, risking my position to interfere, "the show was over, sir. He has caused no lasting harm."

Angrist's eyes bored into me, "clumsiness in a servant is not allowed. He will be punished to teach a lesson to them all."

Though I felt sick with horror at having caused it, even inadvertently, I had to bow my head in agreement.

The servant gave a tiny shriek as the king gestured to the soldiers who stood watching against the wall, "guards, take him out and have him whipped, then cut off his head. As for you, girl."

His eyes turned to the kneeling maidservant, "go back to your rooms and do not return tonight. You are disgraced for letting his folly effect you."

Soon the king settled in his chair and the feast resumed as if nothing had happened. The thought of the poor servant's fate bothered me still. As I looked on Angrist's arrogant face, so complacent in his power, I boiled with anger inside. One day, I thought, I would make him pay a little back for all of the pain he had caused others. Even if it was just by stealing a prisoner from under his nose.

I did a few more little tricks for the assembly, halfheartedly, before taking my leave. Angrist stayed behind, regaling his guests with a long war story. It seemed that the officer had stopped following me, at least for a time, so I took the opportunity to wander down towards the dungeons.

Because of the orders given them concerning me, the guard did not stop me when I stalked past muttering to myself about finding somewhere dark and damp to meditate in.

The dungeons were below the level of most of the keep, down a flight of narrow, rough steps. At the bottom of them a hallway ran to the right and left, lit by a single lantern hanging from the ceiling above. To the right lay a series of dungeons with solid doors studded with spikes, one of which had soft, sorrowful moans coming from inside it.

I hoped that Swiftwing's husband was not in one of those. But to the left were open cells with iron bars in front, for less dangerous prisoners I suspected. Or at least ones who had displeased the king to a lesser degree.

A guard patrolled up and down the hall as well, but he did not question me as I strolled down the hall to the left. As I walked, I peered into the cells casually. One held a fellow with dusty golden locks tangled and matted on his head. He was busily writing on the wall with a stick of charcoal, though whether it was his will or a dreadful poem I could not tell. The only other prisoner was back in the darkest corner of this side of the dungeon, half-hidden in the shadows. At first I looked at him without really seeing him, my mind adjusted only to find Swiftwing's husband, the man with the powerful Runestone.

Gradually, my eyes shifted to see in the dark. I felt my breath catch in shock. The prisoner was Tallray.

He sat in the center of the floor, ignoring the pile of straw that was the only furniture. In one hand he seemed to be holding a small pebble encrusted with some form of green dungeon-slime, while the other hand held a thin wisp of straw which he prodded at it with. He had not noticed me yet.

I looked around once to make sure that the guard was going the other way, then leaned on the bars, "Tallray, what are you doing here?"

"Ah, Nolin!" He looked up, seemingly as little surprised as if I had dropped into his workshop unannounced. He recognized me by my voice, I suppose, as my face was still covered.

"I am studying this bit of microbial action. See the fungus? It may just form penicillin, if given enough moisture. If only I had a micro—"

"Tallray," I interrupted, "why are you here, in this place, in the Dustlands at all?"

"Why, my friend," the Alchemist gave me a smile, "I was looking for you."

"But how did you get here? That tile was sealed back into place, unless you decided to lift it yourself?" I could not keep a bit of sharp derision from entering my voice, though I knew that Tallray was the only Keeper who had tried to stop the others from exiling me.

The Alchemist's tone became much more serious, "that is why I came looking for you. Bad things have been happening since you left, my friend. The stone in the floor would not hold back in its place correctly, even after Tavierfin had mortared it there. It dropped out again, after which we discovered that the door passed it was not working any more. Soon other tiles began coming loose in different parts of the Dark Passages, shutting off doors and making dangerous holes in the floor. Gleeb almost fell through one, while busy compiling notes in his head. Some sort of crazy bandits came through another and Firendaze had to fight them off. You started a chain reaction that is destroying the Dark Passages."

There was no real accusation in his tone, only grave explanation, but I felt the last words like a blow. I had thought that the lifting of the tile was innocent in itself, that the only repercussions of that act had fallen on me, and that all too harshly. Now I was being told that there might be something to the Keeper's insistence that it had been the wrong thing to do, that it had hurt the passages themselves.

Just then the guard walked up behind me and grunted, "hey, what are you doing? You're talking to the prisoner."

He gripped the spear he carried tighter, looking at me as if he was considering using it. Quickly recovering myself, I told him in Amulet's voice, "this prisoner stopped me and claimed that he has a magic stone or relic of some sort on him. I don't know if I should believe him, but he claims that if I bring him better food from the kitchens he'll show me."

"I could just beat it out of him," the guard suggested, his suspicion of me falling away, though his grip on the spear did not loosen.

I snorted with sham amusement, "no, these nomads can be stubborn and I don't want him to lie about its use and get me killed if it is truly magic. I'll bring the food, if you don't mind and won't trouble me when I return."

The guard shrugged, "I don't care what the cellrat eats. As long as he doesn't escape it can't hurt me. Besides, the boss said to let you do what you wanted."

With a nod of agreement, I strode away. In the kitchen, I picked up a warm loaf of bread and a slab of some sort of cold, greasy meat. Along with them, I brought a small bottle of medium-grade wine. I could not make the food look too good, or else the guard would begin to wonder at how friendly I was with the prisoner. At the same time, it had to be good enough to bargain with a nomad and actually nice enough for Tallray.

When I returned to the dungeon, the guard made sure to stay at a respectful distance. Rumor had already spread about my performance 'summoning spirits' up above and he did not want to risk incurring a wizard's wrath. At the same time, he did watch me carefully to make sure that I did not open the cell.

As I had been getting the food ready, my mind had been working on Tallray's story, When I passed the provisions through I asked, "tell me, when did that red-haired 'friend' or yours who lived below the workshop become your wife? Because it is Swiftwing who sent me here to find you. I came in disguise, as Angrist has it out for me already."

Tallray's expression became sheepish, as well as it might, "ah, well, we were married on the evening before you became an apprentice. Remember my wedding coat? I was not able to change before being summoned to the Keeper's meeting. Luckily, they did not suspect why I had a new, fancy suit. But tell me, is she unharmed?"

"That long?" I stared at him, then remembered to nod to show that she was unhurt, "so, I'm not the only rebel. But now we must continue business. Show me the Philosopher's Stone so that the guard does not become suspicious. Yes, I know of it. Swiftwing described it to me as a promise of payment if I rescued her husband, whom she did not name."

Tallray hesitated, before opening the lining on the inside of his jacket and taking out a Runestone. It was about six inches square and an inch thick, pure white as Swiftwing had told me. The Runes on it glittered a living yellow-gold, full of such power that I could feel it from where I stood.

It made my fingers reach for it unconsciously, before drawing them back, "now pretend that you are telling me about it. But actually, tell me more about the Dark Passages and why you came here. Do you know why they are coming apart?"

Tallray's long hands brushed over the stone, holding it half-way towards me as he spoke quietly, "we are not really sure why the stones are falling. Corky looked at them and said that there was a weave made of Elements which he had never noticed before, holding them all together. His idea was that it was broken at some places, but he could not fix them because he only has three of the required Elements. So I thought of you. And decided to come find you in hopes that you could fix the passages, since you have all four. Swiftwing, bless her stubborn heart, would not let me come alone."

"A weave of Elements..." I remembered suddenly what Eoan had told me while dying just a few nights ago. That he had seen the Founders write on the Runestones with every Element, and then fit them together with a web of the same.

Could I replicate the web, even with a command of all four Elements? And was it worth putting it back together for people who had exiled me, who never wanted to have anything to do with me again, just because I was an experimenter?

Seeing my hesitation, Tallray added pleadingly, "please, Nolin. Do not hold a grudge against us. I have come to find you knowing that you are better than that, wishing that you had never been exiled no matter what you did. Help us, my friend. We need you back among us, or else this great work called the Dark Passages will fall to pieces and our lives with it. Please, help us."

I looked at him for a long, level moment, everything in my life weighing in the balance.

I nodded slowly, "I will not come back among you, but the Dark Passages I will fix. Not only that, but I will get you out of here."

The Alchemist shook his head, "it is too dangerous. If you are caught, which you would be with all of these guards and walls, you would be killed and the Dark Passages left to ruin. Fix them before all else. I am safe here, for now."

"I will do both!" I insisted loudly, before remembering to lower my voice, "You must give me the Philosopher's Stone, Tallray. At least for now. I need it in order to put the stones back into place in the Passages."

The gears in my mind were already starting to turn over a plan that would allow me to rescue Tallray, fit the stones back into place and get me my revenge on Angrist, all with one powerful weapon.

I just needed the White Stone in able to claim that weapon, "swiftwing said that you would give it to me if I rescued you, anyways. And the guard will get suspicious if you do not."

With a look like a mother giving up her only child, Tallray passed the stone through the bars to me. I tucked it under my Omberling cloak, turning to walk towards the exit.

"Hey, did you get what you wanted? Is it magical?" the guard stopped me to ask, darting glances between the cell and the bulge under my cloak.

"Somewhat. It may be of slight use, if he is not a complete liar." I shrugged, pushing past him to walk up the steps and traverse the palace to my rooms.

The next day I convinced Angrist to let me go back to the Omberling city to fetch something which I claimed I had left behind, that would make my magic even stronger. At first he wanted to send soldiers with me, even a vehicle to make the trip quicker, but I was just able to dissuade him, explaining that the soldiers would not like to go near the city, and promising to bring him a great, unexpected treasure when I returned. I think it was the last promise which convinced him, though it was also the last promise which secretly held his undoing.

I took provisions with me, enough for two people to live off of for more than one day. No one in the kitchens challenged me, nor the guards at the gate. Angrist had given the command to let me go freely.

It was a relief to walk out of that castle, though on the way I had to pass a group of frightened farmers being herded in to explain why they had not paid the last tax set upon them by the tyrant. But once I was beyond the cliff to the north and out of sight I pulled the hot, sweaty wrappings from my head and turned to look in the direction of the castle for a moment, "you'll pay for everything now, Angrist! By tomorrow's twilight there will be no more poor farmers whipped at your commands, nor servants or Stardwellers, either!"

Tucking the headdress under one arm, I trudged on. It was noon when I reached the hill where Eoan's pyre had stood. The ashes and coals still lay in a pile, cooled and spread out by the winds. The black bottle sat in the center, deformed by heat. Not at a great distance from it, on the far slope of the hill, Swiftwing had set up her camp.

The little heap of our bags made a wind break on one side, while she had scooped out a hollow of sand to make it more protected. The ashes of a small fire lay at the foot of the hollow.

"Did you free him?" She looked up at me when I came to a stop beside her, her eyes and voice filled with a painful anxiety.

"Not yet." I knelt down in front of her, meeting her gaze, "I am sorry that I did not recognize you at first. It has been a handful of years since we met, and then only briefly. Though you could have told me your husband's name."

She looked down at the ground, fiddling with a splinter of wood from the fire, "I did not want you to know who we were at first. I...wanted to test you, perhaps, to see if your heart was good enough to rescue him without a reason."

I felt my jaw tighten into a straight, hard line "then I'm sorry to have disappointed you."

I slid the white Runestone onto the ground between us. She looked up at it in surprise, then at me questioningly, "where is Tallray?"

"I'm going to get him out of Angrist's dungeons soon," standing up, I gestured at the silent city laying below, "but first, I must raise the Omberlings."

Snatching up the stone again, I added, "that fool husband of yours wanted me to leave him in bondage so that I could fix the Dark Passages without risking myself saving him. But that's not how it is going to work. If I can raise the Omberlings, I will do both with their aid. If not, I still rescue Tallray first, I just do it alone."

Swiftwing, of course, had little idea what I meant about the Omberlings. But she trailed after me curiously as I made my way down into the city. She was not lacking in courage, even if it was mostly of the pointless sort.

Once in the main square of Ombreel, I stood in front of the central pillar and considered the indent where the White Stone was meant to lay. I did not know what would happen when I put it in its place. Was it only an unlocking mechanism, to remove the glass so that I could awake and cure the Omberlings manually? Or would it take the stone from me and do everything itself?

Slowly, I held out the Runestone and dropped it smoothly into place. It fell flat into the indent with a soft click. For a moment, nothing happened.

Then the Runes on the stone began to glow brighter and the pillar to shiver. Stepping back for fear that it would fall to pieces, I looked up at the top of the antennea. The metal rod on it had flakes of rust coming off of it, shaken into the air like water off of a dog's pelt. A low, deep thrumming was beginning to fill the air around me.

"Stay back!" I called to Swiftwing, waving her away from the square. She stood near the last houses around it, watching with a pale face. The metal rod shook off all of the rust, showing beneath it a thin line of shining blue. The very tip of the antenna began to glow an intense, neon color, while the thrumming became louder. Soon it was so loud that I could not hear anything else, while gusts of wind whipped around the square, carrying dust with it.

I stumbled further back in surprise as the tip of the rod gleamed white-hot and shot sparks off, long, jagged lines of power like lightening. They reached out all across the city, touching each house in a web of energy. I could hear them crackling above me with maddening energy.

The sound of breaking glass shattered above the thrumming noise, while the spark of Erilaz in me leaped up and burned in harmony with it, so that I almost felt like I was on fire. On instinct, I spread my arms wide and shouted above the noise, "Omberlings, I command you to awake! I call you to life again! Arise!"

More suddenly than it had began, the noise and lightening went away. Everything was ghostly, sharply still. I gazed around, waiting to see what would happen next. Swiftwing had shrunk back against a house wall, hands clasped in front of her and eyes shining.

At first, nothing changed. A minute drew out to a painful point as the dust settled and I heard one last tinkle of glass from far off in the village. With a glance, I noticed that the Philosopher's Stone was still in its place, Runes dimmed now.

The sound of footsteps, light and rustling, began to fill the streets. Something moved in the doorway of a nearby house, a shadow taking form. Shapes silently poured out into the square around me, pulling rags and veils from their faces. My breath caught in my throat as I realized that they were not entirely opaque. I could see through them indistinctly.

Faces were revealed, pale and gray, as misty as a mountain dawn. Eyes like dark slots, mouths just faintly seen, expressions unreadable. Their black robes, made of many layers of thin, fluttering cloth, blew out in the wind around them even though they were less solid than their surroundings.

Their hair was dark, or as pale white as bone. It waved in the air, gentle strands, translucent as a snowflake.

No one spoke. They stood in ranks, staring at me, while I gazed back in wonder. Realizing that I must make the first move, I grasped the Philosopher's Stone.

Holding it up above my head, I declared, "I have the White Stone!"

"It is too late..." the words came from the whole crowd like a sigh. I blinked, uncomprehending until they went on, "too late for us to be cured...too late for life."

The stone sunk down to hang at the end of my arms, my words gone dry and hollow, "too late? Then...you are dead?"

A rustle of nods moved through the crowd, before one figure stepped forward. He must have been tall at one time, though now he appeared as a bent old man with waving white hair. In his hands he held a solid black staff crosswise. Moving slowly up in front of me, he explained, "the magic of our sleeping-bonds did not keep us tied to this world in the way we had hoped. Our bodies went beyond while our spirits and forms remain. Wraiths, uncured and incurable. But still with one oath to uphold. We must obey the commands of the one who brought us the White Stone."

Kneeling, he gave me the black staff. Unlike his hands, it was solid when I touched it. Taking it from his misty grasp, I held it carefully. There was nothing carved on the staff, or marked in any other colors. It was simply a solid black rod with a slight knob at each end, like a marching band's baton. Smooth and cold, I could feel that it was something which had not seen the light of day for many years.

The old man had faded back into the army of ghosts. I looked around at them for a moment, before raising the rod into the Runestone's place above my head, "to Angrist's castle! Follow me."

With a padding sound of many phantom feet, the hoard followed. Out of town, across the dunes, we marched until evening was falling and the castle was beneath us in the valley. Swiftwing had come as well, trailing behind the army as we marched. In the lead, I stopped them just back of the cliff. Beckoning a few forwards, I pointed out Hahstgart and Soleinden below.

"You see that castle? I want it destroyed. Can you do this task?"

They nodded, words trailing from them, "yes, commander. It will be leveled. No stone shall stand on another."

"But do not destroy the city, or kill everyone within the castle. Only those who get in your way: let the others flee. Save all of the prisoners from the dungeon carefully. And do not let the king, Angrist, escape. I want him."

"Your commands will be obeyed." The Omberlings faded back into their ranks, before beginning to pour down the hill towards the castle below. I let them pass me, following behind, while Tallray's wife stayed on the cliff tops.

In a flood of fluttering black and gray, the army of wraiths flowed off of the cliffs. They were a cascade of moving spirits. Their quiet steps were not heard until they were near Hahstgart, their dark cloths camouflaging them in the dusky dunes. But when we neared the fortress I heard the sound of shouts from the wall tops. Men began scurrying back and forth. A horn was sounded to call up all of the troops inside. Hahstgart was on the alert. But it was too late for them.

I don't wish to ever again see destruction like I did that night. The Omberlings could not be stopped with arrow or bullet. They came up to the walls in a black tide and simply pushed them over, cracking the adobe and tearing it apart so that it lay on the ground in crumbs no bigger than my fists. Men fell with it, screaming, or were crushed beneath large blocks before they were destroyed. A brave few tried to stand and fight back in the courtyard, but many fled away from the falling castle across the dunes.

Once the outer walls were gone, the keep was pulled apart so that it fell in all directions like the house of cards it was.

Meanwhile, I stood on a larger chunk of stone that I had ordered the Omberlings to leave behind them, watching with my arms crossed. When it got darker, and most of the soldiers were gone, I lit a small Fire and set it on the stone beside me so that it could be seen who was sending the black tide against the fort. My stolen cloak flapped lazily, cobalt blue in the dusk.

Finally, the keep was in ruins and most of the populace gone, fled away or laying dead. I heard shouting and a detachment of Omberlings approached me, dragging someone in their midst. He was not a coward when it came to a fight, struggling against the translucent hands and flailing out all around him despite being outnumbered by phantoms. But there was nothing anyone could do to harm the Omberlings.

They dropped him in front of my stone and retreated into a tight half-circle around him. Panting, more red in the face than ever, Angrist of the Dust looked up at me. My white hair was gleaming in the fire light, while the Omberling cloak still shimmered darkly down my back. I had not resumed the brown mask.

"You." Angrist's face turned into a snarl, though it was paler than before, "Nerheem. Amulet. You are the same!"

I looked down at him with a sort of horrified fascination. In the darkness, with the red glow of the fire, he looked like nothing so much as a mad beast from a nightmare. I knew that he was an evil man and a tyrant king, but for a moment I could not make any move against him. It was as if he had me captive rather than the other way around.

But then he sprang towards me, hands outstretched like claws as he scrambled up the stone. There was a killing light in his eyes. Without thinking, I drew on my core energy and shot a powerful bolt of it at him. Powerful enough to kill.

With a gurgle he fell back off of the stone, twitching for a moment before laying still on the dusty ground. Angrist, King of the Dust, was dead. I looked away, not wishing to see any more.

Jumping from the stone, I found out where the prisoners were being kept. The Omberlings had saved them as gently as I wished, putting them aside and making sure that they stayed there. I waved them away, letting the terrified prisoners escape. All except for Tallray, of course. He stood looking at me with a blank, amazed expression.

"N-Nolin!" He exclaimed finally, seeming to come awake, "what is all of this? I did not know that you had an army! Especially an army of spirits!"

"I didn't. Not until this afternoon, when the Philosopher's Stone awoke them," I grasped his arm and began to lead him away from the ruins, back towards the cliffs, "they are the Omberlings and will help me rebuild the Dark Passages as well. But for now, there is someone waiting for you up there."

"Swiftwing?" His face lit up when I nodded. Without another word, he darted off to find a way up the stone cliffs to the top.

Chapter 32: Conclusions

That night I spent sleeping near the ruined walls of Hahstgart, surrounded by the standing figures of the Omberlings. They had slept so long that they would not rest again, probably ever, unless someone finds a way to set their spirits free. The next morning we began the march to where the Dark Passages ran closest to the ground, near where I had first entered the Dustlands. Immediately, I saw the problems my experiment had caused. Large tiles lay on the ground here and there, black shapes in the dust. None had cracked, but they were all laying many feet from the Passages above.

Luckily it did not appear that the damage went out over the Dustlands further than the eye could see.

Using a scaffolding of dark beams that they brought out of nowhere, the Omberlings hoisted each tile up between them and carried it to its place. Then, while some of them held the stone in place, others carried me safely to the top of the scaffolding. The most difficult work using the arts of Erilaz began then.

I had to first find the standing web of Elements which held them all together, see it intertwining all of the Dark Passages, before weaving it through the fallen tiles to make it whole again. I worked until my eyes were bleary from staring at the glowing weaves and my fingers trembled from tracing them back together.

Feeling empty, I ate what Tallray and his wife gave me, then fell down to sleep until later that day. When I got up the Omberlings were waiting for me and we continued to work. I had to rest again that night, but the next morning all of the tiles but one were back in their places. I had left the original one out for a time, so that Tallray could return through it.

"You must go back now so that I can seal it up," I told him, feeling tired and irritable from the constant strain of the repairs, "through that tunnel. I'll send a few of the Omberlings to help you up."

"Aren't you going to come with us, Nolin?" He said, an anxious expression on his face.

I shook my head, "No. This is my place now. Go."

"You must come back with me," Tallray made a move as if to grab my sleeve, but I jerked it away, "please, come back. Benji is not old enough to join us yet and we have no other Keeper. We will need you to reactivate doors now. And nothing in the Passages seems as good now that you are gone."

I gave him an ironic look, "do you really think that the others would take me back, even if I pleaded on bent knees for it? No, I am of the Dustlands now. But your secrets are safe with me. Go."

"Please, don't be so bitter! Come back with us," Tallray made a jump and caught my sleeve again, apparently to force me back with.

In that moment all the repressed emotions and turmoil from the past days bubbled up inside me: the loss of Eoan, tension of infiltrating Angrist's castle and shock of defeating him after having raised the Omberlings. All that mixed with my weariness into a dangerous brew.

Anger grew into energy, which I lashed out at him without consideration. A whip of angry power slapped out from me, expressing my feelings. A surprised look crossed Tallray's face and he staggered back, before falling to his knees and crumpling to the ground.

I stared at him while panting, appalled at myself for losing control so entirely. Swiftwing gasped, staring at me as if I had become a monster. In many ways I had.

Throwing myself down beside Tallray, I rolled him over and felt to see if he was still breathing. There was a faint heartbeat and, when I stopped to think, I could hear his ragged breathing. But I had struck him with a high amount of power, which could easily be fatal. In fact, even as I listened his breaths were growing slower and further apart.

"He's not—?" Swiftwing sobbed, joining me beside him.

"Not yet," reaching into my pocket, where I had stored it, I drew out the Philosopher's Stone. There was only one way to save the Alchemist now, using his own creation.

"Omberlings, give me a drinking glass!" I shouted, not caring how they got it. But they seemed to be carrying many things invisibly with them, including a fine Omberling goblet which was swiftly given to me.

Using the tip of my knife, I scraped off shavings from the edge of the stone. They came off like peelings of hard wax, after which the stone healed itself completely so that no mark was left on it.

I mixed these bits with Alkahest in the goblet. It only took a minute before the shavings were gone, replaced with two separate liquids in he bottom of the glass. The top one was the Alkahest, which I poured off back into its bottle using great care to make sure it wall all gone. The second elixir was liquid life. Into it I mixed just a touch of water, before moving over next to Tallray.

"Hold his head up," I commanded Swiftwing, who obeyed palely. I forced the mixture between the Alchemist's teeth, making him drink it. When it was gone, I sat back on my heels.

At first there was no sign of a difference, his breaths only coming in distant jerks now. But after a tense second or two had passed a flush of healthy red passed across his face and he began to stir, breathing strong and normal.

"Thank you," Swiftwing said, tears in her eyes. I stared at her, not understanding how she could say those words at that moment.

"Don't thank me. I almost killed him."

Standing up, I turned as if to go, "I have become a hard man."

Behind me, I heard the woman say softly, "you're a lonely man, Nolin."

I looked over my shoulder, shaking my head, "just hard and harsh. But don't worry: I will never teach anyone to be like me. Or teach the secrets of the Keepers to any another. I swear it."

With that, I walked away to speak to the Omberlings about sealing the last hole once my old companions had gone through it.

EPILOGUE: Reasons and Patterns

The dust storm had blown away by the time the story ended, leaving the little adobe house in peaceful silence. Grains of earth lay thickly on the table and floor, though the two occupants were untouched by it. Hiram looked up with eyes still sharp despite being ringed in darkness from lack of sleep. "coward."

Nolin sighed, "I suppose I am afraid of what would happen if I taught someone everything I know. Not only for myself, or out of jealousy, but because of the lonely life it forces you to lead. Being a 'wizard' is not all about sparkling tricks and poetic battles, Hiram. In fact, there is no such thing as a poetic battle, nor a magic trick that does not cost you a price in the end. But also I am afraid of what would happen to an apprentice if I kept him. As you can see, something bad always happens to anyone near me."

"I still say that you are a coward because of it!" the boy growled, standing up off of the bed, "you can not live without losing sometimes, Nerheem. All true Dustlanders know that."

"True." A small smile curled at the corners of the ex-Keeper's mouth, "but though I swore never to teach anyone to be like me, I did not promise not to tell anyone my story. You have the spark of Erilaz strong in you, boy, and I'm sure you have a clever mind to go with it. Have I really taught you so little in these two days and one night of speech?"

A surprised look crossed Hiram's face, as he held out his hands in front of him. Closing his eyes, he took a deep breath, before unfurling the fingers slowly. On each palm rested two orbs of Elemental energy. Silvery-clear, burning orange, aqua blue and deep, grass green.

"Nerheem," he whispered, opening his eyes to see what he had done, "see what I have done. You are the greatest wizard ever to be seen in the Dustlands. Thank you."

Nolin stood up as well, stretching, "there is yet another reason I do not need an apprentice, Hiram. Though I might 'go beyond' through sudden violence any day, as you pointed out, I can not die by poison, wounds, sickness or old age."

As he spoke, he pulled something out of one of his leather bags. Holding it out on the palm of his hand, he displayed a Runestone about an inch thick and six square, made of pure white stone.

"The Philosopher's Stone." Hiram looked solemnly at it, stretching out a finger to brush it gently, "your friend let you keep it, Nerheem?"

"Tallray did not try to stop me," Nolin shrugged, tucking it back away.

"What are you going to do next, wizard?"

Another brief, bitter-sweet smile crossed the young man's face, touching his eyes with a strange light, "I never could pass up an opportunity to explore a place which no one else has been before. I am going into the Midnight Maw, with the help of the Omberlings, some rope and more provisions. I was only staying here to wait for them, as I sent them back to live at their city last time, until I needed them again. Now a small group of them are on their way to meet me, so that we may see what is down under the Dustlands."

"Good-bye, Hiram. Remember what the story taught you, which is far more than just the arts of Erilaz."

The boy nodded slowly, before turning to go out of the door. Nolin watched him with a mixture of sadness and fulfillment, wondering where his story would lead him now. Not just to be a nomad or villager who ground his days away into the dust, that was for sure.

"And it does feel good to have told someone everything," the wizard murmured to himself, watching the shape dwindle away across the dunes.

END

Don't miss out!

Visit the website below and you can sign up to receive emails whenever Rachael S Lucas publishes a new book. There's no charge and no obligation.

https://books2read.com/r/B-A-XHJJ-YGQQC

BOOKS 2 READ

Connecting independent readers to independent writers.

Did you love *Exile Of Dust*? Then you should read *Dimensions*[1] by Rachael S Lucas!

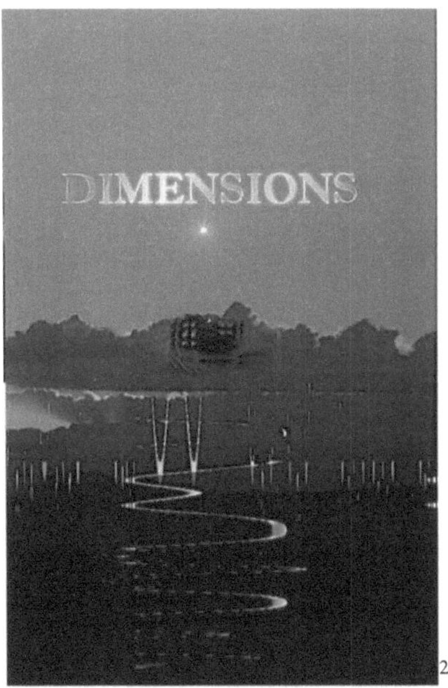

Lenny Staff's life runs on simple wheels in the oppressive city of Belltoh. That is, until his best friend Sara disappears mysteriously, his employer and hero Dr. Devi shuts down shop and the police find out that Lenny is illegally cybernetic...

Enter Jax, a young man with a dimension travelling habit and a flare for riding hoverboard. He hates staying still, especially when someone else is making him do it. And when an evil form of corruption cramps him in a ring of nine worlds, he jumps through Lenny's window looking for help.

---

1. https://books2read.com/u/3R5Jon

2. https://books2read.com/u/3R5Jon

Together with seven other quirky adventurers, one from every dimension in the ring of nine, they travel dimensions to find out what is destroying their worlds, and why.

About the Author

Rachael Lucas is a quiet girl from the mountains of northern California. She loves reading, writing, gardening and Asian art among many other things. She also lives with a varying number of cats and dogs who are always on call for inspiration.